P9-EMP-821

"I DON'T USUALLY HAVE TO BEG FOR KISSES."

"I don't usually kiss men I don't even like."

"That's just the point," he said, the gleam in his eyes intensifying. He angled in closer, and lowered his head close to hers. Once more their lips were only inches apart. Once more Emily felt her breath catching in her throat.

"I think you do like me. And the hell of it is, I like you. It doesn't make any sense, but not much does in this world sometimes."

No, it didn't make sense. But it was true, Emily thought in wonder. She did like him. How? Why? She wanted to hate him. . . .

"Well," she took a deep breath, stunned by her own thoughts, by the wild urges spinning through her. "You did rescue me from the storm, so . . . I'll grant you one kiss and only one," she said in a rush. How prim she sounded. Then she just couldn't stand it any longer. She grabbed the front of his shirt and yanked him toward her, placing her lips upon his.

She'd meant it to be a quick kiss, over and done with in a hurry . . . but something changed as her mouth touched his and she found herself lost in the kiss, hopelessly, dizzily lost. . . .

RAVE REVIEWS FOR
AWARD-WINNING AUTHOR JILL GREGORY
AND HER BESTSELLING NOVELS

ROUGH WRANGLER, TENDER KISSES

"This is the first Jill Gregory book I've read, but if the rest of her tales are as well told as this one, I've got many hours of great reading ahead of me."
— *The Oakland Press*

"Jill Gregory crafts stories against the backdrop of the Wild West and creates characters so real they are easy to understand and empathize with. She bases her romances on how her characters learn to trust in the power of love to heal and ease away the pain of the past. Her faith in love renews our own. Thank you for this invaluable lesson, Ms. Gregory."
— *Romantic Times*

COLD NIGHT, WARM STRANGER

"ANOTHER WINNING WESTERN." — *Booklist*

"An engaging book, supported by a well-drawn cast of townspeople." — *Publishers Weekly*

"YOU WILL BE ENTICED FROM THE FIRST CHAPTER. . . . You will cry and cheer for these wonderfully beloved characters, who will do nothing less than capture your heart. . . . Jill Gregory has done it again. Her talent shines through in this sensually captivating novel—she shows us once again that love can conquer all."
— *Rendezvous*

Books by Jill Gregory

Rough Wrangler, Tender Kisses
Cold Night, Warm Stranger
Never Love a Cowboy
Just This Once
Always You
Daisies in the Wind
Forever After
Cherished
When the Heart Beckons

Once an Outlaw

Jill Gregory

A DELL BOOK

Published by
Dell Publishing
a division of
Random House, Inc.
1540 Broadway
New York, New York 10036

ISBN: 0-440-23549-9

Manufactured in the United States of America

Published simultaneously in Canada

December 2001

10 9 8 7 6 5 4 3 2 1
OPM

To all of my wonderful family—and especially Larry and Rachel—with all my love

Once an Outlaw

Chapter 1

Forlorn Valley,
Colorado

"EMILY, HONEY—YOU SURE YOU'RE going to be all right here on your own? I don't much cotton to leaving you."

The stoop-shouldered giant with the grizzled face and stringy gray hair peered intently at the young woman beside him on the porch of the old log cabin. His seamed face was full of doubt, but in the gold afternoon sunlight that slanted down across the Rockies and made the sky glisten a hot and burnished blue, his niece looked as calm and unruffled as a mountain lake.

"I'll be fine, Uncle Jake," she assured him. "I can take care of myself."

Yet, even as she spoke the words, Emily Spoon felt an eerie prickle across her neck.

She couldn't imagine why. She wasn't afraid of this beautiful isolated patch of land deep in the heart of the Colorado foothills—or of the dark—or of being alone. She wasn't afraid of anything—except losing her family again.

"And don't forget," she added, as a gust of wind swept down from the mountains and blew a strand of midnight hair across her cheek. "I'm not all alone. There's Joey."

"Hmmmph. That little twig of a young'un? You know what I mean, girl."

Her uncle's voice was deep, scratchy, and gruff, well suited to the leathery and intimidating visage of his fifty-plus years, but Emily wasn't fooled. She knew that despite his fierce appearance and his deep-set, squinting eyes that were the color of mud, when it came to his family, those he loved, Jake Spoon was gentle as a lamb.

Of course, there was no doubt that his years in prison had changed him, she reflected, a sadness touching her fine gray eyes as she studied the uncle who had raised her. Before Deputy Sheriff Clint Barclay had tracked him down and arrested him, he'd been larger than life and twice as bold, a man who always thirsted for adventure. He'd been in constant motion, craving hard riding and wild roaming, a good fight, and a mean chase. He'd been drawn to the lure of riches—ill-gotten riches—especially if they belonged to the wealthy and powerful.

But those seven years he'd spent behind bars—and all that had happened to his family while he was gone—had drained him of much of his vinegar and aged him in countless ways. There was a weariness now in the craggy lines of his face, a somber dead look to his eyes, and his smile, once big and crooked and easy, was now as rare as a gold nugget in a turnip patch.

Meeting his searching gaze, Emily felt a twinge of concern. These days Uncle Jake's shoulders always looked as if they carried some invisible, impossibly heavy burden that was too much for him to bear.

And perhaps, she reflected, thinking of her Aunt Ida, they did.

"Of course I know what you mean," she said with a quick smile, patting his arm. "But everything will be fine. So you just go on to Denver and buy the best horses you can find, and as much stock as we can afford. Joey and I will be perfectly all right until you and the boys get back."

"Load up that rifle and keep it at the ready, you hear?"

"I will."

"And if any strangers come by, shoot first and ask questions later."

Emily eased him toward the porch steps. "Uncle Jake, I know how to take care of myself."

At that he nodded curtly and turned his head away, but not before she saw the sheen of guilt in his eyes.

"Please, don't look that way." Emily took a deep breath. "The past is behind us now—all of us. The Spoon family is back together and everything is going to be just like it was."

Well, not quite like it was. Aunt Ida is gone . . .

As if reading her thoughts, Jake swallowed, scowled, and pulled his hat down lower over his eyes. His shoulders drooping, he stepped down off the porch.

"You bet your boots it is, honey," he said gruffly. "No need for you to worry about anything. Once we get back from Denver, me and the boys are sticking to this place. We'll make a go of it—come hell or high water."

A surge of happiness swept through her. He meant it, she was sure of it. Uncle Jake and the boys were really going straight.

We're going to be a family again—together under one roof. And no one is going to take this ranch, this land away.

A breathless joy seized her. As the sun drifted lazily overhead toward the western sky, she watched her brother, Pete, and her towheaded cousin, Lester, lead their horses from the barn.

"Hey, Uncle Jake, let's ride. There's a poker game

waiting for me in Denver—and a great big pot of cash with my name on it." Pete waved his Stetson at Emily, his thin, handsome face alight with excitement. "So long, Sis! See you in a couple of days."

Lester mounted his piebald and rode up to the porch. He was even larger than Uncle Jake, a mountain of a man, with enormous shoulders and a sweet, moon-shaped face covered with freckles. "Keep an eye on the barn door, will you, Emily? I didn't get a chance yet to fix that bolt. Want me to bring you back any fancy doodads from Denver?"

"Just bring yourself back in one piece—all of you." Emily fixed a meaningful gaze on each of them. Jake Spoon nodded and wheeled his horse toward the trail.

"All right, boys—let's ride!"

As he dug in his heels, Pete gave a whoop loud enough to raise the dead, and all three of them thundered off, heading south across the valley.

For several moments, Emily stood at the broken rail of the porch, watching until the three riders disappeared over a ridge. As the dust dissipated in the still, crystalline air, she scanned the entire horizon, her gaze slow and careful. All was peaceful, quiet, and reassuringly empty but for the rolling foothills lush with new grass and buttercups, and the rising, pine-steeped mountains that towered in the distance.

She drew in a deep breath of pure mountain air and hugged herself.

This little cabin, her new home, was tucked neatly away on the banks of Stone Creek, some ten miles from the town of Lonesome, and there wasn't another cabin or ranch house anywhere in this part of the valley. She loved the isolation of it, the sweep and beauty. After years of living in the noisy boardinghouse on Spring Street in Jefferson City, and working as a servant in the vast, cluttered, and demanding household of Mrs. Wainscott, this snug log cabin in Forlorn Valley was a slice of heaven.

Silence as thick as the rich forests that backed the cabin enveloped her, and there was no sign of any person or beast, unless one counted the hawks circling the far-off mountain peaks or the herd of elk crossing the plateau of rocks to the north.

So why do I have this prickly feeling on the back of my neck? Emily wondered uneasily. *A feeling that there is someone—or something—out there. Someone coming . . .*

She shivered, and glanced again at the burning blue sky. There were hours left until nightfall. She hoped by then she'd shake off this foolishness.

"Em-ly. Em-ly, where are you?"

At the sound of the small childish voice, she whirled and hurried back into the cabin.

"I'm here, Joey. It's all right." She smiled at the boy who stood by the hearth, staring at her with wide brown eyes that looked too big for his face. At six years old, Joey McCoy was small for his age, his face thin and pinched, his hair pale as wheat. His long-lashed brown eyes, so like his mother's, were filled with a fear that never seemed to go away.

"I hope you're hungry," Emily said cheerfully, "because I'm planning to fix the two of us a truly delicious supper."

The child merely stared at her.

"You remember my famous fried chicken and biscuits, don't you?" She tilted her head to one side, her voice gentle. "Well, that's not even the best part. For dessert, we're going to have blueberry pie." She crossed the room and knelt beside him, offering a smile she hoped was steady and reassuring. "Your mama's recipe. That's your favorite, isn't it, Joey?"

He didn't answer, only peered toward the window, his small hands clenched at his sides. "When are they coming back?" he asked.

"Uncle Jake and the boys? In a few days."

"So . . . we have to stay here—all alone?" he quavered.

Emily touched the tip of his button nose. "The time will pass in a blink. We're going to be mighty busy getting this place all fixed up."

She watched Joey's gaze shift to take in the small main room of the cabin, with its bare plank floor, sparse furnishings, and the unadorned brass-bowled oil lamps, then it returned, intent and serious, to her face.

"It's nowhere near as nice as Mrs. Gale's boardinghouse, not yet," Emily conceded with a grin. "But it will be, Joey—you'll see." Her smile widened and her eyes began to sparkle. "I'm going to sew some lovely white lace curtains for all the windows, just like Mrs. Gale had in her front parlor. And when I go into town, I'm buying a pretty rug—maybe two."

"That sounds nice," he mumbled. But the little boy was not to be distracted. His brown eyes fastened themselves on her face once more.

"Is that man—the bad man—going to find me?" he asked on a gulp.

"No, Joey, He is *not*." Emily gathered his slight body into her arms. She wished she had the power to make his fear go away. His bones felt fragile as she held him close and sensed his trembling. "He isn't going to find you, Joey, I promise. Not here—not anywhere. You're safe," she said firmly.

"What about Mama?"

"Your mother is safe too. I'm sure of it." She drew back and smoothed a stray lock of pale hair from his eyes. "We tricked the bad man, remember? He can't find either one of you. And soon your mama will come back here to fetch you to a brand-new home—and you'll both be together. And no one will hurt either of you ever again."

"Promise, Em-ly?"

"I promise."

She felt his tense body relax ever so slightly. After giving him one last gentle squeeze, she rose to her feet. "You know, I promised your mother I'd take good care of you until she gets back, and that means I can't let you waste away for lack of food, young man. Think how angry she'd be with me! So you need to promise me something, Joey."

"What?"

"That you'll clean your plate tonight, drink your milk, and eat a great big piece of blueberry pie. Maybe even two pieces. Think you can manage that?"

She hoped to coax a smile out of him, but Joey hadn't smiled much since the day John Armstrong had knocked him across the room and given Lissa McCoy a black eye.

He nodded solemnly.

Emily's heart squeezed tight with pity. If John Armstrong, Lissa's ex-fiancé, ever did show up here, it would be the last mistake he ever made, she vowed silently.

Lissa had been her closest friend during the years that Uncle Jake was in prison and Pete and Lester were on the run. She and Aunt Ida had been unable to keep their Missouri farm going, and when they'd lost it, they'd moved into Mrs. Gale's boardinghouse where Lissa McCoy, a young widow, worked, cooking and cleaning for Mrs. Gale, who had a bad hip and could barely make it up and down the stairs. Lissa and her son, Joey, shared a room behind the kitchen, and it was Lissa who had befriended

Emily and her aunt, and helped Emily find a job as an upstairs maid in an elegant house on Adams Street. From the start, Emily had liked the quiet, cheerful young woman who worked tirelessly without complaint, and who clearly doted on her little boy. In fact, the only thing Emily hadn't liked about Lissa was her beau—a moody, unpredictable man of uncertain temper who worked for the railroad. Emily hadn't trusted John Armstrong, but Lissa had been blind to his true nature—until she became betrothed to him.

Then it was too late.

Now Lissa was on the run, terrified and fleeing from the very man she'd once thought to marry. And Emily was caring for Joey until Lissa had a chance to throw him off the trail, reach California, and try to secure a safe home for them both with her estranged grandparents.

Until Lissa returned for the boy, Emily had promised to keep him safe. And she would, no matter what. But making Joey *feel* safe was another matter.

However much she tried to convince the child that John Armstrong wasn't about to track him from Jefferson City all the way to Lonesome, Colorado, Joey was too caught up in his fear to truly believe her. He refused to step outdoors for more than a moment or two at a time, and he then scurried back into the house as if pursued by wolves.

Who could blame him? Emily thought, her eyes darkening as she remembered the tears and sobs and screams of that awful night. Armstrong had beaten Lissa and terrorized Joey. And it would take time for the memories of fear and horror and violence to fade.

"I have an idea," she said, taking the little boy by the hand. "Why don't you play with the marbles Lester bought you while I sweep the floor? Then you can help me bake that pie."

"I can help you sweep," he offered. "I always used to help Mama."

"Well, fine, then." Emily beamed at him. "I'd love some help. Goodness knows, there's enough to do around here. Another pair of hands will be most welcome."

She sensed he just wanted to be close to her, that he felt safer that way, and she couldn't blame him. The fear John Armstrong had created would not soon be forgotten.

But to her delight, Joey did eat a fair amount of the fried chicken and biscuits she served him later, and a large slice of pie as well. After she tucked him into his bunk in the back room he shared with Pete and Lester, she stood for a moment gazing down at the small boy with the too-serious and too-pale face.

"Maybe tomorrow you'd like to help me with the planting. I'm going to start a vegetable garden out back."

"Out . . . back?"

"You can dig in the dirt and get as filthy as you want. Back on our farm, Pete always loved to do that. He'd find worms and bugs and . . . well, never mind about that—*he* always tried to put them in my hair." She shuddered, then gave a laugh. "He was a terrible boy. Not nice and polite and helpful like you. Still . . . doesn't it sound like fun—the digging part—not putting them in my hair," she added with another laugh.

But Joey quickly shook his head no.

"I want to stay in here," he whispered.

"All right." Emily kissed his cheek. "Whatever you like. But if you change your mind, all that nice dirt and those bugs and worms will be waiting."

He did almost grin then, his mouth trembling a little,

and she saw a sudden, wistful look enter his eyes. "Night, Em-ly," Joey said softly.

"Good night, Joey."

When she was at the door, she heard his voice again, a barely audible whisper over the sudden gust of wind that rattled the shutters.

"Night, Mama," Joey said into the darkness.

Emily's throat tightened. She closed the door and tiptoed out to the main room of the cabin where a fire blazed in the hearth. She turned up the oil lamp, praying all the while that Lissa really was safe and on her way to California to find her family, praying that John Armstrong hadn't found her . . . hadn't . . .

She closed her eyes and gripped the back of the old pine rocker beside the sofa. *Don't even think about that. Armstrong is not going to catch Lissa and he isn't going to kill her. Even though that's what he threatened to do, every day since she discovered what kind of a man he really was and broke off their engagement.*

A sudden gust of wind blew the shutters wide, and Emily started. She gave her head a shake at her own jumpiness and hurried to the window to secure the latch. Then, shivering a little from the chill sweeping down from the mountains, she crossed to the inlaid wood chest in the corner. *Enough worrying,* she told herself. *You have work to do*. Sewing those new lace curtains was first on her list. They'd brighten the cabin considerably—and the old place needed it.

The lid of the heavy chest squeaked as she lifted it. Once the chest had belonged to Aunt Ida—and to Aunt Ida's mother in Boston before that. It was deep and finely carved, made of fine rich oak and inlaid with brass and silver. It now contained all of Emily's precious fabrics: calico and gingham, muslin and wool, yards of linen, squares of sateen and even a bolt each of velvet and silk—as well as scraps, buttons, ribbons, needles, and pins.

It holds something else too, she thought, her heartbeat quickening.

It held her dreams.

All of Emily's hopes and plans for the future revolved around the treasured and carefully accumulated contents of this old chest.

Kneeling down, she rummaged through bolts of gingham and yards of bright-colored calico, seeking the crisp white lace muslin she needed for the curtains, but when her gaze fell upon the cloud of dusky rose silk she'd purchased in Jefferson City the day she'd left, she couldn't resist pausing and lifting it out into the light.

It was gorgeous—the most gorgeous fabric she'd ever seen. Easily as beautiful as anything owned by Mrs. Wainscott. *It's going to make a magnificent gown,* Emily thought, her eyes glowing with anticipation.

She could envision the gown already, finished and perfect, with its elegant fitted sleeves and black satin bustle and gleaming jet buttons. And when the women of Lonesome saw it, she thought dreamily, they would all want a gown just as beautiful, as sophisticated, as irresistible . . .

I hope.

A flicker of exhilaration ran through Emily as she stroked a finger along the silk, the dusky rose shade gleaming richly in the glow of lamplight. Unfortunately, the gown would have to wait, and so would her dreams. *But not for long,* she promised herself. Only until she'd made the cabin cozy and comfortable for all of them.

Because no matter what it took she was going to make a success of her dressmaking business. She would make certain that whatever happened with this ranch, whether

Uncle Jake and the boys succeeded in making it profitable or if they failed, she was going to earn enough money on her own to support all of them. No one would ever have the means or the power to take everything away from them again.

We'll never lose this land like we lost the farm, she thought, clenching the soft silk in her fingers. *And I'll never find myself forced to work as a servant again for the likes of Mrs. Wainscott.*

For a moment, memories of the Wainscott household flooded back. They were all unpleasant. She didn't want to think about that place, or about her employer, Augusta Wainscott, the most demanding and twig-brained woman she'd ever met. Or about her aquiline-nosed son, Hobart, who had a proclivity for pinching servant girls every time he caught one coming around a corner.

She wanted to think about the new curtains, and the rug she would buy for the parlor floor, about filling the house with homey things, like embroidered cushions for the horsehair sofa and for every chair, and pretty gold-framed watercolors to brighten the walls. She wanted to think about a spanking-new stove, and matching china plates and cups, and perhaps even a small pianoforte like the one in Mrs. Wainscott's music room . . .

She froze as she heard a noise from outside.

A small noise.

Like a twig crackling, Emily thought. *Or perhaps just the wind.* But that chill prickled down her neck again, and she drew in her breath.

She ran into the kitchen and grabbed the rifle down from the shelf. Swiftly, she checked the chamber for bullets, then paused and listened again.

Silence.

There was no one there.

Emily waited a bit longer, wishing she could stay put inside the cabin. These log walls were old, but they were thick. They held safety, comfort. Warmth and light. But she had to check, had to be sure. She'd never fall asleep tonight if she didn't know for certain.

Swallowing down the acid taste of fear, she forced herself to walk to the front door. She eased it open, wincing as it squeaked. Her finger curled around the trigger as she stepped out into the cool darkness, the deep shadows lightened only by a fuzzy half-moon and a sprinkling of dazzling white stars.

It was only a matter of seconds before her eyes adjusted to the darkness and she did a quick scan of the yard and the trees and the ridge beyond. No sign of any horses, of any movement at all.

She turned toward the dilapidated barn and the corrals with their broken posts and saw the barn door ajar, swinging wide in the wind.

The barn door. Lester had warned her about that.

She shook her head. So much for noises in the night.

She started toward it, relief flooding her.

And that's when someone lunged at her from behind, wrenched the rifle away as though it were a toy, and clamped a hand over her mouth.

"If you scream, lady, someone's going to die." The low, hard voice growled in her ear. Powerful arms encircled her. Imprisoned her, holding her so tightly she could scarcely breathe. "Now answer me and make it fast. Where are the others?"

Chapter 2

HIS HAND WAS JAMMED ACROSS HER mouth so hard her lips were crushed against her teeth. *So much for screaming,* Emily thought desperately. Twisting and writhing, she fought him, unable to break free.

For a split second, a jumble of thoughts spun through her mind. Was it John Armstrong? Had he somehow followed her and Joey? Or was this some enemy of Uncle Jake . . . or Pete . . . or Lester . . . ?

Or just an outlaw passing through, looking to steal some money or a horse, or seeking a place to hide out? she wondered through the roar of blood in her ears. Or maybe there was more than one . . . maybe a pack of them, like wolves . . .

It didn't matter, Emily told herself, struggling against the panic that threatened to overwhelm her, fighting the bile and the gut-punch of fear. Whoever this was, she wasn't going to let him hurt that little boy sleeping in the back room. She'd stop him. Somehow . . .

Suddenly he began dragging her toward the barn, around the side, and with easy strength pushed her up against the wall. For the first time she had a glimpse of him: a big man, well over six feet, wearing a black Stetson and a gray duster that billowed about his powerful frame. He suddenly eased his hand from her mouth and pinned her against the barn.

"The Spoon gang. Answer me. How many are inside?"

Emily stomped down as hard as she could on his foot.

He grunted in surprise and for a moment his grip on her slackened. It was all she needed. She shoved at him and made a grab for the rifle. He held on without any apparent effort as Emily fought desperately to wrench it away.

"Get . . . off . . . my . . . land!" she gasped, still clinging to the gun, though it was clearly under his control. "I don't know . . . who you are . . . or what you want . . . but if you don't leave now, you'll be sorry!"

He stared down at her and in the faintness of pearly moonlight she saw keen, storm-blue eyes that were colder than glaciers, set within a rough, unshaven face. His jaw was lean, his features sharp and handsome. Heaven help her, she'd never seen a man so handsome. He exuded an overall impression of strength and will and power, perhaps because he was so tall, she thought dazedly—taller than either Pete or Lester or Uncle Jake. But there was something more—something indefinable, something that breathed *danger*.

He looked like a man who always got what he wanted. A man who didn't scare easily—if at all.

Not surprisingly, her threat didn't seem to frighten him. In fact, after she voiced it, he visibly relaxed, though his grip on the rifle remained as firm as ever.

"You're alone then," he said softly.

"I . . . no. Yes. I mean, what makes you think that?" Emily blurted.

He yanked the rifle out of her reach with finality. "If someone else was here, you'd have screamed for help."

"You told me not to."

"Never yet met a woman who did what any man told her to do."

"Especially a man who attacks a woman on her own property in the middle of the night!" Emily was about to kick him again, but one look at those intimidating eyes made her think better of it.

"This your property?" The stranger's gaze narrowed on her. Even through the darkness, only faintly broken by the luminosity of stars and moon, he could see how pretty she was. Blue-black hair, wild and wavy, sweeping to her waist, a slender figure beneath that dark gingham gown, with mouthwatering curves in all the right places, and a face like an angel. But those smoke-gray eyes with sparks shooting out of them were pure devil. Not to mention that soft-looking mouth of hers that was temptingly parted and trembling just a little . . .

What the hell does this gorgeous woman have to do with the Spoon gang? he wondered, and then his stomach tightened. *Don't get distracted,* he told himself. *Or you'll end up dead. Jake Spoon and the boys could still be hidden here somewhere and they'd shoot you in the back just as soon as look at you.*

And this girl would probably fix them coffee while they buried you . . . if they bothered to bury you . . .

He jerked a thumb toward the cabin. "I have it on good authority that the Spoon gang is living here. So just who are you?"

"Who are *you*?"

Emily's heart was still thundering like a runaway train, but some of the fear was subsiding. This was *not* that low-down cowardly bully John Armstrong, thank heavens. She didn't know who he was, but at least he wasn't after Joey. He was looking her over as if she were an apple he was deciding whether to pick, eat, or toss aside as wormy and beneath notice. Her chin came up. He had her cornered here, hemmed in, outsized and outmatched in strength—he had her gun, and she was alone—but she'd be damned if she'd let him see her snivel and cower.

"You heard me," she repeated, icy as Mrs. Wainscott in her haughtiest mood. "Who are you?"

"I'm the one with the gun," he said coolly, "so I reckon I'll ask the questions." He gripped her arm. "Let's just go back to the cabin and step inside and—"

"No!" She wrenched free of his grasp.

"Something you don't want me to see inside?" Those hard eyes pierced her. If she'd been naked, he couldn't have studied her any more closely. "Or some*one*?"

"No!"

Suddenly, he had the rifle up, leveled in the direction of the cabin. "Then let's go. You first."

"They're not here, really." If Joey woke up and saw this man, saw the gun, he'd be terrified. "There's no need to go inside," Emily said desperately.

"I reckon we'll see about that."

He gave her a push toward the door. That's when the moonlight glinted off something pinned to his duster—and she saw it. *A star. A silver star.*

Shock hit her like a brick. "You're . . . the law!" Emily gasped. She stopped dead, fury sweeping through her. "I should have known!"

"You have something against the law?"

"You're damned right I do. Get out of here. Get out right now." Emily's fists clenched. "You can't just barge into someone's home—"

"And here I thought you were inviting me."

He had the nerve to smile, a cold, hard smile that made her long to punch him.

"I'd rather take a bullet than invite a lawman into my home." Her fury was making it difficult to breathe. Her blood seemed to be on fire. *The law.*

"How dare you come here. My uncle served his time, damn you. Now he's free to do as he pleases. You just leave him alone!"

Potent heat, all fury and passion, seemed to blaze from her. Those big gray eyes smoldered as if they would incinerate him with silver fire.

"Jake Spoon is your uncle?" he asked, forcing himself to concentrate on her words, not her beauty.

"I'm not answering any of your damn questions. Give me back my gun and go!"

"I'm afraid it isn't that simple."

"Says who?"

"Says me."

He caught her arm as she made a grab for the rifle. Even through the gingham, Emily felt the warmth and strength of his grip, though he didn't hurt her. But he didn't release her either.

"Let me *go*."

"I'll think about it. Look." Suddenly his voice sounded weary. And patient. As if he were a teacher speaking to a recalcitrant and not very bright child. "I just got back into town. I'm tired. I'm not in the mood to fight with you. I just want to ask your uncle some questions."

"He's not here. You'll have to come back another time—maybe in daylight, out in the open, instead of skulking around in the dark, like a . . . a rat! Unless you're too frightened to ride up and show yourself?"

A short laugh broke from him. Emily realized how foolish she sounded. From the swift, sure way she'd seen him move and the tough, dangerous glint of his eyes, he didn't appear to be a man who was frightened of much in this world. Maybe of nothing.

"I learned early in this job to be cautious," he said softly. "It's what's kept me alive."

"Isn't that a pity?" She glared at him, wishing he would let go of her. His touch was disconcerting. It wasn't just that he was so strong, she thought, it was something else. Something indefinable.

In the darkness, he lifted a brow.

It annoyed her that he didn't seem to mind her animosity in the least. In fact, he looked almost amused. But still wary, careful. Almost as if he were expecting someone to jump at him or shoot at him out of the dark. Something told her that if someone did, he'd be ready for it.

"The thing is, like I told you, I've been away," he continued in a quiet tone. Without her even realizing exactly how he did it, he backed her against the barn wall again, his body hemming her in. "Just rode in this evening. And first thing, before my horse is even unsaddled, one of our citizens tells me Jake Spoon showed up in the general store. He was followed back here, to the Sutter place."

"So? What of it?"

Her tone was defiant, but her heart was sinking down to her toes. Emily had been hoping against hope they could just kind of settle in, blend in, that no one would really notice or care that three members of the Spoon gang were setting up ranching outside of Lonesome. But if folks were already noticing—and following—and sending the sheriff . . .

"We don't want any trouble." She tried to control the quaver in her voice, but it escaped and she flushed, hating the sound of it.

The lawman's cool blue gaze fixed itself on her face.

"Folks in Lonesome don't want any trouble either," he said evenly.

Suddenly he released her arm. Then to her amazement, he handed her back the rifle. "You heard of the Duggan gang?"

She nodded, her fingers clutching the rifle, even though she knew he could take it away again if he chose to.

"They took over Lonesome a while back. The town hired me to clean them out. I did."

"If you want a medal, go to the governor."

For an instant she saw the quick spark of amusement in his eyes, then it was gone. His voice stayed even, maddeningly even. "Lonesome has been quiet since then—a nice, clean, upstanding town—real safe. Folks like it that way. So do I."

"I'm really not interested—"

"So if the Spoon gang has any ideas about—"

"My uncle isn't the head of the Spoon gang anymore," she interrupted. "There is no Spoon gang anymore. We're just a family looking to set up ranching. We don't want any trouble either."

"Jake Spoon and his outfit are bad news."

"Not anymore." Emily met his gaze squarely. A sudden gust of wind lifted her heavy hair and blew it across her face and she shoved it back with a hand that shook, but her voice was steady. "If you and the rest of the stupid town just leave them alone, leave *us* alone, you'll find out that they just want to go straight and make an honest living."

His lip curled sardonically. "Ahuh. And I own a parcel of land in a Mississippi swamp that's just brimming with gold."

"I'm telling you the truth."

"And you are?"

She lifted her chin. "Emily Spoon."

Emily Spoon. There was something spunky and alluring about the name, just as there was about her. *How in hell did Jake Spoon end up with such a beautiful spitfire for a niece?* he wondered, vaguely distracted.

"And who else is living here with you and your uncle, Miss Spoon?"

"I'm not answering any more questions, Sheriff. It's late, I'm busy, and you're trespassing on my land."

At this, his eyes narrowed and he took a step closer. Emily took a step back.

"Got a deed for it?" the sheriff asked, an edge to his voice.

"For . . . what?" Every time he got close, she seemed to lose her train of thought.

"The land."

"My uncle has one."

"Tell him I want to see it." The lawman's tone was curt. The weariness was gone from his face and he suddenly looked cold again, harsh, like a man who's heard too much, seen too much. "Tell him to come into town and show it to me. I have a few questions."

"I don't have any idea when he'll be back."

"Where'd he go?"

"That's none of your business either."

Emily met his hard penetrating stare for a full minute while the stars glowed clear as diamonds overhead. She'd been through a good many things in her life and dealt with all manner of people, but never had she encountered anyone with as determined and steely a gaze as this tall lawman with his dangerous good looks. She forced herself to meet those penetrating eyes, forced herself to keep her head high, her back straight. But she wanted to weep in frustration, because she'd hoped this would all be easy, and it seemed now that it was going to be hard.

Yet she wouldn't weep in front of any lawman. Certainly not this one.

"It's time for you to leave now," she informed him stiffly.

He studied her a moment longer, his expression unreadable, and then touched his hand to his hat.

"Good night, Miss Spoon. If you know what's good for him, you'll see that your uncle brings that deed to town."

Emily stood rigidly, refusing to answer, refusing to budge even as he strode off toward the trees near the little knoll.

So, she thought, her knees trembling beneath her skirt. *He hid his horse far enough away so that no one in the cabin would hear his approach. Then he crept forward on foot, no doubt to scout out how many of the "Spoon gang" were on hand—and where.*

A cautious man. And a smart one.

The worst kind of lawman, Emily thought uneasily. Her stomach was churning. Even now, she could remember the strength with which he'd snatched the gun from her, held her. Standing alone beneath the moon, she felt again the power in those muscled arms.

And heard the deep flat politeness of his voice.

Still she didn't turn away, not until she saw him mount, glance back once more at her and at the cabin—and ride off, a shadowy figure in the moonlight, a man who sat tall and easy in the saddle, riding a dark horse, riding him hard.

It wasn't until she slipped back inside the cabin and bolted the door with shaking fingers that she realized Joey *had* awakened while she was outside.

To her horror, she found him with his face pressed against the window, the shutters drawn back. He was barefoot and trembling, his skin so pale she caught her breath. Tears streamed down his cheeks.

"Don't let him hurt me!" he sobbed. "Don't let him, Em-ly, please!"

"Oh, Joey, no! No one is going to hurt you ever again—it's all right!" Emily set the rifle down and enfolded him in her arms, drawing him away from the window. "There's no danger—nothing to be frightened of. That wasn't the bad man—it was only the sheriff, paying us a visit. And he's gone now. He rode back to town. Didn't you see?"

"Yes, but . . . but I thought—" He took a deep breath, still clinging to her neck with all his strength. "Are you sure he wasn't c-coming for me?"

"I'm very sure. I promise you. You're safe here, Joey. Very, very safe."

Emily spent the next half hour silently cursing the lawman, even as she reassured Joey again and again that there was no danger. It wasn't until she had fixed the little boy a glass of warm milk, tucked him back into bed, and sat with him until he fell asleep again that she realized Lonesome's sheriff had come and gone, scared both her and Joey half to death, left her with a warning . . . and never even told her his name.

Chapter 3

Clint Barclay tossed the dog-eared pile of wanted posters onto his desk and rubbed a hand across his eyes. He leaned back in his chair, trying to block out the loud snoring of the drunken old miner sleeping it off in the jail cell a dozen yards away. Shrieks and shouts of raucous merriment drifted in through the open window of the office, along with loud singing and the banging of piano keys. Sounded like things were getting pretty wild down at Coyote Jack's Saloon. And it was only a little past suppertime, Clint noted.

He figured he'd probably have to head over there and calm things down before too long.

But it wasn't only the miner's snoring or the saloon's rowdiness that kept him from concentrating on the wanted posters, memorizing the faces drawn on each one so that he could recognize any of the outlaws at a moment's notice, if he happened to spot one.

Another face kept appearing in his mind.

A far more appealing one.

The delicately sculpted, prettily oval face of Emily Spoon.

Clint shook his head in bafflement. How come with

nearly every female in this town devoting her spare time to trying to run his life and find him an eligible bride, foisting every daughter, cousin, niece, and acquaintance upon him in an attempt to corral him into marriage, the only woman whose face seemed stuck in his mind was a rifle-toting, icy-tongued beauty from a family of low-down outlaws?

It made no sense at all.

You don't want that *little handful for a bride, that's for damn sure,* he told himself with a grin. He'd be better off with Mrs. Dune's whiny-voiced niece, or Mary Kellogg's sister—or even Carla Mangley, he reflected with a shudder as he thought of the latter young woman's overbearing mother—than anyone related to Jake Spoon.

Still, it dumbfounded him that a family as low and common and crooked as the Spoons could produce such a gorgeous woman. Especially since there was nothing the least bit low or common about her—not as far as he could see. The raven-haired Miss Spoon spoke as finely as his own elegant sister-in-law, his brother Wade's new wife, Caitlin Barclay herself. Clint had just returned from Wade and Caitlin's wedding in Silver Valley, Wyoming, when he'd found out the bad news about the Spoon family moving into town.

But while the eastern-bred and -schooled Caitlin was blonde, cool, and sunny, Emily Spoon with her dark hair and smoldering gray eyes was all fire, earth, and ice.

Clint raked a hand through his hair, thinking of how determined she'd been to wrest that Winchester back from him. No doubt she'd have used it too, if he hadn't taken it away from her so quickly in the first place.

Two days had passed and Jake Spoon still hadn't shown up with his supposed deed to the Sutter place. No one had spotted him in town either. Must be away still, Clint reflected.

But doing what? he wondered suspiciously. If old Jake thought he was going to start holding up trains or banks or stagecoaches in other parts of the state, then hightail it to the fringes of Lonesome and hide out in the Sutter cabin, claiming he'd been ranching all the while, he'd sure as hell have another thing coming.

If he doesn't show up by tomorrow, Clint thought, *maybe I'll just pay Miss Spoon another visit and see if she's still all alone at that cabin.*

Not that she'd ever been exactly all alone to start with. There was the boy—that pale little kid he'd glimpsed at the cabin window just as he was riding off.

Clint wondered suddenly if the kid was Emily Spoon's son. Maybe she was married . . .

And maybe not, he reflected, his mouth tightening. *Maybe she's raising him alone—in the midst of an outlaw gang . . .*

Clint frowned. With her fine-boned features and those unusual silvery-gray eyes, Emily Spoon didn't even look old enough to have borne a child already five or six years old. Not unless she'd borne him when she was sixteen, seventeen . . . but . . .

Either way, it was none of his business, Clint told himself, pushing back his chair. He paced across the small office, his boots scraping upon the floor, and gulped a swig of nasty-tasting coffee that had gone bitter and cold in his cup.

Emily Spoon didn't concern him. It was Jake Spoon and his gang he needed to think about.

But that was part of the trouble. If Jake's niece was living in the cabin, she could well be involved in whatever the rest of the Spoons were up to. He remembered how insistent she'd been that he stay away from the cabin—and wondered if that boy was the only reason she'd wanted to keep him from going inside. It didn't make sense that she'd go to such lengths to hide a child. She could actually have been protecting someone else.

A lover? Clint set the cup down on his desk and frowned. A member of the gang? Maybe the kid's father, maybe he was an outlaw too . . .

Or maybe Jake Spoon himself had really been inside the cabin all along. Playing possum . . .

But he quickly dismissed this last idea. From what he knew about the outlaw, Jake wasn't the type of man to let his niece face down the law on her own. He might be crooked, but he was no coward who would hide behind a woman's skirts. He was hot-tempered and tough as buckskin. He'd have come out with guns blazing before he'd let a lawman get within an inch of his front door—or one of his womenfolk.

Clint sighed and picked up the stack of wanted posters again, but at that moment the door burst open and Hamilton Smith, Lonesome's paunchy, mustachioed banker, tumbled into the office.

"Clint—trouble!"

Clint took one look at his face and panic washed over him. "Don't tell me. Is it Agnes Mangley?" He sat up straighter in the chair. "Did Bessie tell her I'm back in town? Damn it, she's already picking out a wedding gown for Carla, isn't she—"

"No, no, nothing to do with Agnes or her daughter. I mean real trouble," Ham gasped breathlessly. "You'd best get down to Coyote Jack's—*now*. That whole place will be smashed to bits if you don't put a stop to things pronto."

Only a fight then. Clint relaxed. "Hell, why didn't you just say so, Ham?" He sprang out of his chair and headed toward the door.

"It's a helluva fight." The banker hurried after him, struggling to keep up with the sheriff's long strides. "The whole place has gone wild!"

Better that than to have Agnes Mangley on the wedding warpath again, Clint thought, loping toward the saloon. Still, he hoped he wouldn't need the two Colt .45s strapped to his gun belt. Things didn't get out of hand in Lonesome too often—most of the town was law-abiding, and even the miners and drifters passing through had heard of Clint and knew his reputation, so they toed the line as well. But tonight, things were definitely out of the ordinary. Even from the street he could hear mirrors splintering, bangs and thumps, men yelling.

The piano music had stopped.

As he pushed through the swinging doors and surveyed the riotous scene before him through a cloud of tobacco smoke, he saw that chaos reigned. Men were hurling punches right and left, someone threw a chair at a young cowboy in a green shirt and neckerchief, someone else threw a whiskey bottle that smashed into an already-shattered mirror over the bar.

Saloon girls were crammed onto the stairs or tucked into corners, and everywhere fists and oaths flew, while the owner and bartender, Big Roy, haplessly fired shots into the air, shouting futilely for the fighting to stop.

Clint's gaze zeroed in on the man in the center of the fray—the dark-haired cowboy in the green shirt and neckerchief, who had adroitly ducked as the flying chair sailed by. He seemed to be fighting three men at once, and though his lip was bloodied and there was already a bruise over one eye, he was holding his own. At six feet, nearly as tall as Clint, he clearly knew how to throw a punch—and how to take one.

Clint waded in among the brawlers, headed straight at

the young fire-eater. Along the way he pulled Mule Robbins and Squinty Brown apart, warning them that they'd land in jail if they didn't stop right then. Both men stared into the eyes of the sheriff and quickly returned to their senses.

"Hold on, Ed! Break it up!" Clint grabbed ahold of Ed Perkins's massive arm just as the blacksmith was about to hit a bewhiskered miner who'd been losing one poker hand after another every night for a week.

"Settle down, both of you, or you'll find yourself sharing a jail cell for the next week." The steel in his tone froze both men in their tracks. They lowered their fists and backed away from each other as Clint shouldered past.

Thus the room began to quiet and to clear as the sheriff finally reached the green-shirted man who had just doubled over after being punched in the stomach by Slim Jenks, one of the new hands at the WW Ranch.

"That's enough, Jenks," Clint ordered. "You too, Riley—and Frank. Back off."

The WW wranglers stopped, their fists still clenched.

"He started it, Sheriff." Jenks glared at the doubled-over cowboy slumped against a table. "He started the whole damned thing. And just guess who he is!"

"I don't give a damn who he is." Clint's steely gaze shifted from Jenks to the other two wranglers, who seemed determined to get in a few more licks. "The next man to throw a punch gets thrown into a cell. You got that?"

None of the three answered, but neither did they make a move.

"Roy," Clint called to the bartender. "Is what Jenks said true? Did this fellow start it?"

The bartender's gaze met the piercing stares of the

three WW wranglers, then slid to the dark-haired cowboy who groaned, trying to straighten up. "Yep, that's right. He started the whole thing, Sheriff. Didn't cotton to something Slim said to Florry, and he lit into him."

"Then what?"

"Then these two yellow-bellied cowards decided that bastard Jenks needed help and they jumped me," the green-shirted cowboy snarled, and before Clint could stop him he landed a blistering right cross to Slim Jenks's jaw. Jenks toppled backward and went sprawling across the floor. Riley and Frank surged forward—but halted at the sight of the black-handled Colt .45 in the sheriff's steady hand.

"I already warned you that the next man to throw a punch was going to jail and I meant it." Clint fixed the cowboy with a hard look, the type that had made more than one cold-blooded murderer start to sweat, but the cowboy in the green shirt only glared right back at him. Blood dripped from his cut lip, staining the front of his shirt. The bruise over his eye was already swelling.

"Let's go," Clint told him. "We've got laws against disturbing the peace and fighting in a public place. Anyone else want to come along and join him in a cell?" The sheriff's cold gaze raked the three men from the WW Ranch.

Slim Jenks came slowly to his feet and shook his head. "You're right to lock him up! You know who this is? He's Pete Spoon!"

That got Clint's full attention. He eyed the other man intently, then seized his arm. "That true? Are you Pete Spoon?"

"What if I am?" The cowboy wrenched away. "I didn't do a damn thing wrong—and you can't prove that I did."

Clint's gut clenched. Emily Spoon had assured him

that her family meant no trouble. And right off the bat, here was one of the Spoon boys tearing up the saloon.

"You started this fight, Spoon," he said evenly. "And I'm finishing it. Get moving."

He half expected the outlaw to resist, but to his surprise, Spoon merely eyed him resentfully from beneath a shock of dark hair and swaggered his way to the door.

"I might have thrown the first punch, all right," he muttered, "but then they jumped me—three against one." He swung toward the bartender. "You tell him, damn you. Tell him that's how it happened."

Clint saw Jenks, Riley, and Frank all turn to look at Big Roy once more. The bartender's eyes slid away from Clint's as he answered.

"Young Spoon started the fight. That's all I know. He was the one who threw the first chair that smashed into my mirror."

Pete Spoon snorted in contempt. "You sniveling, low-down coward, you're as worthless as they are!"

Clint gave him a push toward the door. "That's enough. Let's go. And the rest of you—clear out of here. *Now.* Unless you're planning to help Roy with the cleanup."

The saloon girls edged out of their hiding spots as Clint and Pete Spoon reached the double doors.

"Thanks, mister," Florry Brown said softly. She pushed a strand of toffee-colored hair behind her ear and smiled woefully at the cowboy in the blood-spattered green shirt.

Pete Spoon shot her back a crooked smile, then winced as his cut lip bled harder. "Wasn't no trouble at all, ma'am."

Once they reached the jailhouse, Clint put his prisoner in the second cell, then scanned the young man as he shut and locked the cell door. In the first cell, the miner snored on.

"Hold on, while I find some liniment for those bruises."

"Don't trouble yourself," Pete Spoon growled.

"Don't intend to." Clint hooked the keys onto his belt. "Is Jake Spoon your uncle?"

"Yeah. So what?"

"So Miss Emily Spoon is your sister."

"What of it?"

Clint regarded him coolly. "She tell you and Jake I stopped by?"

"Mentioned it."

"Your uncle back yet?"

"Could be."

Clint's tone was as hard as the bars that separated him from the outlaw. "Then why didn't he show up here? I'm sure your sister told him I want to see the deed to the ranch."

Pete pushed away from the bars and sank down on the cot against the wall. Gingerly he touched the bruise over his eye. "Ain't no law says we have to come in here and show you the deed to our ranch any time you say, is there, Sheriff? I reckon Uncle Jake'll get around to it when he's good and ready."

"By then, maybe I'll have thrown you all out of town, making it a moot point."

Pete Spoon stiffened, flashing the sheriff a hostile glance. "You can't do that."

"Care to make a wager on that?" Clint drawled. "I don't know yet what you're all up to, but I know you're trouble. And I don't tolerate trouble in Lonesome." Clint swung away. "At least, not for long."

"I didn't start that fight tonight," Spoon called after

him. "That low-down buzzard insulted that girl and I called him on it. The others jumped in against me."

"The bartender didn't back up your story." Clint was digging through his desk for liniment.

"The bartender's afraid of those boys. Maybe you are too," Pete taunted.

Clint had noticed Big Roy's strange behavior and he sensed that Pete Spoon just might be telling the truth. He hadn't had any trouble with Jenks before, but still . . .

It didn't matter. He wasn't about to let Spoon off the hook so easily. He'd been warned not to throw another punch, and he'd done it anyway.

Digging the liniment out of his desk drawer, he returned to the cell and tossed it through the bars to the prisoner stretched out on the cot.

Spoon caught it without a word.

After the outlaw had lowered himself back onto the cot, facing the wall, and Clint had settled back in his chair, he picked up the wanted posters and checked them all again, making sure none of them depicted any of the Spoons.

He didn't know if they were wanted men now. But they had been for a while, back in Missouri. And he remembered hearing something about Pete and Lester Spoon—cousins—mixed up in some gunfighting in Texas a few years back.

An image of Emily Spoon popped into his mind, that cloud of midnight hair framing her beautiful face. "We're just a family looking to set up ranching," she'd said.

Sure you are, lady. And I'm Napoléon Bonaparte.

"Pop! Emily! We got trouble."

Emily was cracking eggs into the sizzling butter in the

fry pan when Lester burst into the kitchen the next morning, his perspiring face so pale his freckles stood out even more than usual.

"It's Pete—I don't think he ever came home from town last night!"

Emily froze.

"What do you mean?" Jake had been helping himself to one of the buttermilk biscuits Emily had already set on a plate in the center of the table, but at these words he paused, his hand in midair as he peered hard at his son. "You sure?"

"He and his horse are both gone. I never heard him come in, and there's not a sign of him this morning." Lester dropped into a chair, wiping his sweaty face with his shirt sleeve. "And usually he's the one to fix coffee first thing—and look, Emily, there's not a drop in the pot."

"Could he have just decided to spend the night in town?" Emily was trying not to panic, but her expression was worried as she turned imploringly toward Jake. "He could have met a . . . a saloon girl, and had too much to drink . . . and . . . maybe slept it off somewhere . . . right?"

"Sure, honey, I'd bet my boots that's all it is." But they left unspoken the more dangerous possibilities: that some bounty hunter might have found him, recognized him from his days of being wanted in Missouri—then decided to bring him back there—dead or alive. Knowing Pete, Emily thought, her heart growing cold with fear, they'd never take him alive.

Or some cocky young gunfighter could have crossed his path—and decided to make a name for himself. Pete would never turn away from a dare or a fight. Her good-looking younger brother was too impulsive and sure of himself—and too hot-tempered.

"Uncle Jake, I'm scared." She swallowed past a lump in her throat and whispered, "Who knows what kind of trouble he's gotten himself into?"

At that moment Joey wandered into the kitchen, rubbing his eyes, his hair still tousled from sleep.

"Who? Me?" he asked, peering at Emily in alarm. He immediately started backing away.

"No, Joey, of course not. We weren't talking about you. It's Pete we're worried about. He . . ." She took a deep breath. "He seems to be missing."

"Did a bad man get him?"

Emily shook her head. "No. Come sit down."

When he obeyed, and was seated across the table from Jake, she returned to frying the eggs. She made a pot of coffee and set out a pitcher of milk and some dishes of butter and jam to go with the biscuits. But all the while her mind was spinning.

By the time she had poured a tall glass of milk for Joey and slipped into her own rather wobbly chair at the table, she had made up her mind.

"As soon as the dishes are done, I'm going into town to find Pete and bring him back," she said.

Her uncle swallowed a forkful of eggs. "Nope, Emily girl. It's best you stay here with the young'un—me and Lester will go."

"You don't want to run into that sheriff, Uncle Jake," she said quietly.

"Sure I do." His eyes blazed. "I want to give him a piece of my mind for coming out here and scaring you like that the other night. And if he wants to see the deed to this place, let him ride up here again in daylight and ask me for it!"

"You see, that's just what I'm worried about. Your temper is even worse than mine." In dismay, Emily pushed her plate away, too distraught to eat. "The wisest thing is for you to steer clear of him—you stay here with Joey and let me find Pete."

She saw his frown deepen and knew what he was thinking: that as the patriarch of the family he ought to be the one to go.

But deep down, Uncle Jake knew as well as she that he needed to lay low until folks in Lonesome got used to having him around and realized that none of the Spoons were going to cause them any trouble. As the one who'd served prison time for stagecoach robbery, the only member of the gang to be caught red-handed with loot from the holdup, he was the most notorious member of the gang and the acknowledged leader. His presence was the one most likely to get folks riled up—especially the sheriff.

Jake hadn't yet had the pleasure of meeting Lonesome's resident lawman, but he knew in his bones that situation would be rectified soon. Still, right now, they needed most of all to find Pete, and maybe Emily *was* best suited to that.

"All right, honey." He nodded. "You go ahead. See what you can find out. Lester, you stick by her—don't cause any trouble, boy, but don't back down from it either."

"You don't need to tell me that, Pop." Lester tugged his gun from its holster and checked it for bullets. "We'll be fine."

Joey's eyes widened and Emily saw the worry in their brown depths. She glanced at her uncle and nodded deliberately toward the boy.

"Say there, son." Uncle Jake's gruff voice took on a jovial tone. "Looks like you and me will have to fend for ourselves this morning. What do you say we take on kitchen duty and wash these dishes so Emily can get on to town? Think we can handle that?"

To Emily's relief, Joey nodded and actually smiled at her fierce-looking uncle as she jumped up from the table and grabbed her bonnet from its peg by the door.

"Take care not to break any dishes—we scarcely have enough to go around as it is," she admonished breathlessly as Lester stomped out the door. "We'll be back soon—with Pete," she added over her shoulder. Then she was hurrying toward the barn on Lester's heels, wondering just what she'd find when she reached Lonesome.

"Good thing that kid takes to Pop," Lester said as he helped her mount Nugget, the golden-maned palomino mare they'd bought for her in Denver. "You'd think he'd be scared of someone who looks like him. He's scared of everyone else. Even me," he said with a sigh.

"Uncle Jake does have a way with kids—he always has," Emily said absently, frowning into space as Lester mounted his dun gelding and they started toward the ridge.

"No need to worry so, Em." Her cousin threw her a swift glance. "I'll bet Pete's just having himself a good time with some pretty saloon gal, or something like that."

"We'll see," Emily muttered. But she prayed he was right as she spurred the mare to a gallop. The vast land swallowed them as they rode hard and fast across the sloping trail, the fierce sun beating down on their shoulders as they headed toward town.

The first places to check were the saloons, Emily knew. Lonesome had two of them, and she and Lester decided to start with the bigger, fancier one—Coyote Jack's.

The moment Emily saw the boarded-up windows, her heart sank. And when she and Lester stepped inside the dim, red-carpeted interior and saw the broken mirrors, shattered chandelier, overturned chairs and tables, the carpet stained with spilled whiskey, she knew.

A saloon fight.

She threw Lester a stricken glance.

"Ten to one it was over a girl," he murmured.

The bartender, still sweeping up broken glass behind the bar, frowned gloomily as they approached, picking their way through the debris. "We're closed. Until further notice, folks."

"You haven't by chance seen a man about six foot tall, wearing a . . . a . . ." Lester's voice trailed off and he glanced at Emily for help.

"A green shirt," she supplied. "He has black hair like mine—it's parted in the middle and there's a scar on his right hand . . ."

Her voice trailed off as the bartender straightened and scowled at them.

"I wish to hell I *hadn't* seen him—but I have." He grimaced. "Beg your pardon for cussing, ma'am. But that fellow's the one who started the fight. In ten years, my saloon's never been torn up this bad before."

Emily swallowed. "Where is he?" she asked, dreading the answer.

The bartender came around the bar and began whisking the broom beneath a table where shards of a broken whiskey bottle were scattered. "In jail. Where he belongs," he said darkly. "Thanks to Sheriff Barclay. He can rot there as far as I'm concerned."

"Sheriff *Barclay*?" Emily gasped as Lester gaped at the man. "Do you . . . mean . . . *Clint* Barclay?"

Clint Barclay. That name was seared into her brain for all time—he was the lawman who'd sent Uncle Jake to prison. The one who'd tracked him mercilessly, arrested him, testified against him in court.

She felt like she was going to faint.

The bartender eyed them both from beneath bushy brows. "Yep. Clint Barclay. You know him?"

"Not . . . exactly," Lester said grimly.

"Well, let me tell you, Clint Barclay's the best sheriff this side of the Rockies. Cleaned out the Duggan gang a few years back. Single-handed too. He's the best damned shot I ever did see . . . Hey, where're you going?"

His last words were drowned out by the slamming of the double doors.

The black-haired girl and the moon-faced man were gone.

Chapter 4

WHEN ARE YOU PLANNING TO LET *me* out of here, damn you?"

As the sour-smelling old miner shuffled out of his cell, past the sheriff, and headed for the door, Pete Spoon gripped the iron bars and glared at the implacable lawman.

"You have twenty bucks to pay the fine for fighting, Spoon?"

"Not on me, but—"

The sheriff cut him off, turning to the miner. "Cuddy, you keep out of trouble. I don't want to see you back here for at least a month."

The old miner, bent and bleary-eyed, waved a vague hand in the air. "Hmmmph. I'm headed to Leadville. They're not so quick to lock a body up over there."

The jailhouse door creaked shut behind him. Ignoring the glowering prisoner who remained behind bars, Clint strode to his desk and dropped the keys inside a drawer.

"How long you planning to keep me locked up?" Pete demanded.

"Until I'm good and ready to let you out." Clint was already reaching for the ledger crammed full of paperwork, all of it demanding his attention. The sun was hot and bright as a griddle full of grease, and the office air was stifling. He wished like hell he was out fishing instead of stuck in town half-buried in work, but there was a stack of correspondence, warrants, and directives from the federal marshal's office that had piled up while he was away at Wade's wedding, and then there was this prisoner to keep an eye on, and the rest of the Spoon gang to consider . . .

The thought had no sooner passed through his mind than the office door burst open and Emily Spoon swept in with sparks flying from her eyes. She was wearing a most becomingly fitted white blouse and a dark blue riding skirt that swished around her ankles as she crossed the floor with quick precise strides. Right on her heels came a huge, burly man in his early twenties, clad in buckskin, with red hair and a neck thick as a bull's.

"Sheriff Clint Barclay!" Emily Spoon spat out the name like poison, her face ablaze with fury and contempt.

"*What?* Clint Barclay?" Pete Spoon lunged up against the iron bars. "Em, is that *him*?"

It was Lester who answered, his hard gaze locking on the sheriff who came slowly, nonchalantly to his feet. "It sure is, Pete. The bartender at Coyote Jack's just told us."

"Morning, Miss Spoon." Clint strode easily around the desk. He towered over Emily, threw Lester a swift, coldly appraising glance, then shifted his gaze back to the woman who stood trembling furiously before him.

"Is there something I can do for you, ma'am?" he asked coolly.

Emily's fingers itched. Oh, how they itched. She wanted to slap him. Or kick him where it would really hurt. Or scratch his eyes out. But she did none of these things. She glared at him, shock and anger and distress raging through her like a wild and uncontrollable storm.

Clint Barclay, damn his cold, ruthless lawman's eyes, stared right back.

"So you're the man who tracked down my uncle and had him thrown in jail."

"That's right." He had the nerve to look as calm as if they were discussing the chance of rain.

"You broke up my family. Ruined my aunt's life! She died calling for him, never seeing him again—"

Her voice quavered and broke, and it was Lester who clapped a hand on her shoulder and said tersely, "Don't tear yourself up like this, Emily. He's not worth it."

"You're right." Emily took a deep breath, fighting for control. But it wasn't easy. Visions of Aunt Ida growing weaker and weaker were embedded in her mind. She'd never forget how her aunt had suffered, her heart failing, her body slowly giving in to death. And all the while, every morning, every night, she'd called out for Uncle Jake, even with her last rasping breath.

"The other night—why didn't you tell me who you were?" she demanded. Her voice shook. "If I'd known—"

"What would you have done, Miss Spoon? Shot me with that rifle I took away from you?"

Clint regretted the words the moment he said them. The truth was, he was fighting against an unexpected surge of pity. He didn't regret putting the leader of a feared outlaw gang behind bars, not for a moment—but he regretted the very real pain on Emily Spoon's lovely face.

"Look," he said quickly, "try to be reasonable for a minute. When I tracked your uncle down six years ago, I was just doing my job. I put lawless men behind bars, and I'll be damned if I'll apologize for that—"

Emily slapped him. The ringing thud of her hand striking his face seemed to echo for one shocking instant through the jailhouse. But it wasn't enough to satisfy the passionate rage swirling through her—her temper wholly snapping, she lifted her hand and tried to do it again.

But this time he caught her wrist and held it fast, his eyes going flat and hard—the eyes of a man without pity.

"I don't think so, Miss Spoon," he said softly.

Lester rushed at him then. "Let her go, damn you, Barclay!"

The hard shove he gave the sheriff should have sent him reeling backward, but it didn't. Instead Clint Barclay only stepped back a pace, quickly releasing Emily's wrist. Then in one lightning motion he landed a bone-crunching right to Lester's jaw, a blow that sent the red-haired man spinning to the floor.

"Lester!" Emily cried in horror.

Lester clambered up dizzily and charged again, but the lawman hit him once more, and he fell back with a grunt, crashing into a chair.

"Emily—grab the keys from the desk drawer and get me out of here. I'll teach him a lesson!" Pete was shouting.

But the next instant, as Lester and Barclay traded blows again, Lester suddenly was knocked to the floor and this time he struck his head. Clint stepped in front of Emily so she couldn't reach the keys in his desk, but she made no attempt to get past him; instead she flew to her cousin and knelt beside his still form.

"Lester! Lester, are you all right?" she asked frantically as his eyes remained closed. "My God, what have you done to him?"

Clint made no reply.

Lester Spoon moaned, and Emily let out her breath in relief, even as she cradled his head in her lap.

"Don't try to move yet. Just wait. Pete, are you all right?"

"I will be soon as you get me out of here and I can say a few choice words to Barclay!"

Clint leaned against his desk, watching Emily fret over the fallen man. "I can hear you through the bars just fine."

"You're despicable!" Emily cried. As Lester struggled to a sitting position, clutching his battered jaw, she scrambled to her feet and faced the lawman.

"You're nothing but a bully!" She was shaking. Never had she seen anyone fight like that. Lester was tough—he and Pete, she knew, had started and finished more than a few barnyard and saloon brawls—but the sheriff had knocked him down as easily as if he were no bigger than Joey.

"You have no idea what you did to my family. And now . . . this! Why is my brother locked up in that cell?"

"He was fighting in a public place. And disturbing the peace."

"Let him out. Now."

"I'm afraid I can't do that, Miss Spoon. He has to serve two days' time, and then there's the matter of a twenty-dollar fine."

A twenty-dollar fine! Emily's heart sank.

"You have twenty dollars, Miss Spoon?"

"I'll get it, damn you!"

"Fine." Clint nodded, pushing away from the desk to stand towering before her. "Bring it in tomorrow, and he's all yours."

Emily stepped toward him again, her hands clenched into fists. Oh, how she wanted to hit him. But it would only lead to more trouble. She struggled once more to control her temper, but rage filled her, and she knew she was trembling from head to toe.

"From the looks of that saloon, I'm sure Pete wasn't the only one who was fighting. Why isn't anyone else locked up?"

"He was the one who started it all."

"I think you're lying." Emily stalked closer. "You're just trying to harass him—and all of us so we'll leave."

"I'm trying to keep the peace. Anyone who can't live peaceably like the rest of our law-abiding citizens can clear out."

"You'd like that, wouldn't you?" Pete yelled from inside the cell.

"Hell, yes. I would." But Clint was watching Emily Spoon's pale, angry face and feeling a twinge of something that made him downright uncomfortable. He didn't know why. He believed in what he did for a living, believed in it down to his very core.

After losing his own parents to a murderous outlaw gang when he was nine, a gang that left him and his two brothers orphaned, he had no sympathy for those who broke the law and terrorized others. The outlaws who'd killed his parents all those years ago had never been captured and made to pay for their crime, but he'd spent his life bringing other lawless men just like them to justice. He'd worked hard trying to make the West safer. Using his gun, his wits, his fists, and his own strength, he'd dedicated himself to protecting people from the human vultures who roamed this land.

But Emily Spoon didn't see things that way. Her loyalties were firmly entrenched with those on the wrong side of the law.

"No, Lester—don't." She grabbed her cousin's arm as

he finally gained his footing and tried to stagger toward the sheriff. "Just stand still a moment. Lean on me."

"Dizzy," he muttered. "Otherwise I'd give him what he deserves . . ."

Noting his glazed eyes and battered face, Emily's stomach clenched. She threw a helpless glance at Pete, watching wrathfully from behind the bars, and then turned her frustration on Clint Barclay.

"See what you've done! He's hurt!"

"If you ask me, he's damn lucky. I could lock him up too."

"Oh, my, aren't you the soul of kindness."

Barclay folded his arms across his chest. "Come back tomorrow with the money, Miss Spoon. Better yet, send your uncle instead—with the deed to the ranch."

"Go to hell!" Pete yelled from behind bars.

"You . . . want to see . . . my pa, you'll have to . . . go to him," Lester said in a thick tone.

Clint's dislike for both of the Spoon boys was growing by the moment. They didn't strike him as being low-down-mean and brutal like the Duggans, or like some of the gunmen he'd encountered over the years, but they were hot-headed, arrogant, and full of themselves—and he had no patience to deal with rough young pups who needed to learn manners and respect for the law.

"Miss Spoon, allow me to get the door. It appears your cousin needs to rest a spell."

He had to admire the way she looked at him. As if she'd skewer him alive if she could and leave his heart for the buzzards.

Miss Emily Spoon had spunk—and just as much arrogance as her brother and cousin. But she was a lot nicer to look at, he had to admit, his gaze flickering over her lush figure and that luxuriant cloud of hair. For a moment he wondered just what it would feel like to tangle his hands in those dark velvet curls that so enticingly spilled down her back and framed her face.

Or to kiss that wide, pretty mouth.

He wondered if she'd taste as good as she looked.

Whoa. Clint drew in a deep breath and dragged his thoughts back to business. This was no ordinary woman, to be admired, enjoyed, perhaps squired to a picnic or church social, he reminded himself grimly.

She was a Spoon.

But he noticed that when Lester leaned on her while they made their way to the door, it was all she could do to support him and he gritted his teeth.

"Want some help?"

"Not from you," she returned scathingly.

Fine. She didn't want his help, he wouldn't offer it again. Even if her damned cousin fell flat on his face in the middle of the street.

As they brushed past him going out the door, he caught the scent of lilacs drifting past. Nice. Real nice . . .

But nothing that ought to make a man's blood surge through his veins, he admonished himself, startled by his own heated reaction.

It wasn't exactly sultry French perfume, like Estelle over in the saloon wore, or that musky, oily rose scent that enveloped most of the other saloon girls at Coyote Jack's.

This was clean, soft, pretty. Like her, Clint realized, grimacing.

Next thing you know you'll be following her, he thought.

But he didn't. He stood still and watched the two of them stagger out of the jailhouse and down the boardwalk toward their horses. Lester Spoon was mighty unsteady and the girl was struggling to help him. Frowning, he wondered how they were going to make it home.

Then he reminded himself it wasn't his job to make Lonesome a soft, welcoming place for outlaw families. Or to see they got safely back to their dens.

He stalked back into the office and slammed the door, trying to block out the memory of the distress he'd seen in Emily Spoon's eyes when she'd spotted her brother in that cell and the way she'd fretted about her cousin.

Pete Spoon's voice barreled at him, hard and low.

"You ever touch my sister again, Barclay—you're going to pay."

But before Clint could reply, his attention was drawn to the window, and what—or more precisely, *who*—he saw bearing down at him, headed straight from Hazel's Millinery to his office door.

"Damn. No!" He yanked the shade down and wheeled away from the window. Little beads of sweat popped out on his brow.

"They coming back?" Pete demanded.

Clint barely heard him. All he knew was that Agnes Mangley and her daughter, Carla, were swishing up the street in yards of bustled muslin and lace and hats with bird's nests in them.

Coming his way.

And Clint knew why.

Swearing under his breath, he sprinted toward his desk, grabbed the keys from the drawer, and rushed back to twist the lock on the office door. Hooking the key ring on his belt he dove toward the back door, ignoring the incredulous stare of Pete Spoon from behind the bars. Just in time he dodged out into the alley, faintly hearing the loud rap on his door and shrill calls of "Sheriff! Yoo-hoo! Sheriff Barclay!"

He nearly tripped over a pile of discarded trash, righted himself with an oath, and sprinted down the alley faster than a jackrabbit, making a beeline for the one place he'd be safe from any or all of the matchmaking ladies in Lonesome—the one place no respectable lady would set foot—the back door of Coyote Jack's saloon.

Chapter 5

EMILY GRIPPED THE KNIFE TIGHTLY and hacked away at the five potatoes on the counter before her, then dumped the slices into the simmering pot of beef stew on the stove so forcefully that boiling water splattered. Behind her at the kitchen table, Uncle Jake was blowing smoke rings into the air as he and Joey played gin rummy, both of them yammering over the intricacies of the game. But she barely heard a word—her mind was too full of the image of Clint Barclay's arrogant face.

I wish I could dump him into a pot of boiling water, she thought savagely.

From the moment she'd returned from town she'd been unable to think of anything but that horrible scene in his office.

Why didn't I bring the rifle along, aim it at Clint Barclay's broad chest, and order him to let Pete out of that cell?

Because then you'd have been breaking the law and he'd have tried to lock you *up,* a small sane voice from within admonished her, but she just scowled and wished she'd done something more useful than slapping Barclay's face.

The man seemed invincible—nothing seemed to penetrate that cool, iron calm of his, the impression he gave of being able to handle anything that came his way. *He's solid,* she thought suddenly, *rock solid.* She had to admit that wasn't a bad quality in a man. But it was in a lawman, she told herself. Especially a lawman trying to drive your family out of town.

She remembered the way he'd gripped her wrist when she'd tried to slap him, remembered the heat of his touch on her skin, the strength in his grip. He'd clamped his hand around her tight enough to prevent her from slapping him twice and from jerking free, but not enough to hurt. Even angry, she reflected, frowning, he'd thought to temper his strength.

Doesn't anything shake him up, make him lose control? she wondered. Not that she wanted him to, she told herself. But it was maddening to confront someone so in command of himself, someone who never lost his temper enough to give anyone an edge.

She, on the other hand, had the Spoon weakness for flying off the handle.

How can you criticize Uncle Jake and Pete and Lester for their tempers, when you can't even control your own? she thought in frustration.

"That stew smells mighty good," Jake said from the table behind her, interrupting her thoughts, and Joey chimed in too.

"Smells mighty good," he repeated. Then his small voice exclaimed, "Gin!"

Jake chuckled. He pushed two marbles toward the boy. "You beat me, son. Good for you. You're a real fine card player."

"Mr. Spoon, can we play again?"

The eagerness in Joey's voice made her pause in the

midst of chopping carrots to glance over her shoulder. Joey's normally pinched little face had lost its tautness for once—his eyes sparkled as Jake handed over his cards and the boy carefully began to shuffle them as he'd been taught.

Oh, Lord, I hope he doesn't teach the child to cheat, or Lissa will never forgive me, Emily thought suddenly, but aloud she merely said, "One more game, you two, and then someone needs to set the table and someone else needs to tend to the chickens."

"Already?" Joey sighed.

"Once dinner is over and all the chores are done, you may play one more hand—if Uncle Jake agrees."

"Do you, Uncle Jake?"

Despite her distraught state, Emily's lips curved up in a smile. *Uncle Jake.* The boy was warming to her uncle nicely. Jake noticed it too, and winked at her from the table.

"You bet, son." He took a drag on his cigar and puffed out another smoke ring. "I need a chance to win back my marbles, don't I?"

She tossed the carrots into the stew, added a can of green beans, and gave everything a quick stir with a spoon, then slipped off to the back bedroom.

Lester was rolled up in his bunk against the far wall, eyes closed. Gently, she touched his shoulder.

"Are you all right, Lester?"

"I reckon."

His voice sounded fuzzy.

"I'll bring you some stew in a bit. Don't try to get up."

"That sheriff sure hits hard," he muttered. "But you wait—next time I'll be the one to knock him flat on his back."

"There won't be any next time," Emily said quickly.

"After tomorrow, you'd best stay away from Barclay—and that goes for Pete too. And double for Uncle Jake," she added, as Lester pushed himself up to a sitting position.

"Did you tell Pop yet about Clint Barclay being the sheriff here?"

"No, not yet." Emily paced around the room, her anxiety mounting again. "I'm waiting until Joey goes to bed. I don't want him getting upset when Uncle Jake explodes." And he *would* explode, she knew, her brows knitting.

"Lester." Abruptly, she returned to her cousin's side and gazed at him imploringly. "Promise that you'll help when I have to keep him from riding into town and shooting Clint Barclay!"

"Pop won't go flying off the handle." Gingerly, he touched a finger to his swollen jaw. "Maybe he would have before. But he's different since prison. He knows how to hold his temper better."

Emily hoped he was right. It was true that her uncle didn't drink liquor the way he used to, as much or as often, and his temper *was* steadier, less likely to erupt over small matters.

But this was no small matter.

"I hope you're right," she said uneasily. "But if he starts to get all riled up—especially since now Clint Barclay has locked *Pete* up in jail—then I expect you to pitch in and help me settle him down before he does anything foolish."

"Don't worry, Em, I'll help you. Not that I wouldn't like to see Barclay get what he has coming," Lester added darkly.

Unexpectedly, Emily felt the sting of tears behind her eyes.

"Em, what's wrong?"

"Nothing. It's . . . nothing."

"You can tell me," Lester said quietly. "Come on—you hardly ever cry."

"I'm not crying." She blinked back the threatening tears. "It's just that when we came here, and I saw this cabin, this land, I . . . I thought we'd be staying, I really did, but now . . ."

Lester struggled to his feet with an effort and went to her, slipping an arm around her shoulders. "Come on, Em, it'll be fine. It's not as if we have to mix much with the sheriff—or the town, either, for that matter. We're all the way out here on our own place. We'll get the ranch going, and everything will work out."

But Emily was thinking also of her dressmaking business. She needed the goodwill and patronage of the women of Lonesome. She'd been counting on her knowledge of society fashions to attract their interest in the gowns she planned to sew. But if the women of Forlorn Valley feared or disliked her and her family, who would want to purchase dresses from her?

No one.

The thought frightened her. Because if she couldn't make a go of her dressmaking business, then everything would depend on the success of the ranch. And if that failed . . .

She couldn't bear to think about that—about the possibility that Pete and Lester might go back to holdups and running from the law—that they'd all be separated, and would lose this land, this chance for a fresh start. She'd wind up a servant again, toiling for another tyrannical socialite like Augusta Wainscott.

She never wanted to go back to *that*.

You'll simply have to make the dressmaking a suc-

cess—enough of a success to support the whole family, if necessary.

Just because the Spoons were at odds with the sheriff of Lonesome didn't mean they had to be at odds with the entire town, she reasoned. But doubt gnawed at her.

"Don't look so glum," Lester pleaded. "Honest, Emily, you don't know how bad Pete and I felt having left you and Aunt Ida to fend for yourself all those years. We want to make it up to you."

"It wasn't so bad, Lester," she lied. "Not for the most part."

For a moment her mind drifted to the Wainscott household. She could still hear Mrs. Wainscott's thin, waspish voice, pecking at her, scolding and demanding, continuously finding fault. And she could still remember what it was like scurrying up and down the stairs with armloads of linens and towels and buckets and brooms. She could remember the smell of lemon polish and beeswax and how it felt to endlessly dust and scour and scrub and sweep—three storys, each and every day. The ache in her arms by midafternoon, the rawness of her hands.

Then caring for Aunt Ida at night.

She saw Lester watching her and, pushing the difficult memories aside, summoned a smile. "It's over now," she said firmly. "It's all in the past. Lester, this is our fresh start."

"Damn right it is."

Emily thought of the tall handsome sheriff with those cynical storm-blue eyes. "And no one is going to ruin it for us," she muttered.

"Em-ly?" Joey hovered in the doorway. "Uncle Jake says that in another minute the stew's going to be all burnt up."

Oh, Lord. Emily spun around and dashed back toward

the stove, thankful she didn't intend to earn her living in a kitchen.

Fortunately, the stew was only simmering wildly and everything tasted just fine. And after a dinner of hearty stew and thick sliced bread and warm apple pie and coffee, after she'd tidied the kitchen and tucked Joey into bed, and picked up her needle and thread to finish stitching the curtains, she waited until Lester had stretched out on the horsehair sofa, and Uncle Jake had added logs to the fire before sinking down on the armchair with a block of wood and his knife, before she told him the name of the sheriff who had locked Pete up in Lonesome's jail. The sheriff who wanted to see the deed to their ranch.

The sheriff who wanted to drive them away from his town.

"Clint Barclay!"

Jake Spoon's thick raspy voice sounded even thicker and raspier than ever as the name exploded from his lips.

"Naw! That . . . can't be." His brows clamped together as Emily bit her lip. "Emily girl—are you sure?"

Filled with dread, she nodded. "I didn't know his name until today, Uncle Jake—"

He surged off the chair, dropping the knife and the wood as he sprang toward the door.

"Uncle Jake!"

"He locked me up and now he's locked up Pete! I'll be damned if I sit here like an old woman while he goes after my family one by one!"

Lester staggered to his feet but Jake was already at the door.

It was Emily who darted after him and grabbed his sleeve.

"No, this isn't the way. It will only—"

He whipped around to confront her and her voice trailed off at the fury in his eyes.

"Let go of me, girl."

She almost cringed before that harsh voice. His eyes were cold, slitted, mean, so unlike the eyes of the uncle who had taken her and Pete in when they were children not yet even ten years old, and along with Aunt Ida had promised to keep them, raise them, love them as his own. This was Jake Spoon the outlaw, robber of stagecoaches. Murder shone from his eyes.

"Pop, come on now, you just stop and think. I told Emily you'd changed and she thought so too, but now—"

"Clint Barclay, Lester!" Jake snarled.

Then his gaze at last truly focused on his niece's distraught face. He saw the tears shining in those wide eyes, the trembling in her lip, and suddenly the violence died out of him as quickly as it had sprung up. The red blinding rage receded, and he gripped the slender hand clutching at his sleeve.

"Emily, don't look like that," he said hoarsely. "I'm not . . . goin' nowhere."

Relief flooded her so powerfully she could barely speak. "That's good, Uncle Jake. It's . . . it's not the way . . . to handle this."

"You're right. Lester, so're you." He nodded at his son, but it was Emily he smiled at. His lips almost cracked with the effort but he did.

"You said before . . . the sheriff wants twenty dollars to cover that fine for fighting."

"Yes." Emily moistened her lips. "And he's insisting on seeing the deed to the ranch."

"I'll bring him what he wants tomorrow," the gray-haired man said grimly.

"Uncle Jake, let me."

"I'm not scared to face him, Emily girl."

"Of course not. But . . . you said yourself when we were traveling out here that you've got little use now for towns or people. And maybe it would be best if you didn't meet up with Sheriff Barclay again—just yet."

"What the hell's the point of waiting?"

Lester spoke up. "To tell the truth, Em, I don't see the point either. Might as well get it over with."

She glanced from one to the other. Maybe they were right. Uncle Jake had served his time, after all. And no good evidence had ever been found against Pete or Lester.

Lonesome's sheriff might be a formidable man, but he could hardly arrest them or order them out of town without just cause.

And she'd make sure he had none of that.

Her gaze shifted to Lester. "All right. We'll go, but you stay here with Joey."

"Em! You think I'm afraid to face that no good low-down—"

"You're not afraid of anyone or anything, just like Pete," she said impatiently. "Though sometimes I wish you were. But I don't want to bring Joey into town yet. He's just starting to get comfortable here at the cabin, and I'm not ready for people to start asking questions about him. There'll be time enough if Lissa doesn't get back soon and I have to send him to school. But for now," she took a deep breath, "under no circumstances can John Armstrong find him, so I don't want to take any unnecessary chances."

"I'd like to get my hands on that weasel who beat your gal friend and the boy," Jake muttered fiercely, momentarily distracted from thoughts of Barclay.

"Let's hope you don't ever get the chance—that none

of us ever sees him again," Emily said fervently. "But I do think that the best way to keep Joey safe is to keep him here at the cabin, quiet-like, for a while. I'll figure out what to say about him in time."

She hooked her arm through her uncle's and led him back to his chair. Lester followed, sinking down on the sofa once again.

"Right now our first order of business is to get Pete released from that jail," Emily said.

"I still think you should be the one to stay here with the boy," her cousin grumbled.

She shook her head. "After what happened today, you'd best stay away from Sheriff Barclay. The less you have to do with him the better."

"I'm not going to lose my temper again."

"That's right." Emily planted her hands on her hips. "Because you'll be here with Joey, repairing the corral posts and building that new shed you promised me."

Jake chuckled suddenly. "Give up, boy. She's got the Spoon temper *and* her mother's stubbornness. I never could talk my sis out of anything once she set her mind to it. Emily not only looks like your Aunt Tillie, she's got the same spine of steel."

"I reckon." Lester slumped back against the cushions and gazed at his cousin, frowning. "But I didn't like the way that sheriff looked at you, Em. You watch out for him."

"What do you mean, how he looked at her?" Jake's gaze sharpened.

"Well, he knew she was a woman, that's what I mean."

"Lester, you're being stupid," Emily heard herself say, but she felt hot color rush into her cheeks. "Clint Barclay looked at me like I was something that crawled out from under a rock—just because I'm a Spoon. But he's going to find out that we Spoons don't scare—or run—quite that easily. Before long, we're going to be as much a part of this town as he is—maybe more."

Yet riding to town beside Uncle Jake the next day, the wagon wheels jolting over the rough trail, Emily felt her confidence slipping. She was dreading the imminent encounter with Clint Barclay and praying her uncle would manage to keep a lid on his temper no matter how much the sheriff provoked him.

They had to get Pete out of jail and start getting accustomed to the town—and the town to them. Before Clint Barclay could turn everyone against them.

As far as Clint Barclay looking at her like she was a woman, well—she was a woman. But Barclay hadn't seemed particularly impressed. She'd had warmer looks from a hitching post.

Which suited her just fine, because despite those keen blue eyes and that lean, masculine jaw, and that broad chest of his, he was the last man on the continent she'd want to be noticed by.

The very last man.

Lonesome's dusty main street was full of people bustling to and fro. Unlike yesterday, when she'd only had one thought in her mind—finding Pete—today she was far more aware of her surroundings. She noticed that the buildings lining the boardwalk boasted almost identical weathered gray facades, that the high blue sky dotted with satin-puff clouds seemed to dwarf the gritty little town, that horses neighed and buggy wheels groaned and children played beneath a tree at the far end of town.

She saw chickens pecking in the alley behind the Wagon Wheel Saloon and a cat drowsing on the doorstep outside Hazel's Millinery. From the second-floor balcony of Coyote Jack's Saloon came the trill of female laughter, and she glanced up to see two women in spangled and feathered dresses, eating apples and calling out to the cowboys who emerged from the feed store with sacks of grain slung over their shoulders.

The largest shop was Doily's Mercantile, Emily noted, but there was also the Gold Gulch Hotel, a livery, the feed store, a bank, and a leather goods store whose front window displayed several fancy and plain saddles, a handsome pair of cowboy boots, and a shelf full of guns: Army Colts, Remington revolvers, derringers.

She didn't spot a single dress shop and with a small flicker of excitement guessed that the only ready-made dresses to be found in Lonesome would have to be bought from the mercantile or through a mail-order catalogue.

That was good.

Uncle Jake reined in the team of horses in front of the sheriff's office, right across from the bank, and as she alighted, she saw that the feed store beside the jail had a sign in the window, as did several other establishments.

POKER TOURNAMENT—Friday through Saturday.
Gold Gulch Hotel
TOWN DANCE—Saturday Night. Come one, come all.

Beneath the words was a row of dollar signs.

Reading over her shoulder, Jake grunted. "Pete and Lester see that, they'll be keen to try their luck." He squinted at the fine print. "Five dollars apiece to enter. We could buy a pile of lumber and nails for fixing the barn roof with that kind of money." He snorted. "Bad enough we have to throw away this twenty dollars just to get Pete out of jail."

"Let's just take one thing at a time, Uncle Jake," Emily soothed him.

"I've got a notion to tear down all these posters before Pete comes out here and sees them."

"There's probably a law against that," Emily murmured with a rueful smile. She gripped his arm as they started toward the jailhouse. "Now promise me, no matter what happens, you won't lose your temper."

"Damn it, girl, I already promised."

"Promise me again."

He pushed open the door. "Let's just get this over with."

Emily's heart thudded as she stepped inside. Clint Barclay was writing in a ledger at his desk, but he looked up as they walked in.

His eyes flicked quickly over Emily, with no display of emotion, she noted, her shoulders tensing. Then his gaze shifted to the man beside her. Slowly, with unsettling grace, like a taut rope unfurling, he rose from the chair.

"Something I can do for you, Spoon?" he asked in a steely tone.

Emily's fingers tightened warningly on her uncle's arm. She sensed his fury at the mere sight of the lawman who had put him in jail. And knew how hard this must be for him.

"We're here to pay the fine for fighting," she said quickly.

Jake dug in his pocket, then tossed some greenbacks on the sheriff's desk. "Let my nephew out of that damned cell."

"You got the deed to the Sutter place?"

"My niece told you I did."

"Let's see it."

"Maybe I just didn't bring it," Jake snapped, his eyes like flint.

"Uncle Jake." Emily glanced over at Pete. He stood

gripping the bars of the cell, watching the exchange intently.

"Please," she whispered, "let's just get this over with."

"Don't show it to him, Uncle Jake!" Pete shouted suddenly. "He has no damn right to ask you for it. I'll stay here till he's sick of looking at my face, but don't you—"

"Pete—hush!" Emily exclaimed.

"You'd best listen to her, Spoon." The sheriff nodded toward the young woman in the clean, pressed blue gingham, the young woman whose midnight curls were tightly subdued by a single braid down her back. "At least she's got some sense."

"Who asked you?" Emily whirled on him. "If you had an ounce of decency in you, you'd open that cell door right now. There's no law that says we even need to show you the deed. We brought it as a courtesy."

Clint Barclay met those shimmering gray eyes and felt a tug of respect. And something else, a pang of conscience. He was giving the Spoons a hard time, but that's because he didn't trust them. Still, Pete Spoon *had* served his time and the fine was paid.

He let his gaze linger on those luminous eyes for one more moment before snagging the keys from the desk drawer.

"Let's see if you can stay out of trouble," he told Pete as he unlocked the door and swung it wide.

For one awful moment, Emily thought Pete was going to refuse to leave the cell, just to spite Barclay, but then he stalked past the lawman, came to stand alongside Emily and Jake, and planted his feet apart as the sheriff handed him back his gun.

"Now I'd like to see that deed." Clint spoke solely to Jake.

His mouth tightly set, the older man yanked a paper

out of his pocket, uncrumpled it, and pushed it at the sheriff.

"No one's lived on that property for years," Clint commented as he scanned the document. "Last I heard, old Bill Sutter got silver fever and headed out to Leadville." He studied Jake intently as he handed back the deed. "Mind telling me how you got this?"

"None of your damn business." Jake stuffed the deed back in his pocket.

"You got anything else to say, Sheriff?" Pete's slate-gray eyes glinted. "Much as we enjoy jawing around here with you all day, we got ourselves a ranch to run."

Emily wanted to poke him in the ribs but instead she stayed very still and held her breath.

Clint Barclay looked from one to the other of them. Despite her straight back and proudly lifted chin, the girl looked pale. Yet those eyes skewered him.

"You can go. For now. But I'm warning you, all of you—and that means Lester too—if there's any sign of trouble, any *hint* of trouble, I'm coming to the Sutter place first. To find you."

"You mean the Spoon place," Emily said quietly. "It's the Spoon place now."

There was a moment of complete silence. Then Pete draped an arm around her shoulders and all three of them headed to the door.

When it slammed behind them, Clint stood for a moment, lost in thought. He hoped like hell he wasn't going to have to arrest the Spoons. The girl was too fond of them for her own good, and worse, she was loyal to the bone. When they went back to their crooked ways—if they hadn't already—it was going to tear out her heart.

He wondered why he should care. Just because she

was beautiful, because she had more spunk and passion in her than a wild filly who'd never known a harness or lead rope? Because of the soft, sensuous glide of her hips when she walked? Or because he remembered how she'd felt when he'd held her close that night at the cabin, how she'd stood up to him with a kind of desperate courage that he'd rarely seen.

Perhaps only once, long ago, had he heard of courage like that—when his mother had tried to protect his younger brother, Nick, from the outlaws who'd held up their stage. His mother had snatched Nick behind her, shielding her seven-year-old son with her own body, showing the same kind of frantic courage he'd seen in Emily Spoon that first night.

Clint returned to his desk, but it was a long while before he was able to focus his thoughts on his work.

Chapter 6

EMILY WAITED UNTIL THEY WERE across the street before she turned to Pete and threw her arms around him. "Are you all right? You look worse than Lester does!"

"You mean this?" Her brother touched the purple bruise above his eye. "It's nothing. Scarcely hurts atall, Sis. And before you start lecturing me, I'll have you know that fight wasn't my fault. I was only defending a lady, and those varmints jumped me—three of 'em—"

"If trouble were money," Emily interrupted sternly, "we'd all be as rich as Midas."

"Especially with a couple of hotheads like him and Lester," Jake added. But he clapped his nephew on the back. "I'm proud of you for not taking any guff from Barclay. Damned if I didn't want to plug him when I walked in that door."

"I thought about it the whole time I was in there." Pete's eyes glinted.

"Oh, you two—there will be none of that!" Emily stared at them in dismay as two women in sunbonnets hurried past along the boardwalk.

Pete pushed back his hat and gave her a weak grin.

"Now don't look like that, Em. I didn't mean it. I wouldn't shoot him in cold blood or anything—what do you think I am? But if we happened to get into a situation where we needed to see which one of us could draw first—"

"No, Pete. I won't have it. And as for you, Uncle Jake—"

"My shooting days are done with, girl. And my stealing days too." He sighed, looking resigned. "Don't get so all-fired worried. I said I wanted to plug Barclay—I didn't say I would!"

"Neither of us did," Pete pointed out.

She closed her eyes and shook her head, then fixed each of them with a stern glance. "I don't want to hear any more talk about shooting anyone. Let's finish up here and get back to the ranch."

"Finish up here?" Pete asked.

"Uncle Jake needs lumber from the mill, and I have to make some purchases at the mercantile. Can I trust you two to go about alone for a while without getting into any trouble?"

For the first time since yesterday, when he'd heard about Clint Barclay being Lonesome's sheriff, her uncle grinned.

"Reckon we'll do our best, but we can't make no promises, Emily girl."

As she watched them amble off, an ache of affection and pain pierced her heart. She walked toward the mercantile, turning her attention to the eggs and flour and beans she needed, and to thoughts of bringing home some licorice sticks for Joey.

With a smile, she reflected that Pete and Lester would each appreciate some licorice too.

A small bell tinkled as she entered the mercantile,

where every inch of sunlit space was crammed with barrels and baskets and crates and bins. An older man with a face like a bullfrog was striding back and forth behind the counter, simultaneously trying to fill the orders of a tiny scrap of a woman with eagle-sharp dark eyes and wispy gray hair piled atop her head and a thin young matron clad in lavender muslin who was trying simultaneously to chat with the older woman, read a long shopping list, and keep an eye on two children who were giggling and darting around the pickle barrels.

"Be right with you," the bullfrog man called out to Emily.

She nodded and continued to peruse the jars of penny candy on a shelf.

"And the poor man has no idea what he's in for after dinner tonight," the gray-haired woman was saying to the matron. As Emily glanced at her, she gave a cackling laugh. "Berty Miller claims she'll get Sheriff Barclay to ask her to that dance this very night or die trying."

"Well, I heard that another one of your boarders, Mrs. Eaves, has sent for her granddaughter all the way from Boston," the young matron replied. "The girl's supposed to be a famous beauty and . . . Bobby, you get down from there right now. Mr. Doily doesn't allow children to climb on top of his counters! And Sally, put that pickle back this instant!" She waved her shopping list in the air to fan herself and chuckled. "Well, I swear if I was still young and unmarried, I'd be tempted to throw out a lure to Clint Barclay myself!" she laughed.

"You'd have to stand in line," the gray-haired woman pointed out. "And watch your back. Agnes Mangley is dead set on Carla marrying him. She told me so last week."

"She bought three new ready-made dresses for Carla

last time she came in here," the storekeeper piped up. "And she's paraded Carla all through town nearly every day since Clint got back from Silver Valley, just trying to run into him."

"Well, one or another of them will catch him soon," the tiny gray-haired woman pronounced. She tapped her fingers against the open copy of *Godey's Lady's Book* lying on the counter. "He's just back from his brother's wedding, after all. That kind of thing gets a man to thinking. And now that nearly every unmarried girl in town has set her cap for him . . ."

"It's only a matter of time," the young matron agreed. "Oh, Rufus, I nearly forgot. I'll need five pounds of coffee as well. And half a pound of dried figs."

Emily had been listening to the women's conversation in stunned silence. So—every unattached female in Lonesome—and some from far away—were out to snag Clint Barclay. *The fools.* Handsome he might be, but he was also stubborn and hard-hearted and impossibly arrogant.

They're welcome to him, she thought.

But just then, the little boy who'd been scampering around the store with his sister stumbled into her, clutching her around the knees and nearly causing her to lose her balance.

"Bobby!" His mother gasped in dismay.

"I didn't mean to, Mama, I fell!"

"It's all right." Emily smiled first at the red-cheeked boy and then at the mother. "There's no harm done."

"I'm so sorry. Bobby, apologize to this lady."

"Sorry, ma'am." He grinned at her, his eyes sparkling beneath the fuzz of white-blond hair, and then dodged toward his sister to grab the rag doll she held.

"Bobby! Sally! Goodness, that's quite enough," the

mother exclaimed as the children began to tussle over the doll. "I won't have you children disturbing people in Mr. Doily's store." She snatched the doll from them both and sighed. "I think you'd best go outdoors now and wait for me. Go on—scoot."

Their spirits not at all dampened, the children raced for the door.

"Keep an eye on your little sister," the mother called out harriedly, and blew a strand of brown hair from her eyes.

"I do apologize," she murmured again as the door thumped shut behind the children. "I'm Margaret Smith and I thank you for being so understanding."

Emily hesitated only a moment. "I'm Emily Spoon. Pleased to meet you."

"*Spoon!*"

She'd hoped no one would notice or comment on her name, but that was not meant to be, Emily realized with a twinge of resignation. The frog-faced man stared hard at her.

"You related to *them* Spoons?" he demanded.

She flushed, but managed to nod with composure. "Yes. I am."

"Oh. Dear me." Margaret Smith's pale blue eyes widened. "My husband did mention something about the Spoons . . ."

Her voice trailed off. The warmth had faded from her pretty, heart-shaped face. She nodded quickly at Emily and turned back toward Rufus Doily. "I'll need two dozen eggs, Rufus, and three pounds of sugar. That will be all for today."

The older woman had turned from the counter to survey Emily curiously. "My brother Syrus, may he rest in peace, was held up by the Spoon gang once. In Missouri. Well, they never were able to prove it was the Spoon gang, nor to find the gold and jewelry that was stolen from any of the stagecoach passengers, but he was told that it was the Spoons."

She seemed to be daring Emily to answer her.

"I'm sorry . . . to hear what happened to your brother," Emily managed to say stiffly. She wished the floor would open and swallow her, but she kept her gaze steady on the woman's sharply piercing eyes.

"We have an excellent sheriff here in Lonesome now," the woman added, her mouth pursing. "He takes very good care of our town and all the people in it. If the Spoon gang thinks they can get away with anything, they're sadly mistaken."

"There is no Spoon gang anymore." Emily's chin lifted. "There's only my family. My brother, Pete, my uncle, Jake, and my cousin, Lester. We're starting over. We're starting a cattle ranch."

"Well, ma'am, if that's true, how come Slim Jenks told me that Sheriff Barclay already arrested one of the gang and threw him in jail?" Rufus Doily said.

"There was a fight, but it wasn't my brother's fault." Emily glanced at the two women and at the storekeeper, her spirits sinking. None of them believed her. "We all want to make Forlorn Valley our home—and to live peacefully among our neighbors," she added doggedly.

"Hmmmph." The gray-haired woman was still studying her thoughtfully, her head tilted to one side. All of a sudden she gave a curt nod, almost to herself, and then, to Emily's astonishment, she fixed the girl with a smile.

"I'm Nettie Phillips, Miss Spoon. I own the boardinghouse down the street."

Emily was almost too stunned by that smile to reply, but managed to murmur, "Pleased to meet you, Mrs. Phillips."

Margaret Smith was gaping at Nettie in surprise.

"Let me tell you something, Miss Spoon," Nettie declared. "My father was a preacher. He taught me early in life that everyone deserves a second chance. So I reckon that goes for outlaws too."

"Your father . . . sounds like a wise man."

"And as for you, why, I don't suppose you were ever a part of their gang, were you, Miss Spoon?"

"No, ma'am, of course not. And please call me Emily." She hesitated only a moment before continuing in a rush. "You should know that not everything blamed on the Spoon gang was their fault. Uncle Jake and the boys weren't perfect and they did wrong, but they weren't responsible for half the things people blamed on them."

Nettie gave her another long appraising look. "Well, now, I'm sure you believe that's true—and maybe it is. All I'm saying is that until proven otherwise, I'm prepared to give them a chance. And to give you one too. I reckon other folks in town will follow suit. It might take some time," she stated, glancing at the young matron beside her, "but I think they will. Don't you agree, Margaret?"

"I . . . I certainly believe that Miss Spoon isn't to blame for anything the men of her family have done." The woman spoke cautiously, as if feeling her way along a treacherous and untried path. "But you see, my husband works at the bank. His father, Hamilton Smith, owns it," she told Emily. Her cheeks flushed. "Naturally we have strong feelings about outlaws who steal other people's money!"

"Naturally," Emily repeated faintly.

Margaret bit her lip. "And yet . . . as Nettie has said—everyone does deserve a second chance . . . I *suppose* . . ."

Her voice trailed off. Abruptly she turned and began gathering up her parcels. She threw Emily one quick, searching glance, murmured "Good day" in the direction of both women, and followed Rufus outside as he carried the sacks of flour and sugar to her wagon.

"Bankers and outlaws don't usually mix," Nettie Phillips remarked baldly. "But give it some time. The Smiths are fair people, like most everyone in Lonesome. Margaret's mother-in-law, Bessie, is one of my dearest friends. I've a hunch they'll come around. So will most folks, I reckon—so long as your menfolk abide by the law."

"You don't need to worry about that." Emily felt a rush of gratitude toward this woman, the first person in Lonesome to show her any hint of welcome. "They're finished with their old way of life. So thank you for your kindness."

"Pshaw." Nettie waved a veined hand in the air. "Are you planning to attend our town dance?"

"I hadn't thought about it. I only noticed the posters today."

"Everyone will be there. And at the box lunch social two weeks from now." The woman waggled a finger at her. "Attending both would be a mighty good way to meet just about everyone in Forlorn Valley."

"I'm not sure we're ready for that yet," Emily murmured, but Nettie shook her head.

"Think about it." She turned back to the counter and began rummaging through the pages of *Godey's Lady's Book*. "It will go a long way toward showing that you've got nothing to hide, that you want to be a part of this community."

Rufus Doily came back in and stalked behind the counter. "Anything else, Nettie?"

"Just a bolt of that nice gray silk in the window, Rufus." She turned and winked at Emily. "I'm going to make myself a pretty new shawl to wear to the dance."

Emily had much to think about as she waited for Rufus to cut the bolt of silk and tally up Nettie Phillips's bill. The woman nodded to her as she left, and Emily watched her go out into the street, feeling hopeful for the first time since she'd discovered that Clint Barclay was the sheriff in Lonesome.

Maybe things would work out yet.

Despite what Clint Barclay had to say about it.

By the time the storekeeper finally got around to waiting on her and filling her order, Emily was pondering the idea of attending the town dance. It *would* be a perfect time to begin meeting people, showing them that the Spoons were just ordinary citizens looking to become part of the town, not hiding out, not plotting bank robberies or stage holdups or murders.

And it would also be the perfect time to show off her new dress: her very first creation. If people noticed, someone might even ask her to make a dress for them for that box lunch social in two weeks, she thought excitedly.

Especially one of those silly girls setting their cap for Clint Barclay.

How ironic, Emily thought, as she paid for her purchases, that the sheriff himself might play a part in boosting her plans for a dressmaking business.

"Guess I'd best carry these out to your wagon for you," Rufus Doily grumbled as he surveyed the sacks of flour, coffee, sugar, the parcels of canned goods, cheese, dried figs, eggs, and beans.

But when she went outside with the storekeeper, clutching an armload of canned goods and a bag of penny candy, she saw that though the wagon and horses had been hitched to a post in front of the mercantile, Pete and Uncle Jake were nowhere to be seen.

"Thank you, Mr. Doily," she murmured as the storekeeper dumped the heavy sacks in the back of the wagon.

"You're welcome, Miss Spoon—I reckon," the storekeeper spat the words out reluctantly, frowning as he stamped back inside.

Emily was too preoccupied by the fact that Pete and Uncle Jake were missing to even notice the cowboy who had stepped onto the boardwalk behind her and stopped short when the storekeeper spoke her name.

She deposited her bundles and shaded her eyes, peering up and down the street.

There was no sign of them.

Emily eyed Coyote Jack's Saloon, with its boarded-up windows. Would they dare go there, after all the damage done in the fight?

Then she saw the smaller, plainer sign for the Wagon Wheel Saloon next door to the hotel and immediately headed that way.

But as she neared it, she heard quick footsteps behind her and suddenly felt someone grasp her arm. Taking her by surprise, the man pulled her clear away from the street and around the corner of the saloon before Emily could even cry out.

"How dare you!" she gasped as she faced him in the garbage-strewn alley. But the scruffy-looking cowboy with the dirty, wheat-blond hair and pale green eyes didn't look the least bit apologetic. His lip curled as he eyed her with distaste.

"Shut up. You're one of them Spoons, aren't you?"

"What business is it of yours?" Emily shook free of his hold, trying to contain the fear pumping through her. "Keep your hands off me. And get out of my way!"

But as she tried to step around him and return to the boardwalk, the cowboy gave a jeering laugh and blocked her path.

"You're prettier than your kinfolk, that's for sure."

"I don't know who you think you are, mister, but you'd better let me pass!"

"Not yet, missy. Not till I'm ready."

Emily went white with anger as he looked her over with cool insolence, his gaze lingering on her breasts.

"I'm warning you. If you don't step aside right now, I'll—"

"You'll what?" Again, that hateful, jeering laugh, full of malice. He grabbed her again, one arm snaking around her waist, pulling her close. "You going to shoot me? *Ha-ha-ha*. It sure don't look like you're packing a gun. What's your name, honey? I bet a pretty gal like you has a real pretty name."

Emily struggled against him as the heavy odor of hair pomade and sweat invaded her nostrils. But squirm as she might, she couldn't break free. "Help!" she shouted, as loudly as she could. "Hel—" But the word was cut off as he clamped a hand over her mouth and, with an oath, pushed her against the saloon wall.

"This is between you and me, Miss Spoon. I got a score to settle with one of your kinfolk. Pete Spoon interfered in my business the other night in Coyote Jack's saloon. He stepped in between me and a certain little gal who works there and I figure I owe him."

Terrified, Emily fought against his restraining hands, but he held her fast, his hand covering her mouth. "He even tried to steal a kiss from her. So I need to teach him a lesson. How about I steal one from you? And you tell him all about it."

Emily kicked his shin as hard as she could and shoved against him with all her might, but he just grunted, and his grip on her tightened cruelly. "Now that wasn't nice, missy. Don't try to act all innocent and upset—a slut like you, trash, from a family of white-trash outlaws. Bet you're used to kissing a lot of men. You ought to be real good at it. Let's just see—"

He dropped his hand from her mouth, and before Emily could scream, he clamped his lips down upon hers in a wet, greasy kiss that tasted of bacon fat and onions. Revulsion pounded through her, unlike any she had ever known, even worse than when Augusta Wainscott's weasely son, Hobart, had caught her alone in the green sitting room and tried to fondle her. She fought wildly and as he shifted his stance to keep ahold of her, Emily finally had her chance.

Her knee shot up hard between his legs, a maneuver Pete and Lester had taught her years ago, and the cowboy gave a choked scream of agony. He released her and slumped backward, rigid with a pain that made his eyes bulge and contorted his face.

Emily started to dodge past him, but his arm lunged out and snagged her wrist. "Not . . . so fast, you . . . bitch!" he panted, dragging her back.

Suddenly she sensed someone behind her—someone closing in fast. A man wrested the cowboy away from her and shoved him backward. With her heart in her throat, Emily saw it was Clint Barclay. He stepped swiftly between her and the cowboy whose face was now white with pain.

"What the hell are you doing, Jenks?" the lawman demanded in a coldly furious tone.

Danger emanated from him. But for once the anger underlying his steely control wasn't directed at her or someone in her family. Emily couldn't help the stab of relief that went through her, even as she rubbed at her sore lips, trying to erase the taste and wetness of the cowboy's filthy kiss.

"I didn't . . . mean nothing, Sheriff," the man bit out. "I was just getting to know Miss Spoon here—"

"Didn't look like the lady cared to make your acquaintance."

"We were just having some fun—"

"That's your idea of fun?" Clint shoved him again and the cowboy went down, sprawling in the garbage of the alley.

Clint glanced at the woman behind him. "Are you all right?"

"You ought to clean up the riffraff in this town, Sheriff," she whispered shakily.

Humiliation was bursting through her. Once free of the Wainscott household, she'd thought she'd never again have to put up with the kind of treatment Hobart Wainscott had meted out to his mother's servant girls. And she'd tried her best to put it out of her mind. But this pale-haired cowboy with his insulting words and nauseating lips had brought it all back to her with repugnant clarity.

She was shaken, sick to her stomach, and wanted only to get away.

The knowledge that Clint Barclay had witnessed her humiliation only made it worse. She whirled around and darted back to the planked boardwalk, her knees trembling beneath her skirt.

When she got there she saw Pete sauntering out of the Wagon Wheel, looking pleased with himself.

"Em, guess what? I just signed me and Lester up for that poker tournament on Friday. Should be a real easy way to win us some fast cash. Then we'll celebrate at the town dance, all of us—" Pete broke off after one glance at her white face.

"Emily! What happened?"

"It's n-nothing."

"Oh, no, you don't. You're pale as a sheet. Tell me right now—did that sheriff come after you—did he give you a hard time—"

"No . . . no . . . it wasn't anything like that." She swallowed as she saw the cowboy—Jenks, the sheriff had called him—limp out from the alley. Clint Barclay followed close behind, his lean features hard and unreadable in the golden Colorado sunlight.

She grabbed Pete's arm and drew him away, toward the horses and the wagon, talking rapidly to distract him. "I was worried, that's all. I didn't know where you were . . ."

If Pete knew what had happened with Jenks, he'd either break every bone in Jenks's body or challenge him to a gunfight. And they couldn't afford any more trouble, certainly not trouble like that.

"Didn't Uncle Jake tell you I went over to the Wagon Wheel?" Pete shortened his long stride, matching his steps to hers. "When we finished loading the lumber in the rig, he said he'd just wait for you outside the mercantile."

"He wasn't there. That's why . . . I came looking for you . . ." She hoped he wouldn't notice the unsteadiness of her voice. Jenks had disappeared, but Clint Barclay remained on the boardwalk near the saloon. "I thought you might be at the Wagon Wheel . . . and I was worried that you'd get into some trouble," she said hurriedly.

At that moment she spotted her uncle. "Thank heavens—there's Uncle Jake now."

But her relief turned to puzzlement as she saw that her uncle was coming out of the telegraph office. Pete turned to look, but he was too late to see Jake tuck a paper into his shirt pocket as he closed the door behind him.

Emily saw, though, and despite the turmoil churning through her, she wondered what he'd been doing. She couldn't think of anyone he'd send a telegraph message to—or anyone who would send one to him . . .

Jake caught sight of them, lifted a gnarled hand in greeting, and headed at an easy amble toward the wagon.

"All set?" The elder Spoon glanced closely at both of them as they reached the wagon. "What's wrong?" he asked sharply. "Emily girl, you look weaker'n a squeezed-out rag."

"That's what I told her," Pete chimed in.

"It's nothing. Uncle Jake, what were you doing at the telegraph office?"

He glanced at her from beneath his eyebrows, then shook his head. "Just jawing with the fellow who works there while I waited. Come on, it's time we headed back."

Emily glanced over her shoulder. Barclay hadn't followed them to the wagon. *Good.* The last thing she wanted was for Uncle Jake and Pete to learn what had happened.

Pete helped her onto the seat, then jumped into the back with the lumber and supplies. As he and Jake began discussing the upcoming poker tournament, Emily scarcely heard.

She was thinking about Uncle Jake at the telegraph office. Something in his explanation didn't ring true—he wasn't a man who went out of his way to chat with strangers. And what about that paper he'd tucked into his pocket?

Something wasn't right. But she forgot about the paper as the wagon rolled through town and she spotted Clint Barclay. Two women, who appeared to be mother and daughter, had waylaid him on the boardwalk. They wore large, elaborate hats, fancy-trimmed gowns, and gushing smiles.

The older woman was chattering nonstop. The younger one stood quietly, tall, slender, and pretty as a sunflower, with golden curls spilling from beneath her bowed, feathered, and beribboned hat. As Emily watched and the older woman jabbered, the younger woman slanted a coquettish smile up at him and laid a gloved hand upon his arm.

But the sheriff wasn't looking at her. As the wagon rumbled past, he was looking at the dark hair and pale face of Emily Spoon.

Emily jerked herself forward, staring straight ahead. Every nerve in her body jangled.

She'd never thought she'd feel grateful to a lawman, *any* lawman. But if Clint Barclay hadn't happened by that alley when he did . . .

She shuddered, and reminded herself that she was safe now and unharmed, except for that disgusting kiss. But it unnerved her to know that even worse might have happened if not for Clint Barclay.

She hated the idea of owing him anything—even so much as a single polite word of thanks.

But the inescapable truth was—she did.

Chapter 7

TWO DAYS BEFORE THE TOWN DANCE, Emily was working feverishly toward finishing her gown when Nettie Phillips came to call, pulling up in a buckboard as the afternoon sun waned in a cobalt sky.

"Figured no one else had come by to pay you a welcome visit, so I decided to lead the way," she announced as Emily hurried onto the porch. Spry as a monkey, she jumped down from the seat, then lifted out a basket draped with a red-and-white checkered cloth.

"Strawberry pie," she grinned, as Emily came out onto the porch. "You'll like it, I reckon. Used to be my husband's favorite."

Stunned to have a visitor, Emily gathered her wits enough to invite the woman in, then wondered what to say when Joey edged into the parlor, looking shy and scared.

"Well, well, why didn't you say you had a young'un? I'd have brought some of my famous sugar cookies. Come here, little man, and let me have a look at you," the woman ordered with her customary candor.

"It's all right, Joey." Emily smiled at the boy as he hesitated and threw her a questioning glance. "Mrs. Phillips is a friend."

Joey inched forward as Emily invited her guest to have a seat on the sofa.

"Joey, eh? You're a handsome boy, aren't you?" She studied him carefully with those eagle-sharp eyes. "He doesn't look much like you," she commented, fixing Emily with a shrewd glance, then she reached into her pocket and handed him a penny. "For good luck," she said. "You put that under your pillow, leave it there all night, and you'll have good luck all year through," she told Joey.

The child's eyes lit like miniature lanterns. He studied her small, wrinkled face, trying to discover if it was a trick.

"Really?" There was deep hope in the single word.

"Would I fib to a fine young man like you? You just try it, Joey boy, and see for yourself."

"Can I, Em-ly?" Joey turned eagerly to her. When she nodded, he broke into a broad smile, one of the few she'd seen since the night John Armstrong had attacked Lissa. "Oh, boy, wait till I tell Uncle Jake!"

He raced into the back bedroom, clutching the penny in his fingers, looking so much like a normal, happy little boy that Emily could only stare after him, her heart lifting.

"He called you Em-ly, so I take it you're not his ma," Nettie remarked, leaning against the horsehair cushions. "Whose is he? Your brother's?"

Emily shook her head, uncertain how to reply in the face of such blunt questioning. Nettie Phillips was nothing if not forthright. She seemed to speak whatever sprang into her mind. But Emily couldn't help liking her, despite her startling candor. The woman had been the only person in Lonesome to make a friendly overture toward her, and she'd brought a smile to Joey's face. Emily sensed her questions were well meaning. She suddenly found herself answering honestly.

"Joey isn't related to any of us, Mrs. Phillips. He's the son of a friend of mine. She . . . had some troubles, and I offered to care for him a while—until it's safe—I mean, until she can take care of him again."

"Troubles? What kind of troubles?"

"It's private, I'm afraid. I can't go into it any further. May I offer you some refreshment? A cup of coffee . . . or some lemonade . . ."

"Pshaw, girl, no. If I'm sticking my nose in where it doesn't belong, just say so. Everyone else does." Nettie turned her head this way and that, birdlike, surveying the cabin, and then gave a satisfied nod. "Very tidy. I like those curtains. This place has been vacant too long—as I told Bessie Smith and her husband today. Folks are talking abut you Spoons, that's for sure, but I put in my two cents and said as we should give you a chance. People hereabouts tend to listen to me—because they know I've got good sense, and besides, they had a lot of respect for my husband, may be rest in peace."

"Did you lose him recently?" Emily asked, now that she could get a word in edgewise.

"'Bout five years ago." Nettie's eyes shone. "Oh, my dear, what a man he was. He was a hero in the War between the States, I'll have you know. Up and volunteered, he did, even at his age. Saved an entire regiment, before he got himself wounded. He recovered though—that he did, and came home to me . . . well, listen to me rattle on. I didn't come here to talk about Lucas or about me. I came to tell you that you'll be making a big mistake if you don't come to our town dance on Saturday. Folks are curious and they want to get a look at you—and the dance is a good place to present yourself in the right light. But I can see that you've already decided to go. Very wise of you."

She was looking at the rose silk gown draped upon the chair, where Emily had been sewing black lace on the bodice when she heard the buckboard coming.

"Yes, I've been sewing a dress for the dance—"

Emily got no further before Nettie barreled off the sofa and over to the chair, bending over the gown. "I reckon you have, missy! Some dress this is too, if you don't mind my saying. Why, this'll take the wind out of their sails. I mean, Agnes Mangley's and Carla's sails, that is. They got themselves mail-order gowns from New York for this dance, but my, my, this pretty dress of yours has them beat."

She dragged her gaze from the soft folds of silk, the exquisite lace trim and sleeves, the graceful pouf of train, and stared with intentness into Emily's eyes.

"You're going to look like a damned princess!"

Flushing with pleasure, Emily spread her hands. "Well, I wouldn't go that far, but I'm happy you like it."

"Like it! Where'd you find the pattern for it, girl? Fetching, that's what it is. As fetching a gown as any I've seen in my day!" Nettie raved.

Through her amusement, and her pleasure that someone besides herself saw the beauty of her creation, Emily recognized her first opportunity as a dressmaker. "Truth be told, there isn't a pattern. I did see many lovely gowns when I lived in Jefferson City, before coming here, and I've always had an eye for fashion. Fortunately, I'm more than a fair seamstress—my Aunt Ida taught me to sew when I was a girl, and—"

"You'll be the belle of the ball!" Nettie declared. "All those gals who've set their sights on Clint Barclay—well! Let me tell you, they're going to turn green with jealousy when they see you in that gown!"

"As a matter of fact, Mrs. Phillips, there's no need for jealousy," Emily said swiftly. "I could sew any number of beautiful gowns for any lady who'd like one. There are countless ideas in my head, and all of them revolve around the very latest eastern fashions," she added.

Nettie Phillips's grin was wide as a canyon. "Clever girl. Enterprising too. I like that. And it's not a bad way to endear yourself to folks in Lonesome, missy. Women here are hungry for new eastern fashions. Especially right now, when we have a passel of young ladies looking for a husband—one particular husband, I might add," she cackled.

"You mean Sheriff Barclay." Emily's tone sounded more grim than she'd intended, but Nettie was so engrossed in her own train of thought that she didn't notice.

"Yes, indeed. Why, Miss Berty Miller, who lives in my boardinghouse by the way, has some right fine gowns, several of 'em bought just to impress Clint, but nothing that compares with this."

"Perhaps she'd like to call on me." Emily smiled and held the gown against her, knowing its cleverly gathered sleeves and gleaming jet buttons would be noticed at once by Mrs. Phillips. "It's too late to sew anything before the town dance—it's all I can do to finish this one for myself—but there is the box lunch social in a few weeks—"

"That there is—we're raising money to build a bigger schoolhouse and get some more books, desks, tablets, and other supplies." Nettie Phillips jabbed a finger at her. "Once folks see you at the dance, you're going to have more orders for dresses than you can handle."

That's what I'm counting on, Emily thought, but she merely smiled and draped the gown back across the chair.

"But poor Sheriff Barclay," her guest mused, returning to the sofa, her old eyes alight with laughter. "If that man thought he was in trouble before, you just wait." She shook her head, grinning. "It's only a matter of time, after all. One of these gals is bound to catch him, you know. Bessie Smith told me today that some of the menfolk are even taking bets as to who it will be."

Emily thought of the way Clint Barclay had come to her defense in the alley, the way he'd shoved Jenks away from her. Then she thought of how he'd treated Pete and Lester and Uncle Jake.

"I can't understand all this fuss over Clint Barclay." Despite her efforts, she couldn't keep the edge out of her voice. "He's not a bad-looking man, I'll grant you that but—"

"Not bad-looking? Are you blind, girl?" Nettie gaped at her, thunderstruck. "Why, I daresay he's as handsome as my own dear Lucas was. And a braver man you'll *never* meet."

"I don't wish to argue with you, Mrs. Phillips, since you *are* my only friend." Emily regarded her hopefully. "If I may call you that?"

"You may." The woman nodded. "And it's Nettie. I do believe I've taken a shine to you."

"Thank you . . . Nettie." Emily found herself smiling. "I believe I've taken a shine to you too. But perhaps we'd best not discuss Sheriff Barclay."

For the first time, Nettie sobered, and leaned back against the sofa cushions. "I heard about how he arrested your brother."

"That's right. And . . . you may as well know," Emily took a deep breath, "he was the man responsible for arresting my uncle seven years ago and sending him to prison."

"Well, well, you don't say. Imagine that." The woman pursed her lips. "I understand how you must feel, honey, but to be fair, it wasn't exactly Clint's fault that your uncle held up those stagecoaches, now was it?"

Emily flushed. "No. Uncle Jake did wrong—he admits it. And he's paid for it. But Clint Barclay . . ." She broke off and turned away, pacing to the window. "Let's not talk about him."

Nettie jumped up from the sofa to pat her arm. "I can see how close to your heart all this is. You love that uncle of yours a lot, don't you?"

"He took Pete and me in after our parents died. He and Aunt Ida raised us, gave us a home. If it hadn't been for them . . ."

Her voice trailed off.

"I must say I like the way you stand up for your kin." Nettie sighed. "And I think it's a fine thing to be looking after your friend's little boy. But I've got to tell you, Emily, you're wrong about Sheriff Barclay. He's a fine man. He faced down the Duggan gang all alone. Five of 'em, the meanest vultures—I won't even call them *men*—you ever did see. And he nearly got himself killed for it. But he rousted them, and cleaned them out of our town."

Maybe so. But he nearly destroyed my family, Emily thought. She was spared from answering, however, when Nettie continued without missing a beat.

"I'll say just one more thing and then I'm done. And I'll say it quick—because I know you have your work to do, and land sakes, so do I. I have to get supper on the table for fifteen hungry people at my boardinghouse—including Clint Barclay, and goodness me, that man can eat." She gave a short laugh. "He lives upstairs of the jail but takes

.eals with me," she explained as she moved toward the .oor. Emily followed her.

"So you just think on this, honey." Nettie grasped the doorknob and fixed Emily with a penetrating gaze. "Maybe you ought to give our sheriff a chance."

As Emily opened her mouth to protest, Nettie shook her head. "The same way you want folks to give you a chance," she said firmly. "You might need him one day, a body never knows. And he's the kind of man you can count on. Damn, honey, why do you think every gal in the whole valley who isn't already hitched wants to get him to pop the question? Think on *that* a spell. I'm not saying you should marry him, heaven knows, but it wouldn't hurt to call some kind of a truce, now would it?"

She obviously didn't expect an answer. Giving Emily's shoulder a quick squeeze, she hurried on out to the buckboard, rattling on about the dinner she was going to prepare and how it looked like rain. When she'd gone, Emily returned to her sewing, still convinced of one thing: she was never going to change her mind about Clint Barclay. She'd spent too many nights kneeling by Aunt Ida's bedside, stroking her hand, feeding her spoonfuls of soup, while the aunt she loved withered away before her eyes and called feebly again and again for her husband.

When Saturday night arrived, the gown was ready. From the moment Emily slipped it on and began to fasten up each of the tiny jet buttons, her pulse began to race.

She hadn't been to a dance since she was fifteen. At that time, she and Aunt Ida had still been struggling to keep the farm, and everyone for miles around knew that Uncle Jake was in prison, that Pete and Lester were on the run. It wasn't a pleasant memory.

Emily had been a late bloomer, thin and awkward, and when she'd finally found the courage to step inside the little Missouri schoolhouse festooned by colored lanterns and bursting with fiddle music, no one had said a word to welcome her.

And not a single young man had asked her to dance.

She'd left the festivities early, ridden home all alone, and returned her mare to her stall in the barn. Then she'd climbed up into her favorite place, the hayloft, huddling in the sweet, hay-scented darkness and thinking about all the young people laughing and spinning across the schoolhouse floor. Later, when she'd returned to the farmhouse, she'd told Aunt Ida that the fiddle players hadn't been able to keep a tune, that the refreshments were sparse, and that the company was boring.

She'd been grateful when Aunt Ida didn't ask her many questions.

Shortly after that night, they'd lost the farm, and moved to the boardinghouse in Jefferson City. She'd gone to work for Mrs. Wainscott—and her days of attending dances had ended.

But tonight she was going to a dance in a new town, where she'd already made one friend. And she was no longer young and thin and awkward. And in this dress . . .

She peered at herself in Aunt Ida's old bronze-framed mirror, which Pete had hung over the pine bureau in her room—and felt a sense of wonder at her own transformed image. If she didn't know better, she'd think she could pass herself off as a young woman of means and education and privilege—not as plain old Emily Spoon.

Her hair had been tamed for once—it was tightly coiled atop her head, held in place with a dozen pearl hairpins that her mother, according to Aunt Ida, had worn on her wedding day. Only a few delicate curls had been permitted to dangle, softly framing her face.

The low-necked dress hugged her body enticingly, but decorously, she felt. The rose silk fell in graceful folds, its rich color accenting the creaminess of her skin and the natural rosy hue of her lips.

The lace sash made her waist look tiny, and it didn't seem to matter that she didn't have matching rose kid slippers but merely plain black ones. The dress was enough.

"Whoa, Emily—don't you look like something the angels dropped down from heaven." Uncle Jake's deep-set eyes shone as she stepped out of her room, feeling absurdly shy. Her uncle set down his playing cards and snatched his cigar out of his mouth—then gave a long appreciative whistle. Joey, in exact imitation, did the same, though only a slight wheeze came from his lips.

"You sure do look pretty, Em-ly!" he added, as if to make up for the whistle.

"It's the dress. It did turn out well, didn't it?" Emily twirled around for them to see, absurdly proud of her accomplishment. Lester came forward, his face scrubbed, his hair plastered with pomade, his good blue-and-yellow plaid shirt buttoned up to his neck.

"I'm going to have to stick by your side and fight off every man in the room wanting to dance with you all night!" he declared, looking worried.

"Don't be silly." Emily tucked her arm through his. "You don't have to stay by me—or dance with me. You go find yourself some pretty girl to flirt with—I'll have Nettie Phillips to talk to, and maybe she'll introduce me to some other ladies in town—ladies who will want me to make dresses for them."

"I promise you, Em." Lester steered her toward the door. "You're going to be doing a lot more dancing tonight than talking. I just hope Pete finishes up at that tournament and gets over to the dance in time to help me."

Pete had made it into the final rounds of the poker tournament, and the winner would be determined tonight in a private upstairs parlor of the Gold Gulch Hotel.

If he won, Emily knew, he'd be raring to celebrate. And if he lost . . .

Well, she'd just have to see that her hot-headed brother didn't get into any kind of a fight with the winner.

By the time she entered the Gold Gulch Hotel, Emily's heart was pounding. She didn't know why. It was only a dance. Just because it was the first dance she'd attended since she'd blossomed into a woman, and because she was wearing a gown every bit as spectacular as one Augusta Wainscott had worn to a ball in honor of Missouri's governor, was no reason to feel so nervous—or so excited.

As if something wonderful were going to happen . . .

Most likely, she told herself, *people will know who you are and stay as far away as they can.*

At first the lobby and dining room of the hotel looked to be a blur of people, lanterns, swirling gowns, loud music, laughter, and stamping feet.

Then the blur dissolved into a throng of people—ranchers and townspeople, miners, gamblers, and merchants. Women in a rainbow of gowns, their faces flushed and bright, men in expensively cut black suits or denim and buckskin. There were three fiddlers and a harmonica player on a raised platform at one end of the hotel dining room, where all the tables and chairs had been cleared to make way for the dancing. Colored lanterns added a festive glow, and against the walls of the dining room and the lobby were refreshment tables draped with white linen cloths, sagging with pies and cakes and cookies, pitchers of lemonade, decanters of whiskey and bourbon and elderberry wine.

"Well, now, Emily Spoon, there you are. My, my, just look at you." It was Nettie Phillips. She had tapped Emily on the shoulder and grinned at her—and Emily drew a breath of relief to find a friendly face.

"And who is this handsome gentleman?" Nettie turned toward Lester.

"May I introduce my cousin, Lester Spoon." Emily kept a firm grip on Lester's arm as she felt him trying to slip away. Always as shy around women as Pete was cocky, Lester mumbled something unintelligible, but resigned himself to waiting as Nettie Phillips took charge of more introductions.

"You've met Margaret Smith, of course." She waved a hand toward the young matron whom Emily had encountered in the mercantile. "But Lester hasn't—and you may as well both meet the rest of the Smith clan," she said briskly as the four people she'd been chatting with all visibly stiffened. "Here's Margaret's husband, Parnell," she indicated a tall, reedy man with a high forehead and spectacles, who made no effort to shake Lester's hand. "And his parents, my good friends, Bessie and Hamilton Smith."

Emily thought poor Margaret looked as if she didn't know whether to greet the Spoons or pretend they didn't exist. Her mother-in-law, Bessie, looked equally nonplussed. Emily took swift stock of the tall, stalk-thin woman in plum sateen. Bessie's white hair was piled atop her head in plump sausage ringlets. Her very pale blue eyes blinked rapidly in her long face as Nettie completed the introductions. Beside her, her short and plump husband frowned, twisting the end of his mustache between two thick fingers.

With a sinking heart, Emily remembered—Hamilton Smith was a *banker.*

"Miss Spoon." The banker sounded grim. "Mr. Spoon." As he looked at Lester, he sounded even grimmer.

Dismayed, Emily wondered why she'd ever thought coming to this dance was a good idea. If Nettie's dearest friends couldn't summon up even a morsel of friendliness upon Nettie's own recommendation, what would the rest of the town do?

Parnell Smith, who had his mother's height and pale coloring, was studying her and Lester as if expecting them both to pull out guns and try to steal his pocketwatch, fob, and Margaret's thin gold wedding ring.

And Margaret—

Emily paused, suddenly noting that Margaret Smith was no longer regarding her with reluctance or wariness, but with interest. Very definite interest. The young matron had begun eyeing Emily's dress.

Her own gown was pretty, a white-sprigged muslin with pouffed sleeves and a square neckline. *But sapphire blue would have suited her better,* Emily thought.

Margaret's eyes had grown round. "My . . . my goodness, what a lovely gown," she burst out. "I haven't seen anything quite so smart since our last trip to New York!"

"Emily made this gown herself," Nettie put in. "It's the latest style back east. She knows all about the latest fashions, yes, indeedy."

Bessie Smith was examining the fragile lace of the décolletage and the tight-fitting sleeves. "Well! I must say, it's quite breathtaking, Miss . . . er, Spoon. You're obviously an accomplished seamstress."

"Bet she could make you a gown just as nice for that bankers' convention you're going to in Denver next month," Nettie remarked.

"I doubt that Miss Spoon would be interested in—"

"Oh, I'd be glad to make you a dress," Emily interrupted swiftly. She added a smile, and was amazed to see Bessie's taut face relax. "I'm thinking of setting up a shop—one day. And do you know what, Mrs. Smith? Black chiffon and sea-foam green would be splendid on you. I see something with a ribboned overskirt, a bodice adorned with seed pearls, and—"

"Really!" The woman stepped closer, her pale blue eyes taking on a fascinated sparkle. "I saw a picture in a mail-order catalogue of a ball gown adorned with seed pearls and gold spangles . . ."

"Oh, yes—that's all the rage in the East," Emily assured her, thinking of the gown Mrs. Wainscott had worn to the theater the night before Emily had left her household forever. "If you'd like to come by our ranch tomorrow, I'd be happy to draw a sketch for you—you could make suggestions, of course."

To her astonishment, Bessie Smith accepted readily, and her daughter-in-law began inquiring about hats and slippers and shawls.

"Well, Mr. Spoon." Deserted by his wife and mother, who both suddenly bunched around Emily Spoon and Nettie, gabbing a mile a minute, Parnell Smith suddenly found himself forced to make conversation with the huge, red-haired outlaw who was shifting uneasily from one booted foot to the other. "We heard you and your family have set up ranching at the Sutter place."

"It's the Spoon place now. And Emily wants to call it the Teacup Ranch—since she's hankering to get herself a full matching set of teacups soon as can be." Lester might have been shy around women, but he'd never been the least intimidated by any man. He glowered at the Smiths, as if daring them to sneer at the name.

"Indeed." Hamilton Smith raised his goblet of brandy to his lips. "To the Teacup Ranch."

There was an awkward pause.

"I trust things are going along well at the . . . er, Teacup Ranch?" Parnell asked stiffly.

"Things are going along right fine."

"Glad to hear it. So long as you stick to ranching, there won't be any problem then." Hamilton Smith fixed him with a hard stare.

"What else *besides* ranching do you think we'd be doing? Care to be more specific?" Lester challenged, his face hot. "Say what you mean, Mr. Fancy Banker! If you have the guts to do it!"

"Now see here," Hamilton exclaimed, his face flushing with anger, but Parnell quickly stepped forward.

"This is a town dance. Not a saloon. If you want to start a fight, Spoon, I'll oblige you, but step outside—"

"Fine with me," Lester began, but suddenly his gaze fell once more on Emily, now surrounded by a whole herd of chattering women. She looked so vibrant, so *happy*. The women of Lonesome were admiring her gown, asking her questions, seeking her advice, and she looked more pleased than he'd seen her in a long time.

If he got into a fight with that Margaret Smith's menfolk, it would ruin everything.

"You want to fight or not, Spoon?" the banker's stringbean son asked with determination, though Lester saw him swallow past his Adam's apple.

"Nope." Lester sighed with resignation. "I don't. Think whatever you want. I don't give a damn." Turning on his heel, he sloped away.

It was the first time he—or Pete, as far as he knew—had ever turned away from a fight. It felt terrible, he thought.

I need a drink, he decided, heading toward one of the refreshment tables set up along the wall. Whiskey was called for. Good strong red-eye. This going straight business was turning out to be a lot harder than it sounded.

Emily didn't even have a chance to notice that he'd gone. The little crowd of women surrounding her kept growing. She caught Nettie's eye and saw satisfaction there, and felt a rush of gratitude toward this feisty old woman who was trying to smooth her way.

And then she spotted Clint Barclay and her breath got stuck in her throat.

He was standing before the blue-draperied window of the hotel's dining room, looking more dangerously handsome than ever, his tall, broad frame encased in dark pants and a white lawn shirt and black string tie. His dark mahogany hair was neatly combed, his lean jaw clean-shaven.

He was deep in conversation with a beautiful little redhead. An unpleasant sensation jolted through Emily as she saw the intent way he was listening to the girl. The redhead's charms were well displayed in a low-cut green gown that hugged her tiny but perfectly shaped figure the way a grape's skin hugs a grape. The girl was laughing, her head tilted provocatively up at the tall sheriff, and he had leaned down toward her as if to catch every word she spoke—or as if to see every charm she flaunted.

And Emily, who'd been speaking to Carla Mangley, the blonde girl she'd seen with Clint Barclay after her run-in with Jenks, faltered in midsentence, forgetting what she was about to say.

"Um . . . I . . . uh . . ."

"Yes, Miss Spoon? Can you or can you not make my daughter a dress and matching bonnet in time for the box lunch social?" Carla's overbearing mother, Agnes, repeated her daughter's inquiry, a hint of impatience in her voice.

Then she too followed Emily's glance and caught sight of the sheriff's dark head bent toward the redhead.

"Oh!" she gasped. "Just what does that Berty Miller think she's doing?" Her rounded and delicately powdered cheeks turned a bright red. "Excuse us a moment," she muttered, and seizing her daughter's arm, ducked away from the little throng with Carla in tow, exhibiting all the determination of a cavalry officer leading a charge.

But Emily never had an opportunity to see what happened when she descended upon Clint Barclay and Berty Miller. Someone tapped her shoulder, and she discovered that the sea of women had somehow parted. She gazed up at the scrubbed, eager face of an impossibly tall young cowboy in a red shirt.

"Wondered if I could have this dance, ma'am?"

She was swept forward into a rousing do-si-do before she knew it, and barely had time to learn that the cowboy's name was Fred Baker—then a sleek man in the elegant garb of a gambler invited her to waltz, followed by a stream of other partners. She caught sight of Lester near one of the refreshment tables, then lost him in the whirl of shifting colors and heart-thumping fiddle music. At last she was so breathless she retreated from the dance floor in search of a glass of lemonade, and it was at the refreshment table that Pete found her, sipping lemonade with several cowboys surrounding her, making flirtatious conversation and awaiting the opportunity to ask her for a dance.

"Yahoo!" He grabbed the glass of lemonade from her, sloshing some over the side as he set it down, then spun her around. "I won fifty dollars! How 'bout that, little sis?"

Emily gasped dizzily as he finally stopped spinning her, and she grinned at him as the cowboys retreated, casting dark looks at Pete.

"Good for you. Now we can buy more stock."

"Stock! How about all of us taking a trip to Denver, staying in a fancy hotel, going out for a big gut-busting dinner—"

"Pete!"

"Come on, Em, we all deserve some fun. This ranching is hard work." He grinned. "See that fancy gambler over there?"

He was pointing to the gambler she'd waltzed with. "Name's Lee Tarleton—he won five hundred dollars. Wish I'd done that, but fifty's better than nothing. Where's Lester?"

Pete scanned the room for their cousin. "Got to tell him my good news."

"I haven't seen him in a while. Oh, look, he's *dancing*!"

Lester was plodding across the dance floor with a woman she recognized as one of the saloon girls who'd been eating apples on the balcony her first day in town.

"Well, good for him. Reckon I'll find *me* a girl to dance with too!" Pete started off toward a knot of young women sitting near the lobby staircase, then turned back. "You all right, Em? That sheriff hasn't bothered you, has he?"

Bothered her? Clint Barclay hadn't even noticed her

presence. She might as well be sitting at home sewing curtains or scrubbing floors for all he knew. Or cared.

"No one's bothered me. But, Pete, maybe you should let me hold on to your winnings—"

He was already gone, though, charging toward the group of young women, and as Emily watched he selected the prettiest one in the flounciest pink dress she'd ever seen and swept her off to join the throng of dancers.

She turned back to retrieve her glass of lemonade and suddenly had the eerie sensation that she was being watched. Looking over her shoulder, she realized that her instinct was true.

She *was* being watched. By a man standing less than ten feet away, holding an empty shot glass of whiskey, wiping a hand across his mouth.

Slim Jenks.

As she met his eyes, he gave a sneering smile, set his shot glass on a table behind him, and advanced straight toward her.

Chapter 8

Watching Slim Jenks head toward Emily Spoon like a snake slithering toward a mouse, Clint swore under his breath.

"I beg your pardon, Clint?" Tammy Sue Wells, the daughter of one of Lonesome's ranchers, seized his arm as he took one determined step away from her. "Wait a minute, honey," she exclaimed in dismay, "where're you going?"

"You'll have to excuse me, Tammy Sue, there's something I have to do."

But another lilting feminine voice intruded before he could take another step. "*There* you are, Clint." Berty Miller pounced on him and hooked her arm through his, slanting him a dazzling smile. "I know you said you have to work tonight and keep an eye on things with all these strangers in town for the poker tournament and all, but we haven't even had a chance for more than one teensy dance yet—"

"Later, Berty." He yanked his arm free without even glancing at her and stalked toward Jenks.

Tammy Sue and Berty eyed each other, then both let out sighs of frustration at exactly the same moment. They looked to see where the object of their attention had gone off to in such a hurry.

But to their surprise, he wasn't walking toward another woman at all. He was headed straight toward that new wrangler from the WW Ranch, and from the expression on the sheriff's face, it wasn't going to be a pleasant conversation.

"I wouldn't go another step nearer the lady if I were you." The steel in Clint's voice halted Slim Jenks in his tracks, only a few feet from where Emily Spoon held her ground.

Clint allowed himself one brief glance at her. He had to give her credit. She was standing straight and tall, regal as a princess—no running or dodging for her. Not that she'd need to—he was damned if he'd let the son-of-a-bitch close to her again—but she hadn't even tried to flee.

His hard gaze centered itself on Jenks once more as the wrangler spun around to face him. "Stay out of this, Barclay. I'm warning you."

"You got that wrong, Jenks." Clint kept his tone low so that people strolling and chatting all around them couldn't hear or notice anything out of the way. "I'm warning *you*. If I catch you so much as breathing too close to Miss Spoon, I'm going to lock you up. You got that?"

People drifted past them, headed toward the refreshment table or the dance floor, laughing, talking. But Jenks and Clint might have been alone at high noon on a deserted street for all the notice they took of their festive surroundings.

"Hell, Sheriff—she's a Spoon," Jenks sneered. "You don't want her kind in this town any more than I do. So what do you care if I have myself some fun with that little piece of—?"

Clint hit him in the jaw. Jenks flew sideways, stumbling into Parnell Smith, who managed to shield Margaret just in time. As Jenks went sprawling across the floor, a gasp went up from the crowd and everyone stopped what he was doing to stare.

Hell. Clint took a deep breath, angry at himself. He hadn't planned on doing that. It was his job to keep the peace at the dance, not to disrupt it. He didn't know why he'd lost his temper with Jenks—it wasn't like him to lose control—but there was no going back now.

He glanced at Emily Spoon. She'd gone as pale as the white linen gracing the table behind her. And she was staring at him as if she'd never seen him before.

But then, everyone was staring at him. Including Jenks, who was holding his jaw and not even trying yet to get up from the floor.

"Sorry, folks." Clint raised his voice so everyone could hear, relieved that despite the anger still pumping through him, he sounded cool and steady. "Nothing to worry about. Go on back to having a good time."

He grabbed Jenks by the back of his shirt and hauled him to his feet. "You—*out,*" he said in a soft, deadly tone.

As he started to escort the wrangler to the door of the hotel, he glanced around for Emily Spoon.

She was gone.

"Don't say one more word," he warned Jenks as they crossed the lobby and Clint shoved him outside onto the hotel's moon-silvered porch. The wrangler spun around and glared at him, his eyes alight with anger, but Clint continued without giving him a chance to speak.

"Next time you won't get off so easy. I'm beginning to think Pete Spoon was telling the truth when he said you started that fight at the saloon."

"You'd believe that no-good thieving outlaw over me?"

Jenks demanded. He clenched his fists. "He's the one you ought to be throwing out of this dance."

"You're the one who wanted to start trouble with the lady."

"Damn it, Barclay, I told you. She's no lady—"

He broke off and backed up a pace as Clint seized him by the shirt collar.

"That's enough, Jenks." Somehow Clint kept his fury leashed, his voice deliberate. "If you know what's good for you, you'll get your sorry hide out of my sight. *Now*."

He stood on the porch, tension gripping every muscle in his body as he watched Jenks stomp away down the street to where his horse was tethered. In the light of the half-moon he waited until the WW wrangler had ridden past the edge of town.

Then he lit up a cigarillo and leaned against the porch post, smoking and letting the chilly night air help cool his anger.

He couldn't help wondering why Slim Jenks had it in so bad for the Spoons. It now seemed likely that what Pete Spoon had said about him stepping in between Jenks and Florry in the saloon was true. But even if Jenks did have a grudge against Pete, why should he pick on Emily?

His eyes narrowed in the darkness, and he took a drag on the cigarillo. Nothing should surprise him anymore, he reflected. He'd seen more than his share of ugliness, brutality, and petty cruelty in his travels across the West—had come up against men who were evil, some who were just greedy, and others plain vindictive and mean-spirited. Jenks seemed to fall into the latter category. Clint doubted that the man would let go of his grudge, and for some reason he didn't understand, the thought of Emily Spoon being the target made his gut clench.

He shouldn't have to worry about her, he told himself—she had her damned uncle and her brother and her cousin to look after her. But he was remembering the half-scared, half-defiant expression on her beautiful face when Jenks had come toward her tonight.

And he was remembering something else. The way she'd looked in that dress. Like a dark gorgeous rose, elegant and soft, Clint thought, a muscle tightening in his jaw as he saw her in his mind's eye. She might have been an heiress, a pampered cultured little flower fresh from the drawing rooms of New York—and not a girl from an outlaw family who tried to pick off strangers with a shotgun.

The others can't hold a candle to her. The thought flashed into his head suddenly. Carla, Berty, Tammy Sue—and all the rest of the women who for some reason he couldn't understand were throwing themselves at him as if he were the last man on earth—none of them could hold a candle to that black-haired spitfire who'd ducked out of the dance after he'd hit Jenks and knocked him to the floor.

He wondered where the hell she'd disappeared to.

The sounds of a scuffle around the corner made him stamp out his cigarillo and sprint toward the fray. In the alley he found two old timers fighting over a bottle of red-eye. He hauled them apart.

"Break it up!"

"I had it first, Sheriff."

"He's lying—it's mine. Gimme that bottle!"

Clint stepped between them, pushing the two men farther apart. "Get a move on. Both of you."

He really didn't want to lock up any drunks tonight, at least not yet. The night was too young. There were too many strangers in town. Between the poker tournament and the dance, the town was overflowing with gamblers, miners, high-spirited cowboys, drifters, men of all ages and stripe from near and far.

Both of Lonesome's jail cells could be full up by morning.

He sent the drunks off with no more than a stern look and a warning, and headed back toward the hotel. And that's when he saw a slender woman in a rose gown standing in the shadows of the hotel porch. She was leaning against one of the porch columns, gazing up at the moon, while from within the hotel came the raucous sounds of laughter and foot-stomping and fiddle music.

She whirled at the sound of his footsteps and looked as startled as a fawn caught in the open by a wolf.

"Don't look so scared. I'm not going to eat you." For one moment, Clint thought she was going to dash back inside the hotel, but then he saw her square her shoulders, stand up straighter, and hold her ground, just as she'd done with Jenks.

"Don't flatter yourself, Sheriff," she said with admirable cool. "I don't scare that easily."

"Reckon I noticed."

"What does that mean?"

He came up the porch steps and paused only a foot from her. Close enough to see the rise and fall of her breasts beneath that pretty rose gown. Close enough to see the moonlight reflected in those fascinating silver eyes.

"You didn't run from Slim Jenks tonight when he came after you in there. And considering what that lizard did the other day—"

"I'd rather forget about the other day!"

He nodded, suddenly annoyed at himself. "Can't say I blame you. Sorry, it was thoughtless of me to bring it up."

She was regarding him warily, suspicious even of his apology. Clint wasn't used to a woman looking at him like that—like he was the enemy. Most people who looked at him that way were hardened men—criminals, gunfighters, common bullies, and the like. What did she think he was going to do to her?

Well, after the way we met that first night outside the cabin, and those arguments in the jail, what else do you expect? he asked himself reasonably. It was just as well. He had no call to be getting to know her, and when you came right down to it, he had nothing to say to her.

She was Jed Spoon's niece. And for all he knew, she was privy to whatever the old buzzard might be planning—*if* he was planning. Clint would've laid odds he was.

"If you'll excuse me . . ." Emily turned toward the door, but for some reason Clint couldn't explain, he stepped swiftly into her path and eased her gently back into the shadows.

"One more thing."

"If you want to know where my brother or my cousin is—"

"I don't. I want to know about you, Miss Spoon."

"Me?" Emily stared at him. "I don't understand."

The moon played softly over her exquisite skin and fine-boned features. Clint felt a wave of heat surge in his blood. What the hell was he saying to her? Why did he feel the need to make conversation with a woman who obviously wanted nothing to do with him?

"I just want to know—if you're all right. I never got to ask you the other day—did Jenks hurt you?"

"Not as bad as I hurt him."

He laughed then—he couldn't help it.

"You're right. He wasn't even in any shape to put up a fight by the time I got there."

Emily swallowed. *That smile.* It was devastating to a woman. It transformed that stern, handsome face—made this rugged man even more intensely appealing, if that were possible.

Which is just plain unfair, she thought, her heart thudding wildly in her chest as those storm-blue eyes lingered on hers.

She ought to go in. At once. There was nothing she wished to say to him. Nothing she could think of, anyway, with him looking so tall and large and sinfully handsome in the moonlight, his eyes keen and warm on hers. She felt an absurd urge to grab his string tie and use it to draw him close to her.

When I ought to be considering strangling him with it.

And yet . . . there was something she knew she should say to him. Not that she wanted to, but her sense of honor demanded it be said.

"I . . . I suppose I should thank you for stepping in when you did the other day. In the alley with Jenks, I mean. And tonight." She took a deep breath, speaking each word reluctantly. "I really didn't want to have a scene at the dance—"

"Just when you're starting to get to know folks."

Her eyes flew to his face. He understood. "Yes. I was having a lovely time until then."

"I reckon you must have a lovely time at every dance," he muttered, thinking of the parade of men he'd already witnessed lined up to dance with her—outlaw kin or no.

Emily wasn't about to tell him that she'd been fifteen and a hopeless wallflower at her last dance. Instead she gave a delicate shrug.

He frowned at her. "The fact is, Miss Spoon, there's no need to thank me. My stepping in wasn't personal. I was just doing my job."

"Of course you were." Her eyes flashed. "The ever-diligent lawman. If you'll excuse me . . ."

But as he yanked open the door for her, and she started through it, what she saw in the hallway not more than ten feet away made her stop dead. Not exactly what she saw, but *whom* she saw.

John Armstrong, Lissa's ex-fiancé, was coming through the hall toward the door. His head was turned momentarily toward the dining room where the dancing and refreshments were in full swing, but at the same instant she saw him, his head began to turn back, toward the door . . .

She spun around, flung herself out onto the porch once again, and stumbled straight into Clint Barclay.

"Ohhh," she gasped as she fell against a rock-solid chest, and his arms went around her to steady her.

She heard Armstrong's boots thumping—thumping right up to the door—he would see her—any moment now, he would see her.

There was no time to think, to plan. She threw herself at Clint, driving them both deeper into the shadows. Flinging her arms around his neck, she did the only thing she could think of to do—she began to kiss Clint Barclay with fervent intensity.

Chapter 9

HIS MOUTH MOVED OVER HERS, warm, strong, sure. In the shadows at the edge of moonlight, Sheriff Clint Barclay encircled her with those iron arms and returned her kiss with every bit as much intensity as she had shown in initiating it.

Sparks burst through Emily, along with a dazzling heat as one kiss led to another—and another—each deeper and longer and somehow more intimate than the last. The idea of kissing a lawman should have made her ill, but instead she felt a rush of sensation, heady and hot and sweet.

For a moment, she forgot about everything—even about John Armstrong. She only knew a deep hunger, a yearning that came from her very soul, a pleasure that left her breathless. The soap and leather scent of him enveloped her. Her breasts were crushed against his powerful chest as he drew her closer, closer still.

Her entire body down to the tips of her toes caught fire.

Oh . . . my . . .

Her heart had gone crazy, thundering like an out-of-control train, but dimly she heard the footsteps thump past them on the porch, heard heavy boots scrape the boardwalk, then heard more footsteps—this time receding.

He's gone. Armstrong never saw you . . . you can stop kissing this lawman now, Emily thought desperately, then panicked at the realization that she didn't *want* to stop kissing him. Using all her willpower, she forced herself to tear her trembling mouth from his.

"We can . . . stop now—he's . . . gone," she whispered and tried haplessly to extricate herself from the sheriff's arms, but he caught her to him and hauled her up against his chest again.

"What if he comes back?"

"He . . ." Dazedly, she started to glance after Armstrong, saw his burly figure striding up the street, and then saw nothing more of him as Clint Barclay yanked her in even closer.

"My turn, Miss Spoon." His low, gentle voice was at odds with his powerful strength, and both sent a shiver racing down her back. Electricity blazed between them as his eyes gleamed into hers.

"Turnabout is fair play," he said.

Then he was kissing her, his mouth slanting against hers with explosive heat. It was too late to protest, to try to pull back. The kiss imprisoned her in a giddy pleasure, as surely as did those strong arms. The first time, when she'd kissed him, she'd found him all too willing and ready to respond, following her lead with only the briefest flash of surprise, but this time she found him taking control, kissing *her,* tasting *her,* drawing out the kiss and deepening it as he tenderly explored the very shape and texture of her lips, as if seeking to know her in a way that was intimate and deliciously new and that defied description.

Blanketed in shadows, they were locked in an embrace that sent dizzying sensations tumbling through her. It was impossible to think with him kissing her like this, and Emily, accustomed to thinking so much and so often about everything in her life, knew an odd exhilaration as Clint Barclay wiped everything but the feel, scent, and taste of him quite out of her head.

Neither of them actually stopped the kiss in the end, it just came to a slow, sweet, shuddering end. They stood like that, their mouths still touching, their breath coming quickly, as the sounds of the dance, the laughter, and the music flooded back.

And so did the dark coolness of the night, the creaking of the porch planks beneath their feet, the sighing of the wind sweeping down from the hills.

And the memory of John Armstrong—here in Lonesome—nearly running smack into her.

"I have to leave." Emily broke out of the spell and pulled back within the circle of his arms. "L-let me go."

"Don't you think you should tell me what that was all about?"

"There's no time—I have to get back to the ranch—right now!"

"I'll take you." His arms were still snug around her. "And on the way you can tell me—"

"No!" Emily wrenched away, panic welling up in her. She had to get to Joey and make certain he was safe. She had to find Pete and Lester, ask them to take her home . . .

"Usually when I kiss a lady she's not in such an all-fire hurry to run out on me." Clint's eyes were amused and yet searching as they settled on her in the darkness. "Maybe you ought to just slow down and—"

But Emily was already darting past him, back inside the hotel, without even a backward glance.

As Clint watched her disappear into the crowded lobby, he felt a stab of disappointment.

I never even had a chance to ask her to dance.

No sooner had this thought flashed through his brain than he was shaking his head at the absurdity of it.

A lawman dancing with Jake Spoon's niece? Not a good idea.

Didn't matter how pretty she was—or, hell, how beautiful—didn't matter how sweet she kissed or how delicious she tasted. Getting involved with a girl like her was . . .

Hold on a minute. A girl like her? You're as bad as Jenks, Clint realized suddenly.

He wondered what was wrong with him. Not only didn't he know why Emily Spoon had kissed him with such ardor, why she was afraid of that stranger who'd come out of the hotel, or why she kept disappearing on him, he didn't know why in hell he'd kissed her back.

"*Sheeeriiff! Sheriff Barclay!*"

The singsong tones of Agnes Mangley broke through his thoughts and galvanized him to action. He vaulted over the porch rail and strode down the street in the same direction that the man Emily Spoon had wanted to avoid had walked not more than ten minutes earlier.

It was almost midnight and the boy was fast asleep.

Jake Spoon crossed the bedroom floor and gazed down at Joey's peacefully closed eyes, at his small form curled up into a ball on the mattress. He stood a moment, listening to the child's soft, even breathing.

Sleep tight, kid, he thought. From the looks of it, that's exactly what the boy was doing. Jake figured a norther could blast the hills and the cabin, and Joey wouldn't hear a thing.

Jake turned quickly on his heel. For a big man, he moved soundlessly across the floor, his boots making the barest scuffing noise as he let himself out of the room, then strode through the cabin and out into the night.

When he pushed open the barn door, heavy darkness greeted him. Then he heard a match strike; a flame sputtered and caught. The man standing in the shadows of the horse stalls regarded him with cold, shining eyes.

"'Bout time you got here, Spoon."

Even without seeing Ben Ratlin, he'd have recognized that heavy, dour voice. A voice he'd heard every day for seven years in prison.

"You're early, Ratlin."

"Damn right I am. We have a lot to talk about. Close that damned door."

As Jake complied, Ratlin turned up the oil lamp that hung from a hook on the barn wall and Jake noted that somehow the huge, bearlike man looked even more dangerous than he had in prison.

There was both ferocity and cruelty in those hooded deep-set eyes—and a kind of hunger Jake recognized and had seen in many men. The hunger for gold, silver, for precious gems. For long-dreamed-of wealth, riches attained by any means.

It was a hunger that afflicted many—and its name was *greed.*

Now that the time had come for Ratlin to finally pull off that big job he'd been talking about in prison the past year, to get his hands on the huge payoff he'd been promised for its successful completion, Jake could smell the blood lust on him, the excitement of the hunt and the kill.

Jake understood it. The kind of payoff Ratlin had promised him for doing his part represented more money than Jake had ever hoped to haul in during all the holdup jobs he'd ever pulled.

And Ratlin's share was even bigger than that.

"We'd better talk fast," Jake said. "My niece could be back from town soon. There's not much time."

"Whose fault is that?" Ratlin sneered. He was as big as Lester, and built like a boar. There were strands of gray in his shaggy black hair and beard, and his oily, swarthy complexion shone in the dimness of the barn. "Don't see why you couldn't meet me at Cougar Pass, like I wanted," he growled. "It's damned risky for me to come here. And all because of some snot-nosed kid?"

"I told you, Ratlin, if you wanted to meet tonight, it had to be here." Jake spoke curtly, his gaze nailing the other man's. "I promised my niece I'd keep an eye on the boy while she was gone. If I'd said I couldn't do it, she'd have asked questions. Now quit wasting time and fill me in. When's the job—and who do we have to kill?"

Ratlin shook his head. "You'll find out—all in good time, Spoon."

"What the hell does that mean?"

"It means the boss hasn't told me I can let you in on the details yet. He's calling the shots, not you, not me. Now what about your son and your nephew? You ask them yet if they want in on the job?"

"Not yet. But they will."

"Just make sure they keep their mouths shut. They

won't be squeamish about the killing part of it, will they? Seems to me your old gang never did shoot no one, from what I heard."

"Pete and Lester will do whatever I tell them to do." Jake Spoon met Ratlin's glittering eyes, his own as hard as rocks. "The killing won't be a problem."

"Good. That's real good." Ratlin nodded approvingly and relaxed enough to offer a tight-lipped smile. "Just make sure you and your gang are ready whenever I give the word."

"Just make sure you understand what I expect in return," Jake countered. "We'll want a thousand dollars apiece if there's killing involved. And that's in addition to the valuables and money we take from the passengers."

"Done." Ratlin shook his hand. "You'll get your money—just so long as there's no one left alive in that stagecoach when you finish," he warned. "I've got another man—an old pard—who'll be riding with us. Any problem with that?"

Jake shrugged. "Not if he can shoot straight and we can trust him. Who is it?"

"You'll meet him soon, closer to the time we pull the job. Until then the less you know, the better. The boss doesn't like to take chances. In the meantime, you need to scout out the stagecoach route between Denver and Lonesome and find just the right spot to—" Suddenly Ratlin tensed at distant sounds from outside—wagon wheels creaking, a horse whinnying. "Who's coming?" he demanded in an irritated whisper.

"Damn." Jake frowned and wheeled toward the door. "My niece and the boys must be back already," he muttered.

Scowling, Ratlin eased open the barn door. "Meet me at Cougar Pass tomorrow just after sundown and we'll finish this," he said in a low tone. "And remember, Spoon, if anything goes wrong, the boss will have your scalp—and I'll have everything else," he added coldly. "Either that or the sheriff's going to lock all of us up so fast our heads'll spin."

"Nothing's going wrong." Jake saw the wagon coming along the trail. He thought he could make out Emily's pale face in the moonlight. She was seated beside Lester. Pete's dun gelding cantered alongside.

"I don't want my niece mixed up in this," he said sharply. "Get out, Ratlin, now."

"I'm going—but you'd better show up at Cougar Pass tomorrow, Spoon—and make damned sure no one follows you."

Ratlin eased out the door and disappeared into the thick gloom of the night. Squinting after him, Jake saw him duck toward the trees beyond the barn—no doubt the spot where his horse was hidden.

He extinguished the lamp and sprinted to the porch before any one of his family noticed him. Slipping into the cabin, he plunked himself with alacrity into a chair even as Emily's, Pete's, and Lester's voices sounded from the yard.

Ratlin's words were still circling through his head, over and over again.

Just so long as there's no one left alive . . .

Emily flew into the cabin with Pete and Lester right behind her. Relief surged through her when she saw that Uncle Jake was snoozing peacefully in his chair, and all was quiet.

"Uncle Jake—is Joey all right? There hasn't been any trouble, has there?"

"Trouble? What kind of trouble?"

As Emily explained, Jake sprang out of the chair in dawning incredulity. "You mean that son-of-a-bitch who beat up your friend—he's here in Lonesome?" he demanded, his fierce brows drawing together.

"He must've come to town for the poker tournament." Pete was pacing around the small room, his handsome face full of frustration. "Damn, I wish I'd known. I'd have given anything to get my hands on him."

"Me too." Lester tossed his hat onto the side table. "Emily, you're still shaking. There's no reason to be worried now. That bastard didn't see you, did he?"

"No . . . no, I'm sure he didn't." Remembering the way she'd managed to avoid *that* made her cheeks turn even pinker though, and both Pete and Lester stared at her curiously.

"Calm down, Sis." Pete patted her shoulder. "It's not like you to get this shook up. Nothing actually happened, after all."

Nothing happened, nothing happened. She'd seen John Armstrong and she'd kissed Clint Barclay. Nothing happened.

"I think I need to check on Joey myself," she murmured and headed toward the back bedroom.

Behind her, she heard Pete say, "I know we're supposed to start rounding up the cattle for branding tomorrow, Uncle Jake, but I'm going into town first thing and see if Armstrong's still there. If he is, we'll have to decide what to do about him . . ."

She didn't hear any more. The sight of Joey peacefully asleep in his bunk against the wall drove everything else from her mind.

He's safe, Lissa, she thought in silent thankfulness as

she touched a hand to the boy's hair. Her heart trembled at his tiny size and vulnerability, the small body curled into a ball. "I'll keep him safe," she whispered into the darkness. "No matter what I have to do."

Tonight she'd had to kiss a lawman.

And not just any lawman. She shivered a little as she moved toward the door, astonished by how pleasurable it had been kissing that one lawman in particular.

Never in a million years had she expected him to kiss her back.

The memory of that kiss made her grow warm all over. It made her breath quicken. What was happening to her?

It's just because you haven't kissed many men before, she told herself. *And none of them like* that.

She slipped out of the room, and instead of facing the three men in the parlor again, she ducked into her own room and closed the door. She stared at herself in the mirror and saw that she looked every bit as tidy as she had before she'd left for the dance. Not a curl was out of place. Clint Barclay hadn't mussed her carefully upswept hair or wrinkled her beautiful gown . . .

So why did she think that everyone who looked at her would be able to see the mark of his kiss?

It was only a kiss, she told herself desperately. Even though she remembered every single second of those dazzling moments on the porch—in Clint's arms—it didn't mean anything.

That's what she told herself over and over as she readied herself for bed, turned down her lamp, climbed in between the cool sheets, and stared at the shadows on the ceiling.

It didn't mean anything at all, she whispered into the darkness. *And it will never happen again.*

But that thought gave her no comfort, and she tossed and turned through the long hours of the night, wondering how one irresistibly handsome lawman had managed to so thoroughly disrupt the logical workings of her mind, her senses—and her heart.

Chapter 10

THUNDER RUMBLED IN WITH THE dawn the next morning and so did a spattering of cool gray rain.

"Looks like a bad storm rolling in—should hit later today, unless I miss my guess." Uncle Jake frowned and turned away from the kitchen window as Lester, still at the breakfast table, smothered the last flapjack remaining on his plate with maple syrup. "We'd best start moving those cattle in before it hits. Soon as Pete gets back," he added, meeting Emily's eyes.

She paused while clearing the breakfast dishes from the table and nodded at him, relieved that Jake and Lester wouldn't be leaving the ranch until they had news about John Armstrong. Flicking a glance at Joey, she was glad to see he was forking flapjacks into his mouth and listening raptly to Uncle Jake, totally oblivious of the true import of his words.

Oblivious of the danger, she thought. *If there is any danger . . .*

She carried the dishes to the counter and turned her gaze to the horizon. No sign of Pete yet, only the gray sky, the hills, and the aspens. She'd burst if he didn't get back soon. She couldn't relax until she knew if John Armstrong was still in Lonesome—or if he had only come to town for the poker tournament and then moved on.

She kept glancing at Joey, smiling at him, trying to appear calmer and more confident than she felt. The boy mustn't have even a hint that the man who had nearly killed his mother and had terrified him was less than ten miles away.

"Think once Pete gets back, I'll head south toward Beaver Rock," Uncle Jake continued easily as Lester pushed back his chair, leaving not even a crumb of the flapjacks, bacon, and biscuits with marmalade that had been piled on his plate. "I'll drop off some supplies at the line cabin up there—meantime, Lester, you round up all the strays you can find around Pine Canyon and bring 'em down to the basin."

"What about Pete?" Lester asked.

"He'll take the creek, follow it all the way to Lizard Butte, pick up whatever strays he—"

"Can I go with *you,* Uncle Jake?" Joey interrupted eagerly.

Emily, Lester, and Jake all turned in astonishment to stare at the boy.

Never had Emily seen Joey's face look so bright, so animated—at least, not since the days before Lissa ever met John Armstrong. A soaring happiness almost blocked out her fears about Armstrong being in the vicinity. Joey was finally breaking free of the cage of fear in which Armstrong had locked him. He'd helped her with the planting in the vegetable garden over the past several days, gone willingly alone to the barn to feed the chickens—including the one he'd adopted and named "Clucker"—and now he even wanted to ride out on the range with Uncle Jake. If only Lissa were here to see how well he was doing!

"Son," Jake said kindly, "wish I could take you up on your offer—but I'm afraid I can't today." The gray-haired man went to the boy, stooped, and lightly ruffled his hair. "Best we work on your riding a mite first. These cattle can be mighty tricky. But one of these days—real soon—you'll come along and give me a hand. I sure could use it."

Joey dropped his head, but not before Emily saw the disappointment in his face.

"Joey," she said quickly, "I need your help around here today."

"You . . . do?" Joey's head came up slowly, hopefully.

She smiled at him. "Yes, indeed. I need to get the rest of the firewood into the shed before the rain hits," she said, with a quick warning look at Lester, who was about to offer to do it for her. "Think you could manage to help me carry it? I'm not strong enough to do it all alone."

"I can do it," he assured her. "I'll help you, Em-ly." But he glanced over at Jake as he and Lester headed toward the door. "But . . . you're going to teach me to ride soon, right, Uncle Jake? Promise?"

"It's a promise, son. Why, if the weather's clear, maybe we'll get started tomorrow after supper. I've got a fine little mare, just the right size for you—you're going to like 'er, boy."

"Pete's back!" Lester announced suddenly, and Emily whirled toward the window to see her brother galloping right up to the back door.

As Emily rushed outside, her brother threw her a quick, reassuring smile. "Things are real quiet and peaceful in town after that poker tournament," he said in a casual tone as he vaulted from the saddle. As Joey ran up to greet him, he swung the boy up and onto his horse's back, holding him there and grinning at Emily, his dark hair falling boyishly over his brow. “Most folks have cleared out already. Why, I couldn’t find many strangers atall.”

Both his words and his confident expression filled her with a dizzying relief. So there had been no sign of Armstrong in town. Emily felt as though she could breathe again without a knot the size of a rock in her throat.

“Well, that’s good.” She almost laughed at her own understatement. “Everything’s back to normal.”

“Looks that way. You know, if you want me to stick around today and . . . help out at the ranch, I will,” Pete offered, obviously ready to stay close if she was still uneasy, but Emily shook her head.

“That won’t be necessary,” she assured him gratefully. “Joey’s going to help me. Right, Joey?”

“Right, Em-ly!”

“So shoo, all the rest of you—get to work. And make sure you come back home before the storm hits. Those clouds are getting fiercer looking by the minute.”

As Jake, Pete, and Lester split up and went on their separate ways, she said a silent prayer of thanks that she had successfully avoided John Armstrong and that the danger was past. Her heart should have been light—but somehow it wasn’t.

Perhaps it was just those ominous silver-laced storm clouds moving in from the west, or the knowledge that running across Armstrong last night might have turned out very differently, she told herself as she whisked through her morning chores. But the fact was that she still felt a weight on her, a weight of worry. Her memories of that encounter with Clint Barclay were as vivid as ever, even in the light of day. She kept seeing his face, remembering the rough, exciting slant of his mouth over hers, the sensation of those strong hands moving lightly up and down her back, the clean male taste of him as they kissed . . . and kissed some more . . .

If anyone in her family found out she'd kissed Barclay . . .

Emily shuddered at the prospect. She couldn't bear to think about that.

And there was no need to think about it. *Because it will never happen again,* she told herself. *Not in a million years.*

She forced her thoughts in another direction. Now that the dance was over and her gown had proven to be such a big success—and thanks in large part to Nettie Phillips's friendship—she had her work cut out for her. There was a great deal of sewing to get done between now and the box lunch social. She had orders for three dresses and two fancy shawls. The women would be coming by the Teacup Ranch to be measured and consulted on colors, styles, fabrics—there was material to purchase, as well as matching buttons and satin ribbons. In addition she had all of her household chores to complete as well . . . not to mention looking after Joey.

Emily felt that Joey's schooling should not be neglected any longer. If she didn't get a letter from Lissa soon, she'd have to see about enrolling him in school, she thought, but in the meantime, she'd work on some lessons with him herself and—

She paused in the midst of sweeping the floor as she heard the sound of a horse's hooves, coming fast.

Could it be Pete or Lester or Uncle Jake returning for some reason? she wondered, her heart thudding.

She wasn't about to take any chances. Dashing to the kitchen, she grabbed up the rifle and held it at her side as she hurried to the porch. At the same moment, Joey scurried out from the barn, his face white.

"Who's coming?" Fearfully he darted up the porch steps to her side. His shirt pocket bulged with the pack of cards he carried everywhere. "Em-ly, is it . . . *him*?"

"No, no, of course not." But a horrible seed of doubt had sprung up in her mind and she strained to make out the rider galloping toward the cabin. He was still too far away . . .

"If it'll make you feel better, Joey, go inside and wait. I'll talk to whoever our visitor is."

"But . . . aren't you scared?"

"No. I'm not scared." Emily gripped the rifle tighter. "Go ahead, Joey, go inside," she said, far more calmly than she felt.

The boy didn't need to be told twice. He scooted through the door and it banged shut behind him even as Emily curled a finger around the safety.

If Pete had made a mistake, and John Armstrong hadn't left town and had found out about a girl named Emily Spoon living out at the old Sutter place . . .

Then the rider at last came close enough for her to see who it was. She very nearly dropped the rifle.

Clint Barclay thundered into the weed-strewn yard and reined in his horse less than ten feet from where she stood.

"Morning, Miss Spoon," he said evenly, touching a hand to the brim of his hat.

Morning, Miss Spoon. Is that what a man said to a woman he had thoroughly kissed the night before? Absurdly she felt the urge to laugh hysterically and stifled it.

"Sheriff." The single word was said with caution and the unfriendliest tone she could muster.

Clint swung down from the saddle with lithe ease. "We need to get a few things straight. I found out the name of that man who spooked you. He's J—"

"That's enough, Sheriff!" Emily interrupted swiftly, horror jolting through her. She knew Joey must be listening inside. "Please—don't say any more."

"Why not?"

He vaulted up the steps and glanced at the rifle in her hand. "Planning to shoot me if I do?"

Emily heard gentle amusement in his tone. But at the same time, there was determination in those penetrating blue eyes, a determination that signaled he wouldn't be deterred from asking her about John Armstrong.

"Joey," she called suddenly. "Joey, it's all right. Come out here, please. There's someone I want you to meet."

At first there was no response, and she thought the boy would be too fearful to come out. Then the door opened slowly and the child stepped out. He walked slowly to Emily and without a word slipped his hand into hers.

All the while he was staring at the sheriff, and she saw that he was noting the glittering silver star pinned to Clint's vest.

"This is Sheriff Barclay," Emily said quietly. "Sheriff, I'd like you to meet Joey."

She looked for the surprise in his eyes when he saw the boy, but there was none.

"Howdy, Joey," Clint Barclay said in a level tone.

"You . . . you were here before," the boy blurted out. He peered up at Emily. "Wasn't he, Em-ly?"

"That's right. He was." She knelt down suddenly and smiled into the boy's wary eyes. "He's a nice man, Joey. It's his job to protect people. So you don't have to be afraid," she whispered.

He nodded, and his small shoulders relaxed. "If John Armstrong came here, Sheriff Barclay would shoot him, right?" he whispered back to her.

She stiffened and couldn't help throwing Clint a swift

glance. She could see by his face that he'd heard every word. His jaw tightened and he looked like he wanted to say something, then he seemed to think better of it, and let Emily answer the child's question.

"He'd help us." She choked out the words, torn between the need to soothe Joey's fears and to keep Clint Barclay from learning any more than was absolutely necessary. Unfortunately, the way things were going, it looked like she'd end up having to tell him the whole story anyway. "That's his job."

"She's right, Joey." Clint hunkered down, going eye to eye with the boy. He smiled, a warm, honest smile that tore at Emily's heart—especially when she saw Joey smiling back.

"I have a sworn duty to protect all the people in these parts from bad men. That means that if I catch anybody bothering you, or Emily, or anyone else, I can stop them. And make sure they can't bother you any more."

"Uncle Jake said he'd stop John Armstrong too," the boy replied, more boldly. "And he's a crack shot."

Clint threw Emily a long look, then straightened. "Glad to hear it. Looks like you're protected from all sides, son."

Protected from what? Clint wondered grimly. But he didn't want to question the child. He'd find out everything he needed to know from Emily Spoon.

"Now that that's settled," she was saying, giving the boy a quick hug, "why don't you finish feeding the chickens and let me find out what I can do for Sheriff Barclay. We want to be all finished with our work and cozy inside the cabin when the storm hits, don't we? And Sheriff Barclay will want to be back in town."

"Okay, Em-ly. Clucker is prob'ly wondering where I went. G'bye, Sheriff."

"So long, Joey."

Clint waited as the boy trotted toward the barn. Joey turned and waved once, just as thunder rumbled in the distance. Clint lifted a hand with an easy smile, hiding his tension and the worry vibrating through him.

"All right, supposing you tell me just who in hell this John Armstrong is?" he demanded as soon as Joey disappeared into the barn.

Emily set the rifle down against the cabin door and plopped her hands on her hips. "It's none of your business."

"After last night, it damn well is my business."

Her cheeks flushed a rosy pink. "If you were a gentleman, you wouldn't bring up last—"

"I'm a lawman, Emily. Never claimed to be a gentleman." He strode right up to her, didn't touch her, just stared down into her eyes. His voice was quiet, determined. "And when something's wrong, it's always my business."

"It's nothing—nothing I can't handle. *We* can't handle," she amended swiftly. Her chin lifted. "My family stands behind me on this."

"Look, you can barely tolerate the sight of me, and yet when you saw Armstrong in that hotel last night, you nearly knocked me over trying to keep him from spotting you. You went to . . . extreme lengths to make sure he didn't recognize you," he added dryly, noticing how those finely sculpted cheeks of her turned an even deeper pink than before. And how her lovely mouth started to tremble.

"Not that I'm complaining," he added softly, and the cobalt glint in his eyes made her suddenly grow warm all over.

"Sheriff Barclay—"

"Clint," he interrupted. "After last night, I reckon you can call me Clint."

"Please stop talking about that," Emily pleaded, desperate to change the subject. "I think it's best if we both forget all about what happened last night. Every single part of it!"

"Yeah, well, I'm not sure that's possible."

Her gray eyes widened and flew to his cool blue ones. Something in their glinting depths made her heart start to pound like a locomotive streaking down a greased track.

"Tell me about Armstrong," Clint persisted. He was desperately trying to keep his mind on business when all he wanted to do was reach out and stroke that mass of shimmering black hair. Why did she have to look so gorgeous this morning, in a plain white shirtwaist and riding skirt—she looked every bit as enticing as she had in that fancy gown last night. It was damned unfair, he decided bitterly.

"Tell me why the sight of him spooked you like that," he said more roughly than he intended.

"It's a long story."

"Then get started."

"How . . . how did you find out . . . his name?" Emily couldn't think of anything to do except stall for time. She didn't want to tell Clint Barclay one single thing, not if she could find a way around it. "I . . . I'm sure I never mentioned it."

"No, you didn't. But after you left last night, I tracked him down. He didn't go far, just to Opal's Brothel. It didn't take long to find out who he was, but I didn't learn much else—except that he gets rough with his women," he added, his expression hardening.

Emily froze at his words, her eyes pinned to his face.

Clint continued grimly. "Apparently Armstrong was

eliminated early from the poker tournament. He was in a foul temper. You don't need to know the details," he muttered, thinking of Lorelei and the bruises on her arms, "but I want to know what he has to do with you. And with that little boy. Is Joey your son?" he asked abruptly.

He'd never intended to ask her that question, but he hadn't been able to stop himself. If she had a husband somewhere, or some other man in her life, he damn well wanted to know about it.

She stared at him for a long moment during which Clint held his breath, watching conflicting emotions swirl across her exquisite face.

"No," she said at last, with a shake of her head. "Joey isn't my son."

An odd relief gripped him. So there was no husband . . .

Not that it matters, Clint thought harshly, suddenly, steeling himself as she turned, paced across the porch and back. He tried like hell not to stare at the gentle sway of her hips beneath her riding skirt.

"Joey's mother is my friend. A dear friend. Her name is Lissa McCoy."

There seemed no point in trying to keep the story a secret any longer. From the way Clint Barclay was making himself at home on her front porch, he didn't appear to be going anywhere until she satisfied his damned lawman's curiosity.

"Lissa is a widow, and she worked in the boardinghouse where my aunt and I used to live." Emily took a breath. "At one point she was betrothed to John Armstrong. Then she found out what he was really like and she . . . she broke off their engagement."

A slow drizzle began—heavy gray drops plunking down upon the weeds and grass of the yard and upon the porch—striking her cheeks, dampening her shirtwaist. But Emily hardly noticed. She was seeing Lissa's frightened, tear-streaked face that night she'd sent John Armstrong away. She was hearing Lissa tell her in a voice that throbbed with fear how Armstrong had warned her he would never let her go.

A distant slash of lightning lit the sky. "Are you sure you want to hear all this?" she asked, glancing up. "The storm—"

"Just tell me, Emily," Clint replied in a voice so calm that some of the turmoil inside her began to ease. "I want to help."

She glanced toward the barn. There was no sign of Joey yet. He was safe and dry there, no doubt chattering to Clucker while he played a game of solitaire. She'd have to keep an eye out for him, but in the meantime she could tell Clint Barclay about Armstrong. It wouldn't be such a bad thing. If Armstrong showed up again in Lonesome, Clint could warn her . . .

The rain was falling faster. "Come inside then." She turned abruptly, picked up the rifle, and went through the door. He followed as a harder downpour began to lash the earth.

Never had she thought she'd invite a lawman—particularly *this* lawman—into her home. She suddenly didn't know whether to treat him like a guest or an intruder.

"Would you . . . like some pie—or some coffee?" she began doubtfully, but Clint shook his head. At her gesture of invitation he took a seat—choosing the armchair where Uncle Jake liked to sit.

This isn't right, Emily thought. *He shouldn't be here. I'll tell him the story quickly, ask him to let me know if Armstrong comes back, and then he'll leave.*

She slipped onto the sofa and smoothed her skirt,

wondering if Clint Barclay sensed the same heat and tension between them that she did. Better not to think about that—better to just tell him what he wanted to know quickly—so he would leave.

"From the moment Lissa ended her engagement, her entire life became a kind of hell," she said, looking at Clint with eyes tinged with sadness. "Armstrong always had a temper—which is something those of us in the Spoon family know all about," she added ruefully, "but Lissa had no idea that Armstrong's temper was violent, or that it was fueled by a mean streak. He'd show up, demand to see her, and knock down anyone who tried to get in his way. He pushed me into the wall once when I wouldn't let him inside the boardinghouse."

She saw Clint's eyes turn to chips of blue ice and continued quickly. "But he saved the worst of his violence for Lissa. He struck her on more than one occasion. Other boarders had to come to her aid, force him to leave. One day he caught her outside as she was returning from an errand—he beat her horribly. She had a black eye and bruises on her throat because he tried to choke her." Emily's fingers clenched around her skirt at the memory.

"I begged her to go to the constables, tell them what was happening, but she was afraid, afraid that would anger him even more. The final straw came just before I left the boardinghouse to come west—to meet Uncle Jake and the boys."

A shudder ran through her. "Armstrong climbed through her bedroom window in the middle of the night, while she and Joey were both asleep. He began beating her, and Joey tried to stop him."

"Go on." Clint spoke tensely.

Emily bit her lip, forcing herself to continue. "Joey

was only trying to help his mother, but Armstrong knocked Joey down, kicked him. Then began hitting him. Joey was screaming, crying—Lissa tried to pull him away, to shield him, but Armstrong was like a crazed man. He . . . he started to choke her—he was actually trying to kill her—and I believe he would have killed Joey too." Emily's own hands clenched into fists. Even the memory of that night left her shaken. "Thank heavens Mr. Dane and Mr. Puchinski, two of the other boarders, heard the commotion and broke into her room in time . . ."

Her voice trailed off. "As soon as I heard the noise, I knew it was him. I grabbed Aunt Ida's derringer—the one Uncle Jake gave her before he went on the run—and I rushed downstairs, but Armstrong was gone by the time I reached Lissa's room. He got clean away." She lifted her gaze to Clint's face. "But Lissa knew—and so did I—that she and Joey would have to leave Jefferson City before he came back again."

"I wish I'd known about this last night." Clint spoke in a low tone that was no less furious for all its quietness. "I'd have given a lot to get my hands on him."

She was startled by the anger in him, an anger clearly directed at John Armstrong.

"There was nothing you could have done," she pointed out wearily. "Lissa isn't even here to accuse him of trying to kill her and—"

"I didn't say I'd arrest him, Emily, I said I'd like to have gotten my hands on him."

She stared at him as the import of his words hit her. She felt a shock at the blazing fury in his eyes. "I don't have much use for men who hurt women," he added shortly.

"It's better this way," she said after a pause, then

jumped as another flash of golden lightning streaked across the sky, followed shortly by a growl of thunder. The storm was moving closer, swooping down from the mountains. "It's Joey who needs to be protected now. Lissa is on her way to San Francisco to find a new home for them both—somewhere where Armstrong will never find them. When she's ready, she'll send for him or come for him—but in the meantime, I'm keeping him safe. The last thing I want is for Joey to ever have to see John Armstrong again—or even to find out that he was right here in town last night," she said fiercely. "Ever since that night he's been frightened of nearly everything. Until recently, he's barely spoken, barely smiled. He's just starting to lose the fear. Thanks to Uncle Jake, he wants to learn how to ride, he goes to the barn himself to do the chores—you saw him—he helps me in the garden now, and we even talked about having a picnic down by the stream. That's the first time he's even thought about venturing so far from the cabin."

Suddenly she noticed that while she'd been talking the sky had turned an eerie greenish-gray. The charcoal clouds roiling above were thicker and more ominous than before. The next slash of lightning brought her to her feet.

"I need to get Joey." A sudden knot of worry twisted through her stomach. "I'm surprised that the thunder hasn't already frightened him into coming back—"

"Let me." Clint reached the door before she did. "It's raining pretty hard already."

He was out the door before she could protest, sprinting across the porch, down the steps, and toward the barn. A moment later he disappeared inside and from the cabin door, Emily watched anxiously for him to come out with Joey. But he didn't.

She started across the porch, hugging herself, but at that moment, Clint emerged from the barn.

"He's not there," he shouted.

The knot of worry tightened and Emily raced down the steps. There was steady, drumming rain now, and it matched the hard beating of her heart as she darted toward the barn to look for herself. Clint was already circling the structure, scanning every direction, when she dashed out again, white-faced, fighting panic.

"Joey!" she shouted into the wind. Lightning zigzagged across the sky and, involuntarily, she cringed. The bolt of thunder that followed shook her to the core.

"Joey, where are you?" she screamed.

"Joey!" Clint's deep voice carried even over the rising wind. There was no sign of the little boy, not in any direction Emily looked. Had he somehow come around to the kitchen door, slipped in without her hearing him? Had he overheard them talking about John Armstrong?

Her throat constricting, she raced around to the kitchen door. To her dismay, it was ajar. But even worse was the deck of playing cards lying beside the vegetable garden, being thrummed into the earth by the driving rain.

Her hands flew to her throat. "Oh my God."

Dashing inside the cabin, she called out frantically, "Joey, where are you?"

He'll be in the back bedroom, she told herself as fear clawed through her. *He'll be huddled under his bed or in a corner, sobbing and terrified, because he heard you say that John Armstrong was in town.*

But Joey wasn't in the back bedroom, or in any of the rooms in the cabin—he was nowhere to be seen.

"I'll check the shed," Clint said grimly.

Emily stood in the parlor for a moment, shock and

horror washing over her. Then she rushed outside, straight to the corral, placing her hands on the split rail fence.

"Joey!" she screamed into the wet gusting wind that swirled around her. "Joey!"

It was there that Clint found her a moment later, unable to discern whether it was tears or just rain that streamed down her cheeks. She jumped when he seized her by the shoulders and lifted wide, panicked eyes to his face.

"He's gone, Clint! He must have heard us talking . . . oh, God, where did he go?"

"Poor kid must have run away." His face was taut. "Go inside. I'll find him."

Find him? With terror pounding through her like an iron hammer, Emily turned toward the open Colorado wilderness, scanning the wild land in every direction, the hills and buttes and canyons, the dipping, meandering curves of the valley, the creek . . .

The creek. A fresh terror filled her. She bolted toward the creek bank, but Clint caught her and swung her around.

"I'll go. Get inside," he ordered. "If he isn't down there I'll . . ."

"Don't you dare tell me what to do!" Her voice throbbed with fear and with fury. "I'll be damned if I'll stay here while you go and look for him!" She shook him off and started to run once more, but he seized her again, this time by the shoulders. He spun her around and gave her a shake as rain poured down around them.

"The storm's only going to get worse, Emily," he shouted over the wind. "You're already soaked. The boy will be fine, I'll see to that—"

"You'll have to hogtie me to keep me from searching

for him!" she shouted back. She pushed him away. "He's my friend's *son,* he's *my* responsibility! I promised Lissa I'd keep him safe!"

Her voice cracked and unbidden tears sprang from her eyes. Furious, driven by terror, she dashed them away and gazed into Clint's eyes, her own filled with a desperate determination. "*I have to find him!*"

As the rain streamed down the brim of his hat, Clint studied the soaked, beautiful girl before him and saw the frantic fear that gripped her. There was no way Emily Spoon would wait and pace helplessly in the cabin while he rode out looking for the boy. Arguing with her was useless. And a waste of time.

"Then we'll both search for him." He grabbed her arm. "Come on!"

But there was no sign of Joey along the creek bank, and Emily stared at the churning water in terror.

He might not have come this way, she told herself, and realized it was a prayer. *Please don't let him have come this way.*

"He could have headed in any direction." Clint pulled her away from the creek. "Let's go—we'll cover more ground on horseback."

"And if we split up," Emily called out as she started at a run for the barn.

Joey was out here in this storm, probably thinking John Armstrong knew where he was—believing that the man of his nightmares was after him.

Why, oh why, had she spoken Armstrong's name aloud when Joey was anywhere around? What was she thinking?

You were thinking about Clint Barclay, that's what, she realized with a rush of guilt. Distracted by Clint, she'd been careless and stupid. It was her fault Joey had run away. Her fault.

My God, what if I don't find him—what will I tell Lissa?

The rain fell in torrents, the wind screamed in her ears, and Emily raced for the barn, every bone in her body shaking with despair.

Chapter 11

FEROCIOUS AS A WOLF, THE STORM snarled across the foothills and tore through Beaver Rock. The wind and sideways-slashing rain drowned out Emily's voice as over and over she called Joey's name. She didn't know the region well—she'd only ridden out this way once before with Pete—but she did recognize the steep ravines that bordered Beaver Rock, the wild and craggy trails strewn with rocks and mountain ash and brilliant purple columbine. In the midst of the storm, a savage beauty gripped this wild stretch of the foothills, but she saw nothing of the rain-drenched wild roses or bluebells, of the beauty of white fir trees or snowberry shrubs trembling in the wind. She saw only the driving rain, the harsh and treacherous hills, the dangerous ravines, where a little boy could be roaming, dwarfed by the huge rocks, terrified and alone on those slippery slopes . . .

She forced herself to ignore the rain and the raging wind that nearly unseated her, forced herself to ride slowly, deliberately, twisting in the saddle to scan every crack and crevice of the slick trails, squinting through the downpour as her mare picked her way below, around, and then up and up toward the crest of Beaver Rock.

Beneath the brim of her hat, and beneath the thick yellow slicker that shrouded the dry clothes she'd quickly changed into before setting out on the search, Emily's heart grew heavier and heavier.

There was no sign of Joey.

Or of Uncle Jake.

She'd checked the line cabin he'd mentioned and had spotted cattle huddling here and there beneath stands of box elder, but she hadn't seen her uncle anywhere. Her hopes that he could join the search and increase the chance of finding Joey had all but disintegrated.

She prayed Clint Barclay was having better luck.

Clint had headed toward Pine Canyon and had promised to keep an eye out for Lester. The more people joining the search, the better, Emily had pointed out as she'd fastened the slicker over her riding garb and led her palomino mare, Nugget, from the barn.

That had been hours ago. And still the lightning and the thunder raged. Her mare was shaking, and reared up in panic at each flash from the sky. If Nugget was this frightened, how must Joey feel? Emily wondered in dismay. The very thought of him wandering out here lost and alone made her want to scream.

But screaming wouldn't help. She had to find him. *Soon.*

"Whoa, girl—easy," she muttered as the mare danced sideways after a particularly loud roar of thunder. "Steady, girl, hold steady."

Desperately she scanned the landscape, a nightmare of solid, rising rock, whirling tumbleweed, driving rain. The wind tore at the new spring leaves and whistled deafeningly in her ears.

"Joey!" she screamed yet again. "*Joey!*"

Something moved—*there*—down in the ravine. Just a

shift of movement, but perhaps . . . Her heart pounding with a sudden hope, Emily spurred Nugget in that direction.

"Joey! Are you down there?"

Clenching the reins, she whispered a prayer of hope as the mare started down the slippery trail. But suddenly she saw that what she'd glimpsed was only a badger—it darted across the trail just as a streak of golden lightning exploded across the sky. Almost simultaneously, thunder boomed, then another flash of lightning sizzled, striking an aspen only ten feet away.

Nugget reared straight up, whinnying in terror, while Emily fought to stay in the saddle.

"Whoa, girl!" she cried, but it was too late. The panicked mare reared up even higher than before, and this time Emily was thrown from the saddle. Pain shot through her as she hit the earth, and small squares of white light danced before her eyes.

Then yet another slash of lightning arced overhead, sending the mare bolting down the trail.

"Nugget!" Emily called frantically after her. "Nugget!"

But the palomino never slowed and as Emily watched in despair, she galloped frenziedly out of sight.

No, Emily thought in dazed disbelief. *No! This can't be happening. I have to find Joey.*

Pain and dizziness washed over her, but she fought them off. Summoning all her determination, she tried to stand, but the agony that squeezed through her ankle as she tried to put her weight on it made her gasp. Tears smarted in her eyes.

Unable to bear the pain, Emily sank to the ground again and peered around her through the driving rain.

I must be about four miles from the line cabin, she

thought bleakly. She knew it might as well have been four *hundred*.

But staying here wouldn't do any good. She had to find some kind of shelter, even if she had to crawl to it. If night fell, and no one came this way to find her, it would get bitterly cold this high up in the foothills. Not to mention that the trail was already swirling with water—it could easily flood . . .

Trying to block out the throbbing in her ankle and the rain soaking her face, Emily gritted her teeth and began to crawl.

"What the hell are you doing here, Barclay?" Lester Spoon demanded. "I oughta horsewhip you!"

Half a mile from the rim of Pine Canyon, with the rain pouring down all round them, running off their hats and their slickers, Lester glared at Lonesome's sheriff. "You scared this boy to death!" he yelled over a blast of thunder. "And in case you haven't noticed, he's hurt fell into a gully, no thanks to you. Now get out of my way, I'm taking him home."

Clint barely spared the freckle-faced giant a glance. He was studying Joey, seated before Lester in the saddle, tiny as a burr. The boy's thin face was dirty and tear-streaked, and a blood-soaked bandanna that must have been Lester's was wrapped around his right hand. Relief that the boy was safe flooded Clint—but so did concern for Emily, searching even now at Beaver Rock.

The storm was worsening every moment—the real brunt of it closing in fast.

"You all right, Joey?" Clint shouted, his horse edging in closer as thunder rumbled. "What happened to your hand?"

"I f-fell, Sheriff," the boy answered on a gulp, huddling against Lester's big frame. "When I was running away from the bad man. He's coming after me, isn't he?" Joey yelled, shrinking against Lester. "I know he is—I heard you and Em-ly talking—"

"Hold on, Joey—you've got it all wrong." Clint's voice was raised so that he could be heard over the wind, but it held steely calm. He looked directly into the boy's panicked eyes. "No one's coming after you. The bad man left town—he never even knew you were here, thanks to Emily."

"R-really? You . . . sure, Sheriff?"

"I swear it, Joey. You're safe," Clint yelled. "Emily will explain it all to you later—right now you need to get home and out of this storm!"

"You hear that, Lester?" Joey twisted around in the saddle to give the big man a wavery smile. "I'm safe!"

"Sure you are." Lester clapped a hand to the boy's shoulder. "I told you—no one's going to hurt you, not while you're with us."

"Is Em-ly mad at me?" Joey shouted at Clint over the rain.

Clint shook his head. "No, but she's awfully worried about you. I'm headed out to find her and let her know you're safe—"

"Find her?" Lester demanded. "What the hell do you mean 'find her'?"

"She's out by Beaver Rock, looking for Joey!"

A sudden violent gust roared all around them, whipping the horses' manes and tossing the leaves on the aspens.

Consternation crossed Lester's face. "Damn! Em's all alone in this storm? This is *your* fault, Barclay!"

Clint was too concerned about Emily to waste any

more time arguing with Lester Spoon. "She's hoping to run into your father," he yelled, turning his horse toward Beaver Rock. "Maybe she will and maybe she won't—but I'm going to let her know Joey's safe. And bring her back!"

"You stay away from her, Barclay! My pop's out there—he'll take care of her. Or I'll send Pete—"

"Do whatever the hell you want, Spoon," Clint shouted, his face grim. "But I'm going to Beaver Rock to find her—*now*."

"Damn it, Barclay—we don't need you to look after—"

But Clint was already gone, spurring his horse toward the foothills. As another streak of lightning split the sky, Joey gasped and ducked his head and Lester muttered, "It's all right, Joey. Emily will be fine."

"You . . . *sure*?"

"That sheriff'll find her. If there's one thing he's damned good at, it's tracking. But he'd better not even *touch* her, if he knows what's good for him."

Then he spurred his horse too, as the sky darkened to a murky green and the rain pounded like nails and the bay horse flew along the trail toward the ranch.

Silver rain pummeled the rocks and the mountains, bent the aspens, and sent the wild creatures diving and digging for cover. Dust and stones flew, lightning raked the savage sky, and the night roared like a lion.

Clint Barclay rode through the fury and the thunder and searched for the midnight-haired woman on a golden horse.

Where before he had shouted the boy's name, now he called out the woman's. "Emily! Emily, where are you?"

The wind snatched away his voice and his words, but he only yelled louder, controlling his skittish horse as he controlled the alarm thrumming inside him.

"Emily!"

Squinting against the rain that streamed from the wide brim of his hat, Clint scanned the wild night in every direction. Not only hadn't he come upon Emily Spoon, either upon Beaver Rock or at the line cabin a few miles away, he hadn't run across Jake Spoon either. He wondered if she'd already found her uncle, if they were both still out there searching in ever-widening circles for Joey. Or had Emily not come across her uncle at all—was she instead out here in the storm all alone—somewhere . . .

But where?

His gut clenched as the unbidden and unpleasant thought occurred to him that maybe she hadn't even made it this far. Maybe something had happened to her along the way.

He rode on doggedly, all of his mind and being intent on the search, blocking out as best he could the battering wind and rain, the crashes of thunder that sounded like cannon fire as they echoed through the canyons and ravines.

A tumbleweed hurled across his path and his horse reared.

Damn it, he thought, gripping the reins and staring through the madness of the storm, *where is she?*

It was possible, he reflected as the rain ran in hard icy rivulets down the length of his slicker, that she'd turned back before he even got here. But he doubted it. If Emily thought there was even the slightest chance Joey was out here lost in the storm, she wouldn't have turned back until she found him.

She was the most stubborn woman he'd ever met.

And undoubtedly the most loyal.

But where the hell was she?

Suddenly a sound pierced the fury even of the storm, a sound Clint recognized instantly.

A gunshot. And it had come from due west.

He jerked on the reins, every muscle knotted with tension as he galloped in the direction of the shot.

He saw her in the next brilliant blaze of lightning that seemed to light up the entire state.

She was huddled in her slicker, on the ground, a gun in her hand. He spurred his horse forward and saw the snake lying dead not five feet from where she crouched, the little derringer gripped between her fingers. It was a prairie rattler, Clint realized in alarm—poisonous as hell.

Her pale face lifted to his and tension shot through every muscle in his body as he saw her drained features, her eyes bright with fear. Vaulting from the saddle, he reached her in two quick strides.

"Are you hurt? Did it bite you?" he demanded, hunkering down beside her.

"N-no—I shot it first. But my ankle—it's twisted . . . Did you find Joey?" Desperately she searched his face.

"Lester found him." Frowning, Clint noted that she was shivering—badly. Her lips were blue. "He's fine, except for a few scraped fingers. They're back at the cabin by now, no doubt warm and dry—which is what you ought to be."

For a moment Emily forgot all about the storm, about the pain slicing through her ankle and the icy chill creeping through her bones even as the rain pelted her face. Joey was safe. *Safe*. Relief filled every part of her, obliterating everything else.

"What happened to your ankle?" Clint asked, slipping his arms under her. "And your horse?"

He lifted her with ease and cradled her against his chest as the wind nearly blew her hat off.

"She threw me . . . and bolted. Spooked by lightning." Emily tried not to think how good it felt to be held by Clint Barclay. Held so effortlessly and easily, as if she were a doll. His warmth and strength seemed to be flowing into her, easing the icy weariness that had eaten into her bones. "I . . . I was trying to find a cave or something . . . I didn't think I'd reach the line cabin . . ."

Clint's arms tightened around her as he felt her trembling all over. Her face was icy white, her teeth chattering. Damn, she needed warm blankets and a good blazing fire . . . fast.

"Well, you'll reach it now," he said grimly. "We'll wait out the storm there." As if she weighed no more than a penny, he hoisted her into the saddle and vaulted up behind her.

Lightning split the sky in a fiery arc and she flinched involuntarily. When Clint Barclay's powerful arms closed around her she could only sag against him with relief.

She closed her eyes then, too spent and weak to do anything else. She blocked out the storm that swirled all around them as they galloped away from the ravine and night began to descend. All she knew was that she was safe. That Clint was holding her, warming her, taking her to shelter.

When they reached the line cabin, Emily half expected to find Uncle Jake inside, but when Clint kicked the door open they found it dry, stocked with supplies, cold as a tomb—and empty.

Where is he? she wondered uneasily, finding it odd

that she hadn't come across him once during all the time she'd been searching for Joey.

"I'll get a fire going," Clint said curtly as he set her down upon the neatly made-up cot on the far wall. He noticed then that her hands were shaking so much with cold that she was having difficulty removing the wet slicker. Swearing silently, he paused long enough to undo the fastenings for her and help her out of the heavy covering. There was a saddle blanket folded at the foot of the bed and without a word he draped it around her shoulders.

"I never should have let you go out to search in this storm," he muttered.

"It wasn't for you to decide." Emily clutched the blanket around her and lifted her eyes to the hard planes of his face.

"Yeah? Well, now I'm in charge. Sit here, don't move, and take it easy."

For some reason, despite the numbing cold, his nearness and his touch as he had wrapped the blanket around her had sent a wave of heat through her body.

"I'm perfectly fine," she murmured defiantly, wondering *why. Why* did this man have such an effect on her? Why did his nearness make her heart do strange little somersaults, and warm her blood, and make it difficult to think clearly?

"I can make coffee while you . . ."

"Move off that cot and I'll hogtie you." Clint's stern gaze brooked no argument. He regarded her warningly for a moment, then swung away to the hearth, already stocked with two thick logs. "The first thing we have to do is get you warm."

If anyone had ever told her she'd be hiding out from a storm in a line cabin with a lawman, letting him make her coffee and a simple supper of hardtack and jerky, she'd have thought they were crazy. But here she was, and she was startled that it didn't feel as strange as she would expect. Despite being cold and exhausted, and her ankle hurting, it was almost . . . pleasant to be here with Clint Barclay.

She felt grateful he had found her and . . . she felt unaccountably but completely safe.

You're delirious, a small sharp voice inside her insisted, as the rain battered the cabin's roof and a roaring wind seemed to shake all four mud-thatched walls. *The sooner the storm ends and you can go back to the ranch, the better.*

"Do you think it's going to stop storming any time soon?"

"Like tonight?" He poured more coffee into her tin cup and brought it over to the cot. "Don't count on it. By sunrise, maybe."

Sunrise? "I can't stay here all night," Emily said firmly. She accepted the cup and felt a current of heat as his hand brushed hers. No, she couldn't possibly stay here all night.

"Why not? I don't bite."

"As soon as the storm lessens a bit, I'd like you to take me home."

As if to mock her words, lightning slashed beyond the single window at that very instant, lighting up the sky and the entire shack as if it were daylight. It was immediately followed by thunder exploding even closer and louder than before, and the downpour suddenly intensified.

"Like I said before—sunrise," he repeated, then flashed her a quick grin. "Come on, you're not *that* afraid of me, are you?"

"I'm not afraid of you at all."

Those cool blue eyes smiled into hers as he lowered his tall frame so that he straddled the spindly chair across from the cot. "Then why are you trembling?" he asked, studying the delicate hands that gripped the cup.

"I'm not. I'm just cold."

But it was a lie because, to Emily's dismay, a tingling warmth was rushing through her. She wasn't cold anymore in the least.

"Tell me about Joey." That was a safe subject. Anything to escape the intensity of those eyes. They looked even bluer in the dimness of the cabin, lit only by lightning and firelight. Even bluer yet against the lean swarthiness of his handsome face, the dark stubble of his jaw . . .

"Where did you find him?" Emily asked desperately, taking a sip of the coffee.

He told her about his encounter with Joey and Lester, adding, "Mostly, he was scared—and wet as a drowned rat. I made sure he knew that John Armstrong had left town."

Emily's eyes mirrored her distress. "I never should have discussed that man while Joey was anywhere around," she muttered.

"It wasn't your fault. I pressed you to tell me."

"I can't bear to think that if he hadn't run into Lester, he might still be out there right now—in this!" She flinched as the rain pounded in a driving frenzy upon the shack's roof.

"But he did run into Lester, Emily. He's safe. And so are you." But he was wondering if he'd have ever found her if she hadn't fired that shot.

"He's been so frightened," she continued as if he hadn't spoken. "And he was finally beginning to get over that fear."

"I know." Clint nodded, his eyes narrowing. "I saw the fear on his face today. Poor kid. It reminded me . . ."

His voice broke off.

"Reminded you of what?"

Abruptly he stood up, went back to the coffeepot, and began to pour himself a cup. "Nothing," he said in a flat voice. "It doesn't matter."

"Tell me." Emily watched him, watched him wrestle in his own mind, trying to decide if he wanted to explain. At last he took a swig of coffee and then spoke in that same flat voice.

"Joey reminded me of my own brother, Nick. The way he looked after our parents were killed."

Tension shot through her at his words. And at the rigid clench of his jaw, the flash of pain in his eyes.

"I'm sorry," she whispered into the silence that followed. "What . . . happened?"

He swung back toward her, straddled the chair once more, and in the firelight, his face looked hard again, as if nothing penetrated that iron calm. "Their stagecoach was held up. Nick was with them." He shook his head, remembering, and Emily sat perfectly still on the cot, watching that sharp, swarthy face as if she too could see the ghosts walking through his mind.

"My older brother, Wade, and I were staying with neighbors while our parents went to Kansas—they wanted to visit my mother's aunt, who was dying. Nick was only seven—the baby of the family—so they took him along. I guess my mother didn't feel right leaving him behind." His big knuckles whitened on the tin cup, then, with an effort, she saw him deliberately relax. "But they never got there. The stage was stopped."

Emily sat very still, no longer hearing the drumming

of the rain, only hearing his voice, so calm, dispassionate, almost detached.

"The outlaws who held them up killed all the passengers—except Nick. Every man, every woman—and the driver. My father tried to fight, tried to save my mother, and she in turn pushed Nick behind her, trying to shield him with her own body. Pleading for them to spare him with her last breath. That's what Nick told us later. For some reason, maybe because she tried so hard to protect him, the bastards didn't shoot Nick. They let him live."

Clint's eyes were slits of deadly blue ice. A shudder ran through Emily as she closed her own eyes a moment, thinking of that small boy, the lone survivor of such a massacre.

"He was the only one," Clint said softly, and she marveled at the steadiness of his tone. "The only one to get out alive. And he came back to us, to me and Wade. When he did," he said, drawing in a deep harsh breath, "he looked a lot the way Joey did today. The way no kid should ever have to look."

Emily swallowed. Words couldn't express the sick feeling in the pit of her stomach. "How . . . horrible. I'm sorry." How silly and feeble those words sounded.

Clint looked at her, his expression unreadable. "It was a long time ago," he muttered.

"But the pain never really goes away." Emily's tone was soft. She was thinking of her own parents, who'd died of the fever, thinking how much she missed them still. For a moment, gazing into Clint's eyes, she thought she felt a flash of understanding between them.

"I hope for Joey it *will* go away someday," he said, his jaw clenching.

Emily was still picturing him as a young boy who'd

lost his parents in such a brutal way. "How . . . how old were you when all this happened?" she asked.

"Nine. Wade was eleven." Clint shook his head. "Suddenly we were orphans. All we knew was that no matter what it took, we wanted to stay together. Things looked pretty bleak on that front—until a man by the name of Reese Summers stepped in."

"Who was he?"

"Reese was my father's best friend. The two of them went way back. After the holdup, Reese came and got us and brought us back to his ranch in Wyoming. A place called Cloud Ranch."

"I've heard of it," Emily exclaimed. Cloud Ranch—one of the largest ranches in all of the West. "That's where you grew up?" she asked, a little awed.

"Yep. It's a great ranch now—Reese built it up from a tiny cabin not much bigger than this one. It was his dream, his life. And it became our home. And he became like a father to all of us."

Suddenly he drained the last of the coffee and swung off the chair. He left the cup on the small table near the fire and came to stand before Emily. "It took time though. It wasn't easy, especially for Nick. That's why I understand about Joey and his fears. After Nick saw our parents and everyone else on that stagecoach killed, he didn't speak for a long time. Not one word. But thanks to Reese Summers, he got over it, and the fear—and the silence—eventually went away."

"Where's Nick now?"

"Who knows?" Suddenly the harshness lifted from his face and he laughed. "He moves around a lot, my baby brother does. He stays in touch, though. He's a gunfighter."

"A gunfighter!"

"Guess it's his way of getting back at the men who killed our parents," Clint said. "The bastards were never found, never identified. Never punished. They're the kind of vermin my brother hunts down." His face was grim again and Emily shivered, suddenly knowing that if Clint Barclay himself ever found those men, he'd make them sorry they'd ever been born.

"And this is your way of getting back at them," she said slowly, looking up at him. Her gaze flicked to the badge glinting on his vest. "It's the reason you're a lawman."

There was a pause. The only sound was the rain drumming upon the roof and the wicked hiss of the wind. "Guess you could say that," Clint said at length. "All I know is it's something I need to do."

A wave of compassion swept through her and at that moment it was hard to hate him for being who he was, what he was. Once Clint Barclay had been a young boy like Joey, scared and alone, torn from his parents. He had become a strong man, determined to fight the kind of brutality that had nearly destroyed his family.

"And Wade?" she asked, to change the subject, a bit unnerved by her own reflections.

"Wade took over Cloud Ranch after Reese passed on recently. Actually, a part of the ranch was left to all three of us, but Wade has the biggest share. He's the foreman and he has the same love for the place and for Silver Valley that Reese had." Again his face softened, just a trace. "He got hitched recently. It was his wedding I was coming back from that first night I met you," he added.

"Oh." Emily's thoughts went back to that night, to how frightened she'd been when Clint Barclay had first grabbed her in the darkness. Now, despite his imposing figure, the fact that he was so tall and so muscular, with that sharply handsome face and those eyes that could cut your heart in two, she somehow couldn't imagine being frightened of him. Not in the way she had been at first. Those gentle kisses had seen to that . . .

She mustn't think about those kisses. To stop herself, she said abruptly, "Well, now that your brother has married, I guess you're planning to do the same thing."

His eyes narrowed. "What would make you say a fool thing like that?"

It was Emily's turn to laugh. "Nearly every woman of marriageable age in this town has asked me to sew her a new dress in time for the box lunch social. From what I've heard, they've all set their cap for you. Though I can't imagine why," she couldn't help adding tartly.

Instead of rising to the bait, Clint just sighed. "Neither can I."

"Well, you must have done something to make them all start chasing you like bees after honey."

He looked startled. "Hell, no. Why would I? I've got no intentions of settling down, not for a long time. If ever."

"Oh, not the marrying type, are you?" Emily inquired coolly.

"Nope, and I never pretended to be. But then most men aren't."

"Your brother just got married," she reminded him.

"Yeah, that was a surprise. But Wade got lucky. He met a perfect woman. Someone perfect for him," he added with a grin. "I wouldn't trade in my freedom, even for a girl as gorgeous as Caitlin Summers—I mean Caitlin *Barclay* now."

"What is she like?" Emily couldn't resist asking. There was no mistaking the admiration in his face when he spoke of Caitlin Barclay. An odd prick of jealousy assailed her. What was wrong with her?

"Caitlin's a looker. Blonde. Elegant. She was raised in Philadelphia—the type at home in the finest drawing rooms—but she's taken to Cloud Ranch like no greenhorn you ever saw. For all of her fancy manners, she's feisty as hell. A little bit like you, in that respect," he added suddenly, his gaze settling on her.

"Well, if you're looking for someone like her to marry, I don't think you're going to find her in Lonesome. At least, I haven't met anyone who sounds so . . . perfect."

She spoke offhandedly but heard the vinegar in her voice too late. Clint shot her a quizzical look. "I didn't say she was perfect," he remarked. "I said she was perfect for Wade."

"And what kind of girl would be perfect for you, Sheriff Barclay?" The words flew out of her mouth before she even realized what she'd said. She saw his eyes narrow on her and darken to the color of a stormy sea.

He took a step toward her. Emily tensed.

Another step. She had to force herself to remain perfectly still upon the cot, to resist the temptation to edge away from him. Her heart was beating so fast she could barely catch her breath.

Clint Barclay across the room was distraction enough—but up close, less than two feet away, well, she thought weakly as he paused directly before her, that was too close for comfort.

He loomed over her, seeming to fill the tiny low-ceilinged shack with his height and broad shoulders. She gulped as she saw that the blue chambray shirt that encased his shoulders was open enough at the neck to show the dark curling hair on his chest. And what an impressive chest it was: taut, muscular, powerful—like all the rest of him, she thought on a gulp.

She tried to tell herself that he was only a man, like any other. But something about him didn't seem like any other man. She'd never felt this drawn to any other man or been so fascinated by the way dark hair could tumble over a brow or by a deep, cool, steady voice. As he watched her intently in the flickering firelight and seemed to be considering his next words, she felt her breath get all caught up in her throat. Those searing eyes pierced her face as the firelight danced crazily—and so did her heart.

Chapter 12

"FIRST OFF, I RECKON THERE'S NO GIRL who's perfect for me," Clint Barclay said flatly. He made it sound like a warning, Emily thought, a chill seeping into her chest. "I told you—I'm not the marrying type."

"So you did," Emily acknowledged with a cool little nod.

"I'm not even the romantic type," he added, his lip curling, "and sure as hell not the settle-down-by-a-fire-and-show-me-the-knit-booties type."

His powerful shoulders lifted in a shrug. "Matter of fact, until I took this job in Lonesome I was always on the move—nearly as much as Nick. Neither one of us has ever stayed put in one town for long."

"So . . . why Lonesome?" Emily asked, sliding back just far enough on the cot so that her back was against the wall. The more distance between them, the better, that's what she figured.

In the dancing orange flames of the fire, he shrugged again. His bronzed face looked hard and unreadable. And mesmerizing as hell.

"By the time I cleaned out the Duggan gang, I'd grown to like Lonesome and a lot of the folks here. They asked me to stay—offered me a nice pile of money to continue protecting the town, so I did."

He stepped back, folded his tall frame back down on the chair again, his long legs stretched out before him, and eyed her with cool amusement. "But as for marrying someone, getting stuck in one place forever . . . hell, no. That's not for me. I'll stay in Lonesome for the time being, as long as I'm needed and folks still want me . . . but that's the most kind of a promise I'm prepared to make."

Why is he telling me all this? Emily wondered. He was going to great pains to make his position on marriage, on promises and commitments, unmistakably clear . . .

She noticed then that he was studying her thoughtfully. "But I reckon that doesn't really answer your question, does it? The truth is, no one girl would be perfect for me . . . and sure as hell not one who set her cap for me and chased me around like a dog trying to herd a stray calf." He gave a snort of laughter, then his gaze rested on her and his eyes gleamed.

He gave her a long, slow look, taking in her still-damp tumbling curls, the blanket draped around her narrow shoulders, the sculptured beauty of her face—studying her with such thoroughness that Emily blushed.

"But if I wanted to find the perfect woman—which I don't—I reckon she'd have dark hair, Miss Spoon. Dark like the night."

"Oh . . . w-would she?"

He grinned, a heartrending grin, and suddenly came off the chair in a smooth easy movement that reminded her of a wildcat coiling to spring. To her consternation, he settled himself beside her on the cot and reached out toward her. His fingers closed over a handful of those loosely falling curls. "Her hair would be thick and heavy, and soft like velvet. The kind of hair a man likes to touch and spread out on the pillow, and breathe in the scent of it."

He drew his hand slowly, and ever so gently, through the lush strands of her hair. Emily wanted to tell him to stop, but her voice wasn't working properly and she couldn't say a word.

"And," Clint continued, his grin deepening as his gaze flickered over her expressive face, "I'm finding that I'm partial to a woman with gray eyes. They're unusual. Sort of mysterious. Especially the ones that look bright as silver one minute and soft as a sunrise mist the next."

He moved almost imperceptibly closer to her, locking his gaze on hers. Emily felt as if she were drowning in the hot blue depths of his glance.

"You . . . you don't say," she managed to murmur in an even tone.

"Yep. And if she happens to be pretty good at shooting snakes and sewing the prettiest dresses this side of the Rockies . . . now that kind of a girl would be just about irresistible."

He leaned toward her, his hand closing lightly around her nape and drawing her toward him.

"Is that all?" Emily's heart was racing, but she had a nonchalant expression pinned to her face.

"Well, if her kisses tasted sweeter than elderberry wine and she had a temper hotter than fire, then—"

"And if she recognizes sweet talk when she hears it and knows it's all chicken poop and hogwash?"

Emily's cold tone and contemptuous words stopped him flat, his mouth hovering only a scant inch from hers. She saw his gaze narrow as she jerked back away from him and smacked both of her hands onto his chest to hold him off. Meeting his eyes, her own eyes glittered like polished bullets.

"How much of a fool do you think I am?"

To her surprise, Clint chuckled. "You're obviously nobody's fool, Emily—"

"Miss Spoon to you."

"Miss Spoon," he said softly, laughter in his eyes. "The fact is, I just thought we might want to pass the time till the storm ends in as pleasant a manner as possible. Like we did last night—on the porch." He shot her another thunderbolt of a smile and leaned forward, but Emily swallowed hard, then shoved him back.

"When hell freezes," she retorted with an effort.

"Now, what kind of a way is that to talk?" He feigned a hurt expression. "After I risked my neck in the storm to come out here and rescue you—"

"That's your job, remember. To help people," she fired back, her eyes flashing. "Now get away from me before I . . . I . . ."

"Yes? Before you what?"

Before I fall into your arms like an addlepated fool, she thought desperately.

"Before I scream!"

"Scream away. We're not exactly in the center of town," he pointed out with a grin. "Who's going to hear?

"Damn you!" she exclaimed, scooting to the far end of the cot.

"You sure that's what you want?" Clint asked.

She wasn't at all sure, but suddenly she understood exactly what *he* wanted. Now she knew what all that talk about never settling down had meant before. This so-called honorable lawman was making sure she didn't get the wrong idea—that she didn't mistake his intentions.

Oh, he wouldn't mind kissing her, touching her, even making love to her here in this ramshackle old shack, just so long as she understood it didn't *mean* anything. Just so long as she didn't *expect* anything of him, like that he might start to *court* her, or think about *marrying* her or fall in *love* with her.

Fury and sharp bitter pain plunged like a knife through her heart.

What did you expect, she thought through the ache in her chest. *Roses and champagne, wedding cake and a golden ring?*

Not for Jake Spoon's niece . . . not for a girl who'd never set foot in a fancy drawing room like Caitlin Barclay must have known, except to dust it and sweep it . . .

"It's a long ways till sunrise," Clint continued softly, "and so I thought—"

"You thought you'd amuse yourself by flirting with me and . . . and kissing me." Emily glared at him. "Because I'm the only woman within fifty miles who isn't trying to drag you down the aisle to the altar—and never would!"

He had the nerve to grin again. God help her.

"You're right," he said calmly. "I know for a fact you'd rather jump off a cliff than marry a sheriff. So I'm safe with you. And you're safe with me. Look at it this way, Emily, no respectable lawman would ever marry into an outlaw family. So . . ."

"So I asked you to move away from me."

"And I'm asking you—what's the harm in us getting to know each other a little better?" Clint eyed her accusingly. "You started it the other night, remember? Maybe sharing one more kiss—possibly two—will settle this . . . hell, this unfinished business . . . between us." His voice grew rough. "You feel it too, don't you?"

"I don't know what you're talking about."

But it was a lie. She did feel something—a tug, a pull, an electricity. She'd felt it from the start, but so much more so when his lips had claimed hers.

"I'll make a deal with you—no strings, no promises, and I won't tell the rest of your family if you don't," Clint added with a husky chuckle that made her tingle.

"Why would I possibly want to kiss you again?" Somehow she managed to sound composed, even disdainful, even though a heated excitement was pulsing through her. "I . . . I only did it once because John Armstrong was about to recognize me—"

"You did it more than once. I have a hunch you liked it."

"You arrogant, egotistical—"

"Come here, Emily."

"Miss—"

"Spoon. I know," he finished for her, smiling amusedly into her eyes. He edged closer to her, and she suddenly found herself at the top end of the cot, wedged between him and the wall. He was leaning across her, giving her that heart-stoppingly masculine grin, stroking his hand through her hair. "I don't usually have to beg for kisses."

"I don't usually kiss men I don't even like."

"That's just the point," he said, the gleam in his eyes intensifying. He angled in closer and lowered his head close to hers. Once more their lips were only inches apart. Once more Emily felt her breath catching in her throat.

"I think you do like me. And the hell of it is, I like you. It doesn't make any sense, but not much does in this world sometimes."

No, it didn't make sense. But it was true, Emily thought in wonder. She did like him. How? Why? She wanted to hate him, but instead she found herself being drawn into the charm of a lazy smile, of those keenly beautiful eyes, of a gentleness and a decency she sensed beneath the brawn and the bravery.

"Well." She took a deep breath, stunned by her own thoughts, by the wild urges spinning through her. "You did rescue me from the storm, so . . . I'll grant you one kiss and only one," she said in a rush. How prim she sounded. Then she just couldn't stand it any longer. She grabbed the front of his shirt and yanked him toward her, placing her lips upon his.

She'd meant it to be a quick kiss, over and done with in a hurry because it made her feel guilty to be doing it at all, but something changed as her mouth touched his and she found herself lost in the kiss, hopelessly, dizzily lost. Her lips clung to his, and the sweetest sensations burst through her, layered by darker, more intriguing ones. And when she at last summoned the will to pull back, Clint Barclay had other ideas and before she knew it, his arms were around her and he was kissing her with a single-minded possessiveness that stirred a primal response deep in her very core. He kissed her as if he couldn't get enough and never wanted to stop, and Emily knew nothing else but that she didn't want him to . . .

A moan escaped her lips as a dazzling fire surged through her. She felt dizzy and warm. Maybe she had a fever, Emily thought dazedly. Or maybe she just liked kissing Clint Barclay more than she'd ever liked anything in her entire life . . .

He shifted position suddenly and the next thing she knew she was yanked down onto the cot and he was sliding his body over hers, and somehow or other he managed not to lift his mouth from hers for an instant.

She didn't know why but an absurd rush of pleasure swept through her and she actually slid her arms around his neck. Dimly she wondered why she had done that, but then she forgot all about it as Clint's firm mouth began to search hers even more hungrily and his tongue slipped inside her mouth, igniting a musky fire. Heat, need, desire exploded within her and Emily forgot the storm, forgot the night, forgot everything but the exquisite sensations gliding through her as Clint Barclay's muscled frame lay upon her, as his hands stroked her face, her throat, and his mouth laid possessive claim to hers. Time fell away, there was only the moment, the bliss, the passion jolting between them, and Emily held him to her with a ferocity she had not known she possessed, her hands sliding down his shoulders, drawing him closer, breathing him in, wanting to somehow absorb all of this dark, gentle lawman into her very soul.

When she thought she would faint from lack of air, he suddenly lifted his head and she stared dazedly into his eyes. "That was . . . much more . . . than just one kiss," she gasped. "You cheated."

"You liked it."

Breathlessly she felt herself studying those firm, warm lips as if hypnotized. "Oh," she murmured, "how could you tell?"

He laughed and she did too. She'd never felt so warm, so close to anyone, so happy, she thought in shock. *So kissed.*

"Don't worry, sweetheart, I can tell," he said and then he was kissing her again. She lost herself in the sweet dark musk of his tongue encircling hers. When Emily felt his hand sliding to the buttons of her shirt she knew that she should stop him, but she couldn't bring herself to. Just a little more . . . see what happens, she thought, and then wonderful sensations filled her as he slipped his hand inside her shirt and found her breast.

This definitely went far beyond one small kiss, but it felt so good Emily gasped. No, it felt better than good. It felt delicious and exciting, and a throbbing heat swept through her every place his hands touched, every place his magnificent body touched hers.

Emily forgot then to think how it felt because she couldn't think—not at all. Because Clint Barclay was stealing her breath, scorching her lips, and stroking her nipple back and forth with his thumb until the world became a warm blurred place, a place of achingly sweet pleasure teetering on the brink of torment.

She heard thunder—or was that her heart? She saw his lean, handsome face close to hers and touched it with wondering hands even as their lips caught fire. His body shifted over hers on the cot, and every single one of his muscles seemed to engulf her soft flesh—then she was lost once more in aching need and a tight, hungry ache settled in her very core. Moaning, she dragged her fingers through the thick silk of his hair, then they found the buttons of his shirt. But as he shifted to make it easier for her to unfasten them, his leg brushed against hers and she cried out in pain.

"What's wrong?" He lifted his mouth from those petal-sweet lips of hers with an effort and saw that her glorious eyes were wide upon his.

"It's my ankle," she gasped. "It's hurting . . ."

Clint swore silently to himself—damn, he'd forgotten about her ankle. He should have gotten that boot off right from the start.

He rolled away from her and leaned back, aware of the hot desire still pumping through him, the urges searing his blood. Hell, she tasted good. And she felt good, soft and curvy and giving in all the right places. Her lush body was just as hot and passionate as her temper, and the sensuous tumble of midnight hair around that delicate face was driving him wild.

He took a deep breath and raked a hand through his hair as Emily, her shirt tantalizingly unbuttoned, struggled to a sitting position.

"Sorry." Clint moved off the cot and took careful hold of his self-control, then focused his attention on her damned boot.

"I'll try to do this fast and gentle," he warned, "but if your ankle's swelled up, we might have to cut the boot off."

"Go . . . ahead." Emily's shoulders were trembling. But not only from the fresh pain shooting through her foot. From everything she'd just felt lying on that cot with Clint Barclay, his kisses drawing her into him in a way she'd never experienced before, his hands roaming all over her body, exploring places no man had ever touched.

Her heart was still racing in her chest. Her lips still tingled from his kiss. If she'd thought Clint Barclay was a dangerous man that first night he'd sprung out at her at the ranch, she now knew just how dangerous he really was.

Thank heavens for the pain, thank heavens he'd bumped his foot against hers. Thank heavens something had broken the crazy spell he'd cast over her before things went any further.

Clint was holding firmly to her boot. His hair was mussed, his shirt partly opened where her fingers had torn at the buttons. She found herself forgetting about the pain in her ankle, staring at his powerful, dark-furred chest.

Now she knew what those muscles felt like beneath her fingertips. She was shocked by how much she wanted to stroke them again.

"Ready?" Clint began to slide her boot off, but as Emily flinched and let out a smothered cry of pain, he froze, frowning.

Her previously flushed face had gone white. Clint reached into his pocket, yanked his knife from its sheath.

"I'll have to cut the boot."

"Go ahead . . . but please, do it quickly," she managed to mutter as circles of pain emanated up from her ankle. But the pain was good, it was distracting her from staring at this impossibly handsome sheriff who had convinced her to lie on a cot with him in a line shack miles from anyone and play with fire.

"Just . . . get the boot off," she whispered, her voice thin with pain.

He worked quickly and efficiently at the leather, but even so, by the time he was finished Emily was clenching her hands and biting her lip and she was whiter than a lily.

"Th-thank you. I think," she gasped.

Next Clint gingerly removed her stocking and frowned down at her swollen ankle.

"You need some whiskey."

"Trying to get me drunk now?" Emily struggled for a light tone. "No wonder my uncle taught me never to trust a lawman."

He shot her the briefest flash of a smile.

"Just like I don't usually have to beg for kisses, Miss Spoon, I don't usually have to get women drunk." He tugged off the other boot and the stocking, and she settled both legs carefully onto the cot once more.

Clint tried not to stare at the glimpse of shapely legs visible beneath the folds of her riding skirt. He forced himself to head to his saddle pack and dig out his whiskey flask.

"This ought to take care of the pain."

Emily didn't argue, for now that her ankle was free of the boot's tight confines it was throbbing even more. The whiskey burned her throat going down, but she drank deeply before handing him back the flask.

Clint lifted it and took a good hearty gulp himself. *Being around her would turn any man to drink,* he thought. *Why in hell do I care so much that she's in pain? And why in hell does she have to be so damn beautiful?* Not to mention sexier than any woman he'd ever seen. Even her slender little toes were sexy, he decided in irritation. But it wasn't her toes that captured his attention just now. She'd forgotten to fasten up her shirt, and it draped open still, revealing the white lace of a chemise that barely covered the creamy mounds of her breasts. He resisted the urge to reach out and remove that damned shirt—and the chemise too. Their little kissing interlude was definitely over, he reminded himself tautly. The trouble was, he'd enjoyed it even more than he'd thought he would.

Maybe you enjoyed it too much, he told himself, alarm suddenly surging through him. If her ankle hadn't started to hurt, they both might have ended up in far deeper trouble than either of them had bargained for.

Staring into her lovely face, meeting those vivid silver eyes as they regarded him warily, he reminded himself sternly that she was Jed Spoon's niece.

Yet confusion twisted through his gut.

Wasn't that the point? She was Spoon's niece—a woman he'd never marry—a woman who'd never in a hundred years want to marry him. An ineligible woman, maybe the only unmarried female in town who wasn't trying to figure out how to throw a rope around him. It had seemed so easy, so natural—the idea of exploring that intangible *something* between them—without her getting the wrong idea.

That's all he'd had in mind. A pleasurable romp, a night of plain old-fashioned roll-in-the-hay passion with the most gorgeous woman he'd ever met—and no strings attached.

But kissing her had stirred something in him, something deeper than he'd expected. Something that scared him.

Scared him? Why the hell should a woman, any woman, scare him?

Maybe because of the quiet way she'd listened to his story about Nick, his parents. Maybe because of the simple compassion he'd seen in her eyes. She touched something in him, something that went beyond physical attraction. Beyond lust. There was much more to Emily Spoon than a magnificent figure and a beautiful face. There was a spirit, a soul, a courage he'd sensed from the very start.

Clint didn't like feeling this way—uncertain, out of control. He always knew what he wanted, how to get it. He always knew. Especially where women were concerned.

But not this time.

It's time to back off, he decided warily. *She's no damned good for you.*

He had to step back, put some distance between them.

"You should try to get some shut-eye," he told her curtly, shoving the flask into his pocket. "The whiskey ought to help."

Emily watched the frown settle across his face, and she saw the exact moment when the coldness entered his eyes. Dismay and an odd loneliness filled her. All the warmth and humor of the man who had poured her coffee and stroked her hair and kissed the daylights out of her on the cot were gone. The cool and in-control lawman was back.

A different kind of pain shot through her. "Good.

When I wake up, we can get out of here." She tried to sound as matter-of-fact as he. "In the meantime, you can put your bedroll there."

She pointed to the far corner, near the hearth.

He gave her a long look. "Fine. That'll be just fine."

Suddenly she realized that her shirt was still unbuttoned. Her cheeks burned and her eyes flew to his face. "Do you mind?" she demanded as she fumbled awkwardly with the buttons.

He shrugged, turned away. "Just thought you might need help."

"The last thing I need is any more help from you." The words came out more sharply than she'd intended. But tension still simmered between them, despite his frown, his shuttered eyes.

As lightning crackled and the rain continued, she watched him spread his bedroll and take one more quick tip of the flask. She lay down on the cot, pulled the blanket up to her chin, and tried not to think about anything—about the pain throbbing through her ankle, the storm thrashing outside, or the man settling himself down for the night not ten feet away from her.

But she couldn't stop thinking about Clint Barclay. About the way he made her feel or the things he made her want.

Spending any more time alone with him, Emily decided, hugging the blanket to her, was *not* a good idea.

And sunrise couldn't come soon enough.

Chapter 13

SUNRISE BROUGHT A RADIANT NEW day, a glowing lilac sky, a breeze scented with earth and flowers—and Pete and Lester Spoon descending on the tiny line shack like two bats out of hell.

"Barclay!" Pete shouted as he crashed through the door. "Where the hell is—*Emily*!"

Relief flooded his face as he saw Emily sitting up on the cot against the wall, her legs stretched out before her, her hair mussed, but a wan smile of welcome on her face.

Behind him Lester gave a whoop. "There you are—well, thank the good Lord. Em, we've been searching high and low since dawn. Nugget showed up and—"

"She did? Oh, that's wonderful!" Emily searched their faces. "But what about Joey—how is he? And where's Uncle Jake?"

"They're both fine," Pete assured her, glancing around the shack. "Uncle Jake made it back this morning just before we headed out. He said he spent the night in a cave near Beaver Rock—the storm came in so fast he couldn't get to the shack. But what about you—looks like Barclay found you, after all."

His relieved expression had turned into a scowl, and an almost identical frown darkened Lester's face. "Were you stuck in here all night with that bastard?" her cousin demanded.

"Yes, but—"

"I'll blow his damned head off," Pete exploded. His hands fisted at his sides. "Where the hell is he, Emily, just tell me and I'll—"

"Shut up, Spoon, and get out of my way."

The voice from the cabin doorway sent both Pete and Lester spinning around. Clint Barclay stood on the threshold, his dark hair glinting in the sunlight, his shoulders filling the doorway. He was holding a rifle and the rabbit he'd shot for breakfast, but before he could even step inside, Pete Spoon rushed at him in a flying lunge that sent them both catapulting out of the shack, with Lester leaping after, shouting something indecipherable as he flew into the heap that was Pete and Clint Barclay.

With a shriek of dismay, Emily hurled herself off the cot. Her ankle burned like fire as she hobbled barefoot across the floor and stumbled out into dazzling sunshine. But the sight of her brother and her cousin rolling in the mud and weeds with Clint Barclay, three sets of fists flying, horrible grunts and yells filling the air, sent a sick nausea into her throat.

"Stop! Stop it! Pete—Lester! Clint! Stop it at once!"

No one paid the least attention to her. Two against one, the Spoons were hammering at Clint and with amazement she saw that he was holding his own, those powerful arms swinging out with rapid-fire punches, his muscular frame holding them off as they sought to pin him down.

But there was already a bruise on his cheek and as she watched in horror Pete kicked him in the stomach.

"Stop!" she shouted, and unable to bear it any longer, she dove into the fray. Still pleading for them to stop, she grabbed Lester's arm, trying to pull him back, even as he shook her off like a gnat.

"Stay out of this, Em—get back!" he yelled.

"No! Stop this right now—you're both being totally ridiculous!" she cried as Pete slammed a hard right into Clint's jaw. Emily flinched as it connected and grabbed at her brother's arm.

"Listen to me," she cried desperately, "there's no reason—"

Clint Barclay threw a brutal retaliatory punch and Pete groaned, stumbling back in a daze.

Emily tried to get between them, but it was at that unfortunate moment that Lester jumped at the sheriff and his elbow struck Emily's jaw.

She gave a cry and floundered backward, then sank to the ground, tears stinging her eyes.

"Emily!" Pete and Lester both shouted in unison, their faces frozen in twin expressions of horror.

"Are you all right?" Lester croaked.

"You damned fools. Look what you've done." Alarm in his eyes, Clint started toward her, but Pete got there first and Lester blocked the sheriff's path, his gun suddenly in his hand.

"Stay away from her, Barclay," Lester warned. "Or I'll plug you here and now."

"Lester . . . put that gun away," Emily gasped. "Right . . . now. Put it away, I said!"

Emily struggled to rise, but even as her brother tried to help her, the tears fell faster and she pushed Pete away.

She was the only one who knew that it wasn't the pain of the blow that hurt. It was seeing her brother and cousin fight with Clint, a reminder of the chasm between them, that made her heart ache.

"I . . . I'm ashamed of you, Pete—ashamed of both of you. You had no right—"

"He spent the night with you, Emily! That gives me every right!" Pete argued, throwing Barclay a furious glance as Emily shook her head. "It's not your fault—don't think for a minute that I blame you, or that Lester does either—but he's . . . he's compromised you and taken advantage of you and I'll be damned if I'm going to let some damned lawman hurt my little sister—"

"Hurt me? He found me stranded in the storm and brought me to shelter, that's all!" Emily burst out. "My ankle was twisted—Nugget had bolted—what was he supposed to do, leave me out by Beaver Rock? He . . . he was nice to me—"

"I'll just bet he was!" Lester snarled, and his finger curled on the trigger of his gun as he spun toward Clint, clearly struggling to control his anger.

Emily felt the blood draining from her face. "Lester, you put that gun away right *now.*" As he glanced over at her doubtfully, she limped toward him, despite the pain, and wrenched the gun from his hand.

Trembling, she turned and threw it as far as she could across the weeds and grama grass.

When she turned back, she finally looked at Clint, and her heart sank. He stood a few feet away, straight and tall, though his shirt was muddied and torn, his face bruised and streaked with dirt. He was breathing hard, as were Pete and Lester, but his eyes were centered on her and they were cold and shuttered and utterly unreadable.

"Nothing happened," she said stiffly. Her gaze was

locked on Clint's, but her words were for her brother and cousin. "Nothing at all. We were just waiting out the storm." A quaver entered her voice as she stood there with her hair streaming in thick tangled locks, the sun gilding her pale skin. "And now it's over, so . . . please. I just want to go home."

Clint's stomach clenched. For some reason that quaver and the quiet tears sliding down her cheeks moved him far more than dramatic sobs might have done, had done in the past with other women, other times. It took all of his self-control not to go straight to Emily and . . . and what? he asked himself scornfully. Put his arms around her? Offer words of comfort?

That would be the worst thing you could do, he reminded himself. *Keep your distance. Emily Spoon is not your concern, and she's got three men in her family to look after her.*

There was dismay on Pete's face, and Lester's as well, as they both stared at her and then exchanged guilty glances with each other. Clint steeled himself to stay out of it as Pete came forward and slipped an arm around Emily's shoulders.

"Anything you say, Sis. Take it easy." He swallowed. "Come on, let's get you off that ankle. I'll carry you to my horse."

Gritting his teeth, Clint watched in silence as Pete swept her up in his arms. His eyes were on Emily's pale face, and he scarcely noticed as Lester threw him one more angry glance before following after them.

And so it was that a short time later Clint Barclay sat alone at the shack's wobbly pine table, eating the rabbit he'd shot, that he'd planned to roast for Emily Spoon, drinking the coffee they'd shared the night before and wishing that things were different.

He wasn't sure *what* exactly he wished was different, he only knew that the shack looked a hell of a lot more dreary and empty and cheerless without her.

And he felt a whole lot more dreary and empty and cheerless without her.

And he knew that he'd never forget the moment when she had sprung to his defense against her brother and cousin.

Nothing happened, she'd said.

It wasn't strictly true. And it wasn't because he hadn't tried.

But he knew what the Spoon boys thought—and they were wrong.

And if they believed their threats were enough to make him stay away from her, he thought, draining the last of his coffee as a lark chirped outside the open shack door, then they were doubly wrong.

He intended to stay away from her, all right—but for his own reasons, not theirs.

Clint drained the last of his coffee, rinsed his cup, and threw one baleful glance at the cot where Emily Spoon had slept curled up all night.

He gathered his bedroll, packed up his saddlebags, and in his mind he heard again her frantic words.

Nothing happened.

Clint scowled at the empty air of the line shack. Emily had lied for him. Lied to her brother and cousin, maybe even to herself.

Just as he'd been doing—lying to himself. He'd been doing it right up until the moment when he saw her get hurt. Until he heard that quaver in her voice.

Because something *had* happened between them. Something he didn't understand. But it was just plain useless to deny it any longer. Because whether he liked it or not, it wasn't over.

Not by a long shot.

When Emily returned home, she hugged Joey and Uncle Jake, and allowed herself to be helped into bed, waited on, fussed over. She listened to Uncle Jake explain about the cave where he'd spent the night, and she'd sat Joey down on her bed and looked into his eyes, and explained to him thoroughly about John Armstrong passing through town, then leaving, without any clue that Joey was there.

She nursed her ankle, and later began taking stock of her needles and thread and ribbons and fabric, trying to ascertain what she would need should the women of Lonesome come calling at her door in search of fashionable new gowns with which to win the heart of Lonesome's sheriff.

And to all appearances, she was calm. Quiet, perhaps, after the turmoil of the previous day and night, but calm—and perfectly herself.

Inwardly, however, she was a raging mass of emotions—the most prominent of which was confusion.

First there was Uncle Jake. He claimed to have been at Beaver Rock when the storm descended in its full fury and to have taken cover in a cave. But she'd been at Beaver Rock when the storm had lashed down full force, and she hadn't seen any sign of him all the time that she'd been searching for both him and Joey. If he'd really been there, why hadn't he tried to get to the line shack? She and Clint had made it, despite the rain and the wind.

So why hadn't he even tried?

Uneasiness filled her as she mulled this question. Because

if her uncle were lying, if he really hadn't been at Beaver Rock in the first place, then where had he been?

And what, she wondered, her stomach beginning to churn, *was he doing?*

But while her worries about Uncle Jake's whereabouts were disturbing, they weren't nearly as tumultuous as her thoughts about Clint Barclay. And her doubts about herself. Why had she allowed all that had gone on between them in the line shack to happen? Why had she kissed him and responded to him the way she had, why had she nearly made love with the lawman she'd sworn to hate?

She didn't understand anything of what she felt toward Clint Barclay. Yes, he had helped her search for Joey, and he'd rescued her from the storm—but he'd also fought with her brother and cousin—and he would toss them in jail without a second thought if they gave him half a reason, she told herself.

Loyalty to her family, as well as wisdom and plain common sense, should keep her away from him, should stop her from even thinking about him. But sense had nothing to do with how she felt, and sense had nothing to do with the way her heart lifted at the sight of him, at the somersaults it did when he smiled, or the way her body melted when he kissed her.

She'd always been sensible, always been smart—even when she lost her temper, Emily never lost sight of where her loyalties or her values lay. Until now. Now everything she'd ever believed about herself seemed to have been washed away by that storm, washed away by the onslaught of hot, tender kisses and Clint Barclay's strong, reassuring arms.

All this was brought home to her even more forcefully that evening, when she was sitting up in bed brushing her hair and Pete and Lester knocked at her door.

"Come in," she said quietly, and as they stepped inside, the single candle burning in a sconce beside the bed cast pale streams of amber light upon their bruised faces.

Clint Barclay had certainly gotten in his share of punches, she thought. Her heart sank like a rock in her chest.

"Don't mean to bother you, but we want to say one thing, Em." Pete's gaze was worried. "It's about Clint Barclay. I know you weren't trying to take his side today against us, but the fact is, that's how it looked. You shouldn't have interfered—we were just trying to teach him a lesson and—"

"Pete, you attacked him—both you and Lester, when all he did was save me from getting drenched all night long on Beaver Rock."

"He didn't do any more than that, Em?" Lester stepped forward, his moon-shaped face flushed with embarrassment. Despite Emily's frown, he plunged ahead. "Sorry to be so blunt, but damn it, Em, this is too important to beat around the bush. Are you saying he didn't try to take advantage of you when the two of you were stuck alone in that shack all night?"

"Of . . . course not. Don't . . . be ridiculous!" But even as she spoke, she felt her cheeks burning.

"I told you before, I've seen how he looks at you," Lester went on, glowering. "And the truth is, Em, men like Barclay want only one thing from a girl like you. Not that you're not every bit as good as anyone else," he said hastily, "that's not what I mean—you're the best, Em, the prettiest, the finest girl in the world . . . but . . ."

"Well, it's *us*—we're the problem." Misery and guilt shone in Pete's eyes. "Face it, Em. You're related to us . . . and that means a man like Barclay won't ever respect you, not the way he should. He'd only use you. The same goes for lots of men. But especially someone like him—"

"You don't have to warn me about Clint Barclay. I'm not stupid. Don't you think I know how the world works?"

"Sure, but—"

"You're trying to protect me, both of you, and I . . . I appreciate it, but it isn't necessary. Clint Barclay isn't interested in me, not in any way." Somehow she managed to sound airy and unconcerned, despite the fact that her throat was dry as dust and her heart aching. "And I'm certainly not interested in him!"

"That's good, Em." Pete shifted from one foot to the other. "Because we know you haven't had much experience with men and—"

"I've had enough to know that I'd never let myself become a . . . a kind of toy or . . . casual amusement for any man—and that includes Clint Barclay," she said forcefully. She set the brush down on the bedside table, hoping they didn't notice that her hands were trembling. "Now please, I'm worn out and I'd like to go to sleep."

There was silence for a moment. Pete and Lester looked at each other. "Well, so long as you're sure." Lester still sounded doubtful.

Pete studied her in the flickering candlelight. "We just want to take care of you, Em. You had everything on your shoulders for too long—the farm, Aunt Ida and all. We're here now. If Barclay or anyone else bothers you, you can just let us know and we'll take care of it."

"I know you will." She swallowed. She'd never even told them how Slim Jenks had "bothered" her, because she knew it would only lead to disaster. But she'd rather eat a lizard every day for breakfast then tell them anything at all about her and Clint.

"There's nothing to worry about," she assured them with a false smile. "Good night."

The moment they shut the door, she blew out the candle and cast the room into darkness, the same kind of darkness that smothered her heart. It was a relief to slip into bed, to lie there upon cool sheets and not have to pretend that what Pete and Lester had said hadn't cut straight through her soul. For she knew the truth of what they'd said, and she'd been telling herself the same thing: Clint Barclay might be more handsome, honorable, and kind than Slim Jenks, he might use persuasion and charm and sweet talk, instead of coarse insults and force, but what he wanted from her was the same. He didn't want her for a wife or even a sweetheart, he didn't want to squire her here or there or court her or treat her with respect. He was only interested in her because she was the one woman in town who wouldn't try to lure him into marriage. Because she was the one woman in town who wasn't respectable enough to be considered a possible bride. He could dally with her in secret and not have to worry about her or anyone else getting the wrong idea.

Just as Hobart Wainscott had cornered her in the hallways of his mother's house when she'd been dusting or sweeping, Clint had cornered her in the shack.

It hadn't meant anything to him. He didn't care about her.

No matter that his kisses were deep and hot and drove everything else right out of her mind. No matter that he touched her with a gentleness that made her wild. No matter that she had been sorry to see Pete and Lester at the shack's door this morning, because—fool that she was—she'd wanted a little more time alone with Clint Barclay.

They were as different as night and day. He'd grown

up on Cloud Ranch, a cattle ranch known all over the West as one of the grandest and most profitable spreads in the country. As Lonesome's sheriff, he was a pillar of the community, devoting his life to upholding the law.

And she was Emily Spoon of the notorious Spoons—dirt poor, a nobody, niece to a man who had served time in prison for stagecoach robbery, and sister and cousin to two others who'd eluded the law only because no one had ever been able to prove they were thieves.

With his big family home in Wyoming, his brothers, and his fancy new sister-in-law, an elegant woman like Caitlin Barclay, did she really for a moment believe that he would ever think of her as anything other than an amusing distraction from all the women in town trying to become his bride?

She'd almost been caught up in the pull of that devastating smile, in the urgent heat of his embrace. She'd almost forgotten who she was while she lay warm and close in the circle of those strong arms.

But now she was home in the cabin, and the storm was over, and the night was quiet and still, and she could hear the voice of truth in her head.

Last night was a mistake, but it was over. Over and done with. She'd keep her distance from Clint from this point on.

Even when she ran into him again, as she no doubt would somewhere, sometime in town, she wouldn't let him make a fool out of her.

And with any luck he'd be married soon, she realized. Surely one of the women in town who'd set her cap for him would reel him in like a big flopping fish.

And the sooner that happened, the better, Emily told herself, dropping her head down on the pillow.

Misery descended on her as she tried to drift into

sleep. She kept thinking of last night, when his hands had stroked her as they lay upon the cot, of the way his mouth ignited hers, and the deep, even tenor of his voice. She was wondering how it would feel to sleep in Clint Barclay's arms, to be held and kissed by him all through the night, to see his face in the morning when she awoke.

And she wondered at the emotions he stirred in her, at the yearning that quivered through her when he was near.

Just forget him, she told herself in frustration as night marched on toward dawn and still sleep eluded her.

Forget about the shack, the cot, the kisses that drowned out the storm.

But Emily knew as she tossed and turned alone in her bed that she could just as soon forget about breathing.

Chapter 14

THE NEXT FEW DAYS FLEW BY IN A rush of visitors and activity, as the women of Lonesome descended upon the Teacup Ranch. In buggies and wagons and on horseback they arrived, some bearing fabric they'd purchased themselves, one or two with older gowns they wanted let out, taken in, and gussied up to match the current style, some with no notion of what kind of gown they wanted but eager to hear Miss Emily Spoon's suggestions.

"I'd love a gown in the style of the one you wore to the town dance," Carla Mangley told her eagerly, as the other women waiting their turn murmured agreement.

"And Carla will also need another gown," Agnes Mangley put in sharply. "Something even more elegant, fit for a ball. It's to be worn at the dinner in honor of her late father, my dear Richard. It's being held in Denver, you know. The governor will be there."

"Yes, I know," Emily murmured, measuring Carla's slender waist. Everyone in town knew all about the Mangleys: they'd become the wealthiest and most socially prominent folks in town a few years back when Carla's father and his brother had discovered the richest silver mine in Leadville. Agnes and Carla had inherited his half of it when Richard Mangley died, and—in case anyone ever forgot how wealthy the Mangley women were—despite their furnishings from Paris and New York, their jewels and gowns and painted carriage, their frequent trips abroad—Agnes Mangley never missed an opportunity to remind them.

"Will you get to meet the governor, Carla?" Tammy Sue asked.

"Of course she will," Agnes answered before Carla could say a word. "Her uncle Frank is on excellent terms with the governor, and naturally will introduce both Carla and me."

The women were all suitably impressed and offered suggestions for Carla's new gown, while Emily listened and measured and planned. So while Uncle Jake and Pete and Lester were doing the spring branding, and Joey tended to his chores and worked on the simple lessons Emily had set out for him, she offered the ladies of Forlorn Valley coffee and pie, pored over sample books, laid out various fabrics, and measured and pinned.

She made one trip to town to purchase bolts of lace, satin, muslin, and silk, and the fanciest buttons and sequins she could find in the mercantile.

She stayed up sewing at night until her eyes ached, and by the time Saturday arrived, the day of the box lunch social, the only gown she had yet to complete was her own—a pale lavender muslin with a ruffled skirt and scooped neck, far simpler than the sprigged and beribboned and lacy confections she'd sewn for the other women. But it suited her well enough, Emily thought with satisfaction, as she sewed the last few stitches of the hem. Besides, she had no desire to outshine her customers—that might be bad for business, she reflected with a rueful grin.

"Mighty pretty." Uncle Jake gave her an approving smile as she hurried into the kitchen, still threading a lavender ribbon through her hair. "Mind if I peek into that box lunch you've fixed? I just might want to bid on it myself."

"No one's supposed to know who brought which box lunch—or whose they're bidding on," Emily informed him, her eyes twinkling, "but . . . Nettie told me that everyone does."

He chuckled.

"So I'll let you have a peek, since I can't think of anyone I'd rather share lunch with than you, Uncle Jake—"

She broke off as Joey raced inside, his face still damp from washing at the pump. "Can I see what's in your box lunch, Em-ly? I won't tell anyone it's yours!"

Jake laughed, and Emily did too, her heart lightening at the little boy's good spirits. She knew he was both excited and wary about going to the box lunch social and meeting the other children of Forlorn Valley.

Several of the women who had come for fittings and then to pick up their dresses had met Joey, so his presence was no longer a secret. Emily had merely explained that she was caring for the boy to help out a friend and to her relief, even Mrs. Mangley hadn't done more than lift her eyebrows. No one had asked questions. No one had made any fuss about it.

So she'd decided that the whole family ought to attend the box lunch social. Joey could meet the other children, and everyone would have a chance to see that Uncle Jake, Pete, and Lester Spoon were not fearsome monsters bent on robbing the good citizens of Lonesome.

"I promise, Em-ly, I won't tell anyone," Joey exclaimed, eagerly eyeing the box on the kitchen table.

The child's eyes lit as he opened it. Emily had lined it with pink silk and decorated it with multicolored bows and some straw flowers she'd clipped from an old sunbonnet. It wouldn't be the fanciest box in town, but she was pleased with the ham-and-chicken sandwiches on baked sourdough, the deep-fried corn fritters, a jar of boysenberry preserves, a beautiful peach pie, and the dozen almond sugar cookies she'd tucked inside, draped carefully in Aunt Ida's pretty white linen napkins, along with a jug of lemonade.

"Ooooh. Can I have this box lunch, Emily, puh-leese?" Joey peered hopefully at her and her heart filled with tenderness and delight. Thanks to Uncle Jake's quiet talks and card games and all the time he spent with him, Joey had even rebounded from the scare about John Armstrong. His appetite was healthy again, and even though he was a bit nervous about meeting the children of Lonesome and Emily's plans to enroll him in school, he was a far happier child than the fear-shadowed boy who'd first arrived at the ranch.

"You can't have this one, Joey, but guess what." Hurrying to the kitchen, Emily reached up to a high shelf and took down another box. This one was decorated in blue calico, and the small wood horse Uncle Jake had whittled was tied to it with a yellow ribbon. "This box is just for you."

Joey stared at the carved wooden horse, his eyes wide. "That's . . . that's . . . Jumper!" he cried excitedly. "I thought you said he was for Lester!"

Jake's smile was as broad as the box."He's all yours, son. Truth is, I was whittling him for you from the start."

Emily helped Joey untie the ribbon, and he clutched the horse in his small fingers. "Jumper!" he breathed, and made a dipping, up-and-down motion with the horse as if imagining it jumping over logs, rocks—maybe even mountains, Emily thought, her eyes suddenly damp with tears.

"And don't forget the fixins in the box. Those are from Emily," Uncle Jake reminded him with a nod.

Joey tore his eyes from the horse and opened the lid of the box to find everything in the larger box duplicated in smaller portions in his.

"Oh, boy! This is *my* box lunch?"

"All yours." She drew in her breath as he suddenly threw himself into her arms.

"Thank you, Em-ly. Thank you, Uncle Jake." His face was muffled against her shoulder but she could hear his words. "This is almost as good as having Mama come back," he whispered against her ear.

Emily held him tight. "Listen to me, Joey, your mother is going to come back—very soon. And when she does, I'm going to bake her the biggest chocolate cake you ever saw to celebrate."

"Really?" He lifted his head at last and his brown eyes shone into hers.

"I promise."

"Oh, boy!"

Emily felt almost happy as they joined Pete and Lester outside in the warm spring sunshine, Uncle Jake carrying her box for her, and Joey proudly clutching his, the small whittled horse stuffed into his shirt pocket.

It was a lovely day for a picnic—the sun blazed in a crystalline sky that stretched in a vast, cloudless canopy across the land. Uncle Jake drove the team, with Emily seated beside him, Joey in the back of the wagon admiring Jumper, and Pete and Lester riding alongside.

Every time thoughts of Clint Barclay tried to intrude into her mind, Emily chased them away, as she'd been doing ever since the fight at the line shack—until they reached the long, sloping meadow where the tiny, crumbling schoolhouse was situated.

As they approached, Emily glanced at all the people seated on the grass or upon chairs, upon logs or rocks, or strolling through the willows bordering the creek, and she spotted Clint at once. Her heart flipped over painfully in her chest. He looked all too handsome in a gray silk shirt and dark pants, his wide-brimmed hat shading his eyes from the sun as he leaned one shoulder against a tree and engaged in earnest conversation with Hamilton Smith, Fred Baker, one of the cowboys she'd danced with at the hotel, and Doc Calvin.

She refused to be caught staring if he happened to glance her way, so she tore her gaze away and instead swept it around the clearing as her uncle pulled the team up beneath a stand of aspen.

She saw Carla Mangley, Bertie Miller, and Margaret Smith, as well as several other women whose dresses she'd sewn, and noted with pride that all of her gowns showed to advantage. Yet, though the money she'd earned from sewing dresses for this one event was a tidy and reassuring sum, the sight of all the women wearing her finery as they set their sights on Clint Barclay made her feel queasy.

She had a feeling she wouldn't be able to eat a bite of her own box lunch today, no matter who won her box.

And which of the ladies of Lonesome will Clint Barclay favor with his bid? she couldn't help wondering. Not that she cared one way or another, she told herself with a shake of her head.

As Uncle Jake helped her down from the wagon, and Joey jumped out, wiping his hands nervously on his pants, she saw Clint turn his head in their direction. He straightened, and she saw his eyes narrow beneath the brim of his hat.

"Clint, it's no use fighting the women of this town—not all of 'em at once," Hamilton Smith pointed out. "As I told Bessie this morning, you might as well just give in and pick a gal to marry. It's going to happen sooner or later, whether you like it or not."

"The hell it will." Despite his firm words, Clint felt sweat pop out on his brow, and it wasn't only because of the heat and sunshine. He was starting to feel cornered, like a calf surrounded by a dozen wranglers twirling ropes toward its scrawny neck.

"How did any of them get a notion that I wanted to marry *anyone*?" he complained. Bitterness chewed through him. "It's not as if I ever said one word about hankering to get myself hitched."

Reluctantly he tore his gaze from the vision that was Miss Emily Spoon in a pale lavender gown that was as fresh and pretty as she was herself, and focused on Ham's plump face, then shifted his gaze to Doc Calvin's owlish one. Fred Baker shot him a sympathetic grin.

"Beats me why women get any notion into their head," the cowboy admitted. "I'm just happy it's you and not me they've set their sights on."

"*I* think it was your brother's wedding that did it," Ham offered sagely. "Even Bessie said to me that once a man goes to a wedding, he's bound to get ideas. Hmmmph, *women* do, that's for sure. But I reckon they think now Wade is settled down, since you're the middle brother, you're bound to be next."

"No, sir." Doc Calvin pushed his spectacles higher on

his nose. "I think it's something more. Folks like having you around, Clint, that's all. They want you to stay put. Lord knows we couldn't find a better sheriff. And women tend to think that if a man's married, happy, he'll stay put." His eyes twinkled behind the spectacles. "They just don't want you to leave, and figure if you get hitched, settle down, start a family—"

"Family!" Clint quelled the almost overpowering urge to vault onto his horse and head for the hills. "Now this is getting out of hand!"

"So." Fred winked. "Which lady's box are you planning to bid on, Clint? Everyone in town is looking at it as a sign of which gal you're going to walk down the aisle—"

"Shows how much they know."

Clenching his jaw so tight it ached, Clint stalked off to rustle up a glass of lemonade. He wished like hell it were whiskey.

Box lunch socials weren't for him. Pretty meadows filled with flowers, the laughter of children, women trying to throw a lasso around him—none of it was for him. He'd rather be parched with thirst and stranded on the hot endless plains without horse or canteen, or ambushed by rustlers or Indians or outlaws, or flat on his face in a snake pit—anywhere but here, in this sunlit meadow doing something as tame and civilized as going on a picnic.

Maybe this job was just getting to be too old, too tame, too civilized. Maybe it was time to move on . . .

Mayor Donahue, a stout balding man in an elegant black coat and an equally elegant mustache, stepped up to the long table that had been set up with all the boxes, twenty feet from the old run-down schoolhouse.

"Ladies and gentlemen, we're ready to begin. Now remember, all of the money raised today is to be used to rebuild and expand the schoolhouse so that our Miss Crayden will have a proper place to teach the children—as well as proper materials. So be generous, fair citizens. The lovely ladies of our town have worked hard on their boxes, as you all can see, and we want to show our appreciation. Don't we, gentlemen?"

The mayor beamed as everyone applauded.

"To start the bidding," he continued, holding up a box decorated with pink-and-blue lace, sequins, feathers, and a cluster of lilies, "here is a splendid box from one of our fine ladies in town. Who would like to share a mouth-watering lunch with the creator of this lovely box?" the mayor intoned.

Seated on one of the chairs between Margaret Smith and Nettie Phillips, Emily watched as one after another of the boxes was auctioned off. She could see Uncle Jake through the willows—he was down by the creek keeping an eye on Joey, who was playing tag with Bobby and Sally Smith. She knew he was probably glad to steer clear of the large public gathering, and no doubt relieved not to have to watch everyone bidding on boxes and being paired off—husbands with their wives, young men with the young women they had an interest in.

She knew he still missed Aunt Ida something fierce. Once or twice at night she'd heard quiet sobs coming from the main room of the cabin, and had crept out to find Uncle Jake slumped in his chair, an old photograph of Aunt Ida clutched to his chest. She always crept back as quietly as she'd come, not wishing to disturb his very private mourning.

Perhaps if he'd had a chance to say good-bye, he

would by now be getting over the loss. But he hadn't had that chance, thanks to Clint Barclay, she reminded herself painfully.

Her attention was recalled to the bidding when she suddenly heard her brother's voice call out a bid of three dollars.

Everyone looked at Pete Spoon, standing nonchalantly beneath an aspen, his thumbs hooked in his pants pockets. A slight murmur ran through the crowd.

Intrigued, Emily shifted her attention to the box being auctioned. Mayor Donahue held up a round hatbox decorated with a pink feather boa, displaying it for all to see. Several more bids from different men quickly followed, and she saw several eager glances directed toward a petite, pretty girl with light brown hair done up in ringlets. She wore a tight blue dress and a hat with sequined feathers pinned to it.

"Who is that girl?" Emily whispered to Nettie.

"That's Florry Brown," Nettie whispered back, a shade too loudly. "She works at Coyote Jack's Saloon."

"Four dollars," she heard another voice call out—a rough voice she immediately recognized.

It belonged to Slim Jenks.

For once the wrangler didn't have a smirk on his face—he looked deadly serious as he bid on Florry Brown's box. She, on the other hand, Emily noted curiously, seemed to pale and shrink into her chair every time he raised his bid.

"Six dollars—and fifty cents," Pete yelled, topping Jenks's latest bid. The other men all seemed to have dropped out.

"Eight dollars." Anger mottled Jenks's face as he threw a glance toward Pete, clearly warning him to back off.

Florry Brown sat perfectly still, not looking at either Pete or Slim Jenks.

"Twenty dollars," Pete called out coolly.

Emily nearly gasped. *Twenty dollars*. Either her brother was wildly smitten with this girl, or his dislike of Jenks was driving him to spend money he could ill afford. But it was typical of Pete, she thought, suppressing a sigh. Despite her dismay at the extravagant bid, she couldn't help hoping that at least it would win Florry's box lunch for her impulsive brother.

"I have a bid of twenty dollars," the mayor intoned. "Do I hear twenty-one?" He paused infinitesimally, glancing around the gathering. "Ladies and gentlemen, this fine box lunch is sold—to, er, Mr. Pete Spoon."

A smile wreathed Florry Brown's face as Pete sauntered up to claim first the box and then her hand. As they started off together, Emily watched Slim Jenks scowling after them. For a moment she feared he'd follow, but just as he took a step, another cowboy clapped a hand on his arm and said something under his breath that made Jenks laugh.

Then he suddenly swung his gaze around the meadow and fixed his glance on Emily. There was no mistaking the malicious gleam in his eyes.

Uneasiness knotted in the pit of her stomach. What if Slim Jenks bid on her box—and she was forced to have lunch with him?

No, Emily calmed herself as a breeze tickled the back of her neck. That would never happen. First, Jenks most likely had no idea which box was hers, and second, Lester was here.

Her towheaded cousin was so shy around women, he wouldn't bid on any box but hers—and she was certain he'd outbid Jenks for the box, no matter what the cost.

So she relaxed and folded her hands in her lap, trying

to glance about her without appearing obvious. There was no sign of Clint Barclay, none at all.

Strange. He hadn't appeared at all during the bidding and certainly hadn't bid on any boxes. Berty Miller had looked quite disappointed when hers had been auctioned off, and the sheriff had been nowhere in sight. Everyone had known it belonged to her because one of the ecru lace handkerchiefs she favored had been pinned on as part of the decoration. And so Berty—as well as everyone else in town—could only conclude that Sheriff Barclay hadn't made himself present for the bidding because he didn't care to eat lunch alone with her.

The bidding continued, and a ripple of expectation filled the clearing when a white satin-covered box decorated with red silk hearts and clusters of wild roses was lifted up by the mayor.

"That's Carla Mangley's box," Margaret told Emily.

"How do you know?"

"She always uses red hearts and roses. Besides, see that double rope of pearls that's wound around everything? Her father gave those pearls to Carla on her eighteenth birthday. That's Carla's box, no doubt about it," she finished.

"Now where the devil is Clint?" Nettie mused. She turned and twisted in her seat. "Isn't that just like a man? All these women go to all this trouble to impress him and he's nowhere to be seen! Where can he have gone to?"

Emily was wondering the same thing herself. But she almost forgot about Clint Barclay when the bidding started and she had her next surprise of the day. Lester stood up, a faint pink color tinging his face, glowing all the way up to the roots of his hair as he bid two dollars on Carla Mangley's box.

If a murmur had gone up from the crowd when Pete

Spoon bid on Florry's box, that was nothing compared to what happened when Lester bid on Carla Mangley's. The crowd buzzed, people sat up straighter in their chairs, and Carla—well, she turned bright red and her pretty mouth opened and closed for a moment like a banked fish gulping for air.

Her mother spun about in her chair, scanning the meadow, the schoolhouse, the creek, and the sloping hillsides shaded by trees.

"Where *is* that sheriff?" she hissed in dismay, as the young outlaw Lester Spoon continued to top each bid offered for the box with the red hearts.

But the sheriff seemed to have vanished into thin air.

"Six dollars," Fred Baker called out.

"Seven dollars." Lester caught Emily staring at him. His color deepened.

Why in the world was her shy, awkward cousin, always so flustered around women, so determined to have lunch with Carla Mangley? she wondered in astonishment.

Again Agnes twisted around this way and that, no doubt searching for Clint. Her daughter, desperate, did the same.

"I have a bid of seven dollars," announced the mayor. "Do I hear any other bids?"

"Doc!" Agnes Mangley elbowed Doc Calvin. "Bid on Carla's box. She can't share her lunch with that . . . that criminal!"

"Seven dollars and fifty cents," the elderly doctor called out reluctantly.

"I have seven dollars and fifty—"

"Ten dollars," Lester shouted.

A hush fell over the crowd. Everyone was staring at Lester, and at Carla Mangley. Emily held her breath.

"Sold." The mayor choked out the words. "To . . . to Mr. Lester, uh . . . Spoon."

Carla and her mother sat as still as if they'd been frozen into blocks of ice. Lester, his jaw clenched, strode up to retrieve the box, tucked it under his arm, and walked toward Carla's chair.

"M-Miz M-Mangley?"

"Mama," she gulped, and threw her mother a helpless glance.

"Eat fast, honey," Emily heard Mrs. Mangley moan.

Lester's flush deepened, but he stood stolidly, offering his arm.

As Emily watched, torn between concern for her cousin's sensibilities and amazement at his seeking out this most unlikely of young women, Carla rose, trembling, and took the offered arm. She marched off with Lester toward a sloping hillside beyond the creek bank as if he were escorting her to a guillotine.

The auction continued, the mayor going quickly through the remaining boxes. Margaret's box was bought by Parnell, and she slipped out of her seat with a smile. Rufus Doily bought Nettie's box, and they too departed.

Emily barely noticed, for she was lost in thought, pondering the strangeness of Lester's actions. *Poor Lester,* she thought in dismay, *if he's developed a fondness for Carla Mangley, he's doomed for disappointment.*

But at least he'll have today, she told herself, and then inexplicably her mind flashed back for a moment to the night of the storm, to Clint Barclay's kisses.

Suddenly she realized that the mayor was auctioning off the very last box—and it was hers.

"Last but not least, we have this pretty box here—and let me tell you, what's inside looks every bit as good as what's outside," he promised. "What am I offered for this box, gentlemen?"

"Two dollars," one of the cowboys she'd danced with at the hotel offered, throwing her a hopeful glance, but the words were scarcely out of his mouth before Slim Jenks's voice rang out.

"Five dollars."

He was smirking at her, and Emily's stomach tightened. With an effort she sat perfectly still, her hands gripped in her lap.

The very thing she'd feared was happening, only now Pete and Lester were both off on their own private picnics—and Uncle Jake, she saw as she glanced toward the creek, was seated under a willow tree, most likely whittling, while Joey and Bobby and several other children chased each other across the hillside. His back was to her and the auction, and she realized with a chill that there would be no one to counter Jenks's bids no matter the cost.

She'd probably made a mistake by not telling anyone about Jenks accosting her in town, but it was too late now . . .

"Seven dollars," another cowboy offered, but Jenks immediately raised his bid to ten dollars and shot Emily a triumphant smile.

Her heart began to race. Whatever unpleasantness Jenks had in mind, she'd have to deal with him alone. She had her derringer—she could shoot him in the leg or the arm or the shoulder if necessary. Still, she had to fight a flutter of panic as it became clear no one was raising Jenks's latest bid. There would be no way out.

"Do I hear seven dollars and fifty cents?" The mayor scanned the spattering of people left to witness the auction. "Well, then, this lovely box is sold to Slim Jenks for—"

"Twenty-five dollars."

There was a stunned gasp from the onlookers, and Emily, along with everyone else, twisted around in her seat. There was Clint Barclay standing behind the scattered chairs, his arms folded across his chest.

Another collective gasp went up. Clint's eyes met Emily's and held hers for a long moment as a flood of whispering broke out and the mayor gave a last chance for other bids. There were none.

"Sold! To our fine sheriff—for twenty-five dollars. Ladies and gentleman, I do believe we've raised a good sum for our new schoolhouse today. Thank you one and all, and please enjoy yourselves on this fine spring day . . ."

Emily heard no more. Clint strode forward, took her box from the mayor, then turned and walked with long steady strides back toward her.

Several townsfolk who had chosen to eat their lunches within earshot of the auction watched agog as the sheriff approached Miss Emily Spoon.

So did Slim Jenks.

Emily could see him beyond Clint's broad shoulder, and the anger on his face sent a chill through her.

His enmity toward her—and Clint—had no doubt deepened today. But she forgot about even this as Clint halted before her.

"Miss Spoon." There was nothing but cool politeness in his face, in his tone. They might have been two strangers.

We are *strangers, practically,* she told herself, her heart lurching. *Except for the kissing part . . . and the touching part . . .*

"Sheriff Barclay." She offered a regal nod.

He tucked her arm in his, but not before Emily caught the steely glint in his eyes. Without another word, he escorted her away from the chairs and the staring townsfolk, across the waving spring grass, and toward a knot of trees.

Chapter 15

Uncle Jed and the boys will be livid when they find out who bought my box lunch, she thought fleetingly, but inexplicably, at that moment, she didn't care. Even the realization of her family's fury couldn't dampen the unexpected surge of happiness that swept through her as she walked at Clint's side.

Neither of them spoke as they passed beneath a shady canopy of trees and he led her toward a gully.

Finally she couldn't endure the silence any more and she broke it. "The whole town seemed to be looking for you during the course of the bidding," she burst out, as the sun poured down and twigs crunched beneath their feet. "Where were you?"

"Around," he said in an offhand tone.

"Hiding." Her lips twitched in a smile. "Clint Barclay, brave sheriff, running for cover from the women of Lonesome." A laugh burst from her, and Clint chuckled too.

"Let's just say I know how to keep my head down when there's danger. And fighting a townful of marriage-minded women is as dangerous as it gets."

They reached a pretty clearing far enough from the schoolhouse so that they couldn't even hear the shouts and laughter of the children. "This suit you all right?" Clint asked.

Emily nodded. It was an ideal spot, a clearing of thick grass, where wild yellow pea grew charmingly among clusters of columbine. There was no one else from town visible, and the silence was delightful. Only the murmur of the wind through the aspens and the cry of a prairie falcon circling overhead broke the stillness.

But there was a saddle blanket folded under the lone cottonwood tree. She stopped short. "I wonder who this belongs to . . ." she began doubtfully, but Clint stooped and picked it up, then shook it out and spread it over the ground.

"It's mine. I set it here a while ago to keep anyone else from taking this spot."

"Do you always plan everything out so carefully, Sheriff?" She tried to keep her tone light.

"When I can—but I'm learning, Miss Spoon, that not everything can be planned."

"Is that so?"

He set her box down upon the blanket and straightened, then fixed those keen blue eyes on her with an intentness that stole her breath away. "That's so."

In the pause that followed Emily wondered if he could hear her heart beating. Being alone with him had too strong an effect on her, and she tried to steel herself against him. She tore her gaze away and busied herself lifting the plates and forks and knives from the box, arranging everything prettily upon the blanket—desperate to do anything but gaze at this coolly handsome man, who could make every rational thought fly right out of her head.

"Joey seems to have recovered just fine," Clint commented as she served him a thick sandwich and the corn fritters. "I noticed your uncle keeping an eye on him."

"Joey's fine now. Thanks in large part to Uncle Jake."

"I don't really see what he has to do with it, Emily. If you ask me, it has a lot more to do with you."

"You're wrong—it's Uncle Jake." Emily swallowed a bite of sandwich. "Despite what you think you know about him, he's always been fond of children, and since coming home . . . from prison . . ." Her voice faltered a moment. "He seems to have even more patience than before. He's taught Joey all sorts of things, he plays gin rummy with him, he even whittled him a horse."

Clint Barclay eyed her skeptically. "Hard to imagine Jake Spoon playing grandpa."

"You don't really know him—or anything about him."

I know he robbed stagecoaches and was damned good at it, Clint thought, but there was no point in mentioning that unless he wanted to get Emily Spoon fired up, like striking a match to dynamite. And he didn't. He was enjoying this temporary peace between them too much for that. So instead, he helped himself to another corn fritter and said, "Why don't you tell me then?"

Surprised, Emily's eyes flew to his face. "Do you really want to know?"

He nodded.

"He's a good man." Her voice was quiet. "He . . . he may have done . . . some wrong things, some bad things, but he's still a good man. Do you remember telling me how Reese Summers took you and your brothers in? Well, Uncle Jake and Aunt Ida did that for Pete and me."

Only the skittering of a rabbit through the brush broke the stillness that followed. Clint's storm-blue gaze held steady on hers.

"Our parents died when we were young—Pete was nine and I was six. And Uncle Jake and Aunt Ida never hesitated. They took us in and raised us right along with their own son, Lester." Emily brushed a crumb from the blanket. "Their farm was small and they were barely scraping by before Uncle Jake got mixed up in holding up stages. There wasn't nearly enough money to go around, but they managed somehow—*we* managed somehow." Her fingers clenched around her skirt as the memories flooded back. "They raised us with love, as if we were their own children, and never once did they complain about the extra burden of supporting us."

She met Clint's gaze levelly. "It was Aunt Ida who taught me how to sew." She paused, her eyes misting at the memory of the frail aunt who had taught her so painstakingly how to thread the needle, make neat stitches, how to measure and cut with pride and precision.

"I know about your handiwork," Clint said dryly. "Just walking up the boardwalk this past week I've heard your name mentioned in snatches of conversation everywhere I went. Seems like everyone is talking about how Emily Spoon is a whiz with a needle. They say you sewed a bunch of dresses for women to wear today—and that you made that dress you wore to the dance last week."

She nodded.

"Mighty nice," he said softly. "You make this one too?"

"Yes, I—"

She broke off as he reached out, touched the muslin at her shoulder, traced his hand down her sleeve. "Beautiful."

Her senses whirled at something in his voice, at the gentleness of his touch. Struggling to keep focused on their conversation, Emily forced herself to rush on.

"I owe whatever sewing expertise I have to Aunt Ida, but I owe Uncle Jake much more. He taught me so many things. Right along with Lester and Pete, I learned how to ride, drive a team, shoot a gun. How to fish and the tricks of bluffing at poker. He taught me how to tell if someone was cheating." Her eyes met his, shimmering pools of silver.

"Not exactly a typical female education," Clint drawled.

"Oh, I went to school," Emily assured him. "I won my share of spelling bees and geography contests. But Uncle Jake taught me something even more important. He taught me that families stick together. That they stand up for each other and take care of each other. I'm sure you and your brothers learned that from Reese Summers, didn't you?"

Her words struck something deep in his core. Yes, he'd learned that from Reese. So had Wade and Nick. He'd never in his life felt alone, even when he was hundreds of miles from his kin—he'd known he had them, would always have them. But it seemed damn odd to be comparing Jake Spoon to a man like Reese.

Clint studied her lovely, passionate face. "It's true, Reese taught us that," he said cautiously.

"Uncle Jake taught us the same. And he taught us that if you go through a rough time, you don't give up. You stay strong, hold onto yourself, ride it out. I suppose that's how he got through seven years of prison," she added tightly.

His shoulder muscles clenched. And suddenly he realized that's how she'd gotten through those seven years too. Dark years, when her uncle was imprisoned, her brother and cousin were on the run, her aunt was sick and dying . . .

It had taken toughness. Strength. Courage.

Emily Spoon had come through hard times. Ridden them out. Now she was trying to live them down.

"Guess I never thought of Jake that way. The Spoon gang was just a bunch of outlaws to me." He cleared his throat. "But they were your family."

"They still are." Emily met his gaze defiantly. "Don't think of me as different from them, Clint. I'm not."

"You ever rob a stagecoach?" He set down his plate, his gaze narrowing on her. "Ever take money that didn't belong to you?"

"No, but I told you—there's more to the Spoons than that—just like your family, the one you found with Reese Summers, was more than ranch work and . . . and trail drives and roundups. A family is more than what you *do*. It's where you belong, it's the people you love and count on—and who love and count on you."

She gave her head a shake as she saw the skepticism on his face.

"Never mind." Gathering up the plates and cups, she began setting everything back inside the box.

He didn't understand. He never would. *And why does it matter anyway?* she asked herself bitterly.

But it did matter. For some reason, she'd wanted him to understand.

When he reached out and covered her hand with his, she jumped as though he'd shot her.

"Emily—"

She jerked away, her eyes blazing. "Forget it, Clint. I don't even know why I tried." She placed the lid on top of the box and scrambled to her feet.

"I want to thank you for buying my box lunch. I hope you enjoyed it," she said formally. But before she could lift up the box he sprang up and grasped her by the shoulders.

"Don't you even want to know why I bought your box lunch today?" he asked roughly.

"No. We should go back—"

"I didn't plan on it—even told myself I wouldn't. But as soon as I saw Jenks was there, I knew he was going to bid on it."

"So you did it to stop him," she said coldly. "I suppose I should thank you—"

"Stop putting words in my mouth, Emily." He gave her a shake. "I did it because I wanted to do it—I'd be damned if I'd let Jenks or any other man win your lunch."

"You . . . would?" Dazed, Emily could only gaze at him in astonishment. "But . . . why?"

It was difficult to think straight when he was this close to her. Touching her.

Clint's fingers tightened on her shoulders. He dragged her against him. A palpable heat flew between them as her eyes widened on his. They were only inches apart, and for once, Clint Barclay didn't look cool and in control. His jaw was taut, every muscle in his powerful body seemed tensed. Heat and tension. It smoldered even from those hot blue eyes. His hand swooped to her hair, twisting in the careful curls, even as he spoke quickly, jerkily, the words seemingly forced from him.

"You know why. You damn well know why. Or do I need to show you?"

She couldn't breathe, could only stand there in shock as Clint Barclay hauled her closer and lowered his head down to hers.

And suddenly he was kissing her. It was not a tender kiss. Not persuasive, gentle, enticing. It was powerful and hungry and raw, scorching her mouth and turning her brain to mush.

Demanding, it drew her in, made her reel, turned the world upside down.

And then he lifted his head, breaking the kiss as abruptly as he'd begun it.

"Now do you understand, Emily?" he asked hoarsely.

"No . . ." Dizzy, she touched shaking fingers to her mouth. It felt bruised, tender, as vulnerable as her heart. "I don't understand anything about this . . . and . . . it's Miss Spoon to you."

"The hell it is. *Emily,*" he growled, his eyes determined, and then he yanked her close again, his arms clamping around her waist. "And I'm damned if I understand either, but I think it's time we figured it out. All of it."

His mouth covered hers before she could argue or protest and then she couldn't do anything but kiss him back and cling to him. Her heart leapt crazily as his lips devoured hers, and as he tightened his hold on her, so that they were no longer two, but one, her breasts ached, crushed against his chest, and she felt herself melting into him, on fire with a need that left no room for thought or reason.

Then somehow they were lying upon the blanket, his body covering hers, his weight pushing her into the thick grass.

"I don't know what you're doing to me, Emily Spoon," Clint groaned. Those simple words made her heart soar, and as his mouth skimmed along her cheek, explored the delicate curve of her ear, and trailed incendiary kisses down her collarbone, she shivered with pleasure and wrapped her arms around his neck, pulling him down to her.

"Nothing half as frightening as what you're doing to me," she gasped.

But there wasn't fear in her voice, there was hunger. Hunger for more. Desperation shimmered in those luminous silver eyes as Clint's tongue awakened hers, as his hands roamed her body.

Seeing the desire in her flushed face, her eyes wide

and soft and yearning upon his, Clint's need drummed through him. Damn, how he wanted her. Knowing she felt the same, the tension in him escalated and he deepened the kiss, taking all he wanted, all she had to give.

All week he'd stayed away from her, every damned night, when the only thing he'd wanted to do was ride out to the ranch and find her—her family be damned. He hadn't wanted much—only to see her, hold her, kiss her.

And make love to her.

The depth of his need for this woman stunned him.

"Don't you wonder, Emily?" he asked, as he pressed his mouth to the pulse at her throat. "About what it is—between us."

"I . . . don't want to know," she insisted. Yet her hands slid down his back, her nails clinging to him. The truth was, she'd wondered constantly, but hadn't found any answers, and all of this was just confusing her more. Despite common sense, and Pete and Lester's warnings, it felt so delicious to lie here with him, knowing that at any moment he might kiss her again.

"It's wrong, whatever it is," she whispered. Her breasts felt hot and achy as they pressed against his hard chest.

"Yeah? Who says it's wrong?"

"Pete and Lester. And Uncle Jake would too . . . if he knew . . ."

"Maybe they're the ones who are wrong."

"But what they say—warning me about you—makes sense. This doesn't."

"No, it doesn't," he muttered. Leaning down, he licked the corner of her lush mouth. "Not a lick of sense," he said softly.

A delicious shiver ran through her. She arched her head back and laughed. "Let me up," she murmured breathlessly, "so I can think."

"Thinking's no fun. This is."

She ought to be pushing him away, but she didn't want to. She was too fascinated by those warm, glinting eyes, by the way her own body was responding to his hands and his lips.

"This . . . is . . . wrong . . ." she tried to insist again, but he cut her off.

"Why, Emily? It sure doesn't feel wrong."

"You're a lawman and I'm—"

"Beautiful. You're so damned beautiful."

There was a catch in her throat. She couldn't take this anymore. "Stop sweet-talking me . . . It's not fair, you only want to seduce me."

A chuckle burst from him. He ran his tongue around the shell of her ear. "You got that right, sweetheart."

"Because . . . I'm not respectable enough to court or to . . . m-marry and so you know you're safe . . ."

"*What* did you say?" Clint drew back, bracing his arms on either side of her and staring down into her face.

"Not respectable? Who ever said that?" he demanded, all the teasing gentleness gone from his voice.

"You did. Sort of. You think because I'm a Spoon that I . . ."

"I said you wouldn't want to marry me. Because you're proud and you hate lawmen. Damn it, Emily, I didn't say I didn't respect you. And as for being safe with you," his voice grew harsh, "that couldn't be further from the truth. Right now, if you want to know the truth, I feel anything *but* safe."

Trembling, she reached out and touched a hand to his jaw. The late-day stubble felt rough against her fingers. "That makes two of us," she whispered, unsure if she was asking for mercy, understanding, or release.

Suddenly a voice broke the stillness of the clearing—a loud, childish voice calling her name.

"Em-leeee! Em-leeee!"

Joey.

Next came her uncle's sharper, deeper voice. "Emily! Where are you, girl?"

Clint let out a stream of oaths and rolled off her, and Emily bolted up to a sitting position. "Oh, no!" she gasped.

Frantically she began smoothing out her crumpled gown, her hands fumbling over the wrinkles in her skirt.

"Em-leee!"

Clint pulled her to her feet and she pushed her hair back desperately just as Uncle Jake and Joey appeared at the top of the gully.

"What is it . . . what's wrong?" she called out, hoping her voice sounded calmer than she felt. "Is everything all right?"

"That's what I wanted to ask you." Frowning, Jake stalked toward the picnic blanket, Joey trotting at his heels.

"Just heard who bought your box lunch, Emily. Didn't think you'd want to be alone with *him*." He jerked his head toward Clint.

"It's perfectly fine with me, Uncle Jake," Emily said quickly. "It's to raise money for the schoolhouse. I don't mind—"

"Neither do I." Clint spoke easily, returning her uncle's hard glare with a steady gaze. "Your niece is an excellent cook. We enjoyed the lunch—as you can see." He glanced down at the repacked basket, and Jake and Joey followed his glance.

"Enjoying the picnic, Joey?"

Joey's head bobbed. "Sure am. Sheriff Barclay, you saved Em-ly from the storm, right?"

"I guess you could say that."

"It's a lucky thing you found her," he said. "She could have been eaten by a bear or a mountain lion. But that's a sheriff's job—to help people. That's what Em-ly told me."

"She's right." Clint knelt down so he was closer to eye level with the boy and met his gaze directly. "I'm just glad I was there when she needed me. I'll be here if you need me too, Joey."

"Thanks, Sheriff." A grin broke over his face, but it faded as he glanced up to see Jake frowning.

"Why're you mad at Sheriff Barclay, Uncle Jake?" he asked.

The older man looked down then into that small, uncertain face. He cleared his throat. "Me and Sheriff Barclay don't see eye to eye."

"We should go back to the schoolhouse." Emily hurried forward and took Joey's hand. "I wanted to ask Margaret for her corn bread recipe."

"Go on ahead." Jake's eyes were fastened upon Clint. "Reckon I'll have a word alone with Sheriff Barclay here."

"Uncle Jake, I don't think that's a very good idea." She glanced uneasily between the two men, but her uncle spoke curtly.

"Take Joey back. This won't take long."

"No. I'm not going without you."

Clint saw the shadow of fear—and determination—in her eyes. Something twisted inside him. This slender, beautiful woman was afraid for *him*.

Amused, yet moved in a way he didn't understand, he shook his head.

"Go back, Emily," he heard himself saying, and kept his tone even. "Take Joey with you—it should be time for the potato sack races. We'll join you soon."

Uncertain, she stared at him, then at Uncle Jake. She might as well have been staring at two mules, she thought. The same flinty determination was stamped upon both of their faces.

"C'mon, Em-ly, let's go." Joey tugged at her hand. "Bobby Smith told me that Mrs. Phillips always gives out sugar cookies after lunch. I want one!"

She let go of his hand and gathered up her silk-decorated box, then threw one last glance at her uncle and at Lonesome's tall, hard-eyed sheriff, trying to still the fear in her heart.

"Don't do anything foolish, either one of you," she ordered, before she let Joey pull her away, leaving Uncle Jake and Clint alone, facing each other in the shade of the cottonwood tree.

"Well?" Clint's eyes narrowed. "Say what you have to say, Spoon."

"I damn well intend to." Jake's lip curled. The still spring air around them vibrated with a keen, high tension. Even the hot sky above seemed to quiver with a dangerous electricity.

"But if you know what's good for you, Barclay, you'll listen real careful. Because I'm only going to say this once."

Chapter 16

EMILY COULDN'T SLEEP. THE CABIN was quiet, her room dark and fragrantly cool with wafts of mountain air floating through the open window. Outside, the moon-silvered darkness was alive with the chirping of crickets and the rustle of countless unseen creatures—soothing sounds that normally lulled her.

But not tonight. Or last night.

It was two days since the town picnic and Joey hadn't been able to stop talking about his new friend, Bobby Smith, about Miss Crayden, the schoolteacher, who'd given him a slate and piece of chalk, about Nettie Phillips's sugar cookies, and about the way he'd almost fallen into the creek.

And Emily hadn't been able to stop thinking—thinking about how it had felt to lie upon the thick spring grass with Clint Barclay's arms around her, the sun glinting off his hair, the sizzling taste of his kisses sending wave upon wave of heat all through her blood.

She tossed and turned as the stars burned brighter and deeper in the sky. Deliberately she turned her thoughts elsewhere, letting other matters crowd through her head. She thought of Pete, who'd headed into town after supper—to visit Florry Brown, she guessed. Lester had turned in early, and she'd never been able to find out much about the box lunch he'd shared with Carla Mangley, or why he'd bought it. Uncle Jake had refused to tell her one word about what he'd discussed with Clint Barclay—not that she really needed to ask.

Dire warnings, no doubt, for the sheriff to keep his distance from Jake's niece.

And then there was Lissa, from whom, surprisingly, there'd been no word yet . . . not even a single letter. That was a worrisome fact that was beginning to gnaw at her.

But most of all, she thought about Clint Barclay . . .

Suddenly she sat up and swung her legs over the side of the bed. She couldn't stay in this room another moment. She needed air, space. A chance to think.

Taking time only to toss her shawl around her shoulders, she left her room and crossed the darkened parlor, clad only in her shawl and thin white nightgown. Outside, the chill wind stung her skin as she huddled on the porch for a moment, gazing at the full glistening curve of a crescent moon. Her heart was full of questions, full of longing. She'd never felt so alone.

Taking a deep breath of the night air, she started toward the barn, oblivious of the chill, of anything but the turbulence within her. She was halfway there when she became aware of movement by the corrals. Startled, Emily froze, her heart jumping in her chest.

Through the glow of the moon, she saw her uncle. Jake Spoon was mounting his horse, ghostly gray in the night. As she stared at him, shock coursing through her, he paused in the saddle, perfectly still, a dark, lone figure outlined against the distant hills.

• • •

Clint had left his horse tethered well beyond the trees and stood beside an aspen, watching the Spoon cabin. A frown creased his face and every muscle was coiled with tension.

He had a bad feeling in his gut. A feeling that things were going to get real ugly before this was finished.

He'd sensed from the first that the Spoons would be headed for trouble, but he hadn't known then just how deep or in what direction they'd wade in. Now he did. Or at least, he would know it all, after he met with Marshal Hoot McClain in Denver tomorrow and found out everything he needed to know about what ornery Jake Spoon was up to—and all about his prison pal, Ben Ratlin.

Right now, all he knew for certain was that things were going to heat up fast around here—and they were about to turn dangerous.

And he knew that even though her entire family was involved up to their grimy necks, Emily Spoon hadn't the faintest idea what was about to happen.

With any luck, Clint hoped he could keep it that way.

When Jake first led his horse from the barn beneath that slip of a moon, Clint hadn't moved a muscle. He watched and waited in the shadows. Until the cabin door opened. Until Emily stepped out.

Jake never even saw her, but Clint did. He saw the wind lift and flutter her hair, saw her pull the shawl around her shoulders as she stood silent and lovely, bathed in moonlight. He swore under his breath. Damn, she was so gorgeous. And completely unaware that she wasn't alone out here in the vast blackness of night.

What the hell was she doing? Clint wondered, his chest tightening. And why did she have to be wearing only that shawl and a nightgown so flimsy it revealed every luscious curve?

The thought of her so close to this dirty business made his blood run cold. He forced himself to stay silent and motionless as she stepped off the porch as gracefully as a wraith and made her way across the shadowy yard.

He saw the exact moment that she spotted Jake just as the old coot mounted his horse.

Damn it all to hell.

What in heaven is Uncle Jake doing out here? Emily wondered in shock even as her uncle lifted the reins. Before she could call out to him, he spurred his horse forward. She stared after him in stunned silence as he rode out of the yard and took off at a gallop, disappearing like a wisp of mist in the gloom.

Dismay surged through her. Whatever he was up to, it wasn't anything good. Memories pricked at her, uneasy memories of things that hadn't made sense. That time she'd seen him coming out of the telegraph office in Lonesome. The night of the storm when he'd claimed he was rounding up strays near Beaver Rock, yet there had been no sign of him anywhere.

And now tonight, riding out in the darkness—to do what?

He promised he wouldn't go back to holding up stages, he promised he'd go straight, she thought desperately, but a terrible suspicion clawed through her.

I have to find out what he's up to. She ran toward the barn with some vague idea of saddling her mare and following him, but suddenly strong arms grabbed her and a hard male voice spoke into her ear.

"What the hell do you think you're doing?"

She was spun around, and found herself staring into Clint Barclay's hard eyes.

"Let me go!" She was so furious she forgot the need for quiet, and Clint quickly shoved a hand over her mouth.

He began dragging her toward the barn, as Emily struggled to escape him. But she might as well have struggled against a grizzly bear for all the good it did her.

"Shut up and calm down," he growled in her ear, as he yanked open the barn door and without ceremony pushed her inside.

Then he stepped in after her, pulled the door closed, and they were locked together in the opaque, hay-scented darkness.

It took a moment for her eyes to adjust to the dimness, and then she could just barely make out Clint's face.

"What are you doing here?" she demanded. "Spying on me? On my family?" Frantically she wondered if he'd seen Uncle Jake ride away.

"I'm here doing my job—keeping the peace." Those polished eyes gleamed at her through the darkness. "Any idea where your uncle went?"

"No, not that it's any of your business. I'm sure he's just going . . . for a ride. Sometimes people like to do that when they can't sleep—"

"I suppose that's your excuse too."

Emily's eyes flashed and her chin lifted. "I hardly need an excuse, Sheriff. And neither does he. You have no right to come on our property, skulk around in the dark—"

"What if I told you I wanted to check on you? That I came here just to make sure you were all right?" Clint's voice was hard, but his hands suddenly gripped her shoulders, surprisingly gentle. "To hell with your uncle, Emily—maybe I was just worried about you."

"You expect me to believe that?" She wrenched free of him. "I don't."

"No?" His jaw set, Clint studied her, fighting impatience. Ironic, he thought, that he was telling her the truth, partly the truth, at least, and she didn't believe him. She had no idea of the effect she'd had on him, of how he thought about her every day, damn near every moment. And even in his dreams. No idea how much he wished they hadn't been interrupted yesterday in the clearing.

There was just enough light to see her pallor, to see the panic and distress in those luminous eyes. It tore at him. And at the same time it set off something fierce and protective and powerful inside him—something he was getting tired of fighting.

"You're a tough woman to convince, Emily. You think the worst of me every chance you get. But maybe you'll believe this."

His arms closed around her before she could do more than gasp, and he hauled her up against him. One hand cupped her chin. And the next instant he was kissing her, a hot, powerful kiss that, like those of yesterday, held no gentleness, no hint of gentlemanly ardor, but was pure need, raw and angry and blinding in its intensity.

She tasted too good to let go, and Clint didn't. He held her ruthlessly, his arms tightening, as if he would crush her to him, leaving no space between their bodies for any of their differences to come between them. Emily was kissing him back, her soft mouth pliant and eager upon his, and he was on fire.

Need pounded through him, and his loins tightened as he drank from those sweet, giving lips and tangled his hands in the fine silk of her hair.

When he lifted his head, her eyes were closed, her face flushed, her mouth still parted. God, she was beautiful.

"Emily."

She swayed against him, her hands gripping the front of his shirt. She could barely think, much less stand. Warmth and wanting flooded her. Passion flowed like wine through her body, and when she opened her eyes, staring into that coolly handsome face, she wanted to pull his head down to hers and kiss him again . . . and again . . .

But there was a gulf between them, one that could never be breached. If he had the chance, he'd arrest Uncle Jake in a heartbeat . . . and Lester and Pete as well.

Worse, if what she suspected were true, Uncle Jake was on the verge of giving him that chance.

The barriers between her and Clint Barclay were too high, she reminded herself, and something splintered in her heart. They always had been, always would be, she thought. The yearning that filled her made her quiver.

She couldn't bear to face him. Couldn't bear to be this near to him, not knowing what she knew, not if what she suspected about Uncle Jake was true.

"No," she whispered. "I can't do this. I won't." Her heart breaking, she pulled away. "Just go back to town and leave me alone!"

On pure instinct she bolted for the hayloft, her favorite childhood place of safety, and flew up the ladder. Even as she spun around in the darkness she heard Clint coming after her and she yanked at the ladder in an attempt to pull it up after her, but he held fast to the other end.

"Forget it, Emily." In an instant he had climbed up to the loft and vaulted into the hay beside her. "There's unfinished business between us and this time I'm going to finish it."

"What does that mean?" Even as she spoke, she edged away from him, deeper into the small, dark space of the loft.

"It means I'm not leaving until I'm good and ready—and neither are you."

"Stay as long as you like, but don't you dare touch me." Despite her cool words, her breath was coming fast. Too late, she remembered she was wearing only her nightgown. And this stupid shawl. She wrapped it more tightly around her, draping it over her breasts, but to her amazement, Clint Barclay reached out in one lightning motion and snagged it from her. With a grim smile, he rolled it into a ball and threw it down into the barn. It landed in a tangled heap on the floor between the workbench and the horse stalls.

"You . . . you . . ." Fury strangled her and she couldn't even force the words out.

"You're free to get it—if you think you can get past me," he invited. "But I've got to warn you, Emily, I have every intention of touching you. All over. Unless you tell me not to, that is."

"I already did," she cried. "Damn you, don't you listen?" She started past him, twisting her body so that her feet would touch the top rung of the ladder, but Clint yanked her back toward the loft, tossed her down into the hay, and flipped her over. He threw himself across her before she could roll aside and stared down into that beautiful, astonished face.

"You didn't mean it," he said roughly. He smoothed a heavy lock of ebony hair from her eyes as he held her pinned beneath his body, despite her efforts to wriggle free. "Tell you what. If I kiss you, and you don't kiss me back, that'll be the proof. I'll not only let you down the ladder, I'll open the barn door for you myself."

"What a gentleman!" Emily pushed futilely at his iron chest. "But I don't want you to kiss me, and if you did I would never kiss you back—"

"You always kiss me back," he corrected.

He kissed the tip of her nose. "That one doesn't count." He brushed his mouth across her cheek, then his lips traveled slowly to the shell of her ear. "Either does this," he said, flicking his tongue over the delicate skin.

Emily shivered all over. Despite her intentions to steel herself against him, the most delicious sensations were sweeping through her. Her body came alive, vibrant with heat and desire and urges that had nothing to do with reason.

Oh, what was he doing to her? She was on fire, beset with a fever, and yet shivering. She was angry as hell that he'd trapped her here, frightened of what would happen to Uncle Jake, determined to avert a disaster . . . and she was melting right here in Clint Barclay's arms.

"This has gone far enough," she managed to bite out in what was supposed to be a hard tone, though it sounded shaky and weak to her own ears.

"No, sweetheart, it hasn't gone far enough, not nearly enough."

"What do you want from me?"

Something in those vivid silver eyes cut him deep. "Damned if I know," he admitted.

For a moment they just stared into each other's eyes.

"But I think we should find out—find out what we both want—from each other." Clint touched her cheek. "Or live the rest of our lives wondering."

He was right, she thought, staring into his face as if she would memorize everything about it, from the hard slant of his jaw to the electrifying intensity of his eyes.

"We owe that to each other, Emily. Even if it's only for tonight."

Only for tonight . . . could she do that? Make love to him . . . only for tonight . . .

"I . . . won't . . . kiss . . . you back . . ." she murmured, her heart hammering painfully. One last time, she tried to squirm free, but Clint held her fast.

Then he leaned down and his lips were only a breath away.

"Let's see."

He kissed her then, deeply, richly, a hot potent kiss that rocked the night. The world spun away. There was only the sweet tang of the hay, the texture of his mouth against hers, the heat and power of his body seeming to flow inside her skin . . .

And a kiss that sizzled through her like none she'd ever experienced before.

Sensations broke through her, sweet and hot. Before she knew what was happening her arms twined around him and she was drawing him down to her, closer and nearer, returning his kiss with an urgency that she couldn't control—turning it into something even deeper, hungrier, more intense.

Their tongues met in a dark, musky battle that made her moan, and it was a long time before Clint pulled back, his eyes glinting.

"Some kiss," he muttered thickly, and then his mouth dropped to her throat and rained warm kisses against the vulnerable whiteness of her flesh. Emily was lost. Lost in a world of deep pleasure and spiraling desire.

When his hand cupped her breast through the thin cotton of her nightgown, Emily tingled with hunger and delight. But that wasn't enough for Clint—he stripped her of the nightgown and surveyed her, all of her, his eyes gleaming in the darkness with admiration and what she could plainly see was raw desire.

"So beautiful," he said huskily. Her body was lush, creamy, perfect—the sight of it filling him with an agonizing need.

Emily saw his intentions, knew what was going to happen, and wanted it to happen, wanted it more than she'd ever wanted anything—but at the same time a pulse of fear threaded through her.

"I've never . . . no man ever . . ." She paused, swallowing, not sure how to explain, but Clint, after one moment of stunned silence, smiled very gently, a smile that magically softened the hard planes of his face. He leaned down to touch his mouth to hers, kissing away her fears.

"I'll try not to hurt you," he vowed, his lips warm against hers. "My God, Emily, the last thing I'd want to do is hurt you."

It was the truth, she saw it in his face, and a crazy happiness leapt through her. "I know," she breathed wonderingly. "I . . . trust you." Somehow, here in this darkened loft, alone with him and the hay-scented night, she did.

"We'll go slow." Raging need throbbed through him, and he would have loved to take her now, quickly, satisfying the roaring in his blood, but he steeled himself to control his passion, to curb the powerful urges and bring her, wild and needy, along with him. "Slow as you want, sweetheart."

He unbuttoned his shirt and Emily slid it off him. Next came his boots, his pants, and then he was as naked as she, his magnificent body looming over her in the darkness.

Emily reached for him, and he grinned, then kissed her mouth—long, lingeringly—then, slowly, each of her breasts. Heat shot through Emily in an aching spurt of fire. She writhed and dug her hands into his shoulders as he began to toy with her nipples, ruthless as an outlaw plundering gold. He rubbed and caressed them until they were diamond-hard rosy peaks at the mercy of his hands and his tongue.

A gasp came from deep within Emily's throat—who would have known that Clint's big, rough hands could do such gentle, wondrous things to her? She moaned, half in torment, half in ecstasy, and he grinned down at her with a purely male triumph that made her burn for more of him.

She strained against him, her body hungering for more as he stroked her, kissed her. A tension built in her, everywhere, especially low in her belly, and between her thighs.

"Clint. What . . . are you doing to me . . . I can't think . . ."

"I told you, Emily, thinking's no fun."

"But . . ."

He went still as stone at the hesitation he heard in her voice. Every nerve in his body straining, the tension coiled tight within him was so powerful it hurt to breathe.

"You don't want to stop, do you?" he asked quietly, his eyes on hers.

Emily gazed up into those eyes, those somber blue eyes that seemed to crackle with their own brand of lightning, and felt a depth of emotion and need she'd never known before.

"I'll die if you stop," she whispered. She felt the surge of his heart.

"Just for tonight," she went on softly, fervently, holding fast to his broad, muscled back with hands that trembled. "I want to forget who I am, who you are. I want to forget about everyone and everything else. We're just . . . Emily and Clint—nothing more. Nothing less." Her eyes were pleading, soft as mist in the dimness. "Can we do that?"

"We sure as hell can." His hands roamed over her. "I'll show you how."

And he did show her.

He stroked her and kissed her and loved every inch of her body until she was nearly blind with pleasure and Emily clung to him with a need that swiftly matched his own. Her delicate hands moved over him shyly at first, then boldly, exploring those hard splendid muscles, touching the great thickness of his manhood, reveling in his grunting reaction to her touch, to the sweat sheening his face.

She felt her own power and beauty through his fierce response to her touches, knew with a rich happiness that he needed her as much as she needed him. And she did need him, all of him.

Passion gripped her, making her breath come in short, fitful gasps. It was hard to breathe, impossible to think. Swept up in a whirlwind of pleasure, all she could do was touch him and hold him and writhe beneath him as he stroked her hair and kissed her lips, and his hand slid between her damp thighs.

"Emily, I want you. I want you so much it's killing me." Taut with the effort to remain in control, he stroked her, watching her face, and inhaled the sweet lilac scent of her skin. Gently he kissed her wildly cascading hair. "I want you . . . now . . ."

"I want you too. Please . . . oh, please . . "

Clint groaned, need pounding through him in nearly painful waves. Emily Spoon's blazing temper had been his first clue to the passion running deep and wild within her, a passion that flowed like potent brandy in her heart and her soul and blazed like flame in her luscious body. Gazing into her face, that exquisite face, breathing in the sweet fragrance of her skin, and feeling her writhing, desperate movements beneath him, was rapidly sending him over the edge. She was warm, moist, and ready for him, and in her glazed eyes he saw a desire as fervent as his own.

He covered her body with his and spread her legs with his thighs. He entered her carefully, stroking and kissing her all the while. At the moment when she gave a stifled scream of pain, his entire body went still, only his heart thumping against hers.

"Emily, Emily," he whispered.

How tender her name sounded on his lips, she thought, and it made the last of the pain fade away. She couldn't tear her gaze from him, couldn't breathe as she clutched at him. His next kiss was the gentlest yet.

"Hold on, sweetheart, we're going for a ride."

He eased farther inside of her, deeper, taking control as he passed the last barrier between them and began to thrust within her. He plunged deep, deeper, thrusting again and again with powerful movements that were sure and strong and possessive, sweeping her into a maelstrom of pleasure. Gasping, Emily's hips began to writhe in rhythm with his taut body. A whirlwind of sensations enveloped her and she clutched at him, her fingers sliding through his thick hair as Clint kissed her until she was dizzy. Scraping her hands down his back and lower still, to his hips, she frantically wrapped her legs around him, bucking and twisting as his movements came faster and harder than ever and a sweet bursting pleasure built and built within, sweeping her into a rising storm unlike any she'd ever known.

Wild frenzy rose within them, and together they held each other and rode the storm, swept up in wildfire and wind and thunder that roared through their blood and made them one. Higher and higher, faster and faster, the chaos spun, and finally the universe fell away and they soared to the brink of heaven. Release brought joy and sweet fulfillment, and slowly, entwined in each other's arms, they drifted like feathers back to earth.

At last they lay sated and dazed in each other's arms. Emily felt as if she were floating, or perhaps dreaming . . . but it was better than a dream. She nestled close to Clint, her head upon his chest, and together they drifted toward sleep.

She didn't really want to sleep. She wanted the night to last. To put off the morning . . .

Suddenly there was a rasping sound and the barn door cranked open. Moonlight flowed in and Emily jolted awake in Clint's arms. She felt every muscle in his body tense and his arms closed around her.

"Shhh," he breathed into her ear as Jake Spoon led his gelding into the barn below.

Emily thought her heart would explode as they lay there together in the loft while Jake unsaddled and tended his horse. When she suddenly remembered her shawl, panic rushed through her.

What if he discovers it lying on the floor? She clenched her hand around the taut muscles of Clint's arm, scarcely daring to breathe.

But in the darkness he didn't discover it. Jake worked quickly, silently, and at last stomped out of the barn and slammed the door behind him.

For a long moment there was no sound but the beating of their hearts.

Finally Clint sat up, gazing down through the darkness again into her pale face. "That was close." He gave her a ghost of a grin and twined a finger in her mussed and silken hair.

"T-too close." Emily couldn't match his smile. Icy coldness washed over her as the beauty of the night dissolved and dark reality returned. Shuddering, she pushed herself up to a sitting position, all too aware of her nakedness, and shifted away from him.

Her uncle's return had banished every last vestige of passion and fire and sweet gentle peace. It had reminded her of everything she'd been trying to forget. She didn't know where he'd gone tonight, but she knew his actions were suspicious—and where there was smoke, she'd learned from the past, there was always fire.

Clint was no fool. Why wasn't he questioning her? Why had he stayed with her instead of following Uncle Jake?

The answer sprang to mind, chilling her. *Because he already knew where Uncle Jake was going. He knows what he has planned. He's just waiting for the right time to move against him, to spring a trap . . .*

Alarm suddenly flooded her. Clint Barclay was a man who liked to be in control of himself and his surroundings. She should have known he wouldn't do anything without a good reason.

She couldn't trust this man—not where her family was concerned. He despised the Spoons and everything they were—just as much as they despised him.

And as far as her heart was concerned?

He had only wanted one night, she reminded herself desolately.

And now that night was over. Dawn was coming; she'd

seen the first opal shimmer of it when Uncle Jake opened the barn door.

She reached for her nightgown, her nakedness suddenly a painful thing, her vulnerability to this man, in every sense of the word, too overwhelming to endure.

"Emily, don't go yet." He grabbed hold of the nightgown and gazed at her, his eyes sweeping over her breasts, up the sleek column of her throat, locking on those eyes that looked too big and heavy and haunted for her delicate face.

"Please, Clint," she said quietly. "It's nearly morning. You saw the sky, didn't you?"

This time as she tugged at her nightgown, he released it. Emily donned it, her hands shaking, but her lovely mouth was set. During all of the passion they'd shared in this loft, he hadn't once said he loved her. Hadn't mentioned a future.

That's because we don't have one, she thought. *We never did.*

Watching her expressive face, Clint's throat went dry. *Let her go,* a voice inside of him warned. *You have a job to do. And love and duty don't mix.*

Love? What was he talking about? Shock jolted through him.

Love.

He couldn't be in love with Emily Spoon. No way. But . . . the hell of it was, he didn't know *what* he felt. He only knew he didn't want her to leave.

But it would be better if she did. Before he got himself—both of them—into something that they couldn't get out of.

Clint felt sweat bead on his brow. The one woman in town who always seemed ready to walk away from him was the one woman he wanted to stay. In this loft, in his arms. In his life.

He started yanking on his clothes. She slipped down the ladder without waiting for him.

"Emily . . ."

She turned as he descended the ladder, clad only in his pants, his shirt open, revealing the powerful muscles of his chest.

"When can I see you again?" Hell, he sounded like some idiotic schoolboy.

Emily looked as closed as a flower that has given up on water and sunshine.

"What would be the point?" she whispered. She held herself together with every ounce of her will. *Don't let him see, don't let him know, she told herself wearily. At least you can salvage your pride, if not your heart.*

The truth was, she had come to love him. To love this man to whom honor was a duty. A man who was as gentle as he was strong, who believed in upholding the law, who dedicated his life to it. A man who had made it clear he was not looking for love or for a wife, or ties of any kind.

A man who went his own way and answered only to himself.

She had to do the same. She had a duty to follow too.

That meant talking to Uncle Jake, demanding to know what was going on. She intended to stop him—whatever he was doing—before Clint Barclay had another chance to throw him in jail.

"Good-bye, Clint." Her voice was soft. Cool. Final.

Part of her prayed he would run to her, grab her, tell her . . . what? That he loved her? That he would try to accept her family, get along with them, that he wouldn't arrest them if given half a chance?

Absurd. His sense of honor and duty would never let him look the other way. He wouldn't be able to live with himself. And she couldn't live with herself if she didn't try to protect Uncle Jake.

She went out into the pale shadows of dawn and closed the barn door behind her.

Chapter 17

"OH, IT'S YOU, MISS SPOON."

Agnes Mangley's voice was colder than a Rocky Mountain stream as she stood in the doorway of her splendid white frame house at the edge of town, frowning at Emily. "I see you have our gowns—at last. Another day would have been too late!"

Emily handed over the box and spoke levelly. "I won't keep you, Mrs. Mangley. I know you and Carla leave for Denver tomorrow and you both must be very busy."

"Indeed we are." The woman sniffed. "Kindly wait a moment and I'll fetch your money."

Well, what did you expect—to be invited inside, asked to join the Mangleys in a cup of tea? Emily thought to herself as she waited on the large spacious porch for Agnes Mangley's return.

It had been four days since the box lunch social, and obviously Mrs. Mangley had not forgotten that Clint Barclay had bid on Emily Spoon's box and her own Carla had been forced to dine with none other than Emily's notorious cousin.

She wasn't taking it well at all, Emily reflected. If only the woman knew how much Emily wished she'd never met Clint Barclay, that he'd never bought her box lunch, never caught her outside in the moonlight the next night, never made wild sweet love to her in the hayloft.

If only Rufus Doily had bought my box lunch instead, Emily reflected glumly.

But it was too late now. She and Clint Barclay *had* made love to each other in the hayloft two nights ago—and she hadn't heard a word from him since.

Don't think about it. Emily had been trying to push the memories of that night away ever since she'd returned to the cabin. But she couldn't, because the memory of all that had happened between her and Clint was written upon her heart. Engraved upon her soul.

And she wanted to see him—heaven help her, to kiss him, to touch him, to make love to him—all over again.

But she wouldn't see him. She wouldn't set foot near that awful jail and his little cramped office that seemed too tiny for the towering lawman who worked there. If he wanted to see her, he would have to come to the ranch. She wasn't about to go chasing after him like . . . like Carla Mangley and Berty Miller and the rest of the women he kept dodging like blazes.

"Here. Thank you kindly and good day."

Agnes thrust the money at her and slammed the door before Emily could even reply.

She turned away and walked up the tree-shaded path leading from the house, then started up the street toward the center of town, but she paused as someone called her name.

"Miss Spoon! I mean . . . Emily! H-hello!"

Carla Mangley jumped from the seat of a swing slung between two trees at the rear of her house and ran toward her. "H-how are you? You came to call? I didn't know . . ."

Emily stared at her. Carla Mangley had never made

much of an effort to speak to her before—except to discuss what kind of trim or sleeves she wanted in her dress. Now the girl was staring at her as if she were her long-lost friend.

"I delivered the dresses," Emily explained, hoping she didn't look as puzzled as she felt. "I know you and your mother wanted them for your trip to Denver. You'll be pleased with them, I hope."

"Oh, yes. The dresses." The girl nodded. "I forgot. It doesn't matter, really," she shrugged, "there won't really be anyone at the Governor's Dinner—anyone that matters," she added, flushing. "Just my Uncle Frank and Mr. Sleech, his mine foreman, and some congressmen, and the governor."

"Do you mean it doesn't matter because Clint Barclay won't be there?" Emily asked directly, but to her surprise, Carla's eyes widened and she shook her head, sending her blonde curls dancing.

"Sheriff Barclay? Oh, no, that's not what I meant at all. I was thinking of . . ."

Her voice trailed off.

Confused, Emily wasn't sure what to say. She nearly tripped over a stone in the road when Carla said casually, "Did . . . did your cousin drive to town with you . . . by any chance?"

"Lester?" Astonishment filled her. "Why . . . no, my brother Pete drove into town with me. Lester is working on our barn today."

"He is? How . . . how splendid of him," the girl breathed.

Splendid? Lester? Emily drew in a deep breath, more bewildered than ever.

"You and . . . Lester . . . enjoyed the box lunch social last week?" she offered tentatively.

Stealing a glance at Carla, she saw a deep orchid blush steal into the girl's cheeks. "Yes. Yes, we did. I mean, I did. I hope Lester felt the same. Did he . . . mention anything to you about it?"

"None of the men in my family has mentioned much of anything to me lately." Emily spoke grimly. It was the truth.

She'd questioned Uncle Jake about where he'd gone the night she'd seen him ride off and he'd refused to give her a satisfactory answer.

"Took a ride, Emily girl. No law against it." Those had been his exact words. And when Emily had demanded to know if he was going back to his old ways, he had looked her right in the eye. *"I made you a promise on your Aunt Ida's grave, girl. Did you forget that?"*

"No, but there are things I don't understand . . . like the night of the storm, when you said you spent the night in a cave . . ."

"You think too much, Emily. You're fretting yourself to death over nothing." There had been an unexpected harshness in his voice. *"You just tend to your business and stay out of mine."*

"But, Uncle Jake—"

He'd stalked away from her without another word.

Pete had been just as closemouthed about his apparent interest in Florry Brown. And when she'd tried to tell him her concerns about their uncle, he'd echoed Jake's words.

"You just mind your own business, Emily. Leave Uncle Jake be."

And Lester hadn't discussed the box lunch social with her at all—he hadn't even mentioned a word to her about Clint Barclay bidding on her box. So she had no idea if he'd enjoyed the time he'd spent with Carla. But obviously Carla had not disliked his company nearly as much as she—and her mother—had expected.

"I'm glad you're not upset that Sheriff Barclay missed out on bidding on your box," she ventured, fascinated by the discussion as Carla fell into step with her as she headed back to town.

"No, not at all. At first I was disappointed, because Mama so wants . . ." She stopped and took a deep breath. "To tell you the truth, Emily," she said in a rush, "Sheriff Barclay terrifies me."

"Terrifies you? Why in the world should he terrify you?" Emily gaped at her.

"He just does." Carla turned to face her and lifted her hands helplessly. "He's so . . . so imposing, I guess I'd have to say. I get all tongue-tied around him, and can't think of a thing to say. I always feel that he thinks I'm stupid . . . and foolish." Her voice quavered. "I've let Mama down something awful by not getting Sheriff Barclay to like me. To fall in love with me, really," she finished miserably. "Mama just has her heart set on me marrying him, but I never wanted . . . that is . . ." She broke off.

"Mama gets *notions,*" Carla said at last, sighing, as if that explained everything.

Amazed, Emily could only gaze at her in wonder. "Do you mean . . . you really *don't* want to marry Sheriff Barclay?"

"I usually try to want what Mama wants," the girl replied softly. "It's easier that way. But . . . to tell you the truth, I want to marry a man who loves me, and I don't think Clint Barclay ever would."

They reached the edge of town, and both women stepped up onto the boardwalk, out of the path of a wagon rumbling down the street.

"I see," Emily murmured, wondering frantically where all this was leading.

And then she found out.

"I thought I might run into Lester before leaving for Denver tomorrow . . . but I guess I won't . . ." She bit her lip. "Would you . . . give him a message for me?"

"Of course." Emily murmured the words automatically, stunned as she noticed the shy blush staining Carla Mangley's cheeks.

"He . . . he asked me at the box lunch social when I might be returning from Denver. I wasn't sure . . . but I do believe we'll be taking the stage home next Tuesday. Perhaps . . ." She took another deep breath. "Perhaps he'd like to call sometime after that? I'd . . . I'd welcome a visit," she finished quickly, her eyes flashing defiantly. "And I don't care what Mama says! You'll tell him?"

"Yes." Emily felt dazed. "I'll tell him."

Carla squeezed her hand, her eyes shining with gratitude. "Thank you. Oh, thank you. Good day, Emily."

In amazement, Emily watched her hurry off.

The notion of Carla Mangley actually inviting Lester to come courting her filled her with such astonishment that Emily forgot about her own problems for the moment and even forgot where she was headed. Lost in thought, she bumped into Doc Calvin, murmured an apology, and continued walking, distracted, until she suddenly found herself directly in front of the last place she wanted to be.

The jailhouse.

The door was closed, the windows shuttered.

There was no sign of Clint Barclay.

She put a hand to the doorknob, then quickly dropped it as if it had burned her flesh. *Walk away before he opens this door and finds you standing here like a pathetic fool,* she ordered herself—and spun around so quickly toward Doily's Mercantile that she collided with Nettie Phillips.

"Goodness, dear, be careful!" the woman chided.

"I'm so sorry," Emily gasped.

"Looking for Clint Barclay, are you?" Nettie grinned knowingly at her. "How very interesting. I don't mean to be nosy, Emily, but frankly, everyone in town is talking."

"They are?" Emily's heart sank.

"Yes, indeedy. There was quite a stir when he bid on your box lunch. Some mighty pretty noses were out of joint—but as I told Margaret that very afternoon, may the best gal win."

"Nettie! I assure you, I'm not trying to *win* anything, least of all Clint Barclay—"

"No?" Nettie peered at her even more intently. "Are you certain about that?"

"I've never been more certain of anything in my life." The words came out even more vehemently than Emily had intended. But they only caused Nettie to tilt her head to one side and smile.

"Hmmm."

It was the shortest sentence she'd ever heard from Nettie Phillips. Suddenly Emily couldn't bear Nettie's piercing gaze one moment longer.

"Excuse me, Nettie, I'm on my way to Doily's Mercantile—"

"He's gone, in case you're wondering," Nettie called out as Emily began to hurry off.

She swung back. "Rufus Doily is gone?"

"No, Clint Barclay," the woman replied, her grin widening. She jerked a thumb toward the jailhouse door. "Denver, I think. Been gone these past few days."

Emily struggled to hide her disappointment.

"Don't have any notion when he'll be back, in case you're wondering," the woman added.

"It's no concern of mine, Nettie." Emily spoke airily.

"Course it isn't," the woman agreed, and then gave a cackle of laughter. "Come along, honey, I'm on my way to Doily's as well. Thought I'd bake a rhubarb pie tonight—and I'm fresh out of rhubarb. Nothing quite so fine on a warm spring night as a rhubarb pie, that's what my Lucas always used to say."

Emily was relieved when Nettie began going on about which of her various boarders fancied her cooking the most, and how Mr. Taylor had spilled gravy all over the dining room carpet and she'd been at her wit's end to scour the stains out.

Emily didn't want to talk about Clint Barclay anymore—not with Carla Mangley, not with Nettie Phillips, not with anyone. She wanted to forget she'd ever met him. Unfortunately, her own mind kept whirling with thoughts of him. She was wondering why he'd gone to Denver, what he was doing there, and when he would be back.

But even these thoughts were at last driven from her mind when Rufus Doily, after filling her order for dried apples, coffee, and beans, told her he had a letter for her.

"From San Francisco, California," he announced, and scurried down the counter to the neat piles of mail he'd sorted earlier that day.

Emily's spirits lifted when she saw the thin, graceful script on the envelope. The letter was from Lissa!

She tore open the envelope and began to read, oblivious of Rufus Doily's stare and Nettie Phillips's keen gaze.

Dearest Emily.

I've arrived safely in San Francisco and have been staying in the home of my grandparents. They've been only too happy to set aside the feud that separated them from my father for so many years, and we are now a family again. They want me to come live with them here and to bring Joey. I'll be coming for him the last week in June and can scarcely wait to see my darling little boy again. How can I ever thank you? Please keep him safe until I arrive, Emily. I know you will. My grandfather is sending an armed escort with me—a man he trusts. I finally do believe that all will be well.

Thank you, my dearest, kindest friend. I will be with you soon.

Your grateful friend, Lissa.

"Good news, honey?" Nettie inquired.

"Wonderful news." Emily's eyes shone. "My friend is well, and she's coming for Joey. Oh, he'll be so happy!" For the first time in days, Emily's heart lifted. She couldn't wait to get home and tell Joey that his mother would be with him soon.

"You'll miss the boy, I reckon," Nettie commented.

"Very much." Emily nodded, a pang going through her. The cabin wouldn't be the same without Joey. She'd miss his noisy card games with Uncle Jake, the way he called her Em-ly, his soft, fervent hugs when she tucked him in at night.

"But it's all for the best," she told Nettie. "He'll be with his mother, where he belongs."

"Could be you'll have children of your own some day

soon. Of course you'll want a husband first," the woman added with a grin.

Emily's throat tightened. More hints about Clint Barclay. Nettie had no idea how far off the mark she was. She had no idea that Uncle Jake might be breaking the law once more—and that Clint Barclay would enforce that law until his very last breath.

Neither did she know how deeply averse Clint Barclay was to marriage. He didn't want to marry her—he didn't want to marry anyone. He'd had plenty of chances to make a declaration of love—he'd never once said the word, or even hinted at it.

What he felt for her was lust, pure and simple. Yes, he'd been tender, he'd made her feel beautiful and desirable and as special as a rose in winter—but then he'd turned away from her, stayed away from her, and left town. Without a word.

He would never be her husband. She would never awaken by his side in the mornings, be swept away by midnight kisses, or cradle his baby in her arms.

A hollow ache more painful than anything she'd ever known began to throb deep inside her.

Good Lord. She loved him. She loved Clint Barclay.

Emily felt almost dizzy with shock at the supreme idiocy of her own foolish heart.

Somehow she managed to speak calmly, bidding good day to Nettie and Rufus Doily, despite the wrenching sadness crashing through her.

She found Pete lounging against the wagon, his hat pulled low over his eyes. Hearing her footsteps, he pushed back his hat, then his eyes narrowed as he saw her face.

"What's wrong, Em?" he demanded.

"I just want . . . to leave this town. Please, let's just go home."

"Okay, Sis. Calm down." He set her parcels in the wagon, helped her onto the seat, then sprang up beside her.

"You want to tell me what's eating you?" he asked quietly, studying her with worried eyes.

"I'm anxious to get started on supper. And . . . there's a letter here—it's from Lissa. I need to tell Joey about it."

"That's it?"

"That's it." If there were one thing in the world Emily knew she couldn't explain to Pete, it was her feelings for Clint Barclay.

She threw one last, fleeting look at the closed-up jailhouse across the street from the hotel and wished she could as easily lock, shutter, and close her heart.

Chapter 18

EMILY KNELT BESIDE THE TALL COTtonwood tree as the school bell rang and straightened the collar of Joey's freshly washed plaid shirt. "Don't forget that you're going home with Bobby after school today to see his new kittens," she reminded him as he started to pull away to join the other children streaming into the schoolhouse.

"And Mrs. Smith asked if you wanted to stay to supper. Her husband offered to bring you back home afterward, if you'd like."

Joey's eyes sparkled. "Yes, please! I want to play with the kittens as long as I can. Bobby said that the littlest one has a stripe down its back!"

"Remember to be gentle with them." Emily gave the boy a hug. "And don't forget to thank Mrs. Smith for supper."

"When I come home, you'll help me get ready for the spelling bee, won't you, Em-ly?"

"You can be sure I will," she assured him. "Go on with you now, you don't want Miss Crayden to mark you tardy."

"I sure don't!"

He gave her one last squeeze and wheeled away, trotting for the schoolhouse door. But he stopped just as suddenly and spun around. "How many days till Mama comes?"

"Nine more days, Joey."

He grinned so widely it appeared his small face would crack. "Whoopee! Bye, Em-ly!"

She watched as he dashed inside just as Miss Crayden was about to close the door. Emily smiled after him before turning the wagon toward home, filled with gratitude at the way Joey had blossomed over the past weeks. He certainly loved Forlorn Valley—especially the Smith children, as well as his other friends at school, and the little cabin on Teacup Ranch. And ever since she'd shown him Lissa's letter and explained that his mother was coming for him, the last sign of his former burdens had seemed to lift from his shoulders.

All had been quiet this past week since she'd received Lissa's letter. Uncle Jake and Lester had nearly finished the repairs to the barn and Pete had been out line riding every day. Margaret Smith had stopped by one afternoon with some muslin for a new Sunday dress, and she'd brought news from town.

Her husband's parents, Bessie and Hamilton Smith, attending a banking convention, were still in Denver, as were the Mangleys for their dinner with the governor, but they were all expected to return on Tuesday. The blacksmith's wife was expecting her fourth child any day now, and Rufus Doily had fallen off a ladder and been stitched up by Doc Calvin.

And oh, yes, Sheriff Barclay hadn't returned from Denver yet either, Margaret reported casually, her gaze searching Emily's as she relayed this news, then she cleared her throat and stood up tactfully to leave.

He can stay in Denver forever as far as I'm concerned, Emily thought that Monday morning as the horse plodded back toward the ranch. She didn't know how she would handle seeing Clint again, how she would manage to pretend he was unimportant to her when she encountered him on the boardwalk or in the mercantile. But she couldn't bear the thought of him knowing her true feelings, of knowing how he'd hurt her by leaving town without a word. The Spoons had never had much in the world, but they had their tempers and their pride.

She was determined to keep mastery of both—even if it killed her.

Deep in thought, she drove toward home—until a sudden flash of movement through the trees caught her attention. Glancing quickly in that direction, she saw a man riding a gray horse across a gully, headed toward the foothills.

The man was Uncle Jake.

Emily reined in, staring. Uncle Jake had planned to go to town today—for more lumber and nails, he'd said. But Lonesome was located in the opposite direction.

She hadn't been able to follow him the other night, but she sure could today. Emily jerked the reins, her mouth grim. She'd have to stay well enough back so he wouldn't see or hear her. She'd risk losing him, but she'd try to track his horse's hoofprints if need be. Fixing her gaze on the burly rider galloping fast toward some unknown destination, she turned the mare off the trail.

She didn't know how long she followed Jake. The sun beat down, the hot, windswept air felt heavy as a blanket, and the ground grew steeper, more rocky and treacherous. So far she had managed to keep her uncle in sight, but as the trail became more winding and steep, it became more dificult for the wagon to follow. At last she pulled the mare to a halt, jumped out, and unhitched the horse, her fingers flying. With every second that passed she feared Uncle Jake would disappear up ahead, but at last she had the horse free and she abandoned the wagon without a second thought. Standing on a rock, she managed to mount and then rode bareback, clutching the mare's mane with trembling fingers. Just as she dug in her heels to urge the horse faster, she saw a flash of Jake Spoon's blue shirt disappear at the slope of a ravine.

"Come on, Nugget," she muttered, and then she was riding hard in pursuit. Since Uncle Jake wouldn't answer her questions, she'd just have to find out what was going on for herself. She had no idea where he was going or what he was up to, but if he was planning a holdup, Emily knew one thing.

She had to stop him.

Keeping well back, she followed him down the ravine, along a narrow rock-strewn trail. Once she saw a bear lumbering across a high ridge to her left, and a hawk wheeled overhead, but she tried not to be distracted by her wild, lonely surroundings. Always she kept her eyes on her uncle's tall hunched figure in the distance, praying he wouldn't glance back and see her following him.

An hour must have passed. They were deep in the mountains. Jake had taken yet another path, one that wound upward and to the north. Emily clung to the mare's mane and followed. When he again disappeared up ahead, she swore under her breath and urged the mare faster.

By the time she reached the spot where she was certain she'd last glimpsed him, there was only empty sky above, a steep hair-raising fall into a glinting silver stream at the edge of the trail, and heaps of rocks and boulders. She paused, looking around, her stomach clenching.

Then she saw a place where the path forked—a small pathway that appeared to squeeze between two rocks. She studied it a moment, then heard the sound of a horse whinnying.

Another horse replied.

Both sounds had come from the direction of that side path.

Her throat dry as sand, Emily turned her mare onto the path and rode slowly, cautiously forward between towering rocks, her ears straining for the slightest sound.

It wasn't long before she realized that she'd entered a narrow pass through the mountains, a pass invisible from both above and below. Faintly, up ahead, she heard men's voices.

She slipped off her mare at a small dip in the path and left her to graze in a patch of grass hidden behind some rocks. Warily she crept forward, taking care to make no sound.

When she finally saw Uncle Jake, he was in a flat clearing thirty yards ahead. And he wasn't alone, she realized, her heart starting to thud. She pressed herself up against the rocks beside her and took a deep steadying breath.

There were two other men in the clearing with him, and all three of their horses. She didn't recognize the first man. He was big as a bear, wearing buckskins and cracked boots, his shaggy black hair and beard half hiding a cruel, swarthy face.

The other man, the one standing beside the horses, taking a long deep drink from a leather flask, she did recognize.

It was Slim Jenks.

The bottom seemed to drop out from her stomach. Emily sagged against the rock wall and tried to squeeze herself between the cracks, slightly around the corner, so that the men couldn't see her from the clearing. She stood perfectly still, frozen with fear and dismay, as she heard the rumble of their voices.

"So the stage should reach Boulder Point by . . ." Jenks's voice was blown away by a sudden gust of wind rushing through the pass.

"Your boys clear on what they have to do?" The man with the black beard strode toward Uncle Jake. Though her uncle was tall, this man with his huge hulking shoulders and great height and bulk nearly dwarfed him. "Make sure those two women get shot first, shot dead—then kill everyone else. They all have to be done breathin', including the driver, before you and Jenks and those boys start helping yourselves to the loot."

Slim Jenks eyed her uncle, the flask still in his hand. "There can't be any witnesses left alive, you got that, Spoon? Not a single one."

"I'm not stupid, Jenks, and neither are Lester and Pete." Irritated, Uncle Jake wheeled away from the cowboy and addressed the black-bearded man. "We've robbed enough stages, Ratlin, to know how to pull this off. Isn't that why you wanted me and my boys in the first place?"

"But you never killed anyone before, did you, Spoon?" Jenks persisted. He stuffed the flask in his pocket and stalked up to the older man.

"Happens I shot a man once after he pulled a gun on me. But I never killed no women," Jake growled, meeting the cowboy's contemptuous gaze. He shrugged. "For a nice pile of money, I reckon it'll be easy enough."

Jenks gave a hard laugh.

"Just remember, none of us get paid, not one red cent, if those Mangley women don't die," Ratlin growled. "That's the whole purpose of—"

The wind swept through then, wiping out his words. Emily hugged the rock, horror crawling over her.

The two Mangley women. Carla and Agnes. She felt as if she were slipping, slipping into a faint, and she dug her fingers into the hard, rough surface of the boulder, trying to hang on, not to faint, to listen, to think . . .

But grief was washing over her. Uncle Jake, who had taken her in, given her piggyback rides, taught her to fish, was planning to murder a stagecoach full of people—and so were Pete and Lester.

Pete would never murder anyone, she thought frantically. And Lester . . . dear Lord, Lester had bought Carla's box lunch. The girl was half in love with him!

No, no, a part of her whispered desperately, *it can't be true.*

But she had heard it with her own ears.

"We get to keep whatever we take off the passengers, right? Plus the thousand dollars apiece Mangley's paying?" Uncle Jake fixed Ratlin with a piercing glance.

Bile rose in Emily's throat. *Mangley? Frank Mangley? Carla's uncle?*

"Whatever you grab off of them is yours." Ratlin nodded. "You and your boys and Jenks can split it all. But don't stick around too long counting it," he warned, "because once Barclay comes after you, you're dead unless you . . ."

He turned away, toward the horses and she couldn't hear his next words. But she'd heard enough. Revulsion and a sick panic filled her.

She started back up the path, her only thought to return home and wait for Uncle Jake, to confront him there. She didn't care what she had to do, she would talk him out of this terrible deed. She would stop him somehow. And then she'd deal with Pete and Lester.

Pain choked her, and she bit back sobs. She'd been living among strangers. How could they? How could they have promised her they'd go straight and all the while they were planning to murder a stagecoach full of people—including women from their own town.

The pain in her chest tightened as another thought came. The Smiths would most likely be on that stagecoach too. She thought of Bessie and Hamilton—Clint's friends—and Joey. He was to have supper this very night with Bobby Smith, Bessie and Ham's grandson . . .

"You headed to Denver straight from here?" Ratlin's voice drifted to her once again, and she froze.

"Yep."

"What about that niece of yours?"

"Going to tell her we've got cattle business down in . . ." The wind snatched his words away, then a few more reached her. ". . . Pete and Lester will be there by tonight . . . we'll plan on meeting up with you and Jenks at the Oakey Saloon . . ."

Tonight. Emily nearly gasped. She had to speak to Uncle Jake now, today. She had to stop him. And what about Pete and Lester . . . what if she missed them, or what if they wouldn't listen to her?

They'd been lying all along—how could she believe they would really ride to Denver and call off the holdup instead of carrying through with it?

How can I take that chance?

She knew the answer. She couldn't.

Clint. I have to get word to Clint.

Lives were in danger. She had to stop the holdup no matter what.

No matter what . . .

Emily wanted to weep, but she had to get away first, she had to think how best to stop the horrible plan that was about to be put into motion. Nothing else mattered now, she told herself as she clung to the feeble remnants of her self-control.

She had to get out of there.

But suddenly she heard someone riding behind her, coming from the clearing, and she scrambled around the rocks, trying to squeeze herself between those that flanked the path. There was a thin opening; she pushed herself into the crevice as far as she could, holding her breath as a rider thundered past.

It was Uncle Jake. Alone. He galloped by in a blur, but not before she saw the harsh set of his face and was nearly overcome by the nightmarish sensation that she was looking at a stranger. Gritty dust flew behind his horse's hooves, and she choked back a cough.

Get out of here, a voice inside her head ordered. *Now.*

She wriggled free of the crevice, but somehow, in extricating herself, she wedged a stone loose and it rattled onto the path.

The sound seemed to echo through the rock.

"What's that?" she heard Jenks ask from the clearing.

Ratlin grunted. "Find out."

For one horrid moment she hesitated, caught between trying to hide and trying to run.

They'd see her on the path if she ran . . . she'd never make it to her horse.

She squirmed back into the crevice again, wedging herself between the rocks as far as she could. All around her the granite boulders dug into her flesh and she bit back a whimper of pain. She longed to reach into her pocket for her derringer, but there was no room to maneuver. She ducked her head and held her breath as Slim Jenks appeared, moving cautiously along the trail. He halted less than two feet from her, glancing this way and that.

Emily held her breath.

Jenks walked a few more feet, following the dust Uncle Jake's gelding had kicked up. For a moment he disappeared along the trail, but she knew he would be back and she forced herself to stay where she was, perfectly still, as if she were one with the very rocks enclosing her.

Her heart was hammering so wildly she was certain he would hear it. Almost it drowned out the sound of his footsteps approaching, his boots scuffling on the rocky trail. "Must've just been . . ."

He broke off, and Emily went cold. She heard him take a step, then another.

"Well, lookee here."

Suddenly strong hands grabbed her, and she was yanked so roughly from the crevice that the surface of the rocks scraped her shoulders. Jenks pinned her against the boulder, his fingers digging into her arms.

"What the hell you doing here? That uncle of yours send you here to spy?"

"No! Of course not! Take your filthy hands off me!"

Jenks's face was dark with anger and suspicion.

"You're lying. You're either spying for your uncle, or for that damned sheriff. Guess I'm going to have to find out which."

He struck her across the face and Emily fell back, pain crashing through her jaw.

"We got trouble, Ratlin!" Jenks yelled. "Spoon's damned niece!"

He seized Emily and began dragging her toward the clearing.

Dazed, Emily could do little to resist, and she found herself suddenly flung before the shaggy-haired giant.

"Hell and damnation." Ratlin's eyes held a hard, cold gleam. "How the hell did you get here, girl?"

Red pinpricks of light still danced before her eyes. She still felt dizzy from the blow, but she tried to speak clearly. "If you know what's good for you, you'll let me go."

"How much did that uncle of yours tell you? I should've known that lousy old coot wouldn't know how to keep his damned trap shut!"

"He didn't . . . he doesn't even know I'm here . . . I just . . ."

"Just what?"

"Followed him. I wondered . . . where he was going . . . he was supposed to be in town and . . ."

Ratlin snatched up a handful of her hair. "You're the one Jenks says is friendly with that sheriff," he spat out. "Is that right?"

"No, I . . . I hate Sheriff Barclay. I don't have any use for lawmen, and . . . least of all Clint Barclay."

"He stepped in one day when she and I were getting acquainted," Jenks sneered. "That was before I knew the Spoons were our pards for this job. And he bought her box lunch at the town social. Paid twenty-five dollars for it."

"Ain't that sweet." Sarcasm dripped from Ratlin's voice, along with an edge of something sinister that sent a tremor through her.

"How much did you hear?" he demanded.

"N-nothing. I'd just got here and my uncle rode past without seeing me. I thought he'd be angry, so I hid behind the rocks. Why was he meeting you?"

She tried to look guileless and confused, but Ratlin's hooded eyes stared at her so raptly she felt he could see through to her skull. For one fleeting moment, Emily prayed he would believe her, but all hope was dashed when Jenks exploded beside her.

"The damned bitch is lying, Ratlin. I'll bet a hundred bucks she heard the whole thing."

As Ratlin's eyes remained on her, a flash of calculation entering them, icy fear descended on Emily. "I reckon you're right," he said thoughtfully. "Either way, we can't take any chances."

Suddenly his thick fingers twisted painfully in her hair, jerking her closer. "I don't know what you're up to, but you made a big mistake coming here, Miss Spoon. I don't like mistakes. Almost as much as I don't like nosy women."

Emily couldn't help the cry of pain and terror that sprang from her lips. Desperately she tried to pry herself free of him, but he swiftly released her hair and seized her arms, hauling her up against the stinking filth of his buckskin jacket as he barked out orders to Jenks.

"Get a rope. We'll tie her up good and tight. I know exactly where to take her until this whole thing is over."

"No!" Panic-stricken, Emily fought against him. "My uncle and Pete and Lester will kill you if you don't let me go right now!" She tried to fumble in her pocket for her derringer, but Ratlin wrestled the weapon away from her and easily pinioned both of her wrists in one of his huge hands.

As Emily kicked uselessly at him, he just grinned coldly down at her. "We'll see about that," he sneered. He glanced at Jenks and barked, "Hurry up with that rope—we have to hide her someplace where the Spoons won't find her."

"She's right, you know." Jenks frowned as he dug a rope from his saddlebag. "They won't like it. Not that I give a damn much what they like or don't like," he growled.

"First off, we don't have to tell them we've got her—not unless something comes up and we need to keep them in line. Say they want more money once the job is done, or they try to double-cross you and take all the loot from the stage." Ratlin suddenly spun Emily around, twisting her arm behind her back. He chuckled as she cried out. "This here gal's our ace. The Spoons kick up any trouble, or don't do exactly as they're told, we just let them know we've got their precious little gal."

Jenks's eyes shone as he advanced on Emily, swinging the rope in one hand. "But say the Spoons don't try anything and the job goes off without a hitch—do we just let her go? What's to keep her from running straight to Barclay?"

"Don't worry about that," Ratlin said almost pleasantly as Jenks bound her wrists before her. He studied the knot Jenks had made, then reached down and tightened it with a cruel yank that made Emily gasp in pain.

"I know for a fact, little lady, that you won't say a word to the sheriff. Because I'm going to see to it—once our little job is done—that you don't ever get the chance."

Chapter 19

EMILY LOST TRACK OF HOW LONG they rode. Through the pass, up to the rim of the ravine, across a winding trail that dipped and rose precipitously, always in the red rock shadow of the mountains.

Her wrists burned as the rope chafed her skin mercilessly and the sun beat down upon her from a peaceful blue sky as Ratlin led her mare in silence and Jenks followed.

Jenks had searched back along the pass until he'd found her grazing mount. The two men had cleaned up the small camp they'd made in the clearing and headed out quickly, smoothly, so efficiently that Emily had the impression that Ratlin and Jenks had worked together before.

But how Uncle Jake and Pete and Lester had fallen in with them, she had no idea. All she knew was that those dearest to her in the world were planning a crime so hideous she could barely comprehend it.

And there was no way to stop it. Not unless she could escape. Even then, every hour that passed would make it that much more difficult to prevent the holdup. Clint was in Denver somewhere, Uncle Jake and Pete and Lester were on their way to some rendezvous there, and she had no idea where precisely the holdup and murder were going to take place.

Despair pierced her heart. It was all she could do to choke back tears. Tears wouldn't help her now.

She needed to stay calm, to stay alert for any mistakes from the men who held her—and to be ready to run if she had the chance.

Thank God Joey was going to the Smiths for supper and wouldn't be coming home after school to an empty cabin. But what would happen when he did come home? From what she'd heard, it sounded as if Uncle Jake and Pete and Lester were all leaving for the rendezvous—the Smiths would eventually bring Joey home, and he'd find no one there to greet him but a vacant cabin.

Helplessness twisted through her.

If she didn't get away and get word to Clint or someone in Denver about the holdup, everyone on the stagecoach returning to Lonesome would die.

And so will you, she thought. She had no illusions about what Ratlin had decided to do. She'd heard the hard truth in his voice. He would kill her the moment he no longer needed her as a possible trump card against the Spoons—the moment the holdup was completed and he knew the job was done exactly as he wanted it done.

No matter what it took, she had to find a way to escape.

Reaching the rim of the mountain, the horses widened their strides, heading across fairly level ground at a good gallop, winding their way through fragrant stands of pine. It was cooler up here and the sun was blocked by the trees. Emily tried to assess her surroundings, but she no longer had any idea where she was.

They halted once to rest and eat jerky and hardtack,

then continued on as the sun slid toward the west and thin low clouds rolled in.

It was hours later when they at last came to a halt and made camp in a shady clearing. Beyond some trees, a clear stream hurtled down the mountainside into a steep canyon full of brush and rock.

"Bet you're ready for some grub," Ratlin remarked as he yanked her down from the saddle and pushed her toward a tree.

"I'm not hungry." Every bone in Emily's body throbbed, and her throat was so parched it ached. But the thought of food made nausea bubble in her stomach. "Could you please . . . untie my hands—just for a while? I can barely feel my fingers, and I . . . I need a few moments of privacy," she murmured. She hated to beg this man, but she'd try anything that might help her get away.

"Please," she added softly, trying to sound piteous.

She thought he'd refuse, but after a slight hesitation he made a grunting noise and set to work at the knot. He ordered her to remove her boots, then told her grudgingly she could venture into the woods, but not for long.

"You'd have to be a damned fool to try to run off barefoot in these parts—your feet would be bloody stumps before you'd get twenty yards. And if you don't come back right quick, I'm coming in to look for you—and I'll drag you back by the hair," Ratlin warned.

Emily knew he meant what he said. And she also knew that it would be impossible to escape him and Jenks here in the mountains, without her boots, without a horse. She'd have to wait and watch for another opportunity, a chance to catch them off guard.

When she returned, she asked him to leave her hands free a while longer, claiming her wrists were painfully sore, but Ratlin apparently decided he'd been generous enough, and promptly tied her wrists again, doubling the knot.

"We don't have time to keep an eye on you, missy, and we can't take a chance you'll find a way to shoot us or take one of the horses. You'll just have to bear it."

He pushed her down onto the grass beneath a tree and ordered her to stay put. Then he set about starting a campfire, while Jenks tended to the horses and fetched water from the stream.

Neither men spoke over their supper of jerky and beans. Emily noticed that Jenks drank greedily from his flask. She knew she should try to eat something, to keep her strength up, but she couldn't. She did drink water when Jenks offered it to her, and after he'd repacked his canteen, she was surprised when he returned to sprawl out on the grass beside her.

"I don't suppose you'd be willing to loosen the rope a little." Much as it galled her, she forced herself to gaze pleadingly into his face. "Please. My hands are almost numb."

Jenks frowned and took another swallow from the flask he dug out of his pocket. He threw a quick look over his shoulder.

Ratlin had disappeared into the trees that led toward the stream.

"Lemme see," Jenks grunted.

She flinched as his hands touched her, but he loosened the knot slightly, though it still dug into her flesh. Then his gaze ran over her, lingering on her pale face, dropping down to the outline of her breasts beneath her wrinkled yellow shirtwaist. He took another swig of liquor. "A shame you came up to Cougar Pass the way you did," he muttered. "A real shame."

"I wish I hadn't," Emily said.

He grinned. "Bet you do. And you know what, it's an even bigger shame that you took up with that sheriff. This didn't have to happen, none of it."

Emily watched him gulp down another swig from the flask. She flexed her wrists—the rope was still tight, but it did give a bit. What she really needed was a sharp rock or a stick.

"I didn't take up with Barclay. I hate him. He arrested my brother—for fighting with you."

Jenks gave a snort. "Yeah, he did. But only because my pards backed me up when I said Pete started it." He stuffed the flask back in his pocket and from his other pocket dug out a misshapen block of wood. Then he pulled his knife from its sheath.

Emily went very still, hardly daring to breathe as he began whittling at the wood, pursing his lips as he worked.

"That's something I don't understand," she told Jenks, trying to appear casual as she watched the glittering blade of the knife. "Pete told me he got arrested after you picked a fight with him."

"So?"

"Why did you fight with him—I mean, if you knew each other and were working together . . ."

"So you did hear us back there in the pass," Jenks said sharply. His eyes glittered as brightly as the blade of the knife.

Emily moistened her lips and nodded. "I heard enough to know that you're all planning a holdup," she acknowledged.

"Yep, I knew it." His lips twisted into a triumphant smile. "Well, the fact is, little Miz Emily, neither of us had any notion we'd be working together back then. I sure as hell didn't. All I knew was that Ratlin was on his way to town—that we were going to pull a big job . . ." He broke off suddenly and scowled. "But I didn't have any notion the Spoons were going to be in on it. Ratlin was the one who brought them in, seeing as he met your uncle when they were both in prison."

Pain squeezed around her heart.

"So," she continued doggedly, keeping her voice even, "you just happened to have a fight with Pete that night?"

"Damn straight. He stuck his nose in between me and Florry." Anger mottled Jenks's face. He suddenly stuck the knife into the grass beside him and tugged out the flask again. "He didn't have no call to do that. I had to keep her quiet, keep her in line, because she found out a few things." He took a quick gulp from the flask. "Things she shouldn't have—about this job. So I pushed her around a little, to make sure she knew what would happen if she blabbed. It wasn't nobody's business. But your brother didn't see it that way."

Once again Jenks raised the flask to his lips, this time draining every last drop of it. "So I had to pay him back—and that's where you came in." He studied her appraisingly, insolently, with a drunken gleam in his eyes that made Emily's stomach lurch. "That day I took you into the alley. And when I saw you at the dance. Remember? And then I bid on your box lunch at the social."

As if she could forget. Emily nodded, saying nothing.

She forced herself to sit perfectly still, as Jenks licked his lips. "I just wanted to get back at ol' Pete. Make him mad. You sure were pretty. And," he added, his eyes skimming over her again, "I had a hankering for a taste of you. So I figured, why not? Figured you'd go running and crying to your brother, and he'd learn what happens when someone gets on my bad side. I always pay back my debts."

"Then you must've been disappointed." The words spilled out more sharply than she'd intended and she quickly softened her tone. "I mean—I never told him."

"Then I reckon you weren't as against the idea as you acted. Maybe you really wanted it all along," Jenks said slyly.

"No!" The word flew from her mouth before she could stop it, and she cursed silently. She took a breath as Jenks's eyes narrowed on her. The knife was still stuck in the grass, only a foot or two away. "I mean . . . I didn't want him to end up in another fight with you. That's all. I didn't want there to be any more trouble."

He laughed then, an ugly sound, at odds with the beauty of the sky as the sun sank in a sea of rose and lavender and gold.

"Oh, there's going to be trouble, all right, Miz Spoon. When all those nice folks on the stage from Denver get held up. That Sheriff Barclay, he's a dangerous man. And he's going to come after your kin. Course, Ratlin cooked up a story—some men in a Denver saloon are going to swear your uncle and the Spoon boys were there the whole time when the stage was being held up. But with Barclay, you never know. Now me—he doesn't know me as anyone other than Slim Jenks, hired hand on the WW Ranch. He'll never even look my way. But the Spoons—they're going to have to be real careful."

Her throat tight, Emily spoke in a low tone, but she couldn't keep a throb out of her voice. "Why does everyone on that stagecoach have to die? Robbery is one thing, but killing—"

"So you did hear all of it, not just about the holdup." Jenks inched closer to her and clamped a hand on her knee. "I knew you were lying," he said triumphantly.

It didn't matter anymore. They were going to kill her

anyway. But Emily suddenly had to know. "You're planning to kill Carla and Agnes Mangley—and all the others on the stage. Yes, I heard. But I don't know why."

"No reason you need to."

His hand slid up her knee, moving along her thigh. Emily tried to flinch away, but he grabbed her by the shoulders and pulled her toward him. "What's the matter, Miz Emily? We've been having us a nice little chat. Now you're turning shy and innocent on me, all of a sudden?"

"No . . . I'm . . . I'm thirsty . . ." She tried not to let her gaze slide to the knife. If she could only get him to walk away, to get his canteen, giving her a chance to get hold of that knife . . .

"Could I have some more water . . . please?" she asked in a rush.

"*Please*. I like that." Jenks beamed. "Maybe," he added, with a slow nod. "Maybe I'll get you some . . . after a while, when we've finished . . . chattin' . . ."

He suddenly yanked her closer and with a chuckle deep in his throat he squashed his lips to hers. Emily lifted her bound hands and tried to push him away, but he only gripped her tighter, his fingers pressing painfully into her shoulders and his mouth sucking at hers. Desperately she bit him, and he swore, but as he drew back he only laughed at her.

"Wild little thing, ain't you? That don't bother me, honey. Because you taste so good. Sweet and hot, just like I knew you would—"

"Get away from me!"

"Like hell. You didn't fight off Barclay, I'll bet. No reason you should fight me. Unless you think I'm not as good as him. You white trash slut, you think you're better than me—"

"Get away from me! Stop!" Emily gasped as he pushed her down on the grass and straddled her. A sharp stone beneath her dug into the small of her back as Jenks lowered himself onto her. "Get—off—"

She broke off as suddenly Ratlin loomed over Jenks and hauled him clear to his feet.

"What the hell are you doing, Jenks?" Ratlin's dark-bearded face was suffused with fury.

"Havin' a little fun, Ratlin. So what? It's got nothing to do with you!"

"We've got a job tomorrow—the biggest job we ever pulled." Ratlin shoved him back a pace, away from Emily. "We've got to pay attention. We've got to be ready."

"That don't mean I can't have myself a little fun tonight." Jenks's gaze slid toward the woman lying on the grass, her face streaked with sweat and dust, her breath coming in shallow gasps.

"She's asking for it," he muttered.

Her skin crawled as he edged closer to her. She struggled to sit up.

"After the job is done—before we kill her," Ratlin was saying calmly, his voice a deep steady growl, "you can do whatever the hell you want with her, Jenks. But not now. No more damned liquor tonight and no women. That stage is going to roll past Boulder Point at ten in the morning. We've got one chance and only one—there can't be any mistakes."

A muscle twitched in Jenks's jaw as he stared down at the dark-haired girl seated upon the grass. "Yeah," he said at last, reluctantly. "All right, Ratlin. You win. Hear that, honey? It's going to be you and me— after the job."

"My family will come after you." Emily glared up at

them both, her eyes shimmering with rage and hatred. "They'll kill you if you touch me. You don't want Jake, Pete, and Lester Spoon for your enemies."

"They'll never know." Ratlin shrugged. "We can fix it so they never find your body." As a shudder ran through her, he sighed. "None of this would've happened if you hadn't shown up where you didn't belong. It's your own fault."

As his calm words and chilling indifference sank in, the sun slipped below the flaming horizon. A cold wind suddenly whisked through the clearing, sending Emily's hair fluttering. She felt icy despair pierce the center of her soul.

Jenks stepped forward and stood over her, a smile playing at the corners of his lips. "But don't think about that part, honey," he said softly. "Not yet. We're going to have us some fun first. After the job's done, I'm going to feel like celebrating. You just think about *that*."

I'll think about it, all right. I'll die fighting you, Emily thought.

The moment they walked away toward their horses, she began edging her body along the ground, toward the knife. But suddenly Jenks swung around. He stalked back toward her and, reaching down, grabbed the knife from the dirt.

"Forgot something." A nasty grin split his face as he sheathed the blade. "You weren't planning to steal my knife now, were you, honey?"

"Not unless I could stick it through your heart," Emily said through clenched teeth.

He laughed, picked up his block of wood, and sauntered away once more.

Emily sat perfectly still a moment longer and then, very slowly, as the men busied themselves checking their ammunition, she inched along the grass once more. She scanned the place where Jenks had pushed her down on the ground—and then she saw it: the small sharp stone that had been digging into her back.

She crawled forward two more steps on her knees and then she had it, clutched tight in her hands.

Not as good as the knife, but it was all she had.

Gritting her teeth, she began scraping the edge of the stone across the rope—back and forth, back and forth.

Again and again. And again . . .

Chapter 20

THE NINE O'CLOCK STAGE RUMBLED out of Denver at precisely two minutes past nine the next morning. The interior of the coach was crowded, as Bessie and Hamilton Smith found themselves wedged alongside a portly hardware salesman from Iowa. Across the aisle, Agnes Mangley and her daughter, Carla, were squashed at close quarters with a loud-voiced man named Simon Sylvester who was seeking investors for a traveling theater troupe.

Agnes Mangley and Bessie Smith chattered at length with one another as the coach jolted along the steep, rutted road. Agnes wished to detail all the attentions the governor had so kindly paid to her and Carla, and Bessie was full of pride and pleasure because the dress Miss Spoon had sewn for her to wear at Ham's banking convention had drawn innumerable compliments all through the evening.

But all conversation ceased when, only an hour into the journey, the sounds of horses' hooves thundered down upon them.

Glancing out the window, the startled passengers saw

a group of men galloping down from the rocky slopes to surround them, and Agnes Mangley let out a piercing scream.

"Outlaws! May the angels preserve us, we're being held up! Shoot them—somebody shoot them!"

Ham grimly tugged a gun from a holster beneath his jacket as Bessie went pale and the other two gentlemen in the coach froze in consternation.

"Mama," Carla Mangley exclaimed in a stunned tone, "be still. They're not outlaws. They're not wearing masks and . . . that looks to me like Sheriff Barclay!"

"What's that?" Agnes shrieked. "Sheriff Barclay?"

Just then there was a shout.

"Driver—hold your fire. Stop in the name of the law!"

Agnes thrust her nose up against the window, peering out as the coach rumbled to a creaking halt. To her astonishment, Sheriff Clint Barclay, dressed all in black, his sheriff's badge glinting in the sunlight, rode right up to the driver's side of the coach.

"What in hell is going on?" Ham Smith muttered as the driver clambered down.

A moment later, Clint swung the door open.

"Sorry to interrupt your journey, folks, but we need everyone to step outside right now."

"Clint, what in damnation is going on?" Ham demanded. "Who are these men? What are you doing?"

"I can scarcely believe it—our own sheriff is waylaying our stage!" Agnes cried.

Clint tipped his hat to her. "Sorry, ma'am, but there's no time to explain. We've got a buggy hidden behind the rocks for the ladies and some extra horses for the men. Deputy Stills will accompany you back to Denver. Do what he says and wait for us there."

"Us?" The salesman for the theater troupe stared at him, bug-eyed. "Who's *us*?"

"Federal Marshal Hoot McClain—and me. We need this stagecoach." Clint's eyes grew hard and flat as he held out an arm to help Bessie Smith as she descended the steps. The driver had already jumped down and was speaking to the marshal and the lanky pale-haired deputy on horseback.

"Come on, folks, there's no time to waste," Clint said as first the hardware salesman clambered out and then Ham followed, staring at him in amazement. "Everybody out—now."

"Well! I never!" Agnes declared as she teetered out of her seat.

"I'm sure Sheriff Barclay knows what he's doing, Mama," Carla said softly.

"Thanks, Carla." Clint nodded at her as he helped her out of the stage.

One by one the passengers found their way to the buggy and the horses the lawmen had provided for their use.

The driver clambered back up onto the seat and Hoot McClain and Clint Barclay turned over their mounts to the deputy, then entered the stagecoach.

"Go ahead," Marshal McClain called to the driver, settling back into the seat vacated by the previous passengers. "Just follow your regular route. Don't do anything out of the ordinary."

"And hold your fire," Clint ordered him. "Leave whatever shooting is necessary to us."

"Anything you say, Sheriff," the driver called down.

He flicked his whip over the horses' backs and the stagecoach rolled forward.

"So far, so good," the silver-haired McClain muttered, ꞏretching out his bowed legs.

Clint stared out the window, every muscle in his body ꞏense as the stagecoach headed on toward Lonesome—and straight toward Boulder Point.

Chapter 21

HIGH ON THE HILL CALLED BOULDER Point, four men waited on horseback. From their vantage point they could see the trail from Denver for miles and they saw the dust cloud that told them the morning stage was on its way.

"Everyone ready?" Jake Spoon asked grimly.

Slim Jenks gave a curt nod as he continued squinting down the road. "We'd best wait till they're about two hundred feet back—right when they round those rocks," he said.

"We know what we're doing, Jenks." Pete Spoon's eyes gleamed beneath his slouch hat. "We've had a lot more practice at holding up stages than you."

"Yeah, well, me and Ratlin have had a lot more practice killing folks than you," the other man retorted. "And today, I'm in charge of that. Once everyone gets out of the stage, I'll shoot the Mangley women first—then you plug the driver. After that, everyone else is fair game."

"Happy hunting," Lester muttered, checking his gun and sliding it back into the holster.

Jenks chuckled, a harsh sound in the clear, dry air. "It always is, boy."

I still don't like Ratlin not showing up." Jake's fierce ws drew together and he fixed Jenks with a penetrat- g stare. "It was supposed to be all five of us."

"I told you—something came up." Jenks didn't add that vhat had come up was Jake's own niece, sticking her pretty ittle nose where it didn't belong. The damned girl had sawed her bonds free in the middle of the night and tried to run off with Ratlin's own horse. Ratlin hadn't wanted to take any chances leaving her alone after that. They were too close to finishing the job, to getting that nice big pile of money. They couldn't risk her getting in the way.

"Ratlin'll meet us at the hideout later to turn over the cash," he told Jake. "Don't you worry about that."

"You sure he and Sleech and Frank Mangley aren't double-crossing us?" Pete's voice was hard, edged with suspicion. "If it turns out I'm risking a noose around my neck for no more'n a sack of dirt, I'm going to be mighty riled."

"No need for anyone to get riled, Spoon." Jenks spat out a plug of tobacco, then leaned casually back in the saddle. "Me and Sleech and Ratlin go way back. No one's double-crossing anyone. Ratlin just had something he had to take care of this morning." He gave a small half-smile, as if he'd said something amusing. "But you can damn well believe he's taking care of business."

"And our alibis—they're all set?" Lester asked.

"Sleech and Mangley took care of that part. There'll be at least five men in the Oakey Saloon in Denver who'll swear you three were there during the time of the holdup. And Florry Brown's going to swear I got hung over and was up in her room sleeping it off all through the night and halfway through today. The WW will fire me for sure, but the law won't be able to pin a damn thing on any of us."

"Especially with no witnesses—not live ones, way," Jake said.

"Ain't it the truth?" A wide grin split Jenks's face.

"Here they come." Pete pointed down to the trail, a they all stared at the stage, a tiny box in the distance as rattled around a curve far below. Moving as one, all fou men lifted the reins of their horses and started down the hill.

They waited until the stagecoach came thundering around the last curve before Boulder Point to spur their horses to a gallop, then they dug in their heels and headed straight toward the rumbling coach.

Jenks, Pete, and Lester fired into the air. "Throw down your guns!" Jenks shouted to the driver. As the stagecoach came to a shuddering halt, the four riders surrounded it, their guns drawn.

"Everyone out!" Slim Jenks bellowed, and the next moment the doors to the stagecoach opened.

But instead of a parcel of terrified passengers clambering out, two men leaped out with guns in each hand and spun toward the outlaws.

"Drop your gun, Jenks." Both of Clint Barclay's Colts were aimed directly at the cowboy's chest.

"What the hell! *Barclay!*"

For a moment Jenks just stared at the sheriff, dumbfounded—then he noticed the other lawman, a slim silver-haired man pointing a Navy revolver.

The blood drained from Jenks's face as he realized the lawmen were only pointing their guns at him. He glanced over at the Spoons and his eyes bulged.

All three of the Spoons were pointing their guns at him too.

Disbelief and then cold fury swept over him. "A damned setup!" he croaked.

Ve don't murder women, you bastard." Jake Spoon's e was as hard and cold as mountain ice. "Throw vn your gun, it's all over—"

Rage and panic took over, blocking out all rational ought, and Jenks swung his gun toward the old outlaw, is eyes glittering with hate. "You damned double-crossing son-of-a-bitch!" he yelled, and fired.

He shot first at Jake, only narrowly missing, then swerved the gun toward Pete, but that was as far as he got before Clint Barclay fired his Colt, hitting Jenks in the shoulder. Jenks cried out, but stayed upright in the saddle and, with one swift yank, wheeled his horse around and tried to run.

Pete and Lester turned their mounts in pursuit, but suddenly Jenks fired back, hitting Lester in the chest.

Clint and Hoot McClain both fired simultaneously, and this time the outlaw toppled off his horse.

As he hit the ground, Pete was already leaping from his saddle and he reached Jenks a moment later. He kicked the gun from Jenks's hand as Clint and Hoot McClain reached the fallen man.

"Where's Ratlin?" Clint demanded.

Bleeding, clutching his wounded shoulder, Jenks glared up at him. "Go . . . to hell!"

"Why isn't Ratlin here with you?" Clint asked Pete as McClain yanked Jenks to his feet. "The plan was to catch them both in the act."

"We're damned if we know where Ratlin is." Pete's brows were knit in a frown. "He was supposed to be here— Jenks said something came up."

"Ha-ha!" His face contorted with pain, Jenks managed to let out a cruel laugh. "Something came up, all right. And you're going to be real sorry when you find out what!"

Clint's gaze narrowed on him. Something ugly knowing in Jenks's tone filled him with foreboding.

"If Lester's dead, you're the one who's going to sorry!" Pete warned, his fists clenched.

"How is he?" Clint called out, glancing back to wher Jake Spoon was kneeling in the dirt, tending to his son while the stagecoach driver looked on.

"Just a flesh wound," the old outlaw replied as he folded his neckerchief and pressed it against the bloody gash in Lester's arm. "But I reckon he needs a doctor."

"Your niece is going to need more than a doctor, Spoon!" Jenks yelled, and suddenly there was a horrible deathly silence.

Clint felt fear grab him by the throat and choke him—for a moment he could only stare in dawning rage at the wounded man before him.

"What does that mean?" Each word was like a pellet of ice.

"You heard me. The Spoon girl. She's with Ratlin. If you don't let me go, Barclay, he's going to kill her and you'll never find him—or what's left of Miz Emily Spoon neither!"

Pete dove at him then, driven by a wild boundless fury, knocking him to the ground. It took the strength of both Clint and McClain to pull him off the wounded man, but finally they shoved him back.

"Hold on!" Clint yelled at him as Pete tried to jump at Jenks again. McClain dragged the outlaw once more to his feet and planted himself in front of him.

"Listen, Spoon," Clint said desperately, "if you kill him, we won't find out what we need to know."

"He's right—the only way you'll find out is if you let me go." Breathing hard, Jenks gasped out the words. His shoulder was bleeding, his face was twisted with pain, but there was a taunting triumph in his eyes. "If you let me go, I'll make sure Ratlin sets her free, but if I'm not back there—"

"Where?" Clint grabbed his bloody shirt collar.

Jenks shook his head. "If I'm not back there in due time, Ratlin will kill her and that'll be the end. Nothing you can do—'cept let me go and—"

"I'll beat it out of him," Pete exploded. His face was ashen and rigid with anger and fear—all of the same emotions that were roiling through Clint as well. "Give me two minutes with him, Barclay," he urged, "and I'll find out where my sister is."

Clint's chest was so tight he could scarcely breathe. Emily—with Ratlin. *If Ratlin's touched a hair on her head, there'll be no place in this world he can hide.*

There's still time, he told himself. *Ratlin doesn't know yet that the Spoons set him up. There's time.*

But not much, he thought, icy fear pumping through him.

"There's not going to be any beating," Hoot McClain said sternly, in his gravelly voice. "We'll take him back to Denver and question him and—"

"By then it'll be too damned late!" Jake Spoon grabbed the marshal by the shoulder and spun him around. "I've co-operated with you every step of the way, McClain—hell, I'm the one who called in the law to keep those women from getting murdered—but I'm not going to stand by and let that bastard kill my niece! You can lock me up for another twenty years if you want, but no one's leaving here unless it's to go after Emily!"

"He's right, Marshal," Lester called, dragging himself up from the ground. "We started this—and now we're going to finish it—our way!"

"The hell you are," McClain flared. "You're not in

charge here, Spoon. I'll throw you back in prison, right along with your son and your nephew, if you don't stand back and let us—"

"Forget it, Hoot."

Clint didn't even glance at the marshal. His gaze was nailed upon Slim Jenks's smirking, pain-twisted face. His voice was quiet, cold, deadly. "Jenks is mine."

"Clint—what the hell are you saying?" McClain protested. "He's probably lying about the girl anyway and—"

"He's not lying."

"You're right, Barclay." Jenks nodded, licking his lips. "I'm telling you the truth. I'm the only one who can save her. And there's not much time. So let me go and—"

"You're not going anywhere." Clint's gun was suddenly pointed at the outlaw's head. He stepped forward as the other men went still, and pushed the barrel against the wounded outlaw's temple.

"What're you doing? You can't—"

"You already admitted that she'll be dead if you don't get back there quick. So there isn't much time. If you want to live, stand trial, take your chances with a judge or prison, then you'll tell me now. But if you don't, well then, we'll just settle this once and for all. You're going to be just as dead as she is."

He jabbed the gun harder against Jenks's temple, his eyes hard as steel when the outlaw winced. "Where is she?" he asked, his voice low.

"You . . . you can't do this. McClain! Stop him!"

The marshal said nothing, only stood tight-lipped, a film of sweat sheening on his brow.

"I'm going to count to three," Clint said.

The Spoons were all silent, their eyes fixed on Jenks,

as a hawk circled overhead and only the whinny of one of the horses broke the stillness.

Jenks stared at the sheriff in disbelief.

"You're lying, Barclay. You . . . won't!"

"One. Two . . ."

"You can't—"

"Thr—"

"Bitter Rock! She's five miles west—at the top of Bitter Rock."

Clint lowered the gun. Jenks stepped back a pace, his eyes still bulging, then Pete Spoon shoved him hard to the ground.

"McClain, do whatever the hell you want with this scum. And get Lester Spoon to a doctor." Clint was already sprinting for Jenks's horse.

Jake and Pete were right behind him. "Bring her back!" Lester called.

"Don't you worry, Lester, we will," Jake bit out.

I'll bring her back, all right—no matter what it takes, Clint vowed. But terror pounded through him, a kind of terror he'd never known. The thought of Emily hurt, or frightened, at Ratlin's mercy, filled him with an agony fiercer than fire, and nothing else mattered.

Nothing other than the fact that he loved her and he'd never told her. There were a lot of things he'd never told her . . .

There'll be time, he told himself frantically as he turned the horse west. He paid no heed to Pete or Jake Spoon, riding hard behind him as they galloped away from the men and the blood and the abandoned stagecoach. He thought only of the woman with the midnight hair that felt soft as velvet in his hands, of her delicate beautiful features and those vivid silver-gray eyes. He thought of how lovingly she cared for Joey, of her loyalty to both family and friends. He thought of how she'd looked at him in the gully when he told her he didn't want any other man to buy her box lunch.

And he thought of the night he'd spent with her, of her passion, her sweetness, and her fire. But he couldn't think of that one wild beautiful night without thinking of all the other nights to come . . .

And he spurred the horse until it flew along the rocky trail toward the crest of Bitter Rock.

There'll be time—time to tell her, to hold her—to make all of this up to her, he told himself, as the horse's hooves flew and he leaned low in the saddle.

He prayed he was right.

Chapter 22

"WELL, HONEY, BY NOW IT SHOULD ALL be over and done with."

Ben Ratlin stood at the cliff's edge, surveying the gorge filled with brush and rocks, while the stream made a clattering sound as it cascaded down the steep sides. "Jenks should be back here anytime."

A leaden weight filled Emily's chest. *Over and done with*. He meant that Agnes and Carla Mangley were dead. So were the rest of the stagecoach passengers. *Bessie and Ham*. Though the morning sun glowed hot, she shivered and leaned back against the tree trunk, chilled and sick.

If only I'd gone to Clint in the first place, as soon as I began to have suspicions, she thought. *Those people would still be alive. They needn't have died . . .*

But how could she have known that Pete and Lester and Uncle Jake were all involved in something so horrible? She'd wanted to believe in them, wanted to trust them when they said they were going straight, starting over, that all they wanted was to be a family again. And even when her suspicions had sharpened—that night she'd seen Uncle Jake riding out in the dark—she'd only feared he might be planning a holdup again, a simple holdup.

That would have been bad enough. But never in her worst nightmares could she have guessed he or Pete or Lester would be mixed up in murder.

The same kind of murder that had claimed Clint Barclay's own parents, she realized, and it seemed like a knife speared straight through her heart.

"Why?" she asked dully as Ratlin turned back toward where she sat a few feet from the campfire. She watched him gulp the last of his coffee across the flames. He'd already shot and skinned a rabbit, eaten it for breakfast, and licked his fingers. Calm as you please. All while waiting for Jenks to return.

"I just don't understand why all those people had to die," she whispered.

"Money, Miz Spoon." Ratlin gave a low, rumbling laugh. "Being old Jake's niece, I'd think you'd know—money's at the core of everything. Me and Jenks and Sleech used to ride together. Different names, different times. Held up banks. A few trains. Did some gunslinging. Took in some nice bundles of money. Easy money. Till I got careless one time and ended up getting caught red-handed." His great shoulders lifted in a shrug. "Ended up in prison—that's where I met your uncle. But Jenks, he didn't get caught—and he went straight, more or less, 'cept for a little rustling on the side. He drifted, working here and there as a ranch hand." His eyes took on a sly glint. "Sleech got a job in a Leadville silver mine—ended up foreman. That mine belonged to two brothers, Richard and Frank Mangley."

Frank Mangley. Disgust broke over her as she realized the implications of his words, added to what she'd heard at Cougar Pass. "Do you mean that Frank Mangley is behind this? He . . . he wants to murder his brother's widow and daughter? Why? Because he doesn't want to share the mine with them?" she asked incredulously.

Ratlin's grin was pure evil. "That's about it, Miz Spoon. Not every family's as cozy as yours. Especially since Mangley found a new vein of silver—worth five times what the rest of it was. The widow Mangley doesn't even know anything about it—I mean, she *didn't* know anything about it. And now . . . she never will," he finished with a dry chuckle.

"You're despicable," she whispered, shaking her head. Dazed horror filled her. "And as for Mangley . . ."

Her voice trailed off. She couldn't think of anything low enough to say about Frank Mangley. Ratlin merely shrugged again and poured more coffee into his tin cup.

"Mangley's a smart man. He worked out this plan with Sleech. Sleech got word to me—knowing I was getting out soon—and to Jenks, who came to Lonesome and got himself a job as a wrangler at some ranch. I brought in your uncle—who, by the way, insisted he wouldn't do the job without his son and nephew. Yep, we put ourselves together a good bunch—all hard men, experienced. And now all that's left is to divvy up the money. And take care of you," he finished matter-of-factly.

"You don't have to kill me. I won't tell anyone—I wouldn't turn in my own family," she said. But it was a lie. Once, perhaps, it would have been the truth, but that was before . . . before the murders. She knew that changed everything, and, she feared, so did Ratlin.

The thought of turning in Jake, Pete, and Lester ripped her apart, but she'd do it if she got away. She couldn't let them go unpunished for cold-blooded murder. They might kill again . . .

A lump of grief filled her throat, so painful she could

scarcely draw breath. But Ratlin just shook his head at her, then set down his cup in the dirt.

"We can't take that chance, honey. Now can we? For all we know, you'd run straight to Clint Barclay. Jenks said you were sweet on him."

A tremor shook her. Sweet on him. "Jenks was wrong."

He cocked his head at her. "Maybe he was, maybe he wasn't. But once he gets back here, I promised him he could have some fun with you. So . . . you'll have a little more time."

Emily fought back the tears that burned behind her eyelids. She sagged back against the tree trunk, closing her eyes. She wouldn't cry. And she wouldn't give up.

The odds were that she'd never get away, never see Clint again, never have the chance to tell him she loved him or to be held once more in those strong arms. She'd never know the fire of his kisses or feel again the beating of his heart against her own.

But she was going to try.

"Could I have . . . some of that coffee?" she whispered. She was pleased by how weak her voice sounded. She made her body go limp, as if she lacked all strength. "I . . . feel . . . faint."

"Faint, huh? Better not. Jenks is gonna want you conscious—alive and kicking, as they say. He likes a woman to have a bit of fight in her," Ratlin remarked. He studied her across the flames, then suddenly reached for a tin cup in his pack.

"Just don't try nothing else. You saw last night, you can't get away. You don't want me to have to raise my fist to you again, do you?"

Emily shook her head. Last night, after she'd cut through the rope and Ratlin had caught her trying to unt his horse, he'd struck her across the face, then tied r hands again, even tighter than before. Her cheek still robbed, but if he believed that would stop her from trying to escape, so much the better.

Her heart pounded as he poured hot coffee into the cup and brought the steaming brew around the campfire to her.

Emily stayed completely still as he set the cup down on the grass and squatted before her, working at the rope.

"Thank you," she murmured. She took a moment to rub her bruised wrists before picking up the cup. Still, Ratlin knelt before her, eyeing her with cold indifference.

"Better drink up quick, because any time now Jenks is going to—argghh!"

He screamed as Emily hurled the hot coffee into his face and then before he could do more than recoil, she shoved against him with all her might. The outlaw tumbled backward, sprawling across the campfire and as flames enveloped him, he screamed in agony.

Emily was already up and running. Ratlin's horse was saddled this morning, and she tossed a foot in the stirrup and swung herself up. The outlaw had rolled from the fire, trying to smother the flames as he writhed about in the grass. She knew if he caught her he'd kill her on the spot, Jenks or no Jenks. Desperately she lifted the reins, barely glancing at him as she spurred the horse toward the trail.

She heard the thunder of hooves coming toward her even before she could see the oncoming rider. Oh, Lord—*Jenks*. Panic raced through her but she kept going, her heart in her throat. Suddenly a horse careened around a curve and loomed on the trail just before her. She screamed and tried to ride past, but the rider reacted like lightning, swerving to block her path and she saw the dark flash of a gun barrel in the sunlight.

"Emily!"

It was all she could do to stay in the saddle as C. reined in and stared at her, a blaze of relief sudder transforming his grim features. Behind him, Pete ar Jake yanked their mounts to a halt.

"Sis—you all right?" her brother demanded.

"Where's Ratlin?" Clint was asking and as her dazed gaze flew back to him, she saw the steely coldness return to his eyes.

There was no time to answer, no time to absorb the shock of seeing Clint and Pete and Uncle Jake together, riding hellbent up the trail—because at that moment shots rang out from behind and Clint charged forward toward Ratlin and the campfire, blocking her from the gunfire as he aimed and fired. Pete and Jake did the same, their mounts leaping forward, guns blazing, and she heard only the thunder of shots, one after another, echoing in deafening succession through the mountain. Gunsmoke filled her nostrils, she heard an agonized shout, and then silence.

From the brush came the chatter of a squirrel. Her horse pranced nervously, and Emily turned him in time to see both Clint and Pete dismount and stalk toward Ratlin, who lay fallen near the campfire. He'd managed to put out the flames and draw his gun . . . but he was the one who'd been shot.

He wasn't moving. His mouth was open, slack. Blood soaked the grass, not far from where Emily had been sitting only moments before.

Emily clung to Ratlin's horse, shaking, her gaze fixed on the bearlike man lying in his own blood. She watched Clint kneel beside him, heard him say something to Pete, who threw a satisfied glance at Uncle Jake, then holstered his gun. Then they both wheeled away from the dead man and walked toward her, and she couldn't do anything more than clutch the reins of Ratlin's horse in hands that felt numb.

"Emily. Are you all right?"

Clint's voice. Gentle. Quiet. Laced with something. Was it fear?

Pete was staring up at her. "Sis. It's over . . ."

"Jenks" was all she could mumble, thinking blindly that she had to warn them. Jenks was coming back . . .

"He's in custody," Clint said. He reached up for her, grasped her gently, slid her down from the horse. "It's over, Emily. It's all over."

She sagged against him, her knees buckling, as weakness and shock took their toll. She felt too dazed to understand what had happened; she only knew that his arms felt safe and strong, so strong as they closed around her.

"The stagecoach," she whispered. "The passengers . . . you don't know . . ."

"I know. I know all of it. Everyone's safe. Thanks to your brother and your uncle here, and to Lester."

At his words, another shock jolted through her. Uncomprehending, she gazed from him to Pete to Uncle Jake, still seated on his horse, his face as gray as his hair.

"But . . . how? I . . . I don't . . ."

Clint's arms tightened around her as he pulled her close and brushed a gentle kiss across the top of her head. "We've been working together to stop the holdup and to catch Ratlin and Jenks in the act. Your uncle has been cooperating with Hoot McClain, the federal marshal from Denver, but he filled me in on the day of the box lunch social—after you left with Joey. We set up Ratlin and Jenks, and now all we have to do is pick up Sleech and

Mangley back in Denver. But all that can wait. Emily . . ."

"You've been working *together*?"

Jake cleared his throat. "We had to play along with Ratlin, sign on for the job. So's we could find out the whole plan and who was behind it," he said gruffly.

"You don't think we'd go along with murder, do you, Em?" Pete shook his head. "We couldn't tell you because we didn't want you involved—"

"*Involved*?" She couldn't be certain she was hearing right. Caught between the urge to weep and the desire to burst into crazed, hysterical laughter, she could only shake her head slowly, as her chest knotted with a new unfamiliar pain.

"We wanted to protect you," Clint said, cupping her chin, tilting it up so that she could see his eyes. They were filled with concern, worry, and tenderness. "We thought the less you knew till it was safely over, the better—"

"Oh, you did, did you?" Emily whispered, a catch in her throat. A dangerous sparkle burned in her eyes. "How *could* you!"

Emily wrenched out of his embrace and stared at him, then at her brother, then at her uncle who looked as frozen as a statue. Her knees were trembling so badly she thought she'd collapse, but sheer will and a sweeping fury kept her on her feet. "I knew something was going on, but I thought . . . I thought you were going back to your old ways," she told Pete and Jake. She rounded on Clint. "And I thought you wanted to arrest them."

"Emily," he began, but she interrupted him, her eyes glittering.

"I was caught in the middle—do you have any idea what I went through?"

"We never meant for it to be like this, you weren't supposed to have any suspicions." Clint's color was ashen. "Listen to me, Emily, when you calm down you'll see—"

"That night . . . that night when Uncle Jake rode out—you *knew*. You let me think the worst, even though you knew it had to be tearing me apart—"

"I was trying to protect you. We'd made a pact to keep you out of it. We knew it would be over soon. We didn't want you mixed up with Ratlin—he's a killer. And Jenks is—"

"I know all about Ratlin and Jenks. Or haven't you noticed?"

She held up her bruised wrists, and saw him glance at them, then his gaze shifted to the mark Ratlin's fist had made on her cheek.

He sucked in his breath.

The anger and hurt in her eyes battered at him, but not nearly as much as the sight of her injuries, the thought of what she'd suffered. His gut wrenched with pain. And with a raw tenderness that was so fierce and overwhelming he could barely see straight.

"Emily, I'm sorry." Were any words ever more inadequate? he thought bitterly. He reached up, touching her face very gently.

"I swear to you, I never meant for any of this to happen—it was the last thing I wanted." He threw a quick glance over at Pete, standing miserable and silent beside him. "The last thing any of us wanted. You have to believe me, you were supposed to be safe, and then we were going to tell you—"

"It's the truth, Sis. All any of us wanted was to keep you clear of this—"

"Don't you dare say another word, any of you." She twisted free of Clint again, stepped backward, and almost stumbled. As Pete reached instinctively for her arm, she knocked his hand aside.

"Don't touch me. Get away from me."

A sick exhausted dizziness was spinning through her head. She hadn't eaten since yesterday, hadn't slept, and the emotional turmoil of death and danger was taking its toll. She'd never felt so weak, so angry, so lost, or so alone.

Even more alone than when Aunt Ida died.

She needed to get away from them, from all of them. Except . . . *Joey.*

A new kind of alarm hummed through her. "Where's Joey?"

Uncle Jake shook his head. "We don't know. We haven't been back to the cabin since yesterday. We left you a note."

Emily couldn't speak. Anxiety and confusion and heartbreak swirled through her. Her head swam. But she pushed the lightheadedness away as she turned back toward the horse.

Clint caught her arm, pulled her toward him. "You're not in any shape to ride back to the ranch yet."

"Don't try to stop me. Or protect me. Or tell me that you care about me. Just let me go, damn you!"

She jerked free and took two steps toward her mount.

And then the air roared through her ears, a sickly gray darkness descended, and the ground rushed up to meet her as she fainted dead away.

Chapter 23

"EM-LY, NOW HOW MANY MORE DAYS till my mama comes for me?"

Joey was galloping around the kitchen table with Jumper clasped in his hand, pretending the horse was running alongside him as Emily removed golden biscuits from the stove and set the pan on the counter.

"Only four more days, Joey. Please stop running, you're making me dizzy."

The little boy drew up short and grinned at her. "You going to bake that big chocolate cake like you said you would?"

"I surely am," she replied, almost but not quite smiling for the first time in days as she blew a strand of hair back from her eyes. "One thing about me, Joey," she added with a caustic irony, which, unfortunately, none of the members of her family were around to hear, "I always tell the truth."

"Oh, boy!"

A week had passed since her capture by Ratlin and Jenks and the foiling of the stagecoach holdup. A long, lonely, empty week. Her physical scrapes and bruises were fading, but the emotional hurts were still as raw and painful as if they'd just been inflicted today.

"They'll be coming back from the range soon—it's time to go wash up." With a sigh she turned her attention to the fragrant pot of beef stew simmering on the stove, thick with meat and potatoes, carrots and green beans.

Joey skidded toward the door. "You going to talk to Uncle Jake and Pete and Lester tonight, Em-ly?"

"What?" She paused in her stirring of the stew and stared at the boy. "I always talk to them."

"Well, you say please pass this . . . and thank you . . . and all that," Joey acknowledged, as he stuffed Jumper into his shirt pocket. "But you don't talk to them like you used to. You're still mad at them, aren't you, Em-ly?"

He rushed on before she could answer. "I didn't mind staying at the Smiths all night that time—and the next day. Really I didn't. Don't be mad at them because of me."

"I'm not mad because of you, Joey." She gritted her teeth. "I'm just upset—because they didn't tell me the truth. They didn't tell me about their plan to help Sheriff Barclay catch those bad men—and he didn't tell me either."

"So . . . you're mad at Sheriff Clint too?"

"I didn't say I was mad at anyone," she said sharply.

"I can tell you are." Joey peeped up at her. "Sheriff Clint came here to see you three times and you wouldn't come out of your room. And Pete and Lester told you how much they liked your pumpkin tarts last night and you didn't even look at them or smile or anything. You've hardly smiled at all lately," he finished. "You always look sad."

"Well, I'm not. I'm fine. So shoo. Out you go."

But as the door banged shut behind him and Emily

plunked the biscuits onto a plate and brought them to the table, her shoulders slumped. She'd tried to behave as normally as she could in the aftermath of her kidnapping, but she was finding it more and more difficult. If not for Joey she'd have left the cabin days ago and gone to live in Nettie Phillips's boardinghouse.

She couldn't bear it here—not anymore. But she couldn't leave, not while Joey still needed her.

Once the cabin had been home, a cherished home, a place she would have protected with her life, filled with those she loved and counted on and trusted. But now it was awful living in these close quarters with Uncle Jake and Pete and Lester. It wasn't that she didn't still love them—it was only that nothing felt the same. They'd lived under the same roof with her the entire time they were planning to trap Ratlin and Jenks and stop the stagecoach murders, but never once had they confided in her or told her what was happening right under her nose.

They had wanted her to believe in *them,* wanted her to trust *them,* but they hadn't trusted *her.*

And Clint Barclay—she couldn't even begin to think about Clint Barclay. He must have known she suspected her uncle of plotting once more to break the law, and he must have known she was frantic with worry, but he'd kept quiet too. All supposedly to protect her.

Tears filled her eyes. The pain inside her sliced deep and hard. It seemed to grow worse every day. She suspected it was never going away.

Love means trust and honesty and faith, she told herself, stomping around the kitchen, setting plates and mugs and flatware on the table. But she had none of that, apparently had never really had it—not with her family, not with the man who had made love to her in the dark, hay-scented barn and mercilessly lassoed her heart. They hadn't trusted her, been honest with her, or had enough faith in her to tell her the truth.

Well, that was just fine. *I don't need them anyway,* she told herself. *I don't need anyone.*

Oh, they'd all tried to explain. Tried to make her understand. She'd heard the whole story, more than once. How Uncle Jake had met Ben Ratlin in prison, and when Ratlin learned that Jake was headed to Forlorn Valley, Colorado, when he got out, to take over a ranch he'd won in a poker game, Ratlin had befriended him.

It turned out Ratlin was getting out nearly the same time—and was headed for Denver. He was looking for some men to help him and some old pards with a job. A job that involved some citizens of a town named Lonesome—and murder.

Uncle Jake had told her how he'd tried to steer clear of Ratlin—the man was dangerous, he'd killed a guard and let another prisoner take the blame—but just before they were both released, Ratlin had cornered him and pressed him to join him and his pards. He'd said they needed some hard, experienced men, who knew how to hold up a stage and get clean away.

Men like the Spoon gang.

He'd promised Jake big money—and he hadn't been willing to take no for an answer. Jake didn't want anything to do with Ratlin or his scheme—he'd never been involved in any killing and, besides, he'd sworn to go straight for good after Aunt Ida died—but he knew that even if he forced Ratlin to back off and leave him out of it, the plan would go forward. People were going to die.

Unless he found a way to stop it.

Going to the law had been hard for Jake—but in this situation, with lives at stake, he'd had no choice. Reluctantly, disgustedly, he'd sought out a federal marshal after his release from prison and told him what he knew, which wasn't much. There was nothing the marshal could do without proof or specific facts regarding the crime, things Jake didn't know.

He'd thought that was the end of it, but the marshal had come up with a plan. A daring plan Jake reluctantly accepted. He'd stalled on giving Ratlin an answer in prison, but now he'd let him know the answer was yes. He and Lester and Pete would pretend to go along with Ratlin and his cohorts—and all the while, they'd be working with the law, with Marshal Hoot McClain in Denver, setting a trap.

Listening to the explanations, Emily learned that only slowly, gradually did the Spoons find out who was going to be killed, when, and why. Frank Mangley, the man behind it, wanted absolute secrecy, and they hadn't known the exact details until only a few days before the actual holdup. At first they'd had no idea that Jenks was one of Ratlin's old pards. They'd guessed, but hadn't known for sure, that the Mangley women were the targets.

The night of the fight in the saloon, Jenks had been trying to intimidate Florry Brown, after he'd let something slip to her about Carla Mangley never getting a chance to marry Sheriff Barclay, even if she caught him, because she'd be dead. Horrified, Florry had demanded to know what he meant, and Jenks had realized he had to scare her into keeping quiet. That was when Pete had stepped in and earned Jenks's enmity—and Florry's gratitude.

But it had taken time and a lot of reassuring coaxing to get her to tell him what she'd heard—and it hadn't been enough. According to the law, in order to make sure Ratlin and his pards were locked up for what they planned to do, they had to be allowed to do it, to get caught in the act.

So the Spoons had continued to meet with Ratlin and go along with the plan. And in the end they'd learned all about how Frank Mangley had grown tired of sharing the profits of his Leadville mine with his brother's widow and daughter. How he'd found a rich new vein, one worth five times the value of the original one—and he didn't care to share it with his sister-in-law. He'd known that if something happened to Carla and Agnes, he'd inherit their shares of the mine. It would all be his.

So he'd decided to kill them both in a stage holdup, making their deaths look like a random act of violence visited upon an entire stagecoach full of people—just a holdup gone bad. No one would suspect that the two women were the targets—no one would possibly suspect that the wealthy and respectable businessman who owned and operated one of Colorado's most lucrative silver mines was involved in any way.

Oh, yes, she'd heard all the explanations, the details. It turned out even Lester buying Carla Mangley's box lunch had been part of their effort to set the trap. No one knew exactly when the women were going to return from Denver—and Marshal McClain needed to prepare. It was a long shot, but Jake and the boys had decided that Pete would buy Florry's box and concentrate on getting as much information as he could from the saloon girl on the day of the social, and Lester would bid on Carla Mangley's box and get a chance to draw her off alone. In the course of general conversation, Lester would try to get some hint from Carla as to when she and her mother were planning to return, information he could pass along to the marshal in order to get a jump on Ratlin.

Emily remembered how Carla had made a point of asking her to tell Lester she'd be returning on Tuesday. Apparently her cousin had done his job all too well—

somehow or other the girl who had everything money could buy had become infatuated with a shy, awkward outlaw who couldn't remember his own name around a pretty woman.

Well, I hope they'll be very happy together, she thought grimly, as she stared into the pot of bubbling stew. *And the same for Pete with his Florry.*

She, on the other hand, was determined never to trust any man again. Particularly drop-dead handsome sheriffs who wooed a girl with kisses and lovemaking in the dark, all the while hatching any number of plots behind her back, plots that involved her very own family—but no one seemed to think that should matter to her . . .

The one thing she'd asked Uncle Jake to explain had been the paper she'd seen him slip into his pocket the day she'd seen him come out of the telegraph office. It turned out that had been a message from Marshal McClain—insisting that Lonesome's sheriff, Clint Barclay, be informed of what was going on and that his help be enlisted. But Uncle Jake admitted he'd put off telling Barclay anything until the day of the box lunch social—at that point, the planned holdup was imminent and he couldn't wait any longer.

So Clint had known since the picnic. He'd known when he came to the ranch and dragged her into the barn and tackled her in the hayloft. He'd known when they'd made love.

He'd been intent on distracting her that night, on preventing her from trying to follow Uncle Jake and messing up all their plans.

Oh, how she wished she could take back that night. She wished she had fought Clint Barclay off, insisted he keep his hands to himself, shown him that she was invulnerable to his touch, his voice, his kisses . . .

Instead she acted like an idiotic lovestruck fool who'd melted into him like a candle lit from both ends—given herself, heart and soul, to a man who didn't trust her or respect her—much less love her—enough to let her in on the truth.

Love her enough? He didn't love her at all. He hadn't said it, not once. He'd told her plain as day in the line shack that he had no intentions of settling down, no desire for marriage.

Which was fine with her, because neither did she. Ever. *With anyone,* Emily vowed, giving the beef and vegetables and potatoes in the simmering pot one last vicious poke with the spoon.

Her spine stiffened as she heard Uncle Jake, Pete, and Lester ride up, heard them talking to Joey out at the pump. When they stomped in, she was composed and calm, her chin notched high as she set bowls of stew around the table.

"Smells mighty good, Emily girl." Uncle Jake gave her a cautious smile from beneath his craggy brows as she marched to her seat beside his and sat down.

Emily picked up her spoon and began to eat.

"Yes, ma'am, it surely does," Lester chimed in heartily.

"After a hard day on the range, it's sure good to come home to your good cooking, Sis." Pete offered his most winning smile.

Joey glanced from one to the other of the grown-ups at the table as a tense silence fell.

Uncle Jake cleared his throat. "You boys going to that there party tomorrow at the Mangley place?" He had adopted Lester's hearty tone.

Pete and Lester said they were.

"Emily? How about you?"

Emily kept eating.

"Emily—"

"No, I am not."

"Oh, Sis, come on. You have to go." Pete broke a biscuit in half. "I hear it's going to be some fancy party—and it's in our honor. Mrs. Mangley thinks we're all heroes for saving her and her daughter." He gave a hoot of laughter. "Bet you never thought that would happen, did you?"

"No, I can't say that I did." Emily continued eating her stew, not looking at him.

"Can I go too?" Joey asked eagerly.

"You sure can," Uncle Jake assured him. "You and me and Emily will all go together."

"I'm not going."

"It won't be the same if you're not there, Emily." Lester's voice was low and full of misery. Sadness flickered in his eyes as he gazed at her across the table. "Besides, Carla told me especially that she wants you to come."

Everyone turned and stared at him—even Emily. His ruddy cheeks turned ruddier.

"What in blazes are you looking at?" He swallowed. "I . . . I happened to bump into her in town this morning," he said defensively, but he dropped his spoon on the floor and then banged his elbow on the table as he reached down to get it.

"We only talked for a minute," he growled.

"A minute. Ahuh." Pete chuckled as he swallowed a mouthful of stew. "Then how come Florry told me she saw you two spooning in the alley outside the hotel? For a lot more than a minute."

Jake guffawed and Joey asked what spooning was. If Lester had been pink before, he now turned scarlet.

"Florry, eh?" Lester's chin jutted out. He jabbed a
ger at his cousin. "You should talk then. You sure are s
ing a lot of her lately."

Pete grinned and winked at Joey. "Why shouldn't I
he said. "No law against spending time with a prett
woman, is there?"

"Is that why Sheriff Barclay keeps coming to see Emily? He wants to spend time with a pretty woman too?" Joey piped up.

Emily choked on a green bean.

"Well, is it?" the boy persisted as Pete got up and smacked her on the back and the coughing subsided.

"I reckon," Uncle Jake said tautly. But Emily shook her head.

"No, Joey, he comes by just to make a pest of himself."

"I thought you liked Sheriff Barclay," the boy said. "I do. The other day, when you wouldn't come out to talk to him, he talked to me instead. And he taught me how to whistle. All kinds of whistles. How to sound like a bird, how to whistle for a horse, how to whistle if you're in trouble . . ."

His voice trailed off as Emily's spoon clattered into her bowl. "Tell me about school, Joey. Did you learn to spell any new words this week?"

"She doesn't want to talk about Sheriff Barclay, pard," Pete told the boy.

"Why not? He likes to talk about her. When he was teaching me to whistle, he said—" He clapped his hand over his mouth suddenly and looked at Emily. "I forgot. He wanted me to tell you something."

"Never mind, Joey," she said, a smile pasted on her face. "Eat your stew. I'm not the least bit interested in hearing what he had to say."

"But he said it was impor-ant. Very impor-ant that I ll you. And I clean forgot," he exclaimed in dismay. Listen, Em-ly, he said he was sorry. Very very sorry."

Emily felt her stomach churning. She'd eaten the stew too quickly—she was going to be sick. "Using a child to . . . to . . . relay his stupid messages to me," she managed to choke out. "It's despicable."

For the first time since the men had come into the cabin, she looked at Uncle Jake. "I want you to tell him to stop coming here, to stop using this innocent boy to try to salve his sorry excuse for a conscience."

"Maybe you ought to tell him yourself, Sis," Pete suggested. He was looking out the window, in the direction of a rider approaching the cabin. "Unless I'm mistaken the sheriff is paying you another call."

"Want me to get rid of him for you, Emily?" Lester offered, pushing back his chair, but Emily, to everyone's surprise, shook her head. She rose from the table and squared her shoulders.

"No. I'm quite capable of getting rid of him myself."

Her face was pale, but she wore an expression of grimmest fortitude. As her family and Joey watched, she stalked toward the rifle, grabbed it, and as Clint rode up to the front yard she marched through the parlor and out onto the porch.

As he swung down from his horse, she saw something that made her go still as stone. Tall, dark, muscular—as gorgeous as ever in a fine blue chambray shirt and dark pants, the man coming toward her clutched a thick handful of flowers, brilliant in the falling dusk, their stems tied together with a pink ribbon.

For a moment something fluttered happily within her, but Emily squelched it immediately. A whole meadowful of flowers wouldn't make up for what he'd done.

"Don't come another step closer," she warned, level the rifle at his chest.

Clint paused for a moment, his eyes narrowing, ap praising. Silhouetted against the distant mountains, h looked every inch as rugged as they did. And just as imposing. But Emily held the rifle steady.

"These are for you," he said evenly.

"I don't want them."

"Emily—"

"Get off my land. You're trespassing and I have every right to shoot you if you don't leave—now."

He surveyed her, his jaw clenched. "Shoot me if you want, Emily, but I reckon I'm not leaving here until I give you these flowers."

"Didn't you hear what I said? Don't come another step!"

But to her dismay, he started forward again, his blue eyes coolly fixed on her.

"Do you think I'll let a little thing like a rifle keep me away from you? We need to talk—"

Emily pulled the trigger, shooting into the dirt at his feet. Surprise glinted in his eyes, but he never faltered. He merely set his jaw even tighter and kept walking. Swearing under her breath, Emily once again fired at his feet.

"Don't think you're going to make me dance unless it's with you," Clint told her, still advancing.

"Stop!" she gasped and leveled the rifle at his chest, but he just vaulted up the steps and took hold of it with one hand, easily wresting it from her. Never taking his eyes from her face, he set the rifle down against the porch rail and then planted himself in front of her.

"Here." Gently he grasped her hand and pushed the bouquet of flowers into it. She tried to pull away, but he

. her easily, carefully, touching her as if she were as gile as the blossoms he'd brought for her. He shifted ɔser to her as the faint shadows of nightfall crept over .e land.

"I want you to have these. Emily . . ."

Clint's voice faded. It was the first time he'd seen her since the day he and Pete and Jake had found her at Bitter Rock, and for a moment, her loveliness snatched away all the words he'd wanted to say. His breath was trapped in his lungs. Damn, she was even more beautiful than he remembered, and what he remembered had been keeping him up nights. Her midnight hair, tossed by the wind, cascaded in a riotous tumble around that delicate face, and the plain gray gown she wore only emphasized her vivid beauty. He gazed at her hungrily, longing to touch her, longing to feel her soft, slender form nestled against his. He fought the urge to catch her up in his arms and carry her into the barn, up into the hayloft, and make love to her all over again, until all the hurt and pain between them was wiped out by the passion.

But since Jake, Pete, and Lester Spoon were all filing out onto the porch, followed by Joey, that didn't seem like it was going to happen anytime soon.

"Let me go!" Emily hissed at him, and wrenched out of his embrace.

"You heard the lady." Jake's raspy voice filled the night. "Back off, Barclay."

"The hell I will." Clint glared at all three Spoon men. "Stay out of this if you know what's good for you."

"You'll leave my sister the hell alone if you know what's good for you," Pete exploded.

Clint clenched his fists and Lester and Pete both started toward him, but Emily sprang forward, getting between them.

"That's enough. I won't have this, do you hear What kind of an example are you setting for Joey?"

All the men fell silent. Clint's gaze searched her f. and for one shattering moment her resolve faltered. S. fought the urge to run to him and throw herself into h. arms. Then she found her backbone again and drew her self up straight and tall.

"Go away," she commanded him icily. She hurled the flowers as far as she could, over the porch railing, into the grassy yard. They landed with a soft thud that made his mouth tighten.

"And don't come back," she added between clenched teeth.

With that she flung an angry look at Jake, Pete, and Lester, grabbed Joey by the shoulders, and propelled him inside the house.

The moment the door was closed, she leaned against it, as the lump in her throat grew hard and tight, as sorrow and loneliness and despair rose in her like floodwater.

She wouldn't cry. She wouldn't.

She took a deep breath—and burst into tears.

"Em-ly!" Joey ran to her and hugged her legs. "Don't cry," he begged.

With an effort, she managed to swallow her sobs. She sniffled and gasped, muffling the sounds of her grief as much as possible. She didn't want any of those men standing out there in the night to know that they'd reduced her to tears—least of all Clint Barclay.

She took a long steadying breath and fought back one last sob. Kneeling, she put her arms around the boy watching her so anxiously.

"I'm b-better now. There's n-nothing to worry about." Somehow she managed a watery smile. "Let's clear the table and you can h-help me wash the dishes."

"Okay, Em-ly." He threw his arms around her neck. "But just tell me—are you crying because you're mad at Sheriff Clint or because he brought you those flowers?" he asked.

Emily's heart split in two. "Both," she whispered desolately. Then she stood up, squared her shoulders, and blinked back a fresh batch of tears.

The thunder of Clint Barclay's horse pounding away from the ranch dwindled, leaving silence between the three men who remained on the porch. Jake lit a cigar, Lester threw himself glumly into the porch chair, and Pete stood scowling into the darkness.

"I've a good mind to follow that son-of-a-bitch and teach him not to pester my sister," Pete growled.

"Want some help?" Lester sighed. "I'll do anything that'll get me back in Emily's good graces. It's hell around here lately, with her being so silent and angry and all. I mean, Barclay wasn't half bad during the holdup—he's right smart, and he can sure shoot straight, but just because he plugged Jenks and got him to tell us where Emily was, he thinks he can come here anytime and make a nuisance of himself."

"Just what the hell does he want with her?" Pete frowned. "That's what I want to know."

"What do you think he wants?" Lester exclaimed disgustedly, shaking his head.

"I oughta horsewhip him."

"You reckon that'll please Emily?" Jake's voice sounded dry in the darkness. "It's what she wants with him that has me worried."

"What's that supposed to mean, Uncle Jake?"

"Either of you boys ever notice the way she looks at him? Or the way he looks at her?"

"No," Pete and Lester answered in unison, sounding puzzled.

"Well, I have." Jake blew a smoke ring toward the sky and watched it rise and dissipate in the clear, cool air. "And I'm not a mite pleased about it. Matter of fact, it turns my stomach. But still . . ."

"What are you trying to say?" Pete demanded.

Jake's gaze pierced each of them in turn as in the distance a coyote began to howl, followed by another, and then another. The mournful cries filled the night.

"Either of you heard that girl crying her heart out these past few nights? Or notice how pale she looks? How sad?" he asked, sounding angry.

"Yeah," Pete sighed. "And I hate it. But that's because she's mad at us, isn't it? And I figure she'll get over it . . . sooner or later."

"She will, won't she, Pa?" Lester asked sharply.

"What she's got, she won't get over," Jake muttered.

A startled silence followed his words.

"I was married to Ida for thirty years and she never got over it—no matter what I did, how many times I let her down, or did something that made her madder'n hell, she never got over it. She loved me, loved me till the end, till the day she died, even though I didn't deserve it."

"What the hell are you saying, Uncle Jake?" Pete glared at him. "You're not talking about Emily and . . . Barclay?" he asked in dawning horror. "You don't think Emily is in love with that . . . that *lawman*?"

Lester froze on the chair, staring at his father incredulously. "No, Pa, no, she can't be."

"Hell, open your eyes. No sense pretending what's there *isn't*."

Pete began pacing back and forth across the porch,

while Lester slumped lower in the chair. "Well, we gotta stop her. Change her mind," Pete exclaimed.

"Change the mind of a woman in love?" Jake gave a curt laugh. "You boys don't know a damned thing about women. Besides," he added slowly, looking at each of them. "Don't you want her to be happy?" His tone was gruff. "To have a home of her own some day? A husband, children?"

"Never thought about it much," Pete muttered. He wanted to hit somebody. Somebody like Barclay.

"Damn it, Pa, she sure as hell isn't going to have those things with Barclay."

"Not at this rate." Jake shook his head. "Did you see how she threw those flowers of his? And he's so busy staring at her he can barely get the words out to apologize. Damn fool. Can't he see that girl's stubborn as a whole pack of mules? By the time he spits out what he needs to say and grovels enough to get her to forgive him, they'll both be older and grayer than me—and I'll be dead. Unless—"

"Unless . . . what?" Pete asked uneasily.

Jake Spoon took a long drag on his cigar, while both Lester and Pete stared at him.

"Unless we give the danged fool some help."

"Now why would we want to do that?" Pete exploded. "Let him suffer. Let him go to hell!"

"And what about Emily?" Lester spoke quietly. "You want her to keep suffering too?"

Pete swallowed. He thought of his sister's drawn face, how angry and quiet and miserable she'd been these past days. The way she'd wept in her room at night when the cabin was dark and still, a heartrending weeping no one was supposed to hear. Emily, who'd cared for Aunt Ida all alone while he and Lester had been on the run, and Jake had been in prison—Emily, who'd worked so hard to make this rough cabin into a home for them all.

"Aw, *hell*." He raked a hand through his hair and spun toward his uncle. "If it'll make Emily happy," he choked. "Tell us what we have to do!"

Chapter 24

CLINT BARCLAY, YOU HAVEN'T heard a word I've been saying." Nettie Phillips poked him in the arm as all around them, chattering people laughed, drank lemonade and elderberry wine, and watched the dancers doing a country jig across the Mangleys' candlelit parlor.

"I asked you why you don't just go over there and ask Emily Spoon to dance," Nettie said as the sheriff turned distracted eyes upon her.

"Any fool can see you're going to burst if you watch one more cowboy take her for a whirl around the floor."

Her words penetrated the dark hell of Clint's thoughts. He tore his gaze from the sight of Emily dancing with Fred Baker and glowered at the frank-talking woman beside him.

"She doesn't want to dance with me."

"How do you know if you don't ask?"

"I did ask. Twice." Clint's lip curled dangerously. "She told me no. Then she danced with Homer Riley and Doc Calvin. Then she disappeared with a bunch of ladies, gabbing all the while about muffs and parasols. Then she danced with Hank Peterson and Chance Russell. She wouldn't even *talk* to me."

"Serves you right," Nettie told him as Agnes Mangley bustled by, making a beeline for Carla and Lester Spoon, huddled in a corner whispering to one another as if they were the only two people in the house.

"You kept that girl in the dark, after all, when you could have saved her a lot of grief if you'd only told her what was going on. Oh, she told me about it," she added airily at his startled glance. "Poor girl needed someone to talk to."

Of course, Nettie reflected, Emily hadn't exactly confided *everything* to her—she hadn't come out and said she was so in love with Clint Barclay she couldn't see straight—only that she planned never to speak to him again—but her feelings for the sheriff were plain as day, at least in Nettie's opinion. She hadn't even planned on attending the Mangleys' party until Nettie shrewdly pointed out that if she didn't come, it would look like she was avoiding him, since the Spoon men and the sheriff were all guests of honor. Did she want to let Clint Barclay know that he could scare her away from attending parties and town functions and dances just because he would be there? Did she want the man to think he had even a thimbleful of power over where she went and what she did?

That had done the trick and Emily had changed her mind about the party. Now the rest was up to Clint, Nettie thought, as she glanced sidelong at the handsome sheriff who had done nothing but scowl and toss back whiskey and prowl the Mangley house like a hungry, restless cougar since the moment Emily Spoon and her family arrived.

"*Men,*" Nettie said pointedly. "You always think you know best for a woman, insead of letting her decide for herself. One of your more foolish and irritating traits, if you ask me. The smart ones learn from their mistakes. Why, my Lucas learned the hard way the first month we were married that . . ."

Clint heard no more as Nettie rattled on—his attention was caught by the sight of Emily being brought a glass of lemonade by Cody Malone.

Was there a man in the room she hadn't spoken to, danced with, smiled upon—except for him? He doubted it. And he doubted his own ability to survive this night without hitting someone.

Trouble was, she wouldn't even give him a chance to explain or to apologize. A chance to even hint at what was in his heart. It was driving him crazy. Feelings he hadn't ever thought he'd feel tormented him. Jealousy, loneliness, despair. Over a woman.

Not just any woman. The one woman he'd discovered he needed in his life was the one woman who wanted nothing to do with him.

Well, I reckon we'll just see about that, he decided, his jaw tightening. He didn't give up when he was on the trail of some low-down smelly outlaw, or a gang of wily scavengers like the Monroe gang or the Barts—he wasn't about to give up on the woman he loved.

That he loved her Clint could no longer deny. That he wanted her in his arms and in his bed and in his heart for the rest of his life was an indisputable fact.

That he'd win her over was an iffy matter. No one he'd ever met had a temper and a will and a knack for holding a grudge like the enchantingly hot-tempered Miss Emily Spoon.

As if she felt his gaze burning into her, Emily looked up at that moment, across the room, and directly into his eyes.

But as he excused himself from Nettie and started purposefully across the room toward her, she turned away and immediately disappeared behind a knot of people.

Clint walked faster, his eyes searching the crowd, and all the while he was completely unaware that he was the object of much attention and conjecture by several other guests at the party.

Hamilton Smith and Hoss Fleagle watched openmouthed as Clint approached the Spoon girl yet again.

"You see what I see, Ham?" Hoss shook his head in disbelief.

"You mean the way Clint keeps looking at that gal? And chasing after her?" Ham sighed over the rim of his crystal goblet filled with elderberry wine. "Mighty sad sight. All these women in town hankering to get him to pop the question, and the one girl he's trying to talk to keeps dodging him like he was a cow pie in a basket of cookies."

"If I ever look that lovesick, shoot me and put me out of my misery," Hoss exclaimed.

And Doc Calvin happened by just then and added his two cents: "Clint's a goner," he muttered sadly.

Several of the other townspeople had taken note of the sheriff's apparently doomed fascination with Emily Spoon as well, but many of the citizens of Lonesome had not even noticed—another development had commanded their full attention. The Spoon boys had suddenly replaced the sheriff as objects of adoration and potential matrimony among the single women of Lonesome. Thanks to their efforts to thwart the plot against the Mangleys, and incidentally saving the lives of Hamilton and Bessie Smith as well, Pete and Lester Spoon were no longer considered outlaws but were hailed as heroes, slapped on the back, welcomed into every conversation.

They were congratulated and complimented, their every utterance listened to with bated breath, applauded, repeated around the room as if it were a nugget of infinite wisdom.

Even Jake Spoon, who stood with his hands in his pockets, hugging the wall, on the outskirts of the festivities, was eventually captured by the throng, hustled to the center of the parlor, subjected to toasts made in his honor, with Agnes Mangley extolling his courage, and every man in the room wanting to pump his hand.

The young women who had previously had eyes only for Sheriff Barclay suddenly were swarming over Pete Spoon like honeybees over a jar of jam. And several had tried to catch Lester's eye, in the hope he would escort them in to supper or ask them to dance. But Lester Spoon seemed mesmerized by Carla Mangley, and she by him. The most astonishing thing about the entire party was the way Agnes Mangley raised toast after toast to the Spoons, fawned over them, insisted they sit beside her, and looked upon Lester's captivation with Carla with obvious favor.

The outcast outlaws of the Teacup Ranch had suddenly become the darlings of Forlorn Valley society. But despite the entire town becoming wholly caught up in this phenomenon, once Pete, Lester, and Jake finally managed to escape and meet in the hallway behind the wide oak stairs, they wasted no time thinking about their new status as heroes.

They quickly got down to business.

"Anyone seen Emily?" Jake demanded. "She was right next to the widow Mangley when I saw her at the supper table, and she and that Margaret Smith were talking about some dress or other she wanted Emily to sew, but then she disappeared!"

"She's in the garden," Pete said. "All by herself. Lester and I saw her slip out and go around back."

"She's sitting right there on the swing, in the dark, no doubt mooning over Barclay," Lester snorted. "No one's around, so if we're going through with this, now's the time," he added.

"But where's Joey?" Pete asked.

Jake grinned. "In the kitchen. He and Bobby Smith swiped a plate of oatmeal cookies and they're hiding out in the pantry eating them all." He guffawed, despite the seriousness of what lay before them. "I told him to stay put—that I had a special job for him to do. So how's about I go get him now—and you boys do your part?"

"Fine by me. This is the only part of this whole damned scheme I'm going to enjoy," Pete said with relish.

"Me too." Lester nodded at Tammy Sue Wells, who glided slowly by, her glance shifting from him to Pete, her hips swaying as she walked. He waited until she slipped into the dining room before continuing. "I'm still not so sure this is a good idea."

Jake's deep-set eyes fixed themselves first on his son, then on his nephew. "If it works," he said gruffly, "I'm not going to like it any more than you do. But it's what makes Emily happy that counts."

Lester sighed resignedly. Pete rocked back and forth on his heels for a moment, wrestling with the strong, contradictory emotions tearing through him.

"Oh, hell," he said at last, taking a deep breath. "If it makes Emily happy, I'd eat a mountain of tumbleweed. So let's quit jawing about it and just get it over with."

His body tensed and straightened as he spotted Clint Barclay, a cigar stuck in his mouth as he leaned against the wall of the parlor, his hard gaze scanning the crowded room, no doubt looking for Emily.

"I want to do the honors," Pete told Lester. "She's my ister."

"I'll flip you for the privilege," Lester quickly counered.

Jake pulled out a coin.

"Heads," Pete said. The cousins watched intently as ake tossed the coin, caught it, and turned it over in his alm.

"Heads," the older man announced.

As Lester swore under his breath, a cold smile touched ete's lips. His gaze shifted again to Barclay and he tarted forward.

"Let's go."

Chapter 25

CLINT'S *HURT?* WHAT DO YOU MEAN he's hurt?" Emily jumped off the swing, her heart suddenly hammering, and peered at Joey through the moonlit darkness.

"I didn't see him, but Uncle Jake said you should come quick—he's in the jail—hurt *bad*." The boy was nearly hopping with excitement, his little face flushed, his arms waving. "Hurry, Em-ly! Uncle Jake said *hurry*!"

Emily raced around the house and up the darkened street toward the jail, fear tearing through her like ripping needles. All evening Clint had been trying to approach her, trying to dance with her, and she'd been avoiding him—outright dodging him as she tried to convince herself she needed to banish him from her life for good. And now he was hurt—what if he'd been shot, what if he'd been stabbed, what if he didn't survive?

She clutched her skirts in one hand and ran along the deserted main street, her feet flying along the boardwalk. Tinny piano music and raucous shouts came from the saloon as she flew past it toward the dim outline of the jailhouse, illuminated in a silvery glow by stars and moon.

reached the building, gasping for breath, pain and clutching at her heart as she burst inside.

Clint's office was in shadow, the oil lamp turned low. first she couldn't see much of anything except Clint's esk, the bookshelves, the metal bars of the cells glinting ust beyond the office.

"Clint! Uncle Jake!" Panic-stricken, she peered through the gloom. "Clint, where are you?"

She moved forward, stumbled over the leg of a chair, and righted herself. Then she saw him.

He was in the jail cell—sprawled, arms akimbo, upon the cot.

"Clint!" Running to him, her heart in her throat, Emily felt a terrible fear descend upon her. What if he was *dead,* what if she was too late . . .

"My darling, what happened to you?" she cried in a broken whisper as she bent over his prone form.

He groaned, stirred. *He was alive.*

"Thank God," Emily breathed. There was no blood upon his white linen shirt, no wound that she could see. Kneeling beside him, she took his hand, pressing shaking fingers to his pulse.

That's when she heard the jail door clank shut and a key scrape in the lock.

She twisted around and saw Pete in the shadows, gazing at her. Lester stood just behind him.

"Quick, he's . . ." Her voice faded as she suddenly wondered why they had shut and locked the cell door. "What are you doing?" she gasped, as a horrible idea occurred to her.

"Pete—Lester—open that door."

"Sorry, Sis. Can't do that."

"Don't be mad," Lester muttered.

She sprang up and ran to the bars, grabbing t shaking them. "You open that door this instant. He's h he needs help, you need to go fetch Doc Calvin—"

"He doesn't need a doctor, Em. I just coldcocked hi that's all." Pete shrugged, trying not to look pleased wit himself as he turned away.

But Lester's expression was somber. "He'll come around soon enough, Em." Sighing, he followed Pete to the door.

"Where are you going? You can't *leave* us here—"

"We'll be back for you in the morning," her brother promised.

"In the morning? No! Stop! What do you think you're—" She broke off as the door slammed shut behind both of them and the next thing she knew another key scraped in another lock. The door to the office, locked from the outside.

Emily gripped the bars and pulled as hard as she could. She shook them, rattled them, kicked them.

She wanted to scream in frustration. She was trapped in there, in this cell. With Clint.

Another groan from the cot had her whirling around.

Clint's eyes opened. Lying on his back, he stared blankly up at her. "What the hell . . . happened . . ."

"You tell me!" Incensed, Emily glared at him. "Are you in on this too?"

"In on . . . what?" He sat up slowly, looking dazed. "What are you doing here, Emily?"

"Joey told me you were hurt—that I had to come immediately—" She broke off, biting her lip. *Why would they do this to me?* she wondered, fury churning through her and, with it, shock. Her family hated Clint Barclay. What possible reason could they have for tricking her and locking her in a jail cell with him for the entire night?

"What are *you* doing here?" she demanded.

Slowly, as she watched, a frown darkened his face and the familiar keenness returned to his eyes.

"Reckon . . . Lester tricked me. He found me at the party—told me that Deputy Stills had just ridden in from Denver. He said Jenks had escaped from jail in Denver and Hoot McClain was organizing a posse. Said Stills wanted me to meet him here and . . . oh, hell."

He groaned again, this time in disgust.

Emily stalked to the farthest end of the cell, which was only about five feet away from where he sat on the cot. "So you came here and then what?" she asked, her stomach doing little nervous jumps and flips.

"I came in the door fast, looking for Stills—then someone hit me over the head and that's all I knew. Must've been Pete," he muttered. A dangerous glitter entered his eyes. "I'll have their hides, the both of them," he growled.

"You'll have to stand in line. I'm going to kill them," Emily muttered. "With my bare hands." She drew a ragged breath. "Why did they do this to me? *Why*?"

Clint looked at her as she stood, her back to the wall as if she wished she could melt right through it and get as far away from him as possible. But she couldn't. She was so near—only two steps away. He suddenly didn't feel like horsewhipping Pete and Lester anymore. Emily wasn't going anywhere and neither was he.

"I don't have a clue why they did it," he said, rising to his feet. The pain in his head was already easing—Pete Spoon must not have hit him that hard after all. But the pain in his heart was still as intense as ever.

"But I'm sure glad they did," he added, and took a deliberate step toward Emily.

She suddenly looked like a cornered doe. "Stay back,"

she warned him, alarm shooting through her. "Don't come any closer."

"Emily—"

"The last place I want to be is here in this cell with you."

"But you came here—fast—when you thought I was hurt."

"I . . . I . . ." Emily bit her lip as he took another step toward her. Her body felt heated, her face flushed. Being close to Clint Barclay always had an unsettling effect on her, but never more so than at this moment, when she knew she couldn't get away. It was difficult to breathe and even harder to think when he was gazing at her that way, his eyes glittering in the gloom, the faint glow of the lamp just barely illuminating the strong handsome planes of his face, the firm line of his mouth, those keen hot blue eyes.

"I thought you were dead, actually, and I . . . I wanted to gloat," she told him in a cold tone.

His brows shot up. "Gloat. Ahuh."

Emily suddenly couldn't remain still another moment. She darted forward past Clint to the opposite side of the cell where shutters enclosed the high window. Reaching up, she tried to unlatch them.

"I'm getting out of here. Someone's going to come down this street, someone leaving the saloon or going to the hotel—and they'll hear me if I scream—ahhhh!"

Clint seized her around the waist and yanked her away from the window before she could unlatch the shutters.

"Forget it, Emily. This is what you get for not letting me talk to you all night. It's justice in a way."

"Justice! I didn't commit any crime. I demand to be let out."

Blue fire suddenly ignited in his eyes. "You think you didn't commit a crime? I say you did."

Suddenly Clint's arm snaked around her waist so that she couldn't twist away. His other hand cupped her chin and tilted it up so that she was gazing directly, inescapably, into his eyes.

"You're a thief, Miss Spoon. The worst kind of thief."

"I never stole anything in my entire life!"

He tugged her closer still. His fingers burned her skin.

"That's a damned lie." His voice was thick, husky. "You stole from me. You stole my peace of mind. My concentration. My regard. My heart."

Emily couldn't speak. Her lips parted, but not even a whisper emerged for she was hearing the words he'd just spoken in her mind—over and over again.

"You don't have a heart."

"Want to bet?"

She moistened her lips. "Don't try to . . . to sweet-talk me. After what you did—"

"I did what I thought was best, Emily—at the time. I didn't want you mixed up with Ratlin and Jenks and Frank Mangley and his damned foreman. We had a plan and you weren't part of it and—"

"You knew what I was thinking! That night when Uncle Jake rode off and you dragged me inside the barn—you knew what I suspected!"

"That he was up to his old ways again." Clint's eyes were solemn. "Yep, I reckoned that's what you thought. But it seemed safer to let you think that a little longer until—"

"You bastard!" She shoved him away from her as a lump rose in her throat and tears sparkled on her eyelashes. Her voice throbbed. "I was torn in two! I wanted so much to believe in him, and in Pete and Lester, but that shook my faith and my loyalty—I didn't know what to do—and then there was everything I was feeling for you!"

"I know, Emily," Clint said grimly. "But don't you see? By then it was almost over and it seemed better to—"

"To what?" she interrupted furiously. "To let me believe that they were going back to their old ways? Only worse? Because that's what I thought, you know! When I overheard Uncle Jake talking to Ratlin and Jenks, I thought he and Lester and Pete were up to their necks in murder. Do you know how that felt? Can you imagine? I was trying to escape, so I could turn them in—my own family. I was going to turn them in—to *you*!"

She broke off on a sob and drew in deep trembling breaths as she fought for control. Pain seared him as he saw the anguish in her face. He hadn't thought about it exactly like that, hadn't realized the true depth of the situation she'd been put into. All he'd wanted was to keep her safe, but he'd hurt her—they'd all hurt her with the secret. Not physically, but in a place more tender and vulnerable than blood or flesh could touch.

"I'm sorry, Emily. So . . . very sorry," he muttered.

Studying her in the feeble light, he took in the shining mass of midnight curls, the creamy fairness of her skin, the full lushness of a mouth that he well remembered tasted of summer berries. But he also saw the faint shadow of the bruises still marring those fine-boned cheeks. The bruises that resulted when Ratlin and Jenks had struck her, hurt her. They had mostly faded but were not completely gone, and the sight of them reminded him that if he'd been honest, if he'd trusted her with the truth, she wouldn't have followed Jake Spoon that fateful day, wouldn't have been captured, tied up, terrorized by men intent on murder.

"I don't make many mistakes when it comes to my work, but this one was a big one," Clint said slowly. "And I'll try to make it up to you, Emily, if you give me a chance."

He reached up and lightly, gently, brushed his thumb across the fading bruise.

She flinched, no longer from pain, only from the effect of his touch.

"They hurt you," he said in a low, tortured voice. "I'll never forgive myself for that."

Emily couldn't breathe as she read the sorrow in his eyes. Her chest felt as if it would explode with a heartrending pain.

"Did he . . . did Jenks . . ." Clint cleared his throat, his own heart pounding, "did he hurt you . . . in any other way?"

She knew what he meant and a shudder shook her. "He k-kissed me," Emily whispered, feeling sick as she said the words. "It was disgusting." She was trembling now, every part of her trembling. "I tried to fight him but my hands were tied . . . and then Ratlin stopped him, told him that afterward, when the holdup was over . . . before they killed me . . . he could . . . he could . . ."

Her voice broke, her face crumpled, and she swayed against him. Clint swept her into his arms, locking her tight against him, as icy pain and a fury unlike anything he'd ever known crashed through him. He wished there were a way he could hold her tight enough to block out every painful memory of her capture, to keep out any hurt or sorrow in the future, to protect her from ever knowing fear again.

But it was too late. She could never forget . . . never forgive . . .

"I'd like to kill him." The words tore savagely from

him, at odds with the gentle strength with which he h
her. "I wish to hell he'd escape—just so that I could tra
him into the middle of nowhere and make him pay fo
ever once touching you!"

Emily laid her head against his shoulder and wept, letting the tears flow. She'd wept alone before, in brief bursts, out of hurt and anger, but now she wept with all her heart, as Clint held her and let her cry, let her pain seep into him, as if he would take it all away if only he could.

When at last she drew a ragged breath and the sobs abated, he handed her his handkerchief and waited until she'd dried her wet cheeks, waited as she sank down upon the cot, weary and spent, her dark hair all atangle.

He knelt beside her, took her hand. "Emily," he said grimly, a great heaviness in his heart. "I don't expect you to forgive me. I know now you won't ever feel toward me even a hint of what I feel for you." He cleared his throat, forcing himself to finish saying what had to be said. "After everything that's happened, I don't blame you for hating me—you have every right—"

"Hate you?" Startled, she stared at him. "I don't hate you, you stupid idiotic man."

His eyes locked on hers. "But I thought—"

"I'm furious with you. Or . . . I was," she added, somewhat puzzled because being there alone with him in this bleak, dim cell had somehow changed everything. The anger that had driven her since her rescue on Bitter Rock had somehow melted away. The barrier between her and Clint might never have been. She'd let out all the pain, all the rage, all the tears, and now they were . . . gone. Simply gone. Like dry, dead dust and withering weeds washed away by a rainstorm. In the same way that a hard, driving downpour cleanses away the dead, parched land, leaving it clean and refreshed and moist with life, she sat there with Clint and no longer saw a man who had withheld the truth from her—she saw the man who made her feverish with his kisses, whose touch made her come alive. She saw the man who'd dried her tears, locked her in his arms, who'd bought her box lunch in front of the entire town. The man who'd made unforgettable love to her in a hayloft and found her on Bitter Rock when she needed him most.

A man who tried to do what was right—but could admit when he was wrong.

The man she loved. And the man she forgave.

"What was that you said, Clint . . . about my never feeling what you . . . you feel for me?" She moistened lips that suddenly felt dry. She felt his hand close more firmly around hers and glanced down at it wonderingly.

"What . . . do you feel for me?" she whispered, a tiny feeble hope like a small hot candle flame springing to life inside her.

The words came easily after all. He'd never said them before to any woman, but he said them to her without hesitation or embarrassment. "I love you, Emily. More than I ever thought I could love anyone." Straight from the heart, his words were as solid and unyielding as the bars that locked them in the cell. His hands grasped her arms, pulled her close, holding her tenderly, but with an urgency that struck through to her soul.

"I love you," he said hoarsely.

A soaring joy rose in her as she lifted her shining eyes to his—as she saw the love in those keen blue depths, sensed the yearning and the hunger within him. The need that was answered by the need in her own heart. She flung her arms around his neck. "Oh, Clint," she whispered, hope filling her, "I love you too!"

Clint kissed her, a hard, possessive kiss that left her breathless and eager for more. She clung to him and pressed her mouth to his, nestling her body against him, reveling in the hard strength of him, in the way she fit against him as he lowered her beneath him on the cot.

"Marry me," Clint said, unbuttoning her dress, his mouth moving over her cheek, trailing down her throat.

Emily could barely think as her fingers fumbled at his shirt. "I don't know . . . your family . . . my family . . . they won't . . ."

"We're not going to marry them, Emily. Damn it, we're going to marry each other. Say yes!"

"Yes!"

"How soon?"

"As soon as I can sew a wedding gown—" She never got to finish, for Clint's mouth descended on hers, his hands began to stroke and entice her, and then they were both lost to thought and reason and any vestige of human conversation.

They spoke with their hands, with their lips, with their bodies and their hearts. They celebrated the love that had bloomed between them against all odds and all reason. Alone in the lamplit cell, locked away from the town, from the world, they held each other and loved each other through the soft hours of the night and into the pale opal glow of dawn.

And it wasn't until the next morning, when they scrambled into their clothes as Pete and Lester showed up to unlock the jailhouse door, that Clint reached into his boot and pulled out a key.

A spare key to the cells, he explained to an open-mouthed Emily. He always kept it on him—just in case.

"And you . . . you didn't deem it important to tell me about this last night?" Emily gasped as her brother d open the door to the outer office and stomped past s desk toward the cell.

Nope. It wasn't important." He chuckled softly. "Not rly as important as spendng the entire night with u—alone in a dark, locked room—with a bed," her in-nded whispered into her ear.

And for once, slipping her hand into his, Emily couldn't disagree.

Chapter 26

LISSA McCOY ARRIVED ON THE STAGE on a warm cloudy morning that held a hint of rain. She flew down the steps in a blue-and-peach striped muslin gown and a fetching feathered bonnet, scooping a waiting Joey into her arms as Emily watched in delight.

Emily's heart was light as she embraced her friend, who looked well, rested, and unutterably happy, despite her untidy chignon and wrinkled traveling dress whose hem was smudged with the dust of her journey.

"How can I ever thank you enough?" Lissa exclaimed, her brown eyes sparkling with tears as she hugged Emily yet again. In her new gown and smart bonnet, she no longer looked like the terrified and desperately poor woman who had fled Jefferson City. Obviously, Emily thought, relieved to see her friend looking so well, Lissa's grandparents had indeed taken her under their wing, and her circumstances had improved considerably.

"You and Joey are both safe—that's all that matters," Emily told her, pressing her hands. "Oh, Lissa, I have so much to tell you!"

"Why, yes, I believe you do," Lissa replied, scooping

up into her arms as her gaze shifted to the man who d beside Emily, the dark-haired, incredibly handsome n whose lean features and confident bearing looked dly familiar.

She cast a questioning glance at Emily, who blushed osily. "I'd like to introduce you to—"

"That's Sheriff Clint!" Joey piped up, his thin voice carrying all the way down the street to the livery. "He and Em-ly are getting married and they said I can come to the wedding!"

"Is that so? Can I come too?"

A new, deep-timbered voice spoke from the doorway of the stagecoach. The rest of the stagecoach passengers had alighted, and now a tall, powerfully built man strode down the steps with a smooth, easy stride. He was dressed all in black, but for the square silver buckle on his low-slung gunbelt. A dark slouch hat slanted low over grim eyes. But his face . . .

Emily froze, staring at that handsome, hard-planed countenance, and beside her, Clint went still as stone.

"Remember I told you my grandfather was sending an escort with me, to keep me and Joey safe on our journey?" Lissa said quickly, setting Joey down. "This is him—Nick Barclay. My grandfather said—"

Her voice faded away as Nick and Clint both began to laugh.

Emily watched in amazement as Clint and his brother clasped one another in a bear hug and thumped each other on the back.

"And this is Clint Barclay—he's our sheriff in Lonesome," she explained a bit breathlessly to Lissa. "He's also my fiancé," she added, her cheeks pink as the posies on Lissa's smart new bonnet. "And unless I miss my guess—your escort is his brother!"

Amid the excited babble that ensued, introduc
were made all around, and Nick grinningly confessed
he hadn't told the woman he was charged to protect t
his brother happened to be the sheriff of the tow
that was their destination.

It turned out that Lissa's grandparents were old friends of Reese Summers, and Clint and Nick had known them both for years.

Nick Barclay bowed low over Emily's hand. "It's a pleasure, Miss Spoon. So you're getting hitched to my big brother? Brave woman. I can't imagine what you see in him, but let me say, he's one lucky hombre."

"I intend to make sure he knows that every day from now on," Emily replied with a saucy smile that drew an approving burst of laughter from Nick.

"Believe me—I know how lucky I am every time I look at her." Clint's arm went around her as he spoke and Emily leaned into him as if her entire body longed for his touch.

Nick Barclay's cool gaze shifted from one to the other of them. He whistled low as he saw how the dark-haired beauty with those entrancing silver eyes looked at his older brother, and how Clint looked back at her—as if he couldn't see anyone or anything else.

"Well, big brother," Nick said slowly, "you're as loco in love with Miss Spoon here as Wade is with his Caitlin, aren't you? I never thought I'd see the day when both my brothers—" He broke off and tipped his hat at Emily. "Begging your pardon, ma'am. But it's a regular shock. I think I need some strong spirits to help me recover."

"Don't feel sorry for him, Emily," Clint said roughly. "He'll never recover. The very mention of marriage makes my little brother break out in hives."

Emily laughed at the two of them. Obviously there

was strong affection between the Barclay boys—every bit as much as between Pete and Lester. But while Pete and Lester, as cousins, could not have looked more dissimilar, Clint and his brother bore a powerful resemblance to each other. Nick had the same tall, muscular physique as Clint, but his hair was even darker and his eyes were a deep gray, so dark they were almost black.

Dangerously handsome good looks obviously ran in the Barclay family, she thought.

"When is the wedding?" Lissa asked excitedly.

"Next week." It was Emily who answered her. "Clint sent telegrams to Wade and Caitlin at Cloud Ranch, and he was hoping to get word to you in time as well," she told Nick with a smile. "So it's lucky you turned up when you did."

"How the hell did you happen to become Lissa's escort?" Clint demanded.

"After the Parkers and Lissa worked out all their differences and settled all their family business, Sam and Lila got in touch with me. They were worried about all the trouble Lissa had in Jefferson City." Nick's gaze flicked for a moment to Joey's rapt face, then he continued, "and they asked if I would get her safely to Colorado and back with her son."

"Joey, you hear that?" Emily knelt down. "The man who's going to travel back to California with you and your mama is Sheriff Clint's brother! Isn't that wonderful?"

"Are you a sheriff too?" Joey asked, grinning hopefully up at the tall man who looked so much like Sheriff Clint.

"No, I'm not, but I can shoot and ride and track every bit as good as my brother here." Nick chuckled, then his face grew sober. "And I can protect you and your mother. No one's going to bother or scare either of you, Joey, I promise you that. And I'll stay with you until you're safely home in your grandfather's house in California."

"That's good," Joey nodded. "But I don't want to leave till after the wedding. Is that all right, Mama?"

"We're not going anywhere until after this wedding." Lissa hugged him and glanced gratefully up at Emily. "I can never thank you enough," she said, tears brimming in her eyes.

"Guess what, Mama! I'm not so scared now." Joey let go of her, stepped back, and gazed at her proudly. "'Cuz I've learned lots of things from Sheriff Clint and Uncle Jake and Pete and Lester. And John Armstrong was here, but he went away and he's never going to find us now—"

"He . . . was *here*?" Lissa straightened, going pale as she looked at Emily in alarm. Nick frowned and threw his brother a quick glance, but Clint spoke calmly.

"He never saw the boy, Lissa. He didn't spot Emily either, thanks to some quick thinking on her part." He threw a swift grin at the woman he was planning to marry, then scooped Joey up and set the boy upon his shoulders, as Joey shouted in delight. "Come on, let's head back to the Spoon place and we'll fill you both in."

"You're going to sleep in Em-ly's room, Mama," Joey explained. "And guess what! She baked a big chocolate cake—and you get to have the first piece!"

"Only if Pete and Lester haven't gobbled it all up by the time we get back!" Emily muttered ruefully.

It was good to have Lissa there, sharing her room during this visit, helping her to prepare for the wedding. In the days that followed they had a chance to catch up on all that had happened since Lissa had fled Jefferson City and Emily had taken Joey into her care. Lissa told her how her grandparents had wept with joy when she'd explained she wanted to patch up the family quarrel that arated them from her parents years ago. How they her to come live with them in San Francisco and p her to raise Joey. And in their three-story man- full of servants, and far from the world of John strong, how she had for the first time in many nths felt safe.

As for Joey, the boy was excited at the thought of get-ng to know the great-grandparents he'd never met. Though he was saddened to be leaving Emily and Sheriff Clint and Uncle Jake and Pete and Lester, as well as Bobby Smith and his other friends, Lissa promised him they would come back to visit, and that all of his friends from Lonesome—especially Emily and Uncle Jake—could come visit him in San Francisco, an idea he quickly warmed to.

Then Emily told her friend all about her first meeting with Clint Barclay, about the box lunch social, and about the plot against the Mangley women. She told Lissa how Uncle Jake and Pete and Lester—along with Clint—were now heroes in the town of Lonesome. She reassured a shocked Lissa that Ratlin was dead and Jenks, Frank Mangley, and Rudy Sleech, the mine foreman, were all in jail in Denver awaiting trial. And she told her how Pete seemed more than a little in love with Florry Brown, and that she wouldn't be at all surprised if Lester was soon walking down the aisle with Carla Mangley—and how she, Emily Spoon, had fallen helplessly in love with a lawman.

"And your uncle—and brother—and Lester—they have accepted him? I mean, Emily, you said he's the man who sent your uncle to prison!"

"They're the ones who brought us together," Emily replied. "Strange as it seems. After working together to trap Ratlin and the others, I think they all came to respect each other, to a point. But Uncle Jake and Pete and Lester

would rather jump off a cliff than admit anythin
than loathing for a lawman. They just know he ma
happy," she murmured, a smile curving the corners
lips.

"Well, any fool can see *that,*" Lissa laughed. Then
sobered and clutched Emily's hands in hers. "I get shiv
all over when I see the way he looks at you. You're luck
Emily, to have found a man like that—a man who love
you so much."

"I know. But it's not half as much as I love him," she replied almost to herself, then she smiled at her friend. "When I came here, I just wanted a fresh start with my family. I didn't want to be alone any more. But I never thought I'd find a man as wonderful as Clint. He's strong, but Lissa, he's so gentle. So caring. And . . . when Jenks told him that Ratlin had captured me, Clint made him tell where I was. Pete told me about it—he said Clint was ready to kill Jenks on the spot. It would have cost him his badge—he might have even gone to jail—but, according to Pete, Clint didn't care about anything else at that moment—except finding me. He loves me even when I'm stubborn and hot-tempered and disagreeable." She laughed. "What do you think of that?"

"That's how it should be, Emily." Lissa's eyes shone. "I'm glad for you. And he's going to faint with pleasure when he sees you in your wedding gown."

"He'd better." Emily's laughter rang out like softly chiming bells. "Or I'll be *most* disappointed."

The days leading up to the wedding seemed to fly by. Emily awakened every morning thinking that soon she would be waking up next to Clint—and she spent every evening with him talking and holding hands and kissing on the front porch.

All the days were happy ones, brimming with friends

ng to visit and offering suggestions for the wedding, e Emily sewed her wedding gown from morning until it. Nettie Phillips and Margaret Smith and Lissa ped her make plans for the reception, which would take ace in the big parlor of Nettie's boardinghouse. Wade nd Caitlin Barclay were due to arrive the day before.

And for their honeymoon, Clint wanted to take Emily first to Cloud Ranch, to see the home where he'd grown up, and then on to San Francisco, to see the sights and visit again with Lissa and Joey.

The morning before her wedding day dawned clear as crystal. Wade and Caitlin's stagecoach was due in at three o'clock, and Emily had planned a big fancy dinner to welcome them. Nettie gave her a recipe for lobster patties and Lissa had one for roasted sage hen with raisin and carrot stuffing and they woke up early and began to scour and clean the little ranch house until every floor, lamp, and stick of furniture shone like a jewel. Then they turned their attention to baking two big peach pies.

At noon Uncle Jake and the boys returned for lunch, and Clint and Nick arrived to see how the preparations were going. Emily fixed enough ham sandwiches for everyone, but after lunch shooed them all out of the kitchen as the women set to work on the elaborate dinner.

"Sure smells good in here," Joey announced after Uncle Jake fetched him home from school. He traipsed toward the windowsill where the pies were cooling, but his mother steered him away, toward the gleaming table instead.

"You must be on your best behavior tonight, young man," Lissa reminded him as she poured him a glass of milk and set a hunk of bread spread with jam before him. "Sheriff Clint's brother and his wife are special guests and you need to use your very nicest manners."

"Joey's manners are always perfectly lovely," E
said quickly, winking at the boy. "But if you play
rummy with Wade Barclay—or Clint or Nick," she ad
suddenly, "remember not to cheat."

"Cheat?" Lissa's eyes widened.

"Uncle Jake taught me how—I can do it so no one ca
tell," the boy bragged.

Emily nodded grimly at Lissa's dismayed expression. "Goodness," his mother said faintly. "Perhaps that's something you'd best forget about before we reach San Francisco—"

"You ain't going to San Francisco, you sneaking little bitch. You ain't going nowhere."

Emily dropped the carrot she'd been slicing onto the floor. It rolled clear across and landed near the toe of John Armstrong's dust-filmed boot.

Lissa's ex-fiancé filled the doorway of the cabin, looking even bigger and more powerful than Emily remembered. He was holding a rifle casually at his side and there was a sheathed knife at his waist. At sight of him, Lissa gave a choked scream, and Joey, seated at the table, froze, his small hand clenched around the milk glass.

Emily felt her heart stop, skip, and start again, thudding fast and furiously in her chest.

Outside the day was lovely, warm, peaceful. A light breeze toyed with the leaves on the aspens, a lark sang merrily, and chickens squawked in the new pen near the barn.

Inside the cabin, the fragrance of the fresh pies was obliterated by the smell of John Armstrong's hair pomade mixed with the odor of his sweat. Lissa's tiny, terrified moan was the only human sound.

Armstrong's lips drew back in a taut, terrifying smile.

‚t happened to hit town, ladies. Passing through on ay to a brand-new job over in Huntsville, and what ɔu know? The whole town's talking about some big ding tomorrow—and all the visitors going to be here it."

He stepped into the cabin and kicked the door closed :hind him. "Just so happened I heard some names I now. Guests of the bride and groom. Lucky stroke for ıe." The smile broadened, growing, if possible, even older. "Not so lucky for you, bitch," he told Lissa. "Or 'our precious brat."

His eyes shifted to Emily, white-faced at the counter, ıer hands closed around the chopping knife. "Or your ıosy friend here. Not too lucky at all."

'Something I need to say to you, Barclay."

Jake Spoon had caught up with Clint and Nick a quarer mile from the ranch. As his horse pranced restlessly, ake fixed the sheriff with a stern look.

"Can't it wait, Spoon? I'm on my way to meet my ›rother's stage."

"This won't take long." Jake ignored Nick, who sat a ›ig black gelding with ease. Instead he studied the sheriff ı moment, his expression unreadable as his eyes pinned he broad-shouldered man who had tracked him down nore than seven years before and sent him to jail.

"If I got to pick who my niece gets to marry, you'd be he last man on my list." Jake spat into the dust of the rail. "But I don't get to pick—Emily makes up her own nind. And she picked you."

"So?" Clint's mouth was a thin line.

"I don't want anyone ever to say I'm not a fair man. I

stole what didn't belong to me, and I paid for it. N
over." He took a deep breath. "I don't want you thr
it in her face."

Beneath the hard words, Clint heard a quaver in Ja
voice. It struck him, not for the first time, but perh
stronger than ever, just how much Emily meant to t
old man.

"I wouldn't do that," he said quietly. "I love her."

Jake nodded. "Reckon that's the only reason I'm let
ting this wedding go forward. Course, there's Emily—
once she's made up her mind, not the devil or rampagin
buffalo can stop her."

"You're right, Spoon—but there's something else yo
should know. Whatever happened seven years ago be
tween you and me—far as I'm concerned, it's over. Yo
served your time. That's good enough for me."

Jake chewed the end of the cigar clamped between hi
teeth. "Something else *you* should know, Barclay. Leste
and Pete—once they ran from Jefferson City—they staye
clean. Did a little gunfighting, some line riding, some scou
work, but they haven't held up a stage since the last job w
all pulled together in Missouri."

"I'm not looking to make trouble for them, if that'
what you're worried about. Damn it, Spoon, I love you
niece. She's going to be a part of me, of my family." Clin
glanced at his brother, who appeared to be studying th
floating puffs of clouds in the pristine sky. "And you an
Pete and Lester . . . well, you're *her* family, so I gues
that, whether we like it or not, that's going to make you
mine too."

"Hmmmph. Reckon that part remains to be seen,'
Jake said gruffly. But a gleam entered his eyes. "Course
you do owe it all to me and I expect you to remembe

I hadn't told my son and Pete to lock the two of
› in that jail cell—"
suppose you told Pete to wait behind the door and
cock me too."
ake guffawed. "Didn't seem to be any other way," he
d with a shrug.
Clint's eyes narrowed. "Take credit if you want for get-
ng Emily to forgive me, Spoon, but you should know,
d never have let her go. I'd have made Emily listen to
ıe one way or another—"
"Hah!"
"And she'd have forgiven me," Clint added coolly. "It
eems to me, you benefited too. She wasn't talking to any
f you until she got over being mad at me—"
"She was talkin'! Not much, but she was talkin'—"
"Excuse me," Nick interrupted, "in case you've both
orgotten, we've got a stage to meet."
"Go on then. Who's stopping you?" Jake reined his
orse around. "Just wanted to make sure we understand
ach other."
"We do." Clint looked at him, a long, measuring look.
Ie nodded. "I'll take care of her, Spoon—the way she
eserves. You don't have to worry about that."
Jake said nothing. Merely studied the other man's hard
alm face, and then gave a curt nod.
"See that you do." He wheeled his horse and started
ack up the trail toward the ranch.

You're going to be sorry," Joey said. He finally released
he glass of milk and pushed back his chair. "You'd better
;et out of here right now. Uncle Jake told me what he'd do
f he ever got his hands on you, and Sheriff Clint said—"

"Yeah, well, they're not here—none of 'em! I sa
all ride off—back to work, back to town." Arm
strode toward Joey, but Lissa darted in front of the
so he couldn't reach the boy.

"No!" she cried. "Leave him alone!"

"You telling me what to do?" Armstrong pointed
rifle at her and Lissa went still.

"No, I am." Emily spoke quietly. She moved forwa
to Lissa's side. "Leave us alone. Just clear out of m
house while you still can. I'm warning you—"

"And I'm telling you that I'm not going anywhe
without this woman and that boy." He swung the rifle to
ward Emily. "I've searched all over and now that I foun
'em, they're coming with me. But not before I'v
taught them both—and you, too, Miz Spoon—a real goo
lesson."

Suddenly Joey dashed around the table and right pa
Armstrong to the cabin door.

As Armstrong spun around, leveling the gun, Liss
threw herself at him. She tried to wrench the gun fro
him, but he held it fast and flung her away, even as Joe
made it outside. Armstrong charged after him, but Emil
sprang into his path.

"No—let him go!" Breathing hard, she faced Arm
strong as he aimed the gun at her, his beefy face suffuse
with rage. "You don't need him. He's . . . just a little bo
It's me and Lissa you want to talk to."

"I want to do a hell of a lot more than talk," he snarle

"Anything—I'll do anything you want, John." Liss
shakily pushed herself away from the wall. Holding he
hands before her pleadingly, she moved toward him
"Anything, you hear? Just leave Joey out of this."

"You've caused me a lot of trouble, woman." Arm
strong was watching her through eyes that shone with an

and a kind of fevered fascination. "You know ong I've been searching for you?"

om outside there came a whistling sound. A long, whistle, followed quickly by several rapid birdlike ps. Then it began again.

Emily caught her breath. That was the danger signal int had taught Joey. As Armstrong turned his head at e sound, Emily began to talk quickly to distract him. Mr. Armstrong, why don't you sit down? I'll cut you ome peach pie and we can discuss this. Would you like offee or—"

"You shut up!" The big man forgot about the whistling nd rounded on her, his mouth twisting. "This is between er and me—you've done nothing but stick your nose in here it doesn't belong. She said she'd marry me and en she changed her mind, and I've got a notion it's your ault."

"No, John," Lissa said as Armstrong suddenly took a enacing step toward Emily. She too raised her voice to peak over the whistling. "I'm the one you're mad at. . . . I never should have run away."

"Damn right. I been through four states looking for ou. Where've you been?" His eyes narrowed. "Someone n that saloon said you came to town with a man. You narried to him?"

"No, no. I'm not married to anyone—"

"Who is he then, you little slut?" Armstrong stepped oward her. "I knew you'd cheat on me! You were always sneaking little—"

The whistling stopped abruptly and in its place came ilence. An eerie, dead silence.

"Something's wrong," Armstrong muttered abruptly. His eyes darted nervously between Emily and Lissa. Sweat dripped down his temples. "Where'd that kid go?

We need to get out of here," he muttered, advanc Lissa. Suddenly he grabbed her arm, and she cried pain.

Emily leapt forward. Desperately she drove the c ping knife into his arm with all the force she could mus

"Run, Lissa!" she cried.

Armstrong screamed in agony as the knife pierced h flesh and blood spurted out. As Lissa twisted free, sob bing, and lurched toward the door, Emily yanked out th knife and shoved the man backward before he could re cover from the shock of being stabbed. She darted towar the door, terror driving her as she stumbled out int bright sunshine, right on Lissa's heels.

She froze momentarily halfway across the porch blinking at what she saw. Nick Barclay stood ten fee from the porch, his gun leveled at the cabin, or rather a the man who had just staggered out of the cabin door, hi arm bloody, his face contorted with pain and fury. Besid Nick stood Uncle Jake, his feet planted apart, his eye grim. Pete and Lester stood on the other side of Nick brandishing their Colt .45s.

They were spread out in a semicircle, surrounding th front of the cabin, and on the porch was Clint. He seize Emily and thrust her behind him, and she realized he ha already done the same to a startled Lissa.

"Hold it right there, Armstrong. Drop your gun!"

Clint's Colt was aimed directly at Armstrong's chest Behind him, Lissa and Emily clutched one another.

"Get out of my way—*Sheriff*!" Armstrong gasped th last word contemptuously. "That's my woman. This is be tween her and me. And that little dark-haired bitch stabbe me. You see this?" He pointed toward his blood-soake arm. "She did that. You oughta arrest her."

"I said *drop your gun.*" Clint's voice was pure ice. Emily had never heard him sound so cold. Her heart pounded with terror for him—he was standing directly between her and Lissa and Armstrong, facing the brunt of the man's fury.

If Armstrong decided to shoot, Clint was at close range, right in his path . . .

"You're surrounded," Nick growled.

"The only way you'll get out alive," Uncle Jake put in, "is if you drop your gun right now. Otherwise, we'll mow you down."

Emily could smell Armstrong's panic. He stared around the semicircle of men, then looked at the lawman confronting him, his gun drawn, aimed, steady. But even as Emily watched the man's eyes, she saw the rage take over, rob him of all rational thought.

"I'm taking you and those bitches to hell with me then," he bellowed at Clint and jerked the rifle up. But even as he squeezed the trigger, Clint fired—and so did the four other men.

Emily and Lissa screamed and held each other as bullet after bullet slammed into Armstrong's body. His bloodcurdling scream penetrated to her very soul and then quickly cut off as he toppled backward, crashing down dead right in front of the cabin door.

For a moment the world shook and spun. Emily didn't know when she let go of Lissa, when she was suddenly gathered in Clint's arms. All she knew was that he was holding her close, whispering her name over and over, and slowly steadily the sickening queasy feeling passed and the ground steadied beneath her feet.

She opened her eyes and saw that Lissa was sitting on the ground beneath the tree, with Joey cradled in her lap and Nick bending over both of them. Uncle Jake and Pete and Lester were lifting Armstrong's body from the porch.

And Clint was gazing down at her, worry furrowing his brow.

"It's over, Emily. It's all over. Are you all right?"

"I was so scared." She clung to him, holding on as if she would never let him go.

"You had good reason." His mouth tightened. "Good thing Joey remembered that whistle I taught him."

"A very good thing," she murmured, resting her head against his chest. "Clint, I thought . . ."

"I'd never have let him shoot you, sweetheart. No way."

"No, I thought he was going to shoot you," she whispered.

Clint stroked her back. His lips pressed a kiss to her forehead. This precious woman who felt so right in his arms, whose courage never failed to surprise him—she'd been frightened for *him*. Powerful emotions surged through him and he closed his eyes, thanking God she was safe, thanking God that she loved him.

"No way in hell, Emily," he told her hoarsely. "No way in hell I'd have let anything come between us. Sure as hell not a piece of scum like Armstrong." His arms tightened as she shuddered. "Especially not the day before our wedding. I got a honeymoon to look forward to—or have you forgotten?"

Oh, Lord. She had forgotten. She'd forgotten everything, her dinner preparations, the stage arriving with Clint's family, even that tomorrow was her wedding day. But as it all came back with a rush, she held tight to this man who was always there when she needed him, this man who had claimed her heart despite every obstacle fate had put in their way.

"A honeymoon," she whispered. "How could I forget?" She gave a shaky laugh, then touched a hand to his face. "I can hardly wait."

"Tell me about it."

She laughed again then as the shock began to fade and relief inched in, relief and the dazed realization that all the danger was past—Lissa and Joey would be safe. Armstrong would never torment them again, they wouldn't have to hide or live in fear. And now there was only the future—for her friend, and for herself and Clint—a bright, loving future, their new life together.

"Hold me a little longer," she whispered, and snuggled against him. "Please."

"My pleasure." Clint pulled her close, so close she could feel the warmth and strength of his beating heart. So close that she tingled and love surged through her, banishing the fear and horror of what had happened on this porch, blotting out everything but this man and the way he made her feel.

"I'll hold you forever, Emily. If you'll let me. Vows or no vows, honeymoon or no honeymoon, you're mine. I'll never let you go."

"That's good," she whispered, smiling up at him as the sun sailed into an orange-gold sky. "Because I'm right where I want to be. Now—and always."

Clint kissed her gently, not caring who was there, who saw, not caring that a man had died on this porch only a short time ago. Nothing could mar this place, this moment, this love he had for this woman. Nothing else mattered, except that they were together, that the future would belong to them both, side by side.

"Always," he whispered back. "I like the sound of that."

"So do I, Clint." She smiled into his eyes and lifted up on tiptoe to kiss him again. Her heart was so full she thought she would burst. "So do I."

Epilogue

One Month Later

THE HOT SUMMER SUN BLAZED overhead as Emily climbed up the hill to the pretty crest of land where her husband was trimming lumber for their new log house. The spot was only a quarter of a mile from the little cabin where her family still lived, and it was deep in the heart of the land that comprised the Teacup Ranch. The creek ran behind it, jumping with frogs, but Emily's gaze was not fixed on the creek, or on the lovely sweep of meadow surrounding the new house, nor the graceful aspens that would stand like sentinels around the fine large house Clint had planned. Her gaze was centered on the man who worked shirtless in the hot sun, the muscles of his chest and arms glistening with sweat, his dark hair tumbling over his brow.

Her husband.

As it always did when she saw him, her heart lifted with happiness. And as if sensing her presence, Clint paused in his work, turned his head in her direction, and a grin lit his face as she ran the rest of the way into his arms.

"You're a sight for sore eyes, Mrs. Barclay," he said after he'd taken the wicker basket from her and kissed her thoroughly.

"So are you, Mr. Barclay."

They spread the blanket she'd brought on the grass near the pile of lumber that would soon be their new home, and Emily set out plates and sandwiches and sugar cookies and a jug of lemonade. After the meal they lay in each other's arms, gazing at the jewel-blue sky and talking of the future they would have in the house Clint was building for them.

Their wedding had gone off without a hitch—Emily had felt as if she were not even walking, but floating down the aisle in the gown of white satin trimmed in palest pink lace, and she'd scarcely remembered to murmur *I do,* so captivated was she at the stunned and lovestruck expression on her groom's handsome face.

Uncle Jake had given her away—Pete and Lester had not frowned at Clint even once—and Wade Barclay and Caitlin, in addition to Nick, had welcomed her with genuine warmth into the Barclay family.

The honeymoon had been even better, and by the time they returned from San Francisco and their visit to Cloud Ranch, Emily had discovered that she was even more in love with Clint than she'd been before. He'd immediately started work on their own separate house, and with Jake and the boys coming to help him whenever they could spare the time, he hoped it would be ready before winter set in.

Emily was busy too—Lester and Carla had set a Thanksgiving wedding date and she was making Carla an elaborate ivory velvet gown that was to be studded with sequins and boasted a graceful satin train.

It looked like Pete and Florry might be making an announcement soon too—but they weren't the only other couple around whom Cupid seemed to hover. Uncle Jake had been spending a great deal of time at Nettie Phillips's boardinghouse.

At the rate I'm going, Emily thought as she lay dreaming in Clint's arms beneath the shade of a tree, *I'll spend my whole career sewing nothing but wedding gowns for the women of Lonesome . . .*

"I have something for you." Clint's voice broke into her thoughts. "Matter of fact, I was going to give it to you tonight at supper . . . I sort of forgot about it for a while . . ."

His voice trailed away and he looked a bit sheepish.

Mystified, Emily sat up and watched as he went to his saddlebag and took out an envelope, then removed a document.

He studied her face as she accepted the paper from him and scanned it.

"But this . . . this can't be!" she exclaimed in confusion.

"It is. It's the real deed to the Teacup Ranch—what used to be the Sutter place."

"But Uncle Jake has the deed—he showed it to you!"

Clint shook his head. "Before old Henry Sutter gave up trying to make a go of the ranch and took off for Leadville to try his luck at finding a big silver strike, he needed money for supplies—and to keep him going until he made his fortune. So . . . he sold the place. To me."

Emily's eyes widened. "To . . . *you*?"

"Yep. I'd been thinking on and off for a while about getting myself a place that was my own, away from the jail. I was getting tired of living in those two little rooms over the office. Toyed with the idea of doing some ranching on the side, hiring on a deputy or two to keep an eye on things in town when I wasn't there. So I bought the place, partly as a favor to Sutter, partly for myself. I figured I could always sell the land later if I decided to move on." He smiled ruefully at her. "But once I bought it, I never did get around to doing anything with it. And then . . . you came along."

"But . . . I don't understand, Clint. If Henry Sutter sold it to you, how did Uncle Jake get that deed?"

"It was a forgery—a fake," Clint said grimly. "I guess when that big silver strike never happened, and Sutter ran out of money, he got desperate. He needed a quick way to get cash—and he somehow found a way to make up some fake deeds to the land. Your uncle wasn't the first to get taken in. A gambler named Ike Johnson showed up last year to survey 'his ranch.' Had a deed just like the one your uncle has. I set Johnson straight and he was mighty disgusted—said Sutter had put the deed up for collateral in a poker game and then lost it. Johnson thought he had a legitimate claim to the place."

"That's what happened with Uncle Jake too!" Stunned, Emily sank down again upon the blanket. "He won it from Henry Sutter in a poker game after he was released from prison. He said it was fate, said Aunt Ida must've helped him win, so he could have a stake to a fresh start—for all of us."

"Maybe in a way she did," Clint said quietly. Silence fell as Clint stuffed the deed back into the envelope and the wind ruffled the leaves on the aspens.

"So . . . all this time . . . you've owned Teacup Ranch?" Dazed, she spoke half to herself. "You made Uncle Jake show you the deed, but you . . . you never told us . . . you could have thrown us off at any time."

Clint dropped down beside her on the blanket, then took Emily's hand and tugged her up and across his chest, his other arm sliding around her waist. "Guess I wanted you to stick around."

"I can't imagine why." Lying atop him, gazing down at that hard, sensuous mouth, seeing the way he looked at her, as if looking deep inside her mind and soul, Emily felt a powerful rush of love and gratitude—for this man and for the path that had led them to each other.

"Don't tell Jake—or Pete or Lester, for that matter." His hand smoothed back her wind-ruffled hair, then twined gently through the thick blue-black curls. "No reason they need to know. I'm giving you the deed, Emily, I want you to keep it—it's a belated wedding present," he said with his lightning grin.

"But, Clint—"

"There's more than enough land here to share. And besides, we're all family now."

Family. She liked the sound of that.

"I guess we are," Emily murmured. "More so than you know," she added softly as Clint began to unbutton her white shirtwaist.

"What does that mean, Mrs. Barclay?"

A smile played around the corners of her mouth as she stroked her fingers across the crisp black hair of his chest, felt those sun-baked muscles clench and burn beneath her touch. She liked the feel of his hard body beneath her, the warmth of him, as they lay in the shade and the hot, peaceful afternoon lazed around them. "It means I have something to give you today too."

His eyes gleamed at her, making her pulse race. "I hope it's what I think it is," he chuckled. He had her blouse off before Emily even realized it, and then made her squeal as he rolled her over so that she lay beneath him. Grinning, he lost no time going to work at the fastenings of her skirt.

"Actually—wait a minute, you brute—it's here—in the pocket of my skirt—" Laughing, pushing his hands away, she managed to tug out what she sought from deep inside the pocket and held it up before his eyes.

"What do you think?"

Clint stared at the tiny yellow knit booties she dangled in her hand. Too stunned to speak, he dragged his gaze from the booties to the exquisite glowing face of the woman he loved.

"I think . . . you're trying . . . to tell me . . ." He broke off and swallowed hard, staring down at her. She was watching him, her beautiful silver eyes filled with hope—and with happiness—and with just a trace of uncertainty as she tried to read his expression.

"Emily, are you . . . sure?"

"Quite sure, my darling," she whispered. "I saw Doc Calvin in town yesterday and—"

Clint gave a whoop and then swooped down and kissed her, a long, deep, melting kiss that banished all the uncertainty from her eyes, and from her heart.

"Guess that means you're happy about it," she gasped when she could speak again.

"Happy?" Clint's grin told her all she needed to know. "Happy doesn't begin to cover it."

"Well, then, maybe this will," Emily murmured saucily, and with her eyes glowing into his, she pulled him down to her, down upon her. Their lips met, tasted, clung. As she kissed him long and lovingly and tightened her arms around his neck, she felt the familiar heat flare in her as their bodies pressed together. A heat hotter than the sun, fueled by passion, joy, and love.

Love.

Love for this man who had changed her life, won her heart, and joined his soul to hers. Love for the home they would have, the children they would nurture, the days and nights they would spend in each other's arms.

Together on the hill where their new home would tand, where their children would laugh and play, where ey would build a future as golden as this day, Emily and lint let the joy and the passion fill them as they cele-rated the most precious gift of all—the gift of love.

About the Author

USA Today–bestseller Jill Gregory is the award-winning author of seventeen historical romances. Her novels have been translated and published in Japan, Russia, Norway, Taiwan, Sweden, and Italy. Jill grew up in Chicago and received her bachelor of arts degree in English from the University of Illinois. She has a college-age daughter and currently resides in Michigan with her husband.

Jill invites her readers to visit her Web site at http://members.aol.com/jillygreg.

"UTTERLY MAGICAL."
—*Romantic Times*

"GREAT FROM START TO FINISH."
"SPECTACULAR WRITING."
—*Rendezvous*

"AS GOOD AS THEY GET."
—*Affaire de Coeur*

Join the chorus of praise for

Jill Gregory

Her stories will win your heart.

Once an Outlaw • 23549-9 • $6.50

Rough Wrangler, Tender Kisses • 23548-0 • $6.50

Cold Night, Warm Stranger • 22440-3 • $6.50

Never Love a Cowboy • 22439-X • $5.99

Forever After • 21512-9 • $6.50

ROM 8 12/01